I0586904

LADY EVE:
STAR MARAUDER

A Time Warden Chronicle

Thomas W. Everson

Welcome to the Crux Arm of the Milky Way, where many species and races are living their lives. This is a work of fiction. Any presumed likenesses of names, characters, businesses, governments, or places is all just coincidence.

Copyright © 2020 2023 Thomas W. Everson

All rights reserved.

ISBN-13: 978-0-9864120-8-0

<u>Dedication</u>

Thank you to my wife, my friends, and my coworkers who have been supportive and been my morale boosters. Your enthusiasm for my stories is exactly why I write.

Contents

Acknowledgements

Thank you to my beta readers Brandi M. (my wife), Lillie B. and Dale C. I take your feedback seriously because I want to do my best job at entertaining people. The stories are what they are because of you.

Thank you to Jake Murray, my cover artist, who always provides nothing but the very best artwork. I wanted Lady Eve to have a powerful cover that would highlight her boldness, her strength, her determination. To say that he exceeded my expectations is an understatement to his ability. I was blown away.

Thank you to Tim Marquitz, my editor, for providing the professional sounding board I need to make sure things flow right. I am a better writer because of not only the technical corrections he provides, but also the outside perspective he brings.

Prologue:
Story of the Reset

"So, tell me about Eve," *she* says as *he* is collecting plates from the table.

He brings them to the sink and begins washing them while staring out the window at the green grass and the apple tree. His brown hair falls into his face, and he has to push it out of the way with wet fingers.

"The cataclysm never happened. Salvoa was never scorched. The desert never existed. Everything that led up to Eve and her bandits never happened," *he* says.

"So, was she even born? Without the cataclysm to shape history, the events that led to her existence wouldn't have happened."

"She was, and she is destined to be that person we first met, regardless of the circumstances. The universe determined she still has a place in it.

"Because of the altered timeline, in the future humanity enters space to join a galactic community of distinct alien beings. There's many, but to name a few, there are the benevolent vraditi, our four-eyed, gray alien acquaintances. They become the police of the galaxy. The elementus are humanoid but born of volcanic worlds and have a tradition of fusing rocks, minerals, and gems to their bodies as they grow. They're industrialists. The QuBE are artificially intelligent robots who take on the forms of various species in order to blend in better. They develop new technologies for all.

"Humans sort of fit their way in anywhere they can. Eve leaves Salvoa at an early age with her parents to be explorers. They're nomads, moving from one space station to another, and then out into uncharted space. Eve, in her typical fashion, is hard-headed, and needs to be in control of her own destiny as much as possible. When she was old enough to go it on her own, she did.

"She started out innocent enough, just doing manual labor, hopping from cargo ship to cargo ship, but she got drawn into the mercenary lifestyle and found her niche. It wasn't long before she was learning nefarious skills. Illicit data trading, espionage, coercion, extortion. Eventually, she started going by Lady Eve."

"Ugh. I hated that name for her."

He laughs. "You and me both."

"Can we change things?"

"Time is complicated. Things are being set into motion to solidify this timeline permanently. Things are going to get bad in the future, and we all have our roles to play."

"What do you mean? Does Auntie already know? Does something happen to us?"

He returns from washing the dishes and kisses her forehead to alleviate her anxiety.

"We have to play out our lives in order to know. I may be a paradox in the timeline, but your auntie says that I don't get to know everything yet. But she did tell me Eve's story, so I'll share that."

Chapter 1
Never According to Plan

The ship banked hard to starboard, dogging the elementus ship hauling two million chits' worth of garocite ore. Once fenced, the inventory would not only ensure they'd have a good cash reserve, but they would also be able to outfit their ship with new armor plating. Darting between the planet and one of its moons, they did what they needed to keep the other ship in their sights.

"Take out their engine before they can hit their Light Drive," Captain Marsi barked.

The left helmsman tapped furiously, issuing flight commands, while the right helmsman commanded the ship's weapons. Light Drive amplified missiles launched from their bay and made a quick skip forward in space to hit the ship they pursued. Their shields took the first two but wavered long enough for a third to get through.

"As soon as we overtake them, open them like a tin can and drop an incendiary grenade in," Captain Marsi directed.

Eve pulled her curly, fire red hair up into a ponytail, strapped on her chest armor and face mask, and readied her hand cannon. The elementus would put up a fight, but she knew the crew would have no issues subduing them.

They quickly decelerated, and the two ships collided. There was no need for the captain to tell them to go. Eve opened their underside bay doors, and their technician descended with a cutting torch. It burned through the target's hull with no problem, and Eve dropped the grenade the instant the chunk of metal fell into the elementus cargo bay.

The marauder crew stood clear of the opening as the blast expanded. When the fire died down, Eve dropped straight in, her seven-shot hand cannon already leveled in her eyesight. The thunder-crack sound was deafening, and the recoil was enough to injure a person if they were unfamiliar with the weapon.

The first shot hit its intended target, the elementus closest to the breech. The ores on their body had been partially fused due to the incendiary grenade, slowing their reaction time. They had no chance to dodge Eve's shot.

The rest of the assault team followed and fired their weapons at anyone not part of their crew. The first wave of elementus were easy to take down, but the ones who'd avoided the blast were mounting their defense. The containers of ore were plentiful, and the two crews used anything and everything as cover.

Shots were fired back and forth, but Eve wasn't caught up in it. Despite being tall and hard to miss, she was adept at moving quickly and quietly. She flanked their foes while the ships shuddered and rocked. Hiding behind a stack of crates at the defensive line, she saw an opportunity. Lining up the shots, she put bullets into a few elementus. They fell, and others began firing in her direction. Hiding behind the crate, she reloaded her gun while *The Fade*'s crew advanced.

They were ruthless, and the cargo hold was quickly theirs. They still needed to get to the bridge to shut down any further attempts to escape. Eve led the way. The simple geometric design of the elementus ships made navigating and finding the bridge easy.

When everyone was in position, she readied another grenade. The control to open the door wasn't responding, and their technician had to cut through. This time, though, the elementus were ready. The moment there was an opening, the defenders tossed their own grenade out into the hallway.

"Scatter!" Eve yelled.

They did their best to hide. Eve was the first around a corner and safe, but another was not so lucky when the blast went off. He fell to his knees and collapsed. The back of his vest and head had been ripped apart by the shrapnel. Eve's stomach fluttered, not from being squeamish but because her own armor might not help if they threw another and she was caught in the blast.

Creeping around the corner and along the wall with soft steps, she pulled the pin on her grenade and lobbed it into the opening. It clinked across the floor several times, and then exploded. Assuming the elementus were now vulnerable, she signaled the marauders to charge in. Weapon fire was exchanged, but the elementus had nowhere to go or hide. One by one they were picked off, and then the bridge fell silent.

Eve comm'd Captain Marsi through her *Trauna* earpiece, "Ship secured. Moving back to the cargo bay. Ready the hoist."

Back amongst the containers, Eve saw the technician was already cutting a hole large enough to fit the cargo through. Their ceiling clattered with a *bang*, and the infiltrators moved to hoist it out of the way.

It was an easy job as the majority were augmented with artificial body parts, which allowed greater lifting strength. Eve was among a few who had opted not to become enhanced. Still, she pulled her weight and lent a hand.

The loading of the cargo was quick and smooth. They hustled, assuming the elementus activated a distress beacon. If they didn't clear the area soon, they'd surely meet the gun-end of a Galactic Police ship. When the last container was aboard, the crew grabbed onto the crane and were hoisted back up.

Clear of the bay door, they shut it, and the ship decoupled. *The Fade* accelerated away with its Cruise Drive at maximum to avoid the explosive decompression of the elementus ship.

"All hands, prepare for evasive maneuvers!" Captain Marsi said.

The crew rushed to return to their bridge posts. Eve was first in, and she took position at a weapons console. On the view screen, rounding the planet was a police heavy cruiser heading for them. Pulse lasers hit their shield. *The Fade* shook, but the shield held.

"Get us to the bulk path!" the captain shouted.

The Fade banked, and they headed out into the solar system while dodging the beams. The cruiser tried to overtake them, but it had more mass to move. *The Fade* outpaced them. The location where the bulk path would open was two *astronomical units* away, and the helmsman punched in the trajectory.

"As soon as we're on the other side, we're going to launch the decoy, double back, and activate the Light Drive," Captain Marsi said.

Their Bulk Drive fired up, and the subspace tunnel out of the system opened. It shimmered like an opal.

Once inside, they knew they'd be safe from weapons fire until they made it to the other side.

They'd never risk collapsing the path, Eve thought.

This path would take them a hundred light years from Tor Galom space. They would have enough time to prep the ship to turn and burn. Captain Marsi delegated assignments, and Eve was put on maintenance duty. After removing and storing her tactical gear in the cargo hold, she and Dovik headed to the engine room.

While interconnected through the synthetic Vradix crystal chassis, the Cruise, Light, and Bulk Drives were three separate engines. They each pulled a different amount of material from the crystal to convert it to usable energy. With one drive in use, it left the other two free for diagnostics.

"I'll take the Cruise Drive," Eve told Dovik.

He grunted and nodded.

They went about making sure all the parameters were in the correct ranges. *The Fade* had recently undergone heavy engine maintenance, so Eve didn't anticipate anything being out of the ordinary. After she finished her task, she checked on Dovik.

"All good?" she asked.

"Tip top shape."

Staying busy, Eve poked around the other systems through a remote console. The remaining ship armaments were at fifty percent. The vibration load on the inertial dampeners was nominal. Shield emitters were functioning. *The Fade* was in its best form, as Captain Marsi expected.

"You ever think about having your own ship?" Eve asked.

"Psht, been with the cap ten years. I'm comfortable where I am."

"Not me. One day, I'll have a ship and crew of my own. I'll give you all some competition," she said and guffawed. He laughed.

With their task finished, Eve leaned back against the console, her arms supporting her and her long legs stretched out. She caught him stealing several glances, and while she enjoyed the attention, he wasn't her type.

Eve knew what she wanted and how to get it. Equally adept at taking by force or by seduction, she felt there was nothing she couldn't *eventually* get. Captain Marsi had been a good teacher in that regard. Before joining *The Fade* two years ago, Eve relied on strength, guns, and willpower. Marsi had shown her more subtle ways to affect outcomes depending on the situation.

While they'd shared a bed on many occasions, Eve denied herself the attachment. A long-term relationship with Marsi didn't line up with her end game.

Gotta keep my eyes on the future. My future as captain of a ship.

Eve pushed up off the console after a few minutes and headed back to the front of the ship. She climbed the stairs to the bridge, noticing how Captain Marsi watched her from her chair. She sat at a command console.

"Everything good, Eve?" Captain Marsi asked.

"*Lady* Eve...and I'd have told you if it wasn't," Eve quips with a quick kiss to the air in Marsi's direction.

"And *I've* told *you*, I'm not calling you that." Captain Marsi smirked.

The time in a bulk path depended on how far they were going but was always a little contentious because, once inside, they didn't have control.

"We have a little under two hours in this bulk path, so everyone but Torp take an hour to rest up," Captain Marsi ordered.

Eve didn't hesitate. She immediately left and headed for her bunk. In order to accommodate room for the cargo hold, the rooms in the ship were small. She shared a bunk with another crew member, but it didn't bother her. She threw on an eye mask and set her earpieces to muffle external sound.

It felt like only minutes had passed when Captain Marsi came over comms informing the crew to return to their stations. The clock was ticking until their exit back to normal space, but she figured she had enough time to grab a nutrition drink from the kitchen.

While others walked the hall toward the bridge, she headed the opposite direction. In the kitchen, she pulled a bottle from their cooler and guzzled it down. It had everything nutrition-wise a human needed to survive. It was no substitute for a hearty meal, but it didn't taste terrible, and it was quick.

Still not pressed to get back to her post right away, she stopped off at the ship's only bathroom. There was only one person waiting ahead of her. Because the ship was small, and their crew were all human, they had a traditional bathroom rather than a vraditi purification chamber.

Once she was done, she washed up and headed to the bridge. Captain Marsi addressed her as soon as she climbed the stairs.

"Torp swapped our transponder onto the probe. You're in charge of programming the flight path. Range is six AU on this model, so make it count."

"Aye, Cap."

At her console, she charted the path for the probe based on the known celestial bodies for the system they were about to enter. Six AU would get the probe to the other side of the system's red giant star, giving them plenty of time to escape.

Reaching the end of the path, the mouth of the anomaly opened, and normal space became visible. Eve was ready. The inertial dampeners adjusted while they decelerated. She launched the decoy and, as soon as it was away, the miniature Light Drive on board engaged. *The Fade* spun about and warped away.

They'd cleared a couple planets before the vraditi ship emerged. Even if they scanned and saw two distinct trails, the transponder the Galactic Police had identified was heading toward the sun. Eve peeked at *The Fade*'s path, and they were heading to hide on the dark side of a moon.

"Any sign of pursuit?" Captain Marsi asked.

"None," came Torp's reply.

"Good. Continue on course."

The Light Drive disengaged as they closed in on the moon. It was slowly being eaten away by the gravitational pull of its planet. Decelerating, the Cruise Drive kicked on, and Torp guided them through a rocky debris field to hide in the darkness.

"Start hibernating non-essential systems," Marsi ordered.

Eve went through the procedures for her console, as did the others. Little by little, the area became darker. Torp's station and the external scanner display were the only ones left fully active. He was a good pilot; touchdown was nothing more than a gentle bump.

"That's it," Torp turned and told Captain Marsi.

Nestled into a crevasse with minimal lighting, the only system still fully active was environmental. Though everything would appear to be powered down, they could have everything up and running again in a matter of moments if needed.

A red giant, a handful of various sized planets, hundreds of moons, an asteroid belt. The Galactic Police would have a tough time finding them tucked away once they discovered the subterfuge.

The system was like so many others Eve had seen, just with its own little quirks. When she was dragged off Salvoa by her parents to go exploring the cosmos, she became well-versed in different astronomical objects and phenomenon.

During her layovers on Emex space stations, she saw many different avenues of living. At some point, she got it in her head that, one day, she would command her own ship and crew. She'd see the galaxy on her terms. The idea of action, adventure, and money became a driving force.

When she was old enough to jump ship and hold her own, she did. The lessons she learned were tough. Arduous work only paid the bills and kept you alive. You had to be an opportunist to actually gain anything, even if it meant breaking galactic law.

The crew watched the radar to ensure they were in the clear. Eve zoned out. The quiet was broken when Captain Marsi made a ship wide announcement.

"All hands to the cargo bay."

After deactivating the internal comms, she instructed Torp.

"Torp, after the celebratory congratulations, go get some rest. Mikael will cover the helm."

"Yes, Captain."

Only emergency lighting along the floor was there to guide their path. The bridge crew made their way down the stairs and aft through the narrow hall. In the bay, Captain Marsi grabbed steins and tapped a keg Eve knew the captain had been hanging onto for several months. The team huddled, and Captain Marsi filled and passed out drinks.

"Good work, everyone. After we fence the loot, we'll be taking shore leave for a month at Starreach Station. *The Fade* will get some much-needed armor upgrades. You'll all be free to do whatever. Since our haul was so large, everyone will get a bonus."

The crew cheered and toasted. Eve had been splitting her cuts between saving for her own ship and slipping some to her parents' account anonymously as a *doner* for their expeditions.

If I could get over the guilt of ditching them, I could save it all for myself.

Barely into their celebration, they were rudely interrupted by an explosion rocking the crevasse they were hidden in. Chunks of the moon smacked into the hull hard.

"Stations! Now!" Captain Marsi yelled.

The crew dispersed. Because she'd hadn't eaten anything solid recently Eve's head swam, and the corridor wobbled in her vision. A direct impact of *something* buckled the hull above them. At the bridge, they powered up the ship, and it hummed to life.

"Shields! Get us the hell out of here!"

Marsi didn't really need to give that order. The crew had already brought the shields online and fired up the Cruise Drive.

"Status!"

"One ship. Transponder IDs as freight. They're marauders," Eve replied.

The Fade pulled away from the moon, and the viewscreen lit up. Their attacker was a unique ship, one they had encountered but never crossed weapons with before. The hull was shaped like a *rayfish* from the oceans of Salvoa. Its primary weapons were railguns, and the projectiles were hammering the shields hard.

At the helm, Torp and Mikael worked to maneuver the ship free of the corner they were backed into. They needed space to activate the Light Drive to warp away.

Eve brought the commands up for firing control and readied everything. She dropped half their mine supply but didn't activate them yet. As the enemy ship neared, she hoped the sudden burst would knock critical functions offline and slow them enough to allow getaway. *The Fade* was hit hard from behind. The ship shook and the Cruise Drive faltered.

"*Fek!*" Captain Marsi swore.

They were hit again, and again. This time, the drive shut down altogether.

"Can we warp?"

"They targeted the Light Drive and condensed fire. It's inop!"

"Maneuver us around. We're fighting them head on!"

They spun on what little Cruise Drive power they had. Eve targeted their ship and fired. The missiles homed in on their ray-like ship. It banked and pushed nose down. Their railguns fired, trying to take out as many missiles as they could. A few landed, but its shields held.

The enemy ship re-targeted *The Fade* and condensed railgun fire again. The projectiles pierced their shielding and tore through the ship. The vacuum of space threatened to kill them all, but backup shielding kicked in and patched the holes.

"Their rail heatsinks can only handle so much! Keep us from blowing up before they overheat!"

Eve launched another volley of missiles. Again, they were able to outmaneuver a few while taking a couple on the nose. The enemy's shields wavered. Then, they entered the mine field *The Fade* had left behind. The launch bays reloaded, and as soon as the target was locked, Eve launched. Ten seconds before impact, she detonated the mine trap.

The enemy's shield faltered. The mines detonated at the aft while the missiles hit the front. It was a success, but they were still coming. They were clearly not going to give up, even if it meant their destruction.

Before the next missiles were loaded, they took another barrage of concentrated, nonstop fire. They were gambling everything that they could take down *The Fade* before their heatsinks were too hot to allow it to fire anymore.

Stupid! They're risking everything for what?

"Bank starboard!" Captain Marsi yelled.

The helmsmen did what they could, but the Cruise Drive was now offline. It was clear they weren't going to escape. Since they'd gone all in, Eve tried to get them to back off with mutually assured destruction. She launched everything available. The missiles and mines were ejected toward the oncoming ship, but they plowed ahead.

The detonation shook *The Fade* hard, and systems overloaded. Main power was lost, and emergency power came on. Atmosphere was venting, and they didn't have long to survive. The enemy's gambit paid off.

"Armor! Weapons! Prepare to be boarded!"

The crew grabbed flashlights and headed to the cargo hold. Once there, they donned their gear. The enemy ship had grappled onto their underside. Unlike their tactics of cutting in through the hull, the lower cargo bay doors were being forced open. Eve and the others took up defensive positions behind crates and readied weapons.

Eve wasn't sure how many to expect, but her hand cannon was ready, and she had a belt pouch full of ammo. She hadn't anticipated the first one to breach would be AI, a QuBE. A robotic humanoid body jetted up and flipped midair, its feet magnetically attaching to their ceiling. They had a thick riot shield to hide behind while taking shots at the crew with their rifle.

The Fade's crew fired at the shield, trying to flank and get a shot from behind. Though they moved fast through the cargo bay, the QuBE was deadly accurate with their precision shots. One by one, the crew fell. Eve hadn't tried to move around the backside. Instead, she went for a locker where they housed an illegally modified *Rekwa* mining laser.

Getting to it's easy. Just have to not get shot.

Eve made a break for the weapons locker while Captain Marsi held the line. Out of the corner of her eye, she saw additional invaders boarding. The remaining of Captain Marsi's crew turned their attention to the new combatants while Eve retrieved the laser. A quick switch on, and it hummed to life. She'd need to be careful as discharging for too long would also burn right through their hull.

She leveled it at the QuBE on the ceiling and fired. The purple beam lit up the interior. The energy burned through the riot shield and the entity in a matter of moments. Eve hoped it would turn the tide in their favor, but as she was about to rejoin the rest, Captain Marsi took a bullet to the head. The combat helmet she wore probably saved her life, but there was no checking now. She was on the floor.

"Fek!" Eve said under her breath.

"Throw down your weapons!" a woman bellowed over the gunfire.

No one did. *The Fade's* crew continued to fight. One by one Eve's companions fell. If it weren't for being separated Eve might have also been shot. They were outmatched and defeat was imminent.

If they're not taking any prisoners, I need a place to hide. Maybe I can stow away in the cargo and escape at their next destination. If they find me, I can't look like a combatant. Need to ditch my gear for now.

Eve ducked behind containers and quickly stripped down to her regular clothes. Trying to be quiet she shoved the gear toward the lockers and looked for a container she could slip into. The enemy crew was making their way around, hunting for anyone left.

Sneaking around the backside of some containers where she was hidden from view, Eve climbed inside one and shut it. The metallic smell of the garocite filled her nostrils. The battle died down outside, and commands were being issued to begin retrieving the cargo.

Chapter 2
Conniving and Surviving

They were rough with the containers, and Eve felt the gravity shift as they brought her container onto the other ship. She thumped against the side and was nearly pinned by the garocite. Voices were muffled by the container, so she wasn't able to get full conversations, but it sounded like they were going to search the containers to verify contents.

It meant she only had minutes at best before she was discovered. Without knowing the layout of the ship, or the crew complement, it seemed bleak. But she wasn't going to give up, not without a fight. She waited for the voices to lessen, and then popped the lid open a crack. They were still loading the cargo. Captain Marsi and crew were nowhere in sight.

Shit. I wonder if anyone else survived.

Unlike the human crew of *The Fade*, her captors were various species. A warrior vraditi, tall and muscular, protected head to toe in gold-colored armor. A human woman with cybernetic limbs had a rifle slung over her shoulder. She, too, was wearing combat armor, though less flashy. And another QuBE, this one with vraditi-like features. They only had two eyes, unlike the vraditi, but they were built like one of the taller warrior race.

They were taking inventory of the crates, and she could hear them a little better now.

"This should be the full cargo from the elementus ship," the QuBE said, their digitalized voice vibrating amongst the containers.

"Intel said there were ten people aboard *The Fade*. We're missing one," the woman said. "Find them."

Fek. Gotta move.

Eve waited for their backs to be turned and did her best to climb out without a sound. It didn't matter. The QuBE heard her with its advanced hearing. Before she could get clear of the lid and slip away, she was caught. The QuBE pointed her out, and the woman moved swiftly, her artificial legs carrying her faster than a normal human.

Eve was snatched up by the collar of her shirt and lifted with the woman's augmented arms. She couldn't see her captor's face through their helmet and had no way to judge their demeanor.

"Stop! Please!" Eve pleaded, feigning meekness. "Who are you? What do you want?"

The QuBE approached. "Another for Captain Kohan to decide on."

The woman bound Eve's hands with cuffs and shoved her hard toward the forward side of the bay.

"Please, I'm just the cargo loader. What do you want with us?" Eve pretended to be near tears.

"Fekking shut it," the woman snapped.

Led through the cargo bay, she was marched past several dead bodies of *The Fade*'s crew and the remnants of the QuBE she shredded with the Rekwa mining laser.

Near the forward cargo bulkhead was the kitchen and dining area. It was clean and appeared well-stocked. On the left and right side of the bulkhead were doors that led up through the ship. They took the left one. In the curved hallway, Eve made mental notes.

There were several doors and a small hallway with the label "Munitions" midway through on the left side of the long hall. On the right wall were two doors, one near the aft of the hallway, one near the forward. At the far front was a door to the bridge area.

The layout was somewhat similar to *The Fade*'s. Two pilot consoles side by side in the center-front area. Four auxiliary consoles, she assumed for managing the systems of the ship. The captain's chair and console were elevated and centered so they could see out of the enormous window. It was an interesting design choice, and a point of potential failure to have a window, but it made for great viewing.

The curvature of the window and hull would reduce the stress while hitting high velocities, so long as they didn't enter at a weird angle.

Two elementus were at the helm. She couldn't get a good look at them, or what their status was based on the materials bonded to their bodies. The captain of this ship was in his chair, checking his console. Handcuffed and knelt in front of him were two members of *The Fade*. Marsi and Torp.

She's still alive?

"I'll pay you back for this," Marsi spat. "You wiped out almost my whole crew!"

Marsi's face brightened just a little bit when she locked eyes with Eve. Eve shook her head just the slightest amount to indicate that she shouldn't act familiar.

Just pretend you don't give a shit. That's all you gotta do. They haven't killed us, so we might still be able to get out of this.

"Dad, we found another. Dumb *chulk* was hiding in a cargo container." The woman sneered.

Eve bit her tongue.

The captain turned in his chair and looked Eve over. He was a broad, balding man with a dark red beard. He had a hardened look, which said he'd been in space most, if not all, of his life. Space had a way of adding years to people, especially due to the extra radiation not filtered by shielding.

"Please, I don't know what you want," Eve continued to play the innocent card.

"Soon as we're in range of the next relay see if they any have contracts out on them," he commanded his daughter. "Maybe we can get a bonus."

"Aye, Captain," she replied.

She sat at a console and input commands. The QuBE and vraditi from the cargo hold appeared and also took stations while their captain continued looking on.

"Nine, secure the prisoners in the empty room."

"Yes, Captain," they replied.

One by one, the remaining crew of *The Fade* were led out, with Eve being last. Taken into the opposite hallway, she took note of the symmetry of the ship. The interior was perfectly mirrored between left and right. Though knowing that wouldn't help in the short-term, it at least armed her with what she'd need to navigate in the event she could break free of her restraints.

We can't let them turn me in for a bounty. Need to escape at the next station. The Fade's gone, and my time with Marsi has run its course. Need to find my next ship.

She was shoved into a nearly empty room with Marsi and Torp, and the door was closed behind them.

"How did you survive?" Marsi asked.

"I made myself look like a non-combatant, and then stowed away in a crate," Eve replied. "Needed them to not see me as a threat so they wouldn't search or strip me."

"I'm glad you survived. We need to get out of here and get revenge," Marsi said.

"Torp, you doing okay?" Eve asked.

"I will be when we get back at these fekkers," he grumbled.

"One step at a time." Eve plopped down to the floor. "Help me get my boot off so we can use the electromagnetic coil in it. It should have enough charge to pop the lock on the mag-cuffs."

"Those aren't spacewalking boots," Torp observed.

"Nope. Customs to augment the artificial gravity on ship. Helps keep my legs toned," Eve replied and winked at Marsi.

Marsi complimented her, "Good thinking."

Dropping down, Marsi sat with her back to Eve and scooted close so that her bound arms could reach Eve's right foot. It took a little time due to the awkward positioning and Marsi not being able to see what she was doing, but together they got it done.

Eve turned around so she could reach the boot. She fumbled behind her back to separate the sole. Because they were customs it meant she had to be able to service them herself to ensure they functioned properly, and she had engineered a way to open it up with little effort. She dug into the rubber where the tabs were and pulled hard. Feeling around the components, she was careful to avoid the capacitor.

"Okay, scoot over here with your cuffs to me," Eve directed.

Marsi was already on the floor with her, and she came close. Eve felt the cuffs out with one hand while moving the sole of the boot with the other. It took a little time to find the right spot on the mag-cuffs to unlock them, but when she did they popped open. Marsi reciprocated on Eve, and then on Torp.

"Now what?" Torp asked.

"I'm improvising," Eve replied while reassembling her boot and putting it back on. "Something, something, take their captain hostage."

They examined the door. The room clearly wasn't designed to be a holding cell of any sort, as it had a keypad for entry, exit, and locking. Eve tried pressing buttons, but there was no response. It was disabled on this side.

"Can you do anything with it?" Eve looked at Torp.

"Eh, maybe?"

He pulled at the panel, attempting to open it. Leaving Torp to tinker, Eve grabbed up the cuffs she was wearing. Examining them, she wondered about their strength. They could hold normal humans no problem, but the enemy captain was the only normal one in their group.

We only have three people against their crew. If we could shackle the captain and the two elementus, we might have a chance. The woman, the vraditi, and the QuBE would be the real issue since they all have superior strength.

"What are you thinking," Marsi asked.

"The ship seems symmetrical. It's likely the rest of the rooms on the outer edge in either hall are bedrooms, spares, or storage. These are also too small for a captain. Best guess is that his is in the center of the ship."

"Hostage or kill?" Marsi asked.

"Maybe both. Might need collateral to get off the ship at their next port."

Marsi put her hand on Eve's shoulder and gave her a conniving smile. "Do what you do best."

It took him a bit after tearing the paneling apart to get at the wiring, but Torp found a way to bypass the lock. Eve put her ear to the door. It was quiet except for the hum of the engine.

Eve kicked her other shoe off and nodded at Torp. Silently, she signaled for Marsi to turn left out the door, and she'd turn right. If there was anyone out there, they'd attempt to overpower them. He opened the door, and they sprang out into the hallway. It was empty.

"They have no foresight. Must not have anticipated we could escape," Marsi whispered.

Eve sped to the opposite hallway wall and slunk along the curved interior back toward the bridge. At the door on her left, immediately before the one to the bridge, she examined the keypad. It was also locked. Backtracking, she waved for Torp. He followed her footsteps exactly.

"Get it done," she commanded in whisper.

He fiddled with it, and now more familiarized with the system, it took him considerably less time to break in. Unlocked, he put the panel back together, and she patted his bare arm in appreciation.

"Head back and hide. Tell Marsi she'll know if I succeed," she said leaning in.

He disappeared back into the holding room, and they shut the door. Eve entered the room she hoped was the captain's. The lights automatically came on, and inside was a well-organized collection of items from different civilizations. They didn't appear to be priceless artifacts, but the lack of dust indicated sentimental value to their owner.

Trophies of conquests maybe? Not a bad idea for when I have my own ship.

Against the rear wall was a disheveled bed with a few pieces of clothing strewn about on it. They weren't the captain's size or style, though. They were most certainly his daughter's.

No matter. I can make this work.

Rummaging through the daughter's items, she found a small, sharp knife. Eve shut the lights off and hid behind a partition that separated the bedroom area from a personal console to lie in wait.

It felt like an eternity. The hum of a Bulk Drive was white noise she could easily fall asleep to. They were making their way through one of the many shortcuts set up by the vraditi. Depending on their destination in the Crux arm of the galaxy, they could spend hours in the path.

Startled when the door opened, Eve readied to strike. There was movement and, after a few moments, she peeked around the partition. It was the captain's daughter.

The woman grabbed casual clothing from the wardrobe next to her bed and threw it down onto the end. She stripped off her combat gear. The extent of her body modifications was extreme. Both arms and legs were completely cybernetic, grafted directly into the fair skin of her body.

The woman began pulling her blonde hair out from a bun, and while her arms were raised seemed the perfect opportunity.

Ignoring the artificial limbs, she's tiny. Looks young, probably inexperienced. I should have no problem taking her down.

Hubris aside, the woman's back was to her. Eve tiptoed across the room, but either her shadow was noticed or her presence was sensed. The woman spun to confront her. Her chance for surprise gone, Eve burst into a short sprint and knocked the woman onto the bed.

With Eve lying on top of her, and the knife digging into her throat, the woman had no choice but to surrender.

"Test me," Eve warned.

"You're going to regret this," the woman snapped.

Eve smirked and leaned into the woman's face to keep her voice low. "I think we can come to an understanding. You got the cargo, trashed our ship, and killed most of our crew. Now, it would only be fair if I could repay that by killing the captain's daughter, but then your daddy would kill me for sure."

"How are you going to hold me hostage *and* make demands? The moment you let me up, I will snap your neck." The woman seethed.

"Maybe I start by disabling your limbs," Eve said and ran her free hand over an area where flesh connected to synthetic. "I mean, I'm pretty sure I could do that *before* you snap my neck."

Exposed and in a vulnerable state with Eve on top of her, the woman turned the color of a red dwarf and conceded.

"What do you want, chulk?" she snipped.

"You have a mouth on you, don't you?" Eve said. "My demands are simple. At the next port of call, I'm walking off this ship with the other two. No authorities, no bounties."

"And how do you plan on getting my father to agree to that? If you hurt me, he'll kill you."

"If he's a *good* daddy, he won't risk you being hurt in the first place. He'll do what I want."

Eve was confident. While they were all mercenaries, she bet he'd have a personal code that wouldn't unnecessarily put his daughter in harm's way.

"I'm going to activate your comms so you can call for help," Eve said.

She moved her free hand up toward the woman's ear, and she started to struggle. Eve pressed the knife harder against her throat.

"Ah, ah, ah. Don't make me kill you."

A trickle of blood had formed at the edge of the knife. It pooled and ran down the side of the woman's neck, staining the sheet. She stopped struggling, and Eve double tapped the Trauna in her captive's ear.

"Go ahead. Scream and yell for help," Eve taunted.

"Someone better get their ass to my fekking room now! One of the prisoners got loose, and she's got a knife at my neck!"

Within moments, the room was stormed by Captain Kohan, Nine, and the tall, four-eyed vraditi. Rifles were leveled at Eve, but they saw the precariousness of the situation. Eve smirked as a *gotcha*.

"You *really* ought to teach your daughter to mind her mouth. If she hadn't called you *Dad*, I wouldn't have thought to take her hostage. In fact, you're who I wanted."

"What do you want?" Captain Kohan asked.

"Safe passage to wherever the hell you're landing next, for me and the other two."

He appeared to be contemplating it and looked to Nine.

"Thoughts?" Captain Kohan said.

"Though there is a significant G.P. bounty on their captain, it's not worth risking Faun's life."

"I meant can you kill her before she hurts my daughter."

"Kill her anyway!" Faun snapped.

"The chance is slim. I don't believe that I can," Nine replied.

Captain Kohan nodded and scowled.

"It's your call, *Cap*," Eve said with a smirk.

"Your passage and freedom are secured."

Does he have an honor code? Is his word his bond?

Eve winked at him. "I need a guarantee because, the moment I let her up, you could kill me and my shipmates."

Captain Kohan's grimace showed his patience was wearing thin.

"There's no guarantee, but I promise that if you don't give up now, I *will* kill you, regardless. Nine, it's my order that this woman, and her two shipmates, are not to be killed or turned in for bounty. See her back to the room."

"Yes, Captain."

It was as good an agreement as she would get, and Eve slowly let the knife up. Being that she was covering the daughter's mostly naked body with hers, she moved slowly getting up, wanting to allow her some modesty. Captain Kohan seemed to read the situation and motioned for the vraditi to leave, then turned around.

"Faun, get dressed and then we need to have a word..." the captain said to his daughter and stepped out into the hallway.

Eve rolled off her and put her feet on the floor. She wasn't a step away from the bed before she was struck from behind. A sharp jab to her left kidney sent her to the floor, ready to vomit.

"Fekking chulk!" Faun raised her voice. "He didn't say anything about not kicking your ass."

Faun kicked her in the ribs. The full brunt of the cybernetic limb caused Eve to exhale hard.

"Faun!" Captain Kohan was firm, his voice booming off the walls. "Enough. Get dressed."

Faun let out a *tch,* and Nine picked Eve up and slung her over their shoulder. Nine carried her back to the holding room, and when the door opened Marsi and Torp took defensive stances. Nine stepped into the doorway and laid her down on the floor. While they were bent over, Marsi's foot shifted forward indicating that she was contemplating making a move. But she didn't. Nine left, and Marsi came to her side to help her sit up.

"Well, you're not dead. So, I assume we're going to prison."

Eve shook her head, still trying to recover.

"Well, you were carried in. That doesn't look good. Did you negotiate?"

"Yeah," Eve rasped out. "Took the captain's pretty little daughter hostage and used her as collateral to buy passage."

"Do you think they'll actually let us go?" Torp asked.

"We'll have to wait and see. Their captain seems a little rough around the edges, but I get an air of integrity from him."

"Good girl. Did you catch where we're headed?" Marsi kissed her cheek.

"Emex Station Eight."

"Elementus controlled." Marsi scratched the side of her head. "We're not likely going to find a new ship there for a reasonable price with all of the taxes. We'll probably be better off buying passage to a salvage yard to find a hull to build up to our liking. Unless you two squandered your bounties from previous jobs, the three of us should have enough to get back into business."

She did, but buying into a ship wasn't the same as having her own. It meant her cuts would be greater, and she might be able to captain her own sooner, but she wasn't convinced this would be the right move. While they waited to reach their destination, Eve continued to contemplate her future.

They knew when the ship exited the bulk path by the sound. The hull hummed differently when the Cruise Drive fired up. It wasn't possible to gauge how fast they were going without instruments, but Eve knew the space station wasn't far from that path.

About a half-hour passed, and the ship slowed. It began a cycle of moving and stopping, indicating they were in queue to dock. Eve stood and readied to be forced off the ship. She looked down at Marsi.

She doesn't have a ship anymore. Might be a while before she gets one again. This relationship may have run its course.

Nine entered the room and waved for them to follow. They were led out through the cargo hold, where the tail section of their ship opened, its ramp down. The crew was already busy offloading the garocite containers into the bay. Faun saw Eve and sneered. Eve flashed her a cheeky grin and blew her a kiss.

Captain Kohan was on the deck, talking with a well-ornamented elementus who seemed to be taking inventory. He eyed Eve.

"So, you wouldn't have grabbed my gun from *The Fade* before blowing it up, would you?" Eve asked him, interrupting their conversation.

"All of your cargo was forfeited," he said sharply. "Get out of my sight."

Damn. I really liked that gun.

Nine led them across the hangar. Eve expected that at any moment G.P. would come out and arrest them, and Nine would collect a bounty. But, when they were far enough from the ship, Nine stopped following. They were free.

Emex Station Eight was one of the more frequented hubs in Tor Galom space. As far as Eve could recall, no one but elementus were allowed on their planets Tor Galom Ig and Tor Galom Aq, and so they were required to come here to do business.

She also knew because it was a popular destination, it also made it a good place to pick up work. Granted, not their last job in which they were supposed to secure the garocite *from* the elementus, but she figured there would be something she could do to kill time while determining her next move.

"I'm going to sniff around, find out where ships are going, and if we can catch a ride," Marsi told them. "In the meantime, we need replacement weapons and gear."

"Aye, Captain," Torp replied.

"Hey, Torp, go on ahead," Eve said.

Just gotta rip the bandage off.

Torp headed toward the entrance to the main city. Eve put her hands in her pockets and gave Marsi a half smile. Marsi looked concerned.

"So, I need some time to reevaluate where I'm going next," Eve said with deadpan tone.

"What?"

"I'm probably going to hang out here on station for a bit. Might pick up some contract work."

"We lose the ship, and you're out? What about the two years we've spent together?"

"We had a good run," Eve said and put her hand on Marsi's shoulder. Marsi immediately shrugged it off, and grimaced.

"Don't placate me. I thought *we* had something."

"We did. We had *fun*. Now, the fun is over, and I'm moving on."

Marsi's face became red, and Eve couldn't determine if it was from anger or embarrassment. Ultimately, any action by Marsi wouldn't change her mind, and she wanted to leave on good terms.

"I'll see you around," Eve said with a wink and another pat to the shoulder.

Marsi cursed her as she heading off toward the main city entrance. With nowhere to be, her stroll was leisurely and her eyes wandered around the hangar. It was fairly standard, much like every other one she'd been to in her life. Bland, lots of ships, cargo of all sizes, and an uncountable amount of people of all spacefaring species.

Past the bulkhead doors, the scenery took on a different feel to it. A large overhead ceiling had lights that gave off the same hue as a red dwarf. The ceiling and walls were highlighted with volcanic reds and crusted grays and blacks. While the ambiance was dimmed, it still made for a spectacular sight. The elementus seemed to prefer all things that reflected their very name, elemental.

While the base construction of the walls and ceilings were elementus in design, the buildings were open to the stylistic whims of whomever owned it. That created a vast sea of design choices to look at. Illuminated signs beckoned patrons into the businesses, and there was no rhyme or reason to what business was where. A hotel was placed by a pharmacy, a weapon store by a food mart, and an organized fighting ring by a jeweler.

When she was still exploring with her parents, she was always intrigued with the bustling about of all the species. Her dad had to have known the dangers of independent station cities as he always had his sidearm on him when entering and kept Eve reined in.

Eve wandered beyond the first street, which catered to the people on quick layovers and started searching some of the more poorly lit streets for a bar to have a drink at. Something that would feel more her style. One with a familiar name drew her in: The Fate Weaver. It was one of many mercenary bars with the same name and a place one could pick up work anonymously.

Inside the seedy bar were many patrons, most concealed with cloaks, masks, and partially closed combat helmets. Some, however, openly flaunted who they were, as if challenging others to try and collect any potential bounty on them. Eve was the latter type. She was confident if someone tried to start something with her, it would end with her foot on their neck.

She sat at a back table and motioned for the tapster to bring a drink menu. Before one of the leather-clad men of the establishment approached, she was joined by a tall, familiar vraditi. It was the one from the ship she'd just disembarked.

"What do you want?" Eve cut right to the chase.

"To drink," he said in his language, with Salvoan overlaid so she could understand.

The tapster came over, dropped a tablet on the table, and returned to the bar. Eve picked it up and scrolled through the menu to find something stiff to drink. Her mood was leaning toward a distilled root alcohol. She ordered two shots of Pentin Spirits, a minty, sour, and salty flavored alcohol. She dropped the tablet onto the table, and the vraditi picked it up to order as well.

She eyed him while he scrolled the menu for his own drink.

"I meant with me. You followed me," she said and crossed her arms.

"You are strong and cunning. I respect that. I drink with those I respect."

The tapster came back with their drinks, and they weren't on the table half a second before Eve knocked the first shot back. It tasted exactly like it smelled, rough. The aftertaste was where it got better. The vraditi picked up his pitcher of frothy, amber alcohol, and drank straight from it.

"Got a name?" she said.

"Ruzat."

"All right, Ruzat. Your boss send you after me?"

"No."

She slammed back the second shot, ordered two more, and a plate of Ralu, small fried meat cubes. Ruzat was halfway through his pitcher and ordered again. When the tapster came over with the next wave of items, another pitcher and a saucy plate of meat and vegetables, she made sure to speak up.

"I'm not picking up your tab," she told him with slurred words.

"Your drinks and food are on me," he said and raised his pitcher in honor.

She downed the third shot and shoveled a handful of the cubes into her mouth.

"Even better. Thanks," she replied with a grin. "So, how'd you get in with Kohan?" she asked. "Been with him long?"

"I threatened his life. Nearly got caught by the G.P. because of an illegal trade deal, one that he brokered. I tracked him, we brawled, and I kicked his ass. The G.P. caught up to us though and we escaped on his ship. Been with him since."

"Sounds like a hell of a ride."

"What about you? How long have you been with your captain?"

"Two years, but I'm a free agent. Merc all the way."

Silence fell between them. Her head swam, and she couldn't tell if the bar had gotten louder or if her tolerance for noise had lowered. Ruzat sat there staring with his four black eyes. It felt like he was trying to size her up.

"Why are you staring?" she asked and drank the last shot.

"What is next for you?"

"Haven't figured it out yet? Why?"

"You are capable. Resourceful. We are down a crew member."

"So, your captain *did* send you after me..."

"No. I will call him. Tell him you should join us. You will be better than another QuBE."

She thought about it.

It's an idea, I suppose. I'd be on a fully functional ship and stay gainfully employed.

"Fine. Call him." She waved her hand dismissively.

Ruzat stood and headed to the bar for a moment, and then exited. Eve picked at the meat cubes, and then put her head down in her arms. It felt like moments but could have been an hour for all she knew when she was tapped heavily on her shoulder. She looked up to see Ruzat and Captain Kohan.

"Is this a joke?" Captain Kohan asked Ruzat.

"I knew you would not come down if I told you it was for her. She is for hire, capable, and has a warrior spirit. Better replacement for Gali because she is flesh."

Captain Kohan pulled Ruzat aside, and they whispered in a heated conversation Eve couldn't hear. Kohan crossed his arms and shook his head. Ruzat persisted. Eve spoke up loudly so they would hear her.

"If you don't want me, whatever, no problem. I'm content to join whatever other ship comes my way. That's kinda the point of being a merc."

Kohan turned to her and returned her cadence, raising his voice.

"Joining my ship isn't as simple as signing the roster. We bust our asses to complete whatever job it is we're doing, and if you want to join us, you have to prove you can, too," he snapped.

"So, what do I have to do, *your Eminence*?"

His brows furrowed, and he scowled, but there was no rebuke as she expected.

"Pick up a level three contract and complete it. Membership fee to join *Skyfire* is fifty thousand and one chits and proof of the completed contract. You have one and a half galactic days to get it done and get to the ship."

He was firm, and she knew it meant time was ticking starting right now. She was drunk and he was challenging her. She wasn't going to let him lord a failed attempt over her.

"Forty-five hours? Psht. I'll see you soon," Eve slurred and winked.

Captain Kohan turned in a huff and left. Ruzat nodded to her, and then followed Kohan. The captain wasn't impressed now, but when she stepped up on deck again with the completed contract in hand, he'd acknowledge her as the right choice to fill that slot on his ship.

Drunk, she hobbled up to the counter where the tapster was cleaning the bar.

"Gimme a menu."

"You've had enough," he replied.

"Not that menu, chulk. Let me see the *other* menu."

He pulled a tablet from underneath the counter, entered something into it, and slid it over. To the uninitiated, it was a list of exotic beverages. In reality, they were job contracts. There were normal merc contracts, ones that didn't require anything illegal. Then, there were her tastes. Gun for hire, illicit cargo hauling, espionage, theft. Nothing was really off limits as a contract. If you were up to something illegal, all you had to do was not get caught by Galactic Police.

Clicking over to the third-tier tab, she swiped through, looking at the prices. Each was a hidden reflection of what the reward was. A five hundred chit contract would yield a fifty thousand chit payout, and a level three contract had a minimum payout of fifty thousand and one.

The first drink was called Microchip and cost five hundred fifty. She wasn't a techie, so she swiped to the next one. Six hundred chits would get her Infiltrate and Interrogate, and it sounded right up her alley. However, when she tried to purchase, it resulted in an error message: "This drink is no longer being served."

"Piece of trash!" she muttered.

Scrolling again, she came to one called Skyway Heist for seven fifty. Not wanting to miss this contract, she mashed her finger on the purchase button. The transaction went through, and she was taken to a payment screen. She tapped her wrist near the scanner so it could read a subdermal nano-chip that accessed her account.

The transaction complete, the tapster took back the tablet, and she waited. He brought her another drink, this time on a coaster. She picked up the glass and drank. It was water. Taking the coaster, she pocketed it and headed out from the bar. When she was clear of the area, she retrieved it. There was a location printed on it.

Heading over to a Wayfinder station, she input the location, and it gave her directions.

Chapter 3
Will Merc For Transport

When she arrived at her destination, she was in a back alley. Her level of caution and leeriness was piqued because she lacked her hand cannon, and she typically didn't attempt contracts after drinking so heavily. It didn't stop her, but she knew the only defense she had right now were drunken swings and kicks.

When she reached the halfway point through the alley, a shrouded figure entered from the other end and walked toward her at a quick pace. Though there was no one else, it was a possibility they weren't her contact. Eve stopped and crossed her arms, her right foot planted firmly behind her.

The figure came close, and no words were exchanged. The cloaked elementus reached its rocky hand out and handed her a cheap, palm-sized tablet. It was one that could be picked up at any market for a hundred chits and weren't traceable to an individual.

When it was firmly in her hand, the being walked away, and she checked it. There was a dossier on her target, and two photos. The first picture was of a well-dressed man with a neatly trimmed beard and moustache. The second was a closeup of the items to be pilfered adorned on his neck and ear.

Target: Keron DeLovo

Items of Interest: Latticed garocite & platinum necklace with briolette cut garnet and matching earrings.

Optimal Location of Interception: Tor Galom Mining Exhibition Hall

Optimal Time of Interception: 22:00 - 30:00

Additional Intel: DeLovo will be moving between different mining expedition crews looking to hire. Security at the venue will be high.

She pocketed the tablet and headed back to the street to find another Wayfinder station. When she arrived, she looked at the time. It was now 27:42. She figured there was no way this contract was for today, but she'd head that way and start a stakeout.

While walking through the city, she stopped in on a second-hand clothing shop that suited her tastes. A fully tattooed, human, woman nodded at her as she entered, and then returned to patching up a leather jacket. Eve approached and leaned on the countertop with her palms.

"Help me put together an outfit. Functional and able to fit a tactical bodysuit under."

The woman set her project aside and sized Eve up with a look. Being a tall woman, she knew it would be harder for the shop owner to find something her size.

"What's your style?" the shop owner asked.

"Functional but alluring. A bit grunge."

But she moved from behind the counter and began digging into stuffed racks.

There was no haste in her step, but she was efficient as she moved from rack to rack and threw things over her arm. She made a few trips back to the counter to set things down, and then back out to the floor to pick up more. Finally, she stopped bringing things over and laid everything out.

There were certain items that immediately drew Eve's attention. One by one, she pointed at the pieces that would become her ensemble. A white cutoff tank top with a big pink X spray painted on; a cropped leather bolero jacket; black cargo pants; a black studded belt; combat boots.

The woman rang up the total on her tablet, and it came to ten thousand chits with tax and station surcharges.

"Got any gloves?" Eve asked.

The woman pointed to a rack, and Eve picked out a cheap set that fit. The pair added another three hundred to the total. Eve scanned her chip to complete the transaction. She slung her new garments over her shoulder and headed to the changing room. The clothing fit well, though the bolero was a little tight against her chest. She opted not to fasten it with the straps. Without a tactical bodysuit underneath, her midriff was a little cold.

Need to get one. Can't have exposed skin in combat.

The shop owner handed her a tan canvas bag to put her old clothing and shoes into, and Eve haphazardly chucked them in.

Back out on the street, she consulted a Wayfinder and found a few hotels in the nearby region of the Exhibition Hall. They were only an hour away by foot, and it gave her time to get used to the new boots.

As the queen of her own destiny, it was important to her that she feel confident in everything she did, and new clothes definitely helped set the tone. She walked with purpose; her head held high. She loved the feeling.

Along the way, she stopped by two other places. One for a bowl of noodles and broth, the other for combat gear.

Inside the weapon's store red lights beamed down, and it felt as if she'd walked into a sauna. When she saw the silverish ore adorned elementus staffing the store, she understood. Their internal temperatures ran much hotter than humans, and they liked to keep their room temperatures high.

She was already starting to sweat. Moving quickly, she priced what she needed. The tactical bodysuit was going to cost thirty thousand chits alone, and a new hand cannon was another twenty. A riot mask and binoculars were five each. After the taxes and station surcharges, it would be well over sixty-five thousand. She choked a little. It had been a long time since she'd had to buy gear.

I wonder if Captain Kohan has my gun. Bet I could get it back from him! But if I'm going to rob DeLovo I need something. I wonder how hard it would be to dual wield hand cannons.

After browsing, she brought a black bodysuit her size, a budget pair of binoculars, and a higher end black riot mask over to the elementus at the counter. A nice gun with a long barrel and extended magazine caught her eye in the locked case at the counter.

"Give me that one," she stated.

The elementus unlocked the case and pulled it out, rang the items up, and then caught her off guard.

"Place your hands on the pad and state your full name for identification."

"What?"

"To register the gun," they said and pushed a wide hand-scanner tablet toward her.

Still a little fuzzy from the alcohol, she'd forgotten legitimate establishments required it in order to purchase a gun. Marsi was on a wanted list, but was *she*? If she was, the sale would be denied and authorities would be called. She decided not to push her luck.

"Never mind the gun. I'll just grab that tactical knife." She pointed to a seven-inch blade in the next case over. "My new boss will have a gun he can register to me."

The elementus didn't bat an eye and returned the gun to its case, then grabbed the knife Eve had indicated.

"Fifty thousand, two hundred and five chits."

"I'll give you forty-five for the lot."

"The prices are non-negotiable," the elementus said and looked up casually from their computer terminal.

"They are if you want me to spend my money here. Or I'll go down to the next shop and tell them you're offering discounts and get one from them."

They sighed and re-rang her up. Forty-nine thousand even. It wasn't much of a discount, but it was better than nothing. She paid, grabbed up her gear, and stuffed it in the canvas bag. On her way out, she blew the elementus a sarcastic kiss for the measly discount.

Two space battles, sleep-deprived, and tipsy, she needed to crash. The first hotel she stopped into across from the Exhibition Hall was mediocre, but it would give her the best vantage point to scope out the area.

Red lights in the lobby beamed down. She removed her jacket and held it with her bag. The elementus at reception had greenish minerals and rocks adhered to their body.

"I need a room," Eve said through a yawn.

"Do you have a reservation?" they asked, their mouth in a slightly crooked smile.

"No reservation. Just give me something on this side of the building, with a window."

"Our non-reservation rate is two thousand chits."

It was an outrageous amount, but she didn't really have a choice, nor did she have the energy to fight with them over it. She nodded, and they processed her in. The elementus handed her a room key with the room number embedded in it.

"You have rented the room for one galactic day. We do serve a light breakfast of seared *alor* root, hot *inani* berries, and *plesian* flat bread from 06:00 to 10:00."

None of the food sounded appealing, and she was sure the alor root would leave her with a nasty stomachache. Without a further word to them, she waved them off and followed signs for the elevator.

Fifth floor, room five-oh-two. She entered but didn't turn the light on because her head had started to pound. A hangover had begun to set in. Before doing anything else, she adjusted the temperature to human conditions.

Tossing her bag and jacket on the floor next to the bed, she headed to the window to look out at the city. The Exhibition Hall was on the other side of a park, and she had a perfect vantage point. The rest of the scenery was moot for her mission, but the wonder of a lively city inside a space station wasn't lost on her.

Near the bed there was an alarm clock, and she set it for ten hours. She only took off the leather bolero before planting herself face first into the bed.

She slept heavily. When she awoke to the alarm, it had already been beeping at her for ten minutes, and she had been completely unaware.

She smacked it hard to silence it and groaned while forcing her stiff muscles to do as she willed. Up and off the bed, she shuffled to the purification chamber room. Stripping down, she tossed her clothes to the side, and set the chamber's settings to human.

Inside, the chamber door closed, and it filled with the cleansing goo raining from the top. As it completely filled, she reminded herself to exhale as it reached her mouth to make the intake easier. The cycle ran, and then when the gelatinous substance was evacuated, warm air blew over her to finish the job.

She collected her clothing and returned to the main bedroom. Tossing the clothes on the bed, she pulled out the tactical bodysuit and slipped into it. It was snug, and even more so when she zipped it up over her chest, but that was how she liked it. With it on, she felt far more protected than without.

Throwing her clothes on over it, she admired the look in the mirror. All she had to do now was find a way to corral her red curls, which had frizzed out.

Grabbing the binoculars, she poked them out from between the curtains. It took her a minute to get her bearings, but she got a clear line on the Exhibition Hall and the parking garage next to it. Between it and the hotel was a park that she'd have to cross. It was mostly open field and short foliage, with a skyway running alongside it. She didn't anticipate too much difficulty.

Vehicles were flying into the parking garage, but when she looked at the clock again, it was far too soon for her target to be there.

Must be the miners getting set up for their show.

There was a computer terminal in the room, and she figured some research on the guy couldn't hurt. Looking up DeLovo, there were a handful of business-related articles about him, all of which gave her the impression he was predictable and punctual. But what she was really looking for were pictures. Anything which might tell her how he'd be arriving.

In the second article, she found him posed in front of a building, and in the background was a gaudy, two-story vehicle similar to a bus.

The picture looks like it might be on Salvoa. Would he be vain enough to bring it all the way out here? Better research it for a way in, just in case.

She couldn't find any information about his vehicle, but looking up similar models gave a little insight to the design. The first level of the bus was accessible through one of three doors. There were two cab doors and a main entrance. The second level had no direct way up from the outside. Inside were stairs leading up to it.

Could I climb the bus to the top without being seen? I guess it all depends on how tight security is.

After getting a bite to eat out at a street vendor, she returned to the room and cut up the black bed sheet to make a tattered headscarf. She covered her hair, and then put on the riot mask. Looking in the wall mirror, she was confident she wouldn't be identified.

The time was nearing when DeLovo was supposed to be arriving. Taking off the mask, she sat at the window with the binoculars up and watched every vehicle going into the parking garage. It was strenuous on her eyes, but she wasn't going to take her attention off the area for more than a moment.

An hour past the time on her dossier, a vehicle similar to the one in the photo came down from the skyway. It entered past a guard shack, and she lost sight of it. Waiting, her eyes didn't leave the area from the garage to the Exhibition Hall entrance. DeLovo appeared from a side door to the garage, surrounded by four bodyguards.

By the time I get over there, he'll be inside and thoroughly engaged in whatever it is he does. Might have to jog a bit to make sure I get there in a reasonable time in case he comes out early.

She strapped the knife to her waist and pocketed the contract tablet. Her jacket and everything else went in the bag, including the destroyed sheet. After canvasing the room for any other evidence she might've left, she slipped out of the hotel quietly.

She kept a brisk pace across the park of alien grass and plants toward the Exhibition Hall. Along the way, she ditched the sheet into a trash bin. The bag was significantly less bulky and a lot lighter.

There was a rugged look about her. She knew she could pass as a worker for a mining expedition. It wasn't a problem being seen climbing the steps of the Exhibition Hall; after all, she was a mercenary. After that, she needed to use discretion. There were many people of various species milling about on the steps. When she reached the top, she contemplated going inside and finding a way to ambush him there, but there were too many eyes.

Maybe I can catch him off guard in his own vehicle. If I lie in wait, I could snatch the items after he takes off, and then bail. Just need to be careful about guards and guns.

Turning toward the garage, she made her way to the side door. It was locked, but she didn't have to wait long for someone to come out. Pretending to have been reaching for the door when they were exiting, she moved out of the way.

"Oop. Excuse me," she said and held the door for them.

After they'd passed, she slipped in. The first thing she did was to scan for cameras. There were a few, including one directly over her head. Retrieving the mask, she put it on and slipped through the darker areas of the garage.

Avoiding the cameras wasn't terribly hard, but the longer it took to find DeLovo's vehicle, the more chances she had of being caught. Rather than search each individual floor, she predicted someone who had a vehicle like that would probably have it parked higher up.

He's wealthy enough that he'd park in VIP, away from potential underclass who might want to rob him.

In the shadows, she made her way from one level to the next. Whenever possible, she slunk directly under cameras.

Haven't seen any patrolling guards. Perhaps they're too confident no one will try anything here.

Finally, at the top of the complex, she understood why. The lower levels were exactly as she'd thought, less important. The top level was far more protected with cameras, as well as guards. Eve took her time surveilling and watching the pattern of the cameras and guard movements.

DeLovo's vehicle was midway down the garage, and getting there while avoiding detection would be difficult. Eve hoped that his model of the vehicle was like the ones she researched.

There are rails on top. Might be my lucky day.

Crouched, she watched for the right moments to move between vehicles. Hugging the wall, hiding in the shadows as best as she could, she avoided the cameras directly overhead. So long as a guard wasn't passing, when the cameras on the walls and pillars across on the other side panned away she moved.

The guards were clearly comfortable with their positions, as they meandered while patrolling. Midway down the garage, she stopped to reevaluate the movements. She'd reached an area where guard paths overlapped, making it a little harder to move. Patient, she held still while waiting for them to move on.

When she reached DeLovo's vehicle she noticed a camera positioned on the wall directly in line and above the vehicle.

Shit.

It panned left and right, and she timed it. Ten seconds from one side to another, with a very brief two-second pause at each side.

I have almost no time to climb up to the top before it comes back and I'll still have to duck out of sight, too. Can't cut the cord because it would probably instantly draw attention.

The patrol passed, and the camera panned. Eve tossed her bag up to the top first. It made it over the railing and landed with a soft *thud*. She assessed the cab's front end which sloped up to the top. It was a steep climb, but she felt it was doable.

It took another five minutes for the right timing between the guards passing and the cameras. As soon as the camera above her head passed the midway, she scrambled to climb the cab. Once there, she swung her legs over the railing and dropped out of sight. Out of view, the only thing she'd likely left as evidence were bootprints.

Still, she dared not to move for a few minutes. On the floor of the vehicle's second level, she scouted her surroundings. Purple velvet couches and a minibar, but not a lot else. To her right was a set of steep stairs down into the main cabin. With no one having come for her, she felt it was safe enough to slide down and hopefully hide out until DeLovo returned.

The décor was similar inside, in that DeLovo appeared to like the color purple. Purple lights were strung across the ceiling, and a mirrored ball hung in the center caused the light to dance. It was gaudy. She liked a little luxury, but not this much.

Passing the bar next to the stairs, she laid on the couch. The time spent alone with her thoughts waiting was painfully boring. All she hoped was that this would go well, and she'd be on her way to the next job on a new ship.

Patience turned to boredom. She couldn't do anything to pass the time for fear she might move something that would be noticed. She lost track of time and startled when she heard voices coming near to the door. She sprung up and tiptoed over to the bar to hide. With four bodyguards sure to bear down on her if they got the chance, she needed to make sure she was the first to act.

Behind and under the counter, she was hidden from view. One voice was doing all the talking, and it didn't sound like it was to anyone in his company.

"The Miners Union is milking the contracts. The larger crews are forcing an across-the-board ten percent pay increase on their costs," he said with contempt. "There's been a significant increase in materials for building ships, and they smell the money to be made. They want a higher cut. Fekking chulk."

There was a *bang* from the other side of the bulkhead, where the cab was. The engine hummed to life, and the vehicle lifted off. DeLovo continued his conversation while his driver made their way out from the garage.

"Yeah, I'm sending a counteroffer to a few of the crews. Just need to figure out which of them is the weakest link, and then their whole union will burn themselves over who can bid the lowest. Uh-huh. All right. I'll keep you apprised."

DeLovo sighed, then groaned. It was quiet for a few minutes, and she could tell they'd made it out to the skyway. They accelerated, and someone stood up.

"Drink, Mr. DeLovo?"

"Yeah. Get me a bottle of Gowarian ale."

The chiller was directly next to where she was, and it meant her discovery was imminent. With one of the guards in the driver seat, she figured a four-on-one fight would be okay as long as she was able to use the one coming as a shield and secure whatever weapon he had.

As he rounded the corner, Eve sprang to her feet with her large knife in hand. It found a home in his side. Caught off guard, she was able to confiscate his sidearm with ease.

"Down! Get down!" she yelled while kicking out his knee.

Jumping behind the guard, she put his own gun to his head. The other two guards scrambled to cover DeLovo and pulled their pistols out. Eve made sure her head was directly behind the man's whom she held captive.

"No one needs to die today," Eve said. "All I need is your fancy looking necklace and earrings."

"Who the fek do you think you are?" DeLovo seethed. "Shoot her!"

They didn't hesitate and fired their weapons into her hostage. Thankfully, he was bulky enough that she was safe for a moment, but not if they kept firing. She took aim from behind his slumped body and fired a round directly into the skull of the guard on her left.

"GET IN THERE!" DeLovo screamed.

The vehicle swerved and decelerated. The other guard rushed forward in an attempt to tackle Eve over her cover. He landed on her, and they wrestled around behind the bar, out of view from DeLovo. They struggled, him holding both her wrists so she could use neither the knife nor the gun. Her knee found his groin, and he dry-heaved. His grip weakened, and she did it again.

DeLovo appeared around the side of the bar with a gun and aimed. Eve hid completely under the man on top of her. DeLovo unloaded his magazine. It was a dozen bullets. When she knew he'd have to reload, she poked out and fired a shot into his knee. He collapsed and screamed in pain, gripping his now shredded kneecap.

Her time was running out. The vehicle had stopped, and there would be another guard to deal with in a moment. Eve shoved the man off her and leapt up. Kicking the gun from DeLovo, she looked down in contempt.

"Psht. I *said* no one had to die. You just *had* to complicate things," she mocked him while fighting to get the earrings out.

He fought her with bloody hands, but she pistol-whipped him in the temple and knocked him out. Her job was much easier now that all but one person was out of her way. With the gun in her belt line, and the earrings and necklace shoved into a pocket, she bounded up to the second floor and grabbed the bag she'd thrown up there earlier. The surefire way to escape would be to jump and run.

They had set down in a field near an artificial lake. Sirens of Galactic Police vehicles sounded, and her best option to get away would be to jump in the water and ditch the mask and makeshift headscarf. Over the side, and down the sloped cab, she bolted toward the lake. Ripping the mask off, she skipped it like a flat stone in the opposite direction she'd be swimming, and jumped in.

Once under the water, she untied the headscarf and pushed it down below her. She wasn't the best swimmer, but she had amazing control of her lungs. She trained both for controlling her breath in case of a low oxygen environment and for pushing out as much air as humanly possible in the event of being temporarily exposed to the vacuum of space.

There were lights overhead, and she wondered if she'd gone deep enough to be obscured. Her boots and the bag gave a significant amount of resistance as she kicked her legs, but her lengthy arms pulled her along. When she felt far enough away, she surfaced, took a breath, and dove under again.

The far end of the small lake came up quickly, and she smacked into it with her hands, skinning her knuckles on a rock. Turning over, she poked her face above the water and let it roll from her eyes before opening them. She had made it a long distance from where DeLovo's vehicle was set down and where the police were searching.

Not wanting to draw too much attention, she slowly slipped from the water to the grassy embankment. Behind her was a park with bushes and trees, which she figured would make for decent cover to get away. Coming up to the first tree, she hid and let the water drip off.

There were a handful of peoples milling about the park in a few different directions, but none of them paid any attention to her. Rather, they were intrigued by what was going on across the lake. It didn't take her long to get away from the park and back onto the streets.

A thought occurred to her, then, and it caused a panic. Patting her pockets, she fished for the cheap palm-tablet. It was waterlogged, and inoperable. Shaking it, Eve tried drying it off, but it was useless. The tablet was busted.

Damnit. I need to find a repair shop and see if it's even fixable. "Shit!" she swore out loud. *Maybe I can report the success back at the bar.*

There was a Wayfinder station nearby, and she consulted the map to find The Fate Weaver. It was a fair distance away, and she'd already started to chafe from the little bit of walking so far. She didn't want to waste any time and hailed a private ride car from the terminal.

It was there within a few minutes, and she climbed in. Before the elementus driver even noticed she was drenching their seat, she barked her destination at them.

"The Fate Weaver."

The vehicle lifted up and spun around. It was a ten minute ride, and they'd made it back to the larger street that led back to the hangar of the station. From there, she'd have no problem finding it. The fare came up, fifty-five chits, and she scanned her chip on the payment screen. It cleared, and she got out.

Back at the bar, she headed immediately for the tapster behind the counter. The tablet made a small *plink* as she laid it down, and she waved him over.

"I bought a contract yesterday, and I need to mark it complete."

He slid the same tablet over he had the other night, and it asked for her to connect her tablet to read the information. With her tablet dead, she had no way to link them.

"You have any other way of completing it? My tablet's fried," she said, tapping on hers.

"Whatever tablet you were given has a unique ID. Without it, you can't mark the contract complete."

"What about fixing it? I need to get this done so I can get the fek out of here."

He eyed her, annoyed, and scribbled down a business. She looked at the time and still had a few hours to kill before *Skyfire* would disembark. She snatched the paper and her tablet up and headed back out. Thankfully, the shop she was looking for was right down the street. When she got in there, she approached the amber and metallic elementus at the counter and held the tablet out expectantly for them.

"I need this fixed. I'm in a rush."

The elementus took it and spoke with a soft voice.

"Repair fee is four hundred, plus a three hundred rush fee."

The pad's value wasn't even worth close to that, and she'd already spent a significant amount trying to get this contract completed, but there was no other way.

"Six hundred," she negotiated.

They eyed her for a moment, and then nodded. Disappearing into the back, she figured it would be a while. There were no seats, so she slumped against a wall and closed her eyes. It was an hour or so before the elementus called out for her.

When she reached the counter, they handed her the tablet, and she confirmed it was working. Satisfied, she paid and rushed back to the bar. At the counter again, she waved the tapster over. Eve didn't need to say anything. They brought what she needed, and she clicked onto the confirmation screen. Tapping her tablet to the bar's, it asked if the job was complete. She clicked *yes*, and both screens went blank.

Now, she only had to wait. Time was running out for her to make it to the ship with the payment and proof of completed contract. Every time someone came in, she looked over her shoulder. Of course, she didn't know who she was looking for so, really, it was just a reaction. The tapster also gave no indication in his interaction with patrons.

A woman dressed in a large, brimmed hat and a casual flower print dress sat next to Eve. They eyed each other, and the woman smiled at Eve.

"Come here often?" she said with a sultry voice.

"Nope."

"Well, lucky for you I do. And I happen to know they have a private room we could talk in."

Eve's curiosity got the better of her, and she took a good look. The woman was obviously well off and didn't fit in at this out of the way bar. She had blue lipstick on, and a light eyeshadow to match. Not quite Eve's type, but she could acknowledge beauty.

"Come," the woman said and grabbed her hand.

Eve grabbed her tablet, stood, and followed, figuring this was her client. The woman led them to a back room and closed the door. It was a small, dimly lit room with red sheer curtains hanging around a few couches. The woman led Eve to the couch, and they sat.

"Tell me…what was Keron's facial expression when you took the jewelry?" the woman asked, blissful.

"Before or after I shot him in the leg?"

"Oh! Tell me everything!"

Eve recounted her exploits, and the woman was attentive. She held out her hand after Eve's story was over. The jewelry passed to the client's hands, still wet, but the woman didn't care. She put it on anyway. Again, she put her hand out, and Eve dropped the tablet in it. With a few finger swipes, and then waving her hand, she handed it back.

Eve verified the completion of the contract and payment. Seventy-five thousand. Transferring the excess to her personal chip, she left the exact fee of fifty thousand and one for Kohan. On her feet, she was ready to head out. The woman grabbed her hand.

"I have a place you can get cleaned up and wash your clothes."

"Next time. Got a ship to catch."

Out of the room, and onto the street, she jogged toward the docking bay. From the entrance, she could still see the ship. The crew were loading the last of a few small boxes. Faun, Ruzat, and Nine were on the platform while Captain Kohan and the two elementus were taking the boxes they handed up. Faun saw her coming and protested loudly.

"What in the fek are you doing here?" Faun paused and recoiled, appearing to hold back a gag. "What *is* that smell?"

"I'm part of your crew now, Princess," Eve said with snark and winked.

The damp clothing was rubbing sores onto her thighs, but she wasn't going to show her discomfort. Upon climbing the ramp, she handed the pad over with the verification of completed level three contract and the fee. Captain Kohan checked it.

"Good. You're on a probationary period—"

She cut him off with impertinence, "Great. I'll get started. Let me know which room is mine and when I can clean up."

"No! This isn't going to happen." Faun approached her dad, crossed her arms and stomped a foot. "I refuse to work with..."

Eve drowned her out as she strung together a string of graphic insults. Down the ramp, she began helping load the final few boxes.

Chapter 4
Second Impressions

After loading supplies, Eve introduced herself to the two shipmates she had yet to formally meet. The elementus.

"I'm Lady Eve," she said, forcing the title.

The two were different than most of the other elementus she'd had dealings with. They both had refined metals bonded on their bodies, but one was clearly of a higher stature than the other.

"Hello, Lady Eve. I am Balok Tecto."

Balok's head and torso were bonded with smooth, dark, and polished ore. Their shoulders were covered with large amber colored crystals, and their arms and legs were covered with reddish-gray rocks.

"And I am Virid Tecto."

The biggest tell Virid was from a better clan was that their head was bonded with a crown of various-colored gems. They were prominent only to the point that they stuck out from the platinum ores bonded to most of their body. Their arms and legs matched Balok's.

"Siblings or mates?" Eve asked unabashedly.

"We are fused with the blessing of the Elementus Suprus," Balok replied.

Eve took it to mean they were married but had no idea if the Elementus Suprus was clergy of some kind or a government figurehead.

I'm sure it will come up at some point. They seem quiet, though, so I might have to probe some.

"Virid, file the flight plan out of the hangar. Balok, prepare the ship for de-dock," Captain Kohan ordered.

The crew made their way to the bridge, with Eve following directly behind Kohan. The two elementus sat at their stations and attended to their duties. Everyone but Eve had their console to sit at. She took a chair at an empty one.

They were soon under way toward the two-tiered shield, which kept the hangar pressurized. Ships of all sizes were headed to and from the docking bay. Because *Skyfire* was a frigate class, they were able to easily squeeze in between mid-tier cruisers and a few larger cargo barges.

They were put into a holding pattern while waiting for the port to clear. When it was their group's turn, the first shield was lowered, and the ships advanced. When all were in, the first shield raised and the second shield dropped. Out and away from Emex Station Eight, they headed out past the shipping lanes.

"Set a course for the Orn system. Our next contract is another cargo run."

The ship arced away from the station and activated their Light Drive. Captain Kohan continued to give orders to the rest of the crew, starting with Eve.

"Since our other QuBE was killed in our raid on your ship, we're down a weapon operator. You have experience in tracking and targeting?

"You point the open end, click, and *boom,*" she said with a wink.

He sighed. "You're taking their position as right gunner. You'll also do whatever else I need, and will cooking and cleaning."

He turned to Faun.

"Take her back and show her our weapons setup, run through the console commands."

"Absolutely not," she said with a huff, and it looked to Eve like she wanted to stomp her foot. "Why bother giving her any responsibility. She's cannon fodder."

Captain Kohan wasn't pleased with the insubordination, as his reddening face indicated, but he didn't say anything further.

Nepotism or favoritism? Both, probably.

"Nine, assign her the empty room, show her around, and start teaching her the weapon system. She's under your supervision."

"Yes, Captain."

Weak. Daughter can't follow orders. Father can't control his daughter. Maybe I should have stuck with Marsi. Or maybe this will be a chance to finally commandeer a ship of my own.

Eve was content with biding her time until she knew if she'd be able to stage a hostile takeover. Finding out whether this group was loyal to the current captain, or if they were loyal to the money would be key.

Nine led her through to the cargo hold to retrieve some spare bedding, and then back to the room she'd been held captive in. Without an actual bed, it was going to be rough until she could buy one and get it on board. She tossed the blanket and pillow haphazardly into the room.

I'll set it out later.

"As directed by the captain, you will learn our systems. It is imperative you understand the capabilities for our continued survival."

"Before that, I need to clean up. Where's the purification room?"

They showed her to a small room to the aft in the right hallway. Closing the door behind her, she stripped and threw her clothing and bodysuit into the washer-dryer combo. While it was going, she jumped into the purification chamber to clean up. When she was done, she checked on the clothing. It had already started its dry cycle. Leaning against the wall, she waited five minutes.

Dressed and ready to go, she exited the room, and Nine led her to the munitions room on the right side of the ship. Inside the short hallway was a ladder up to a gunner pod. Nine led her in, and there was hardly enough room for both of them to move. They directed her to sit in the seat with a wave of their arm.

"Our artillery are two railguns and plasma proximity mines. Your role will be using the computer targeting and manual firing of the railgun."

They spent hours going over the controls. The main takeaway was that the railguns were powerful, and a couple direct shots would cause most shielding to falter. But because it was a railgun, each cannon had a limited number of shots before the heatsink needed to cool. Accuracy was key.

Once she proved she understood the system, and Nine was satisfied, they showed her how to reload both the railgun and mines inside the munitions room.

Done in the munitions area, they headed aft. Passing the bulkhead, they returned to the cargo bay, and she was shown around the kitchen and dining area. Most of the space was for the kitchen appliances.

Coolers, two ovens, a stove. What little space was left was occupied by a long table with bench seats.

There's hardly enough room to move. I won't be able to have anyone in here to help. Maybe if I am purposefully bad at cooking, they'll give the duty to someone else.

Eve wasn't a gourmet chef, and she liked her food salty. Cooking for others, especially non-humans, would be a trial. In a cupboard near one of the coolers were cookbooks for various species next to a mess of spices.

I guess I'll need to read those?

Though the brief training was out of the way, Nine had her continue to shadow them as they entered the left hallway and through a door to the right. It was immediately opposite the one in the right hall but, instead of a purification room, there were stairs leading to the underbelly of the ship.

The engine room was bigger than she expected for such a small craft, though it made sense because most of the spaces on the upper deck seemed small. The multi-staged drive spanned the length of the ship and had multiple accessways to get to the different sections. The setup of drives were Bulk, Cruise, then Light, with the synthetic Vradix crystal chamber in the middle to supply the power to them.

"As *Skyfire*'s first officer, I handle the more mundane ship details so Captain Kohan can focus on running the ship, crew, and contracts," Nine stated as they leisurely headed back toward the bridge. "This includes overseeing the maintenance of our propulsion systems."

"Why's Faun not first officer?" she asked while examining the crystal chamber.

"I assumed the role when Nital, Faun's mother, died in childbirth. Since then, Captain Kohan has indicated he prefers a QuBE as second in command due to our efficiency. Faun will become captain when Captain Kohan dies."

"I see. So, I guess I better get on her good side at some point," Eve thought out loud.

Nine gave her a rundown of the engine, but she'd worked on enough of them that she hurried them along. Back on the bridge, Nine took a place at a console. The other crew were at theirs, leaving Eve to watch out the forward window. Sometime during her instruction, they had entered a bulk path.

"How long 'til we reach our destination?" Eve asked.

Captain Kohan only turned his head slightly to acknowledge her.

"A few hours. We'll have a mission briefing and meal at 16:00. Go rest for an hour, and then prepare a meal."

This wasn't the glamorous part of being a marauder, or mercenary, or whatever she was, but it would replenish her chits. And she was alive.

The rest was short-lived as she had no clock in her room to gauge how long she'd been there. Restless and not wanting to anger her new captain, she got up and headed to the kitchen. It was 15:00.

Browsing the cookbooks, vraditi ate like humans, so she didn't anticipate there'd be an issue cooking for at least four of them. Balok and Virid were a different story. Anything under scalding was considered cold and unpalatable.

Eve did her duty and cooked a simple meal for the crew. At 16:00 promptly, the crew entered the dining area. Except for Nine. It made sense to her to have them on the bridge while the others ate.

The food set out, Eve joined them and sat next to Balok, across from Faun. Faun sneered at her, and if she could shoot daggers from her eyes, Eve was sure she would. It was entertaining, and she intended to antagonize Faun for fun. But not yet. She'd wait until it was only the two of them.

"The next contract is for hauling minerals and plesians. We're to deliver them both to the Khet system. Eve, since you're the F.N.G., you're on babysitting duty."

"What?" Eve said.

"We should only have them on board a few days. Watch them, feed them, clean up after them."

The plesians were a unique species. Their bulky, furry, four-legged bodies made them look like some sort of livestock, but their brains were uniquely developed. They could be specialized in a specific subject, skill, or area, and reach near genius but would forget many other things, sometimes including the ability to care for oneself. There were caregiver plesians for that. Eve likened it to a pet you could train.

The rest of the briefing was on roles. Eve was to help load the cargo containers first in order to create a pen for the plesians, and then they'd load the beings. Only one of those crates was to be food for them, and it was only enough to last three days maximum on their FTL trip from the Orn to Khet systems.

The group finished their meals, and Eve was left to clean up. She hated the menial jobs, but she would do whatever she needed to move up in Captain Kohan's favor so she could worm her way out of them. The rest of the time until reaching their destination was theirs to do what they wanted, and Eve headed for her room for a little more sleep. It didn't feel like any time had passed when a ship-wide announcement came on and stirred her.

"Thirty minutes to destination," Captain Kohan said.

Eve lay there, allowing herself to become aware. Stretching, she rolled her hip and cracked her back. It relieved some of the aching from being on the floor. Up and out into the hallway, she headed for the bridge. Faun was also just coming out of her room, and she side-eyed Eve.

"Just because you weaseled your way onto this ship doesn't make you crew. You're hired help. A servant."

"Whatever you say, Princess," Eve replied.

Faun stomped toward the bridge, and Eve kept a spiteful stride. Faun sped up to break away, but Eve wouldn't let her. Increasing her pace, she grinned.

If it's this easy to get under her skin, this is going to be fun.

"Fek off!" Faun snapped.

"We're going to the same place."

It looked like Faun was trying really hard not to break into a run. All Eve had to do was take bigger steps. Faun grunted, and they burst onto the bridge together. The crew looked at them. Eve returned to her casual demeanor while Faun continued to stomp to her station.

"Brace. We're entering the atmosphere," Balok said.

Eve leaned against the wall, and there was a slight rocking motion. The inertial dampeners made it more like gentle swaying of a ship on the sea. The pilots were adept and, within a few minutes, they were landing near a mountain range.

"Prepare to disembark," Captain Kohan ordered.

Everyone but the Tectos headed for the cargo bay. By the time the crew got there, the aft door had dropped open. Wanting to earn her keep, Eve was the first off the ship onto the cold planet.

Stationed near a semi-hidden mine entrance into the mountainside were heavily armed elementus soldiers wearing armor fused to their bodies. There was a couple dozen crates separated from about a hundred more. Captain Kohan took the lead.

"We're here for pickup."

An elementus with near gaudy levels of armor fused to their torso and legs stepped forward.

"Proof of contract."

Kohan handed over a tablet, and they verified. A curt nod came from the soldier, and Kohan waved for the crew to start loading the staged cargo containers.

Eve followed Nine. While the QuBE was able to pick up the container without help, she was forced to use a levi-lifter to get under them and pull them along. It lifted them a meter off the ground and hovered along as she pulled it up the shallow ramp.

It was a couple hours' work to get the containers loaded and organized to block the plesians from getting past. When they finished, the soldiers brought out the four-legged creatures from the mine and led them over. They all had gear on, which looked like a hybrid of a hardhat and a combat helmet. When they spoke, it was translated through microphones.

"Where is Garr going?"

"Why has Zeon stopped working?"

"What is that?"

The plesians were vocal and confused. The soldiers poked and prodded them along with the ends of their rifles right up to where Kohan was. The *Skyfire*'s crew took over, and they had to employ similar tactics to get them on board.

"Stop. Bilt doesn't want to go up there."

"Where is Celm's family?"

"Hello. Wena is Wena."

Eve slapped their hind quarters with a 'hyah' to keep them moving along, and they complied with grunted complaint. Once into the ship, they sort of meandered in circles.

"Why is Pols here?"

The whole group followed the line of thinking, and each one asked why they were there. They became agitated and, to get control, Kohan whistled loudly. They paid attention.

"Enough! Your debts aren't paid. You're being transported to your next job."

They quieted to a murmur, and the cargo door was shut. Kohan looked at Eve, pointed at her, and then pointed at the plesians. The rest of the crew headed for the front of the ship. In short time they were skyward again. Eve couldn't see where they were but, because there was a distinctive difference between artificial gravity and the gravity of a planet, she knew when they'd left the atmosphere.

Being the only bipedal lifeform now in the cargo hold, she became the focus of the plesians. They swarmed her, looking for their next orders.

"What does Wena need to do?" one asked.

"Relax. We're not at the next destination yet," Eve said loudly so the whole group could hear.

They were silent for a few moments, and as if they'd forgotten, they began asking where they were going. Eve was not amused at her babysitting duties and headed to their food container. Opening it elicited an immediate response from the plesians, and they became ravenous. Eve wasn't sure why because the food was condensed pellets about the size of her arm, and as dense as bone.

One by one, she handed them out. The plesians surprised her when they stood up on their hind legs and grasped the pellets with their powerful paws on their forelegs. Thinking about it, she wondered why it was surprising, considering they could be trained to work mining equipment.

When all were fed, she closed the lid and sat and watched. At some point during her zone out, the Bulk Drive had kicked in, and they were heading to their next destination.

Several hours passed, and she was called on to prepare a meal for the crew. As they had done last time, everyone but Nine came to the dining area, ate, and then returned to their posts. Eve cleaned up after the messy crew, and then the messy plesians. It was beneath her, but she wasn't going to let menial chores break her spirit. In the end, she'd either win them over or conquer them.

The plesians would occasionally become restless, but Eve learned they were easily calmed with pats to their flat foreheads. At least until they dropped out of the bulk path. There was a pause before the ship moved, which was abnormal. Staying in front of the exit of a bulk path could be deadly if another ship were to emerge.

The ship shook as if it had been hit. Before Captain Kohan could even tell her, she leapt over the containers, bolted from the cargo bay, and headed for the railgun she'd been assigned. Comms came alive in her ear.

"Battle stations! Galactic Police are trying to disable us!" Captain Kohan yelled.

On the targeting screen were two ships. Outside the dome above her, she could barely see the cruisers. Sleek, black, narrowly oblong ships, about one kilometer long. Outside of the scanner, the only way she knew they were there were because the light from the windows was different than the light of distant stars and galaxies...and the high-powered lasers being fired.

The *Skyfire* shook when the nearest cruiser hit them with a couple pulses and tried to detain them with a gravitational beam. *Skyfire*'s shielding held and the beam had no effect.

Kohan had left comms open, and a broadcast was sent out.

"Surrender. You are being detained by the Galactic Police for transporting illicit cargo," came an even toned voice through ship's comms.

Eve lined up a shot at their beam emitter to try to disable it. The Cruise Drive fired up, and they pulled away, forcing her to realign. She fired twice. Their shielding absorbed the impact, shimmering against the darkness of space. The Tectos were trying to maintain distance to disallow the ships from grappling.

"You are being detained! Power down your weapons!" came the voice, more authoritarian this time.

Firing two more shots, she watched the level on the heatsink. It was still in good margins. She lost sight of the other ship while focusing on the one, but the scanner showed it circled toward their underbelly. They were going to pinch them.

"Balok, Virid, evade by any means necessary. Faun and Eve, put holes in the ship on us!" Captain Kohan commanded.

"Final warning. Power down or we will be forced to destroy your ship!"

Eve fired three shots in a row, trying to hit the same spot as before while *Skyfire* banked and dodged. The cruiser returned fire. *Skyfire* would lose in the long term because it was two on one.

Her heatsink was halfway, and Faun had started firing, too. Concentrating fire to where Faun was aiming, they tried to wear the shield down. Eve's cannon neared the red-line, and she barked over the comms.

"Right heatsink nearing max. Hold it steady so we can tag team!"

The pilots stopped weaving as much, giving a much steadier shot. It also put them in a bad spot, but they needed to risk for reward. As she put the heatsink into cooldown with rapid fire, they were pelted with laser bursts. The hull shuddered.

Faun concentrated fire and broke through the first G.P. ship's shield. Eve deployed mines. Watching the radar, the second ship didn't have time to avoid them. She remotely detonated and knocked the second off course. Small shockwaves sent shrapnel shooting toward the top cruiser.

Hopefully, it hits something vital.

The second ship recovered and *Skyfire* slowed. They were caught with a gravitational beam. The Tectos attempted to accelerate, but it was no use.

Desperate, Eve deployed the rest of the mines loaded in her launcher. One after another, she felt the shockwaves rock the aft end of the ship, and hoped she wasn't putting holes in their own hull.

The ship rolled, giving line of sight for the railguns. Eve's was ready for a few more shots. Taking over manual aiming, she picked what she thought might be the bridge of the second G.P. ship. She unloaded half a dozen, and an alarm sounded. Her gun shut down.

"What the hell do you think you're doing?" Faun admonished loudly.

"Stop wasting time and finish it up!" Eve barked back.

Faun responded by unloading on the same area Eve had. The shielding fell and a projectile ripped through the cruiser hull. A mayday went out, and the first ship stopped to aid their ally. *Skyfire* was free. The Light Drive kicked on. Stars and galaxies became blurs.

Chapter 5
Insubordinate On Purpose

Because they'd been ambushed by the G.P., they deviated from the original plan. They'd already been through a few bulk paths and lost days to try and shake any tail they might have.

This meant Eve had to caretake longer than intended. Restless, she showed up several times on the bridge unannounced to give *status updates*. Faun protested every time, and Kohan ordered her back to the cargo bay.

Back on the bridge in defiance she made note of the system they'd entered, Altosia. Quietly observing the monitors, trying to avoid Faun's gaze, the system only had a few planets. Their course was headed for the largest, labeled Melosa.

They rounded the gas giant to one of its moons, swapped to the Cruise Drive, and began an atmosphere entry. It was a lush, rigid moon. The peaks and valleys made it look like green ferrofluid. The Tectos took the ship lower, and a vast network of caves came into view. The ship slowed and banked around so the aft end was facing a large cave. Finessed into a tight spot, they touched down.

Eve snuck back to the hold and waited for the crew to come back. The bay door dropped open, and the ship powered down. Captain Kohan appeared first, with the crew behind him.

"Unload the cargo into the cave to shield from tracking signals," Kohan ordered. "We need to scan everything. That ambush wasn't a coincidence."

"Maybe someone sold us out," Eve uttered.

"Maybe *you* sold us out," Faun shot back.

"Shut up, both of you," Kohan retorted, and that silenced them. "It would be a tracking device. I want all of the cargo scanned, plesians included."

The *Skyfire* crew unloaded the plesians first, and then the mineral containers into the cave. It was a poorly outfitted hideaway, with barely enough that a few could survive here for a brief time. Safe from orbital scans, Kohan handed Eve a portable scanning device and pointed at Nine to help her. They scanned and moved the plesians one by one. Faun and Ruzat checked the containers, and the Tectos discussed their status with Kohan.

"Our transponder was pinged," Virid said. "We have one spare transponder chip left. We will need to find a counterfeiter at our next stop."

"Save it for after we figure out what was chipped. It's likely we were tracked to this system, so we need our current transponder to read the same while we take the tracker to a new system and space it."

"We can't sustain the cargo here long," Balok mentioned. "Our best choice would be to make a few small bulk path jumps to be rid of the tracker. We won't be able to return until we change the transponder. Will the cargo survive?"

"We don't have much choice," Kohan said.

About halfway through the lot of plesians, Eve's scanner emitted a tone. Moving around the plesian, the scanner triggered on their right shoulder.

"Why does the thing beep at Wena?" the plesian asked.

Nine silently led Wena away from the pack, and Eve continued. When the scans were complete, everything else was found to be clean.

"Found the tracker, Cap," Eve said.

Nine brought Wena forward.

"Wena is not a tracker. Wena mines."

Eve analyzed the registered signal, and then showed Kohan. "It's a long-range tracker embedded near the bone."

"Wena does not have a tracker near her bones," she insisted.

"Load it up and let's move. Assume as soon as it's out of the cave, the Galactic Police will be picking its signal up. We need to get rid of it."

They forced Wena toward the ship, and when she cried out in fear, it upset the other plesians. They wanted to come to Wena's aid. While Nine corralled her up the ramp, Faun and Ruzat held them at bay while Kohan issued orders.

"Ruzat, Faun you are staying with the cargo to safeguard it. Nine, Virid, Balok, and Eve with me on the ship."

"What?! Why am I staying here?" Faun protested.

"Because the G.P. are pursuing this chip. In the event we're picked up I'll need you and Virid to figure out how to get us out of prison. And I need you to keep the cargo secured."

"Babysitting? Give that trash job to Eve!"

"I need someone here I can trust, and who can keep our cargo *in* the cave," Kohan snapped, clearly irritated by her insubordination.

This caught the attention of the plesians.

"Is Daxa mining?"

"Where is Pit's tools?"

Faun was visibly frustrated and chucked the scanner she held at the feet of the nearest plesian. Because of the extra power put behind the throw from her cybernetic limb, the scanner shattered and scared the pack.

"Quiet!" she yelled.

There was no positive resolution between father and daughter. While Eve thought it might be humorous to poke at it by teasing her, she bit her tongue out of fear Kohan might change his mind and leave *her* here.

On board *Skyfire*, they powered the ship back up. Without Faun on the bridge to pitch a fit every time Eve came up, she felt comfortable sliding into an open console. The controls were oriented differently, but nothing she hadn't seen before. Balok and Virid gracefully led them back out of the atmosphere and plotted a course back to the last bulk path. Once in space, Eve scanned the system.

"No hostiles in the area. What's the plan, Cap?" Eve asked.

"Assuming the G.P. will be ready and waiting for us, we're not going to have time to drop back to the mining base and settle this. We have to space it."

Gross.

Even Eve wasn't that cruel. She might leave Wena somewhere to fend for herself, but ejecting was just heartless. Not that she would admit any of that.

"There's no value in her death. If we come up short on the inventory, we're likely to get docked pay. Lend me Nine, and I'll dig the tracker out," she offered.

"Are you a surgeon?" Kohan side-eyed her.

"No, but it'd be worth the effort if I succeed. Lend me Nine."

"No. You should know damaged goods are near as bad as missing goods. Go reload the railguns and get me an inventory of the mines."

Eve sneered at him.

Fek him. I'll do it anyway, and he can't stop me unless he spaces me, too. It'd be barbaric to space an innocent creature just to get rid of a tracker.

Leaving the bridge in a huff, she gave him a curt "Aye-aye, Captain," on the way out.

Passing the munitions hall, she continued into the cargo bay where Wena had laid down. When they saw Eve, she stood up and whimpered.

"Why has Wena been taken?"

"You have a tracker in your arm...leg...whatever your limbs are. I need to get it out."

"Wena does not."

Not wanting to argue, Eve grabbed the scanner from the locker and brought it over. Turning it on, she scanned Wena on the right shoulder as before. It beeped.

"You hear that? That means yes you do. I'm going to get it out, but I need you to sit down and don't fight me."

Wena sat and whimpered. She fidgeted while Eve approached the lockers again to begin collecting the things she might need. A scalpel, a suture kit, and an antibiotic kit to prevent infection. She needed a numbing agent, but they didn't have any. The kitchen had alcohol, though. Grabbing a bottle of Gowarian ale, a particularly potent alcohol from her planet, she packed it on top of her already precarious tower of items in her other arm.

Returning, she sat the items down next to the furry being, and it triggered Wena.

"Wena does not like knives!" she wailed.

"Shh!" Eve looked over her shoulder at the door. "I don't care if you don't like it. I need to get the tracker out."

"No! No knife!" She got up and stomped to the corner of the cargo hold.

"If I don't do this, the captain is going to space you. Do you understand what that means?"

There was a blank look on Wena's face.

"He's going to put you outside of the ship, into space, and you will die."

"Wena does not want to die!"

Wena sobbed and shook her massive head. Eve had made it worse, and their anxiety was grinding on Eve's nerves.

"Well, then you need to get over here and do what I tell you, got it?"

She still wouldn't return, so Eve grabbed up the ale, popped the cork, and walked over. Without a word, she shoved the bottle into Wena's mouth and dumped the whole thing upside down. The look of disgust on Wena's face showed to Eve that she was about to spit it out, and so Eve clamped her mouth shut.

"Uh-uh. Swallow."

She refused, and so with one hand Eve held Wena's mouth shut, and with the other she massaged her throat in an attempt to make her. It worked, and she let go.

"Wena does not like that!"

"Just let it kick in. It's medicine."

As Eve turned around to go get her items, her heart felt like it jumped into her throat when she saw Nine standing there. They had snuck up on her.

"What are you doing?"

"Disobeying the captain's orders," Eve said and walked past them.

"Why?" Nine asked.

"As artificial life, would you even understand?" She gave no room for response. "Sometimes killing is pointless. The plesian's death serves no purpose if I can extract the tracker and achieve the same goal. Now, unless you're going to help me or detain me for mutiny, piss off."

Nine stayed put. She picked up the scalpel, and Wena lost it. Eve motioned for Nine to hold her still.

"No! No! No sharp objects!"

Nine complied, and with their superior strength held Wena from squirming or escaping. Eve used the scanner to get a closer pinpoint on the tracker, then shaved the hair from Wena's arm and sterilized the site and blade.

On the initial incision, Wena cried out, though it was all she could do. Eve dumped the bottle of alcohol in her mouth again and continued. Careful not to cut more than needed, she pulled the skin away so she could start digging in. The blood made things slippery, but she was able to grab a pair of forceps and begin wiggling them into the tissue.

The pain must have been too much to bear, because after vomiting, Wena went limp and collapsed. At first, Eve was frustrated because she had to sit down on the hard metal floor to continue, but realized it made her job easier. No squirming meant Nine was able to help more readily.

"Grab the scanner and guide me. I'm pretty sure I'm not looking for some glowing, blinky-light beacon."

They did as instructed.

"To the left ten millimeters, straight down to the bone."

Following the guidance, she plunged deep into the tissue. She had to pry the muscle open some, and turned her head several different angles to see if she could catch a glint of the foreign body. Shoving gauze in there to soak up the blood helped, and the grain-sized tracker was revealed.

Pulling it out, she let it drop to the floor and began triage on the open wound. Nine grabbed the tracking device and crushed it between their fingers.

"I will report your success to the captain," Nine proclaimed, and walked away.

"No, don't worry. I've got this handled," she said loudly and rolled her eyes. It was too late. Nine was already gone, but she hoped their robotic hearing would pick it up anyway.

The stitches weren't professional, but they would do the job. While bandaging, Wena roused. She turned violent quickly, and swung her hind leg at Eve, catching her in the side. Wena growled and grumbled incoherently. She got up and stumbled around. The bandage unraveled. Blood was already starting to show through.

"Hey! Sit the hell down! You're going to break the stitching!"

Eve tried to move in to continue bandaging.

"You...hurt Wena," she slurred and swiped at Eve again.

"You don't want to die, right, Wena?"

"No."

"Then let me finish bandaging your arm and stop moving so damn much or you *will*."

That stopped her, and Eve was able to finish. By the time the cargo hold was mostly cleaned up, she was a complete mess. The hum of the Bulk Drive gave her confidence that she had time to get cleaned up. The blood had stained her clothes but not the armor underneath. *Whatever...I'll buy more after we get paid.*

Not wanting to be spaced before she had a chance to take over the ship, she made her rounds to the gunner pods and did what Captain Kohan had originally told her to do. Sure that she would be asked if she had, she entered the bridge with a smug grin. Kohan turned around and scowled in displeasure.

"Are those railguns reloaded?"

"Aye, Cap. Reloaded and ready to go. Twenty mines remain in the cache."

"Next time you disobey my orders, I'll throw you off the ship."

She gave him a mocking salute, and then took a bridge station. He eyed her the whole way, and she knew she had him hooked into her. Whether he knew it or not, his disdain was a way for her to control him.

They dropped out of the bulk path, and the Galactic Police were there. Without hesitation the Tectos engaged the Light Drive, and there was no pursuit. Eve figured the old transponder got changed out, and so now they were just another ship passing through.

Out of abundance of caution, they took a few added bulk paths to ensure they weren't being followed, which extended their time away. They made a quick stop at an Emex Station to pick up some food for the plesians, and then returned to Melosa's moon. As soon as they landed and the cargo door was down, Faun approached and was furious.

"Where the hell have you been?!"

"We had real work to do, like performing surgery, destroying the tracker, and ditching the G.P.," Eve gloated.

Faun ignored her and stormed past Kohan. The rest of the crew reloaded the cargo, and within a few hours they were ready to go. Eve was stuck caretaking again. Wena hung on Eve's every footstep, telling the other plesians of how Eve saved her from 'being outside the ship.' Like a young sibling, Wena wanted to help her with giving out the food. Eve was too tired to fight her so, instead, she gave the food to Wena, and let her do the walking back and forth. *Leaders delegate, anyway.*

The trip to the drop off location compared to the recent events was uneventful. Eve had snuck up to the front a few times to keep track of their progress, getting better at eluding Faun's sharp gaze. Despite the hostilities between her and Faun, she found herself admiring her backside. Before her mind could wander too far, she would slink back to the cargo hold.

Upon arrival, Captain Kohan made a ship-wide announcement, "Prepare for a rough landing. Weather patterns are choppy."

Eve knew this was solely for her, and she did her best to prepare the plesians.

"Everyone, huddle together and lie down. In case of turbulence, don't panic."

All the plesians did as they were told, except Wena who stood by Eve's side. Eve motioned for her to also sit. The ship only hit a few bumps, and then landed without problem.

The cargo door opened, and the ship's drives powered down. The crew joined Eve, and they were met at the entrance to the bay by an elementus with a manifest. Immediately, their contact began dictating to Captain Kohan.

"The scheduled delivery was a galactic week ago. You have forfeited half of your commission."

"The hell I have," he kept his tone even. "You were set up by your seller. One of the plesians had a tracking chip, and the G.P. were waiting for us to drop out of a bulk path."

"Not our problem. Should have scanned the cargo upon loading."

"I should charge you extra! We had to deal with the tracker, burn a transponder, and buy extra food for the plesians so you could even *get* your shipment. All I want is our full commission."

"You will take half, this is non-negotiable. If you do not relinquish our property, we will take measures to secure it."

The others from the elementus crew brandished weapons at them, leaving the *Skyfire* crew with little option but to retreat. Observing the situation from far back, Eve took note of the mobile factory ship nearby. *Bet there's some good stuff in there...*

Captain Kohan begrudgingly waved for his crew to unload. Wena was the last plesian off, and the lead elementus spoke up again.

"This one is damaged. We will not accept them. You will be docked the cost of their contract."

This sets Captain Kohan off. "Absolutely not! You wouldn't even fekking have your cargo if we hadn't done what we needed. You're not going to dock us any further, *hammerhead*."

A gun was stuck in Kohan's face, and he didn't flinch. The elementus spoke.

"You will be docked. Either you take them and try to sell their contract elsewhere, or we will put them down and charge you the cost of disposal."

Wena looked back and forth between the two of them. She whimpered, but when Eve rested her hand on her shoulder, she calmed.

"What am I supposed to do with it?" Captain Kohan seethed.

"Not our problem. Please, imprint to complete the revised contract."

Captain Kohan was bright red, and Eve knew he was thinking about retaliation. Approaching, she turned her back to the elementus and whispered to the captain.

"She's trainable, and you don't have to share rewards with her. Just negotiate whatever her current contract is. As for the loss we're taking, let's take it off their corpses later."

He walked over to the elementus, snatched the pad from him, and input his biometrics. They were allowed to leave without further incident, and the moment they were back on board the ship, Eve was scheming.

"It's a mobile weapons manufacturing facility. Those guns were fresh," she told Captain Kohan as they walked to the bridge.

"Are you suggesting we raid them?" he replied.

"Exactly. I'd put money on that whole operation being a setup. It's a good swindle; hire cargo for full price, then muscle them into half price by siccing the Galactic Police on them with a fraudulent claim of stolen merchandise."

"Roguish. Wish we'd thought of it first," Faun said.

"The anti-air cannons will make it difficult to approach," Ruzat informed them. "We would need to infiltrate on foot."

While waiting on the captain's official determination, the Tectos initiated launch and took them exo-atmospheric. Captain Kohan sat in his chair and scratched his beard. The idea of retaliation was planted, and Eve was already planning for multiple outcomes. Raid, hide weapons for herself, usurp Kohan, take over *Skyfire*.

It might still be too early, but there's no harm in planning for the future.

"Virid, plot a course for landing as close as you can without detection. Balok, take us out of the solar system. Make them think we've actually gone, and then disable the transponder," Captain Kohan ordered.

The Tectos nodded and set about their duties.

Chapter 6
Burning Bridges

In the cargo bay, the crew readied themselves with combat gear. The only one who would be mostly unprotected would be Wena, but there was nothing that could be done about it currently. Eve figured if she survived this, they might get her armor later.

"Ruzat, Eve, and the plesian—"

"Wena's name is Wena," she interrupted.

"You are Team One. Nine and Virid are with me as Team Two. Faun is ranged support, and Balok is staying on board. Comms active, keep in contact, stay with your squad."

"Wena does not have comms."

With a wave of his hand, Captain Kohan directed Nine over to her. Nine came and tinkered with her helmet's settings. Kohan activated crew comms.

"Audio check."

"Reading you clear," Faun replied.

"Good. Balok, wait for our word that the anti-air security is down, then hop the ship closer."

Laid out on a crate was a topographical map of the area. The factory ship was dead center, with a dozen satellite buildings around it, and guard towers securing a fence line. Captain Kohan pointed several things out, starting with a brighter colored area on the massive ship.

"There's significant power usage coming from here, indicating the assembly line. These satellite buildings are likely security, operations, administration. There is one building which has had many elementus in and out. Team One will break the front line to that building, Team Two will follow up to disable any installation defense."

The plan was a smash-and-grab. Get in, do as much damage as they could, steal cargo, and escape.

"I want everyone geared up in ten," Captain Kohan ordered.

Eve lived in her armor, so she only needed to grab a weapon. Digging into the cache, she pulled out a familiar sight. Her hand cannon was amongst other items from Marsi's ship.

"Oh, I missed you!" she whispered to it.

She wanted to say something snarky but kept quiet. Pulling a holster belt with an ammo pouch, she strapped it on. The hand cannon slipped in with ease, and she felt whole. After grabbing handfuls of her caliber ammo and stuffing them in the pouch, she approached the cargo bay door.

All but Wena were clear on their intent. She kept asking what she was supposed to do, and Eve's response was, "Do what I say, when I say, and you'll be safe."

The ship's bay closed after they exited, and all of the light vanished. Before their eyes adjusted, Kohan was leading the way with a portable terminal on his arm. Half of the screen was the map, and the other half had a night vision view of what was ahead of them. It was a rocky and unfriendly terrain. Having landed several kilometers away, she groaned internally about blisters she knew would form.

They came upon a ridge where they could look down on the facility. It wasn't well lit, but there were lookout towers anyway. Captain Kohan scanned with his armband terminal. Between the stationed guards in the towers and the patrols, getting in would be a little bit of work.

Eve was forming a plan, but before she could finish, Faun began directing.

"Ruzat, Eve, and Wena, get down there and neutralize the patrol on my mark," she said while setting up her sniper rifle on its legs.

It didn't make sense to Eve for the two biggest members of the team to be part of the stealthy section, but she did her best to keep Wena close.

"Stick next to me. Get ready to tackle anyone who isn't me or Ruzat," she whispered as they made their way down the embankment.

When they neared the perimeter, they crouched near rocks nowhere big enough to hide them. Eve put her hand on Wena's neck to keep her calm.

The guards were coming around, and if Faun didn't make her move soon, Eve would take charge. Turning sideways, Eve watched a guard and kept her eye on where she thought Faun's muzzle flash would come from.

"Where's our signal, *ma'am*," Eve whispered through the comms.

Ruzat tapped Eve's shoulder, and he pointed to the guard coming from his direction. The patrol would soon be on their position, and it would be too late for surprise. Nodding at him, she counted down from five on her hand.

Before she could give the signal, there were two flashes from the hill they came from. Faun's bullets shattered cameras on the building, which caught the attention of the patrol.

"There's your signal, chulk."

Eve gave the signal to Ruzat, and they sprang up and charged. The elementus were caught off guard, but still attempted to fight.

If they hadn't been trying to keep a low profile, and preserve the element of surprise, Eve would have pulled the hand cannon and blown a hole right through whatever rock and metal covered the elementus's body. Instead, she used weight shifting techniques to throw and slam her opponent.

A third flash came, and above they heard the bullet hit what sounded like stone. An elementus slammed into the ground at high velocity in between the two scuffles.

Eve put hers on the ground and knocked them out cold with an elbow drop onto their head. It wasn't the smartest move because their jagged edges hit the tendon in her elbow. She swore under her breath and stood up to help Ruzat, who didn't need it. He was already dragging his guard off to low brush. She motioned for Wena to help.

Together the three of them hid the bodies as best they could and approached the fence. Ruzat produced a small plasma cutter and cut the chain-link in a wide enough circle for them to fit through. The rest of the crew came down the embankment and breached the perimeter.

"Could have done with a little more heads up," Eve snipped.

"I was focused on doing my job. Mind the business that *pays* you," Faun quipped back.

"Clear comms," Captain Kohan snapped.

The satellite building in front of them was what Captain Kohan believed to be security. The groups split to either side of the door, hugging the wall. Nine was the closest to the entry keypad and held his hand over it. Faster than her eyes could track, Nine tried an incredible number of codes. The door's electric lock clicked, indicating success.

"Team One first, clear the hall. Team Two, clear the first couple rooms. Find their security ops."

Eve had zero hesitation, and Ruzat was right beside her. Guns ready, they burst in the door. They caught a gold colored elementus by surprise, and Eve raced Ruzat to the trigger. She had her hand cannon up, and the trigger pulled before he could aim his shotgun.

The elementus had a fifteen-centimeter hole carved through them, and they dropped to the floor. There was no time to wait and see if more would come; they already knew the answer.

"Wena, come!" Eve ordered and rushed farther into the hall.

Well-armed elementus came around a corner, and they were ready for them. Eve took the left, Ruzat took the right. The firefight was quick and dirty. Head and neck shots for Eve, torso shots for Ruzat. Clear, they moved farther in and were in line with the hallway where the elementus had come from, and where the next door was.

"Wena, watch our..." Eve hesitated and wondered if she'd know what she meant. "Wena, stand to the side and watch that hall. Tell us if anyone is coming."

"Wena understands."

Team Two took the right side of the door while Eve positioned to kick it open. Captain Kohan pulled an incendiary grenade and nodded at her. A few swift motions, and the door was open, the grenade was in, and the two teams were clear of the entry. Inside the room there was yelling and scrambling, but they had nowhere to go but out.

The few who did decide it would be better to exit were swiftly gunned down. The grenade went off, and Eve was the first one in with her hand cannon leveled at the closest security operative. BANG.

The rest of the two teams entered, save Wena. The remaining standing security was dealt with, and Nine moved over to a console which had the least amount of damage. They quickly got to work, and their hands and fingers moved faster than her eyes could track.

Turning around, she motioned to Ruzat to follow, and they left to guard the room. Wena looked back at Eve.

"What was that loud noise?"

"Don't worry about it. These elementus have the rest of your kind. Do you have family in the group?"

"Wena does not have family here. Wena does not know where her family is."

Eve didn't reply, by choice. There was a simplicity to Wena which tugged at her heart. She didn't like it, and she sure as hell wasn't about to show it. Before getting lost in her own introspection, she purposely willed her focus back to the task of raiding the facility.

"Anti-air cannons disabled," Nine said over comms.

"Balok, drop the ship closer. We'll comm when we're ready to start loading," Captain Kohan ordered.

"Yes, Captain. Long range scans show an elementus cruiser a couple sectors over, and it spears they might have altered course heading toward this star system."

"Confirmed," Nine said. "They were alerted to the breech. We have an hour at the most before they arrive."

Captain Kohan pointed down the hall and spoke to Ruzat. "At the end there's a tee. At intersections take two rights and a left. Grab anything and everything."

There was no hesitation between his last word and their movement. The three jogged, with Ruzat in the lead. At the first corner, Ruzat poked a curved scope around to see. He motioned with his hand to hold.

"Ten," he whispered. "Two rows, overlapping pattern."

Eve acknowledged with a nod and leaned down to Wena to give her the next task.

"When I tell you to go, I want you to run around the corner and yell 'help me, help me,'" she whispered. "Run behind the elementus and wait until you see me. When I come out, I want you to tackle them from behind."

"Wena is afraid of pain."

"They'll be distracted. I'll get to them before they hurt you. Can you do it?"

She nodded, and Eve prepared.

"Go!" she whispered.

Doing as instructed, she ran out and yelled, "Help! Wena needs help!"

There were no gunshots, nor cries of pain from Wena. Waiting a few seconds for Wena to get in position, Eve wasn't around the corner half of a second and Wena pounced on two elementus closest to her from behind. Eve had a perfect opening. Her bullets hit their marks and their group was down by five. The attention was back in her direction.

She ran up to a doorway and hid in the alcove there, keeping their attention by sticking her gun out and firing. Her targets were specific to ones not in Wena's line of fire. While they were distracted Ruzat came around the corner, his long legs carrying him at a speed which amazed Eve. He barreled straight for the rest of the security force. The elementus fired on him, but he saw through their aim and was able to preemptively dodge the bullet path.

Ruzat body-checked one and let out a grunt which echoed down the hallway. Eve stepped out, aimed, and fired at one on the left before he could shoot Ruzat. Wena tackled another, and Ruzat dispatched the last with his shotgun.

"Twenty us, five them," Eve boasted, knowing Faun could hear.

Ruzat looked at her confused.

"Body count. Team One versus Team Two," she told him.

"Stop exaggerating and get back to work," Faun said over comms.

Eve gave Ruzat a pat on his arm. He nodded and waved them on. They continued to the room with the given directions and found a cache of crates.

Ruzat holstered his shotgun and picked up two crates. As he was about ready to leave the room, Eve cleared her throat and pointed to a levi-lifter in the back corner. They loaded it up and it took both Ruzat and Wena to move it. He pulled, she pushed, and Eve took point leading the way.

There was a commotion from deeper in the facility. Comms chatter confirmed it was Team Two taking down hostiles. While the security forces were distracted, it gave Team One a shot at an easy exit. When they made it, *Skyfire* was there waiting for the call to open the cargo bay door.

"Balok, lower the cargo ramp," Ruzat said.

The door's uplocks popped free and gravity aided it down. They ran the load of cargo up and shoved it to the side to make sure there was room for more. They reentered the facility and proceeded to make a second run at the ammunition. Midway through loading up Captain Kohan called to them.

"Team One, converge on us at the assembly plant in the manufacturing ship. Take the south-east entrance, path is clear."

"Understood," Ruzat replied.

"Wena, push this out to the ship, and then stay there," Eve motioned to the levi-lifter and ordered.

Wena nodded and they split. Eve followed Ruzat out of the storage room and weaved their way through the building toward the far side. There were quite a few dead elementus lying in the path, making it easy for the two to follow.

She and Ruzat worked well together. They were efficient. On their way to meet with the others, they got caught in a firefight with a few elementus at the end of a hall. Neither of their weapons had the range they needed to take the security forces out. She motioned for them to enter an office.

"Captain, we're pinned. It's going to take us a few more minutes to get to you," Eve said for the comms, and then directed Ruzat. "Can you punch through that wall?"

He shrugged. "We will see."

He knocked on the wall, listening to what it was made of or what might be behind it. Sheet metal. He cocked his mighty fist back and thrust it forward. If he weren't wearing armor, she imagined it would have hurt. The wall dented, and he grunted in satisfaction.

Leveling his shotgun at it, he unloaded three spaced out shots into the wall. At the current range, it cut through with ease and left the metal weakened. He used his shoulder to bash the hole larger, and then strained to pry it so they could fit through.

Taking care not to snag themselves, they ducked through and continued to the next wall. Through a few of them, Eve figured they were close enough she might get a better shot. Poking her head out of the office, she peeked around the corner to where the elementus had taken up their defensive position. They weren't in view, but she knew they hadn't moved on.

"I can get a shot off and run up to the next doorway. Once I'm there, I'll cover you while you move up," she whispered while reloading her firearm.

He nodded and when she peeked again, she saw the briefest glimpse of an elementus at the corner of the intersection. Aiming for the wall directly where she knew they were, she hoped her bullet would have enough penetrating power. Point. Aim. Shoot. Run. She executed her plan, not caring if she hit her mark. As she ran to the next door, she fired several more shots down the hall for good measure, and when she got there reloaded.

Giving Ruzat the signal, she stuck herself out there and timed her shots five seconds in-between to give him the room to move closer. Reloading once more, he signaled, and they rushed forward together. The elementus tried to seize the opportunity, but failed because Eve and Ruzat's guns were already leveled in their direction.

The hall filled with a cacophony of blasts. When the smoke cleared the elementus lay dead, Ruzat had been grazed on his side, and Eve was unhurt. Ruzat breathed in deeply and made no attempt to stop his bleeding.

"You good?" she asked.

"Fix me up when we are back on *Skyfire*. Finish the mission."

She nodded. They exited the other side of the security building and followed the path to the ship in the middle of the mobile base. A door was open, and light was flooding out. Inside was another slew of bodies, none of them their crew. Gunshots were heard further into the building, and all they had to do was follow the devastation.

"Captain Kohan, we are in the building," Ruzat said over comms.

"Flank the west hallway and enter the central manufacturing plant. We're pinned on the east side. Anvil-and-Hammer."

"Understood."

They moved cautiously but quickly. The hallway was clear, and Eve hoped the elementus weren't planning the same thing. After passing numerous hallways and doors, they reached the manufacturing floor entrance. More gunfire confirmed the location was correct.

The duo checked their ammo and reloaded as needed. Knowing they each had limited shots before reloading, Eve thought to propose an all-out attack.

"Left, right, left, right. Alternate shots. You have what, seven shells in there?"

He nodded.

"When we're out, don't reload. Rush 'em."

He nodded once more, and she prepared to open the door. It was locked, and without Nine with them there was no hope of them breaking the code for the entry pad. It meant Ruzat would break it down, and Eve was going to be the first to fire.

"Cap, we're in position. Give me a target," Eve said.

"Upper scaffold, seven hostiles."

"Got it."

Eve pulled her gun into the ready position. Without knowing how high the scaffolding was, she would need time to acquire a target, aim, and fire. She took a cleansing breath, and then gave Ruzat the signal. The door buckled and slammed open when he rammed it.

In the heat of the moment, it was like time slowed for her. Her gaze shifted up about six meters to the scaffolding held up by cables. Seven were what Kohan could see. There were two more on each of the outer edges. Leveling the sight, she aimed a hair to the right and fired her first shot. They had the attention of the elementus.

Her bullet buried itself into her first target, and she readied the next. Ruzat fired a shot at several elementus taking shelter in a barricade of crates. They were met with retaliation and had to take shelter behind assembly line machinery. The sounds of metal on metal were close to Eve. She stayed out of the line of sight.

Captain Kohan and the others capitalized on the split attention and fired into the ones grouped up on the ground. When attention was redirected again, Eve stuck her head out. She lined up her next shot and pegged an elementus on the scaffolding who looked like they were aiming for Faun. It gave Faun enough time to place her rifle on its legs and adjust her scope.

A stray elementus tried to get around the other side of the machine where Ruzat was sheltering, but he was ready for them. He pulled the trigger as soon as they rounded the corner. The pellets spread and only half hit their intended target, the rest ricocheting off the metal panels. Ruzat chambered his next round.

Eve dashed across to where he was and caught a glimpse of Nine and Captain Kohan in a closer position, picking off ones in the group. Virid provided distraction and cover, while Faun sniped a couple off the scaffolding in quick succession.

Eve took charge and signaled Ruzat to alternate their shots. A set of stairs up to the scaffolding had grabbed her attention, and Ruzat followed. *If we can get the high ground, we can get the ones in the middle on the floor,* she thought.

It was clear to the top. The closest elementus was five to six meters away, which gave them plenty of reaction time. She rushed headlong toward them with no chance to steady her hand to get a shot off. They noticed and turned to aim at her, but it was too late. The gap was closed, and she jammed the barrel of her gun in between two grafted ores.

While the two toppled, Eve pulled her trigger and put her last bullet into their chest. They tried to shoot her, but the bullet ricocheted off vents overhead. She holstered her gun and picked up the rifle.

Aiming down into the group of elementus on the floor, she began firing not to kill, but distract so the others could move in and take them out. It worked and the rest were quickly overwhelmed.

"Captain Kohan," Balok's voice came on over comms. "Our window to escape is closing. The elementus ship has entered the star system and are heading this way."

"Understood. Be ready to lift off the moment the cargo hold is closed."

"Yes, Captain."

"You heard him. Don't bother looking in crates, just grab and go. Load up as much as you can pull with a levi-lifter and haul ass to the ship," Kohan ordered.

One levi-lifter per person meant a significant haul of crates. They worked together to make sure their efforts were expedient. Kohan led them through the factory to a docking door. Outside, more shots were fired at them, and they took refuge behind the crates. Faun propped her rifle up and fired.

"Go! I'll cover!" she said.

Kohan didn't hesitate. They continued their convoy of levi-lifters around the facility and toward *Skyfire*. The ramp was down and Wena saw them coming. She bounded down on all fours and helped push one by one. Kohan ran back down toward where Faun was. Eve followed.

Faun was pinned and couldn't pop her head up to get a shot off. Eve leveled her stolen rifle at the flashes and fired until she was out. The air quieted.

"Cover!" Eve barked at Faun and grabbed the levi-lifter handle and pulled with all of her might.

Setting up, she stood on the forks of the lifter and placed her rifle on top of a crate. Taking aim, she fired, chambered, and fired again. Kohan fired blindly into the darkness. The elementus resumed firing. *Don't let me get hit in the back...*

Reaching the ship, Wena helped one last time and the four of them climbed the ramp. Kohan hit a nearby console to close the door. It hadn't even fully closed when Balok accelerated.

"Brace, brace, brace!" Balok yelled through the comms.

Skyfire banked hard, and there was an impact to the underside of the ship. Everyone was thrown off their feet except Nine, who ran for the left hallway. Those who remained tried again to get back up and start moving toward the bridge, but the ship rocked violently a second and third time.

"Elementus have commenced orbital bombardment. Secure yourselves for evasive actions," Nine said.

Eve grabbed Wena as best as she could, pulling her to the side and out of the way of crates. They made their way to the right hallway while the others headed to the left side. There was significantly less room to be thrown once in there, but it also meant smashing into the walls. The two reached the entrance to the munitions hallway, and Eve ran to the gunner pod.

"Right side gun coming up," Eve announced once she was inside.

"Save the ammunition," Kohan replied. "Balok, Virid, plot our course toward the nearest bulk path out of elementus space and immediately engage the Light Drive."

They did so, and Eve watched out her window. Never before had she seen what happened to close proximity matter outside the warp bubble when the drive was engaged. The ground seemed to curve in on itself, rolling like a tsunami. And then it was gone. Not destroyed, but out of view because they were in warp.

Eve let her head fall back and she closed her eyes.

Chapter 7
Return on Investment

Hitting an elementus manufacturing plant was sure to put them into the sights of whoever was running the operation. But, for now, they had escaped with minimal wounds and a considerable number of crates. Eve patched Ruzat up while they drank together and celebrated victory, recounting their past exploits with one another. *Skyfire* set off toward an Emex station on the outskirts of QuBE territory.

Even using the bulk paths, it would take a significant amount of time to get there. The two species-controlled spaces were on opposite sides of the 'band' of the Crux arm in the galaxy.

Though they'd stolen product likely worth over what they had been stiffed on, it would take time to fence. When they opened a crate, Kohan scowled. Pulling a rifle out, it wasn't a normal weapon. It looked like a high-end pulse beam rifle. The stock was wider though. Kohan examined, and the crew waited. There was no magazine or energy cartridge. Not even a place for them. Opening a panel on the stock, they found a crystal as an energy source. It glowed light pinkish-purple inside its gold chassis.

"Vradix crystal...it's a Rekwa weapon," he declared.

This was different than the Rekwa mining laser Marsi had on *the Fade*. The mining tool had been modified to disable the safety features which disallowed use on anything organic. These, however, were designed specifically as weapons. Regular guns were relatively easy to buy and sell. Regulations were significantly more relaxed because their devastating power was limited. Rekwa mining lasers were highly controlled, and a weapon was illegal for anyone to own. Anyone caught with the technology without proper licensing faced extreme punishment.

"This is vraditi technology. Elementus are not licensed to manufacture these," Virid said.

"What the hell are we supposed to do now?" Faun sighed.

Picking a rifle out, Eve examined it. It was larger and heavier than a standard rifle and balanced more toward the aft end. The buttstock had an area cut out for resting comfortably against the shoulder. The trigger guard was four times the size of her finger, and to pull the trigger would take two.

"Could these have been commissioned by the G.P.?" Eve asked.

"Unlikely," Nine replied. "They would be lethal, and the vraditi wouldn't use them. These look like they were manufactured with military specifications."

"For who?" Eve asked, knowing none of them had the answer.

Captain Kohan used his wrist computer to scan the weapons. Eve caught a glimpse of the screen, and he was taking pictures as well as readouts of the energy coming off the open chamber with the crystal.

"We're making a detour to Melosa's moon and doubling back toward human space. I have a fence there that can help." Kohan said. "Settle in. It's going to be a long trip."

For Eve, it meant keeping an eye on Wena, making meals, organizing the cargo hold, and otherwise being bored. Now Wena was unofficially-officially part of the crew, Captain Kohan gave her quarters...in Eve's room. Sharing had not been in Eve's plan, at least not her room. The only reason Eve didn't fuss was because she saw

Wena as a resource, the first loyal subordinate. She wanted to make sure when the time was right for her to take over *Skyfire* she had strong allies.

Once they had unloaded their cargo at the caves, they bounced through a few systems via bulk paths and entered one of the longer subspace tunnels, which cut straight to Salvoa. The known history was that as soon as humans had become spacefaring with faster-than-light drives, the vraditi appeared through it. A thousand years prior, an agreement was struck that if humanity adhered to galactic law, they would be allowed to use the paths.

A thousand years was a long time, and while Salvoa and most humans did in fact follow galactic law, people like Eve found ways to be more opportunistic.

"Lady Eve," Wena said and broke the silence in the room.

"Yes?"

"Can I go to the bathroom."

"You don't have to ask me when you need to shit. Just make sure you listen for any comms announcements."

Wena nodded and left. Eve saw an opportunity to relieve some stress. *Captain or daughter?* she thought. Kohan was capable of procreating, that much was obvious, but she didn't have faith he would satisfy *her*. Faun on the other hand had exciting potential. Eve assumed with the robotic limbs, Faun would have figured out how to be both gentle and rough when needed.

Getting up from her bed, she headed down the hall to Faun's room. She hit the call button on the door's keypad. Faun took her time, and when the door opened, she squinted from the darkness of the room.

"What the fek do you want?"

Assertive as always, Eve came right out.

"When's the last time you had someone in your bed?"

Faun was taken aback for a split second, and then returned with as much vitriol as always.

"None of your business. Get lost."

"Do you want to reset the clock?" Eve stepped into the doorway and rested her shoulder on the frame. "Nothing special, no attachment, just some stress relief."

Faun's grimaced face was hard for Eve to read, and she hoped it wasn't going to be that difficult in the throughs of passion. Eve took another step closer, and Faun took a step back as an invitation.

Eve smirked and closed the door behind them. There was a dim light coming from Faun's bed area, the glow of a control panel. By the time Faun had made it back to her bed, Eve had removed her outer clothes and was working on her bodysuit. Faun stripped her nightwear off and laid on the bed.

Eve stole what glances she could in the dark at the cybernetics merged with supple pink flesh while she finished disrobing and tying her curls back loosely. The hue of the control panel illuminated her curves.

Climbing onto the bed on hands and knees, she moved over Faun and went right into foreplay. She ran a hand up Faun's chest, stopping briefly to stimulate her nipple and watch it harden, and then continued up to her collarbone. Leaning down on one elbow freed her body weight. Leaning in, she kissed Faun's neck and caressed toward the pelvic area, searching for any of her personal erogenous zones. It was the inside of the thigh. Faun let out a small noise of anticipation, and Eve tortured her with that.

Eve moved her fingers closer and closer with every caress until Faun squirmed for her to finally do it. She started with fingers, playing, and building anticipation. Leaning down, she pressed her lips to Faun's and at the same time let her middle finger move to the most sensitive spot. Faun let out a moan through their kiss.

Faun's hands finally came up off the bed. One grabbed Eve's head to pull her in for a deeper kiss, the other went to Eve's hand and forced her to press harder and move faster. The pace quickened and Faun's hand reached for Eve's lower region. Surprisingly, despite the robotic prosthetic, the artificial flesh on her fingertips was soft.

Faun pushed Eve over, and they continued on their sides. Faun slipped a finger inside Eve, which was met with little resistance due to how wet she was. She moaned and followed her lead. Their motions were now fully carnal as they pushed and pulled against one another, making noises, and enjoying the pleasure. Faun's body tensed. Her breathing quickened, and her focus on Eve broke. Eve took it as a sign and stopped only long enough to flip around so they could pleasure each other orally.

Her tongue and lips took over. Faun bucked enthusiastically. Eve climbed over Faun, and she reciprocated. Eve intensified her focus, and it didn't take long for Faun's whole body to begin shaking. Faun took her mouth away to breathe, and the heavy moan echoed off the walls. When she calmed, Eve turned around and straddled her face to get her turn.

Pressing her hands against the headboard, she moved rhythmically while Faun's tongue pressed hard. The more the feeling built, the harder it was to keep rhythm. She compensated with speed until the moment her body could no longer hold back. Her thighs squeezed Faun. Faun pulled her legs open more and continued. The wave of pleasure coursed through her body, and she let out several loud moans.

When the orgasm subsided, she waited for a moment. Her legs felt like jelly, and she feared that if she didn't recover a little before moving, she'd fall. She pulled herself off Faun and turned to sit against the headboard only long enough to finish enjoying the high of having good sex. Getting up, she put her clothes back on, minus the bodysuit, and headed for the door. Before she left the room, she glanced back at Faun who was still laid out on the bed.

One step closer to having her on my side...

After going to the bathroom and cleaning up, Eve returned to her room. Wena was there waiting for her.

"Are we there yet?" Wena asked.

"Let's go find out."

The two of them headed to the bridge. Only Nine was there, at the helm. They were checking all of the systems at once, and Eve envied that ability. *It would probably be information overload for anyone except a synthetic.*

She stepped up to Nine, snapped to attention, and saluted sarcastically.

"Lady Eve, reporting for duty."

"You do not have to salute me," they said, briefly looking at her before returning their attention to raw data on screen.

"I know. It wasn't meant to be serious," she said and sat in one of the pilot seats. "What's our estimated docking time?"

"Two hours."

Eve saw an opportunity to re-educate Wena into something other than a miner. While the plesian's giant paws and fingers would be of little use in pressing the buttons on the smaller consoles, she felt it would at least be important for her to be able to understand how the ship worked.

"Wena, what do you know about flying through space?"

"It's dark."

"What about the ship we're in?"

"It lifts us up to the stars."

"Do you know how?"

Wena shook her head. Eve pulled up the displays for all three engines.

"Each engine is built for a specific job. The Cruise Drive is for going slow, the Light Drive for going fast, and the Bulk Drive for entering the space tunnels like we're in right now…"

It took the whole two hours to get through a basic explanation of how the drives were independent but also interconnected. Wena had many questions, some she asked a couple times. *How much teaching do they have to go through to begin to remember the new stuff and forget the old?*

"Attention to all crew; we will be dropping out of the bulk path momentarily," Nine announced on comms.

Watching through the forward window, the shimmer of the Bulk Drive's bubble against a black backdrop ended, and the stars reappeared as they emerged to normal space. Directly in front of them was Emex Station Fifteen, and a whole hub of ships coming and going. Most of them were Salvoan in design, with a handful of other types from other species.

The rest of the crew appeared and took their stations, Captain Kohan taking over the command chair from Nine.

"Transponder back online," Virid said. "Identified as medical cargo transport."

Eve continued pointing out things to Wena and saw out of the corner of her eye that Faun had looked over. Eve pretended not to notice.

"Docking request sent and approved," Balok stated. "Proceeding to hangar one-four-two."

Much like all of the other Emex Stations, the station was tailored mostly for the resident species. The hangar signs greeted them in Salvoan languages. The elaborate interiors were typical of humankind, flared for whatever mood the original architect was in. They kept things clean, but nowhere near as immaculate as a vraditi station. As the crew disembarked, Kohan addressed them.

"Nine, you're on ship watch," he instructed. "Eve and Faun, you're with me. The rest of you are restocking essentials. No extras."

They dispersed, and Eve took to Kohan's left side, keeping stride with him while they headed from the hangar to the city. He was focused, and even with the short amount of time she'd been with them it was apparent he wasn't a small talker.

How much can I pry without pissing him off?

"So, how long have you had *Skyfire*?"

"Twenty-two years."

"Ah, so Faun was born there?"

He gave a quick nod.

"What happened to Faun's mother?"

"Died a long time ago."

It'll be like pulling teeth if I try to keep getting it this way. Maybe he needs alcohol to loosen up.

She let the conversation drop and just walked. He led them down into the city streets where it was crowded. Above the tall buildings with neon signs flew vehicles of all sorts in a well-orchestrated traffic pattern. Though it had been at an early age her parents had taken her from Salvoa, the atmosphere provided a small nostalgic feeling.

They approached a Wayfinder, and he ordered a lift. When it arrived, they climbed in, and he punched in their destination on a terminal. They were lifted into the traffic and brought up to speed.

The air in their taxi was awkward for no other reason than the three of them all had strong personalities, and no one wanted to share more than they had to. Eve stared out the window and watched the city below pass by. Kohan did the same while Faun rested her head against the seat.

Eve was surprised when the vehicle brought them down into an affluent section of the city. They landed on a street where people looked the exact opposite of what she envisioned a fencer for stolen goods should look like. Still, the moment they were on the ground Kohan hopped out without hesitation. Eve and Faun followed, trying to match his pacing which had already put him ahead.

He didn't have to push his way through the crowds, as they parted for him. *Is he a somebody or a nobody? Either would make sense.* Following his footsteps, both Eve and Faun got different types of stares and glares from different people. None of it mattered in the grand scheme. To her, these were people she might someday steal from or exploit for her own gain.

Kohan brought them down a street to a tucked away restaurant which had a classical feel to it. There were a few people coming and going from it but was mostly ignored. There was a door attendant at a podium to the entrance. His expressionless face gave away no signs of dissatisfaction or distaste in their approach.

"Do you have a reservation?" the door attendant asked.

"Juniper."

The door attendant nodded with acknowledgement and opened the door for them.

"Your table awaits at the far rear left."

Past all the normal patrons, at the far back was a tucked away booth. The red-dyed suede which lined the seats was soft to the touch, and the lighting was enough to see and be seen. Once seated it was fifteen minutes before they were joined by a wiry looking man with unkempt hair and an augmented reality eye piece. Kohan slid a tablet to him without a word, and the man looked it over. The first words out of his mouth were nothing about the contents.

"Big bounty on your head. A hundred million chits from the Elementus Dynasty. Sentient species trafficking, attacking an elementus outpost and stealing high value elements, murder...is this what you took from them?"

"The whole thing was a setup from go," Kohan replied. "G.P. got tipped off, got chased halfway across the galaxy, and then the elementus cut our pay. We liberated that from the elementus' facility."

"There will be interested parties, including those you stole it from. Consider if you put these into circulation, they could be used against you in the future."

"Profit margins?" Kohan asked.

"It'll take time to move them, and the risk of being caught is high. To make it worth it for me, my cut will be fifty percent."

Eve thought it was too steep and would have negotiated, but Kohan didn't reject it.

"Blind auction, quantity of ten. Minimum bid, a hundred million chits. Once you confirm payment, we'll coordinate the drop," Kohan said and stood.

Eve had been in the trade long enough to know the fencer would find buyers.

"I'll be in touch..." the fencer said and paused. His eye darted back and forth reading something on his eyepiece. "A G.P. warrant just came across the station broadcast with your crew's profiles and ship configuration. You need to get out of here before you can't."

Kohan ushered them out and back toward the street they came from. Eve thought about what the fencer had said about the weapons being used against them.

"We need to keep some of those for our lockers," Eve said.

"Agreed," Faun chimed in. "Two big targets on us isn't good."

Kohan didn't acknowledge or agree, just returned them to the posh street they came from and ordered a lift back to the hangar. While they waited for their ride, Kohan tapped his ear and spoke through comms.

"Get back to the ship with whatever you've picked up, now. I want everyone ready to go the moment we're back."

"Some of the supplies aren't due to be here for another hour," Ruzat responded.

"If they haven't arrived by the time we're back, we're leaving it."

"Aye, Captain."

The vehicle arrived and as soon as they entered, Kohan barked at them to get them to their destination as quickly as they could. The feelings Eve had were intense. Her heart pumped from the thrill. When and where would they meet someone trying to collect on the bounty?

Would they have to continue running from system to system from the G.P.?

"Captain, trouble. G.P. is approaching the cargo bay," Ruzat said.

"Disable them. Nine, prepare for launch as soon as we're aboard. Eve and Faun will get on guns and blow a hole through the hangar shields."

Dropped off, the three sprinted toward where the rest of the crew were engaged. The current forces were small, but more police would arrive shortly. The vraditi used their ships as cover while the crew shot from the top of the cargo bay.

Using ships and cargo as cover while moving, the police didn't sense the three of them coming. By the time they were alerted it was too late. Faun took the middle three and knocked them around. Two vraditi on the right-hand side pulled out electrified batons and swung them at Eve.

She blocked some blows while others hit her combat suit. It took the hits, and the insulation redirected the current to the platform. The officers had overextended in their swings which gave her opportunity to counter. Grabbing the wrist of one of the officers, she bent their elbow in a direction it wasn't meant to be and used the baton on the other officer's bare neck. They convulsed and dropped. With her fist already in a ball, she punched the other in the cheek which sent them to the ground with a thud.

Her area was clear, which meant forgetting everything else and get on board the ship. More G.P. shuttles were on approach to the platform, sirens blaring. Kohan was right behind her heading up the ramp, but it was no time for congratulation. Straight to the right gunner pod, she began spooling up the railgun's chamber. There was a cacophony of running, and moments after they passed, the ship lifted off and screamed toward the exit. Ships already in the shipping lane got out of the way while they barreled through, chased by G.P. shuttles attempting to stop them.

There was no reason to think station police would lower the shields even if they were at full speed. Despite the distance still to the exit, Eve targeted the inner shield and fired. It shimmered, and she fired again causing it to waver. Faun fired hers twice, and Eve another. The first shield dropped, and they both fired at the second until their heatsinks maxed out. The shield didn't fall.

"Brace!" Kohan yelled over comms.

The ship didn't collide as the shield disengaged moments before impact. When Eve looked over her shoulder out her dome, she saw the chaos of mere seconds of vacuum. The hangar blew everything nearby toward space. The inner shield came back up and pressure was being restored.

They let us go to avoid mass casualties. That's getting added to the warrant.

A vraditi G.P. battleship had positioned above the exit and lobbed a volley of missiles at them. *Skyfire* arced hard, and Eve began launching all of the mines in her control as chaff. There was a rapid fire *kachunk* sound below her as the quantity depleted to zero. She rotated the pod one-eighty and checked her heatsink. It had cooled enough for a shot. The targeting computer did most of the work while she pulled the trigger and hoped for the best. It hit a mine. Plasma explosions lit up the area and engulfed many of the missiles. Only a few made it through to hit the shield.

They'd bought enough time to find a trajectory out. Their Light Drive activated, and everything blurred. Eve knew there was going to be a significant delay in the battleship chasing them because of its mass. The alignment time and energy needed to get it up to speed meant a head start for *Skyfire*.

"Two smaller ships are pursuing," Nine announced. "They will drop out of FTL moments after us."

Eve wanted to be on the bridge but knew she was needed at her post, ready to fire again.

"Heatsink at fifty percent and dropping," she announced.

"Balok, Virid, find the nearest bulk path and get us into it."

"Yes, Captain," they both said.

The ship slowed and entered in a hard-to-starboard maneuver which put them into a Y-axis spin. The G.P. ships pursuing followed, and Eve tracked them. With the maneuver it was hard to keep a lock, but it didn't stop her from taking a shot.

She hit their shielding and they returned fire with their own railgun. The shield absorbed it. Faun fired twice; one hit and one missed. The second G.P. ship fired and missed as *Skyfire* engaged their Light Drive again.

Faun came on comms. "They're going to keep pursuing. We need to disable one like before and hope the second stops to help."

"Agreed," Kohan said. "Before we enter the path, all fire directed at one. Disable or destroy."

Again, they came out of FTL in a stomach-turning move. Eve aimed for where the ships would be coming from. The first emerged into normal space. Eve and Faun fired almost simultaneously until their heatsinks maxed out. The G.P. ship didn't have time to react, and the shield faltered. *Skyfire*'s projectiles tore through, leaving gaping holes in the hull.

Skyfire pulled away, and as Faun predicted, the second ship came to the aid of the first. They entered the bulk path.

Even if another ship jumped into the path now, we'll be gone before they emerge. Let's hope there's no G.P. waiting on the other side.

Resting her head back, the tension released from her shoulders, and she slouched. Closing her eyes, she performed breathing exercises to slow her heart rate and let the adrenaline work its way through. After a few minutes, she left her station and headed to the bridge. Faun came in from the other hall at the same time, and Eve gave her a nod to express approval.

"Once we exit this path plot a course to Melosa's moon. Nine, perform a continuous scan for G.P. comms, and help them in avoiding detection. Take detours as needed," Kohan ordered.

The three of them worked at their consoles while Faun approached her dad.

"We need a second ship. Everyone looking to cash in on the bounty is going to come after us," Faun said.

"One step at a time. That's a problem for tomorrow. For now, we regroup and run battle drills."

Chapter 8
...Consequences?!

Eve was bored at the hideout and took initiative to keep herself busy. She did her duties without too much griping, but the more exciting activities included visiting Faun's bedroom and test-firing the Rekwa rifles. The power in the rifles was devastating. They burned through organic matter like it wasn't there, and rock melted into magma. There was a significant difference between the rifles and the mining rig she used. Both were deadly, but this was much more focused.

Who has a need for these? Are the elementus planning to invade something?

In order to stave off monotony during the downtime, she'd even stolen a well-worn book from Faun's room. It wasn't the book that had originally caught her eye, but the "bookmark" twinkling in the light. It was a necklace with a heart-shaped Vradix crystal as the centerpiece.

Reading wasn't normally her pastime, but the title of the book, "Purest of Heart," was completely counter to what she thought Faun would read. She thumbed the crystal and stared at the ceiling.

What was the author thinking? This girl is completely unrelatable, and the job class system sounds horrible. I couldn't imagine some test deciding what I did for the rest of my life.

After Captain Kohan sent encrypted transmissions of the weapons at work, it took a month for the auction to happen. The winner was paying twenty million chits per rifle, double what the minimum bid was. With the stock of them they had stolen, it was a veritable gold mine.

Kohan laid out a plan which ensured they would get paid without risking the merchandise being stolen, being caught, or dying along the way. While coordinating with the fencer, *Skyfire* set out to the Garimn System, a trinary star, multi-planetary system which offered the protection of immense gravitational waves. The G.P.'s larger ships would have significant trouble navigating due to their sheer size, while *Skyfire* and any other smaller ship would be able to get in and out relatively easy.

Eve, Ruzat, and Wena were dropped off with the weapons on the ninth planet, Illion. They took up a room at a mining outpost tucked against desert mountains. Their job was to keep the crates secured until payment was made, then activate a tracker for the buyer to follow. Kohan left them there with enough chits to survive while the rest of the crew headed to Starreach station to take payment and deliver the location.

"Can Wena go walk?" Wena asked, pacing about their room, bumping into the cargo crates.

"Stick close by and listen to your comms," Eve said with her eyes closed.

Eve was laid out in her bed. Her head was pounding, and she attributed it to having too much to drink the night before. She hadn't known there was going to be a bar at the tiny outpost, so she'd brought her own half-keg of ale. Ruzat had also drank his share but was up and about just fine.

"Is it ok for her to go by herself?" he asked.

"If you think she needs a chaperone, feel free to follow her in circles."

The room appeared to spin. She became sweaty and clammy, and every muscle in her body ached like she'd done an intense obstacle course training. Nauseated, she tried to run for the bathroom but tripped over a crate and fell. Ruzat let out a deep, vibrating laugh, and Eve shot him an evil look. Trying to get back up, she tried to balance herself against a crate only for it to move. Ruzat laughed again.

"Why the hell did you move it?" Eve yelled at him.

"I didn't do it! You did!"

"Shit!"

Standing back up, she headed to the bathroom and vomited in the wash basin. Turning on the water, she washed it down and doused her whole head. She felt like she was burning up. After rinsing her mouth, she stumbled back toward the beds and tripped. Instinctively she put her hands out to catch herself and put a hole through the door frame.

Caught off guard, she wasn't sure how to react. *Is the construction that flimsy?* Ruzat took notice too, and he watched her carefully. Eve returned to her bed doing her best to not falter again. Ruzat stood and walked over to where she lay and hovered. His rare jovial nature disappeared, and his stoic face had returned.

"How long have you felt sick?" he asked.

"I don't know. I thought it was the alcohol."

"Alcohol doesn't make you strong."

Something caught his eye, and he reached over to the half-hidden book to snatch it up. He pulled the heart necklace out and studied it in the light.

"This is a pure Vradix crystal. Did you get this from the weapons?" he asked.

"No, I stole it from Faun."

"This is why you're sick. Handling these barehanded has been known to alter genetics in a small portion of human populations."

"Every human has heard the myth about the crystals granting superpowers. It's childhood blather."

"It isn't. There was a surge of humans gaining powers long ago when your species discovered the crystals on Salvoa. Eventually you used them to develop your first Light Drives.

"The humans who acquired powers relabeled themselves Alkosian, after our word *alkos.* Then, when the *tarak* appeared from their dens deep underground, fear drove the regular humans to conscript the Alkosians to fight. It's why our species took the entirety of crystals from your planet and provided you with the synthetic ones. We had to stop you from destroying yourselves."

Eve remembered learning about the war, but the truth that it was people with special abilities was omitted. What history remembers was the huge loss of life, as the lizard people are near two times the size of the average human. Even with abilities, she couldn't fathom fighting one without the thought of being tossed like a rag doll.

The true history was one thing to try and absorb. The reality that the crystal somehow altered her was another thing altogether. *Am I still human? Is 'Alkosian' a species or a race?* Myth or not, she didn't want this if it meant she was going to be nauseated all the time.

"Is there a cure?"

"I am not sure. After the war, the Alkosians disappeared without a trace, and no new ones appeared because there were no more Vradix crystals on Salvoa."

Miserable, Eve lay on the bed and soaked it with her sweat. Ruzat brought her wet towels to help, but it only lasted so long before it heated up and felt like she was being steamed to death. An idea came to mind to use the room's purification chamber to hopefully cool down.

After a soak in the *orakos* gel, she felt mildly better. Not even a fraction of normal, but small improvements were better than none. Gradually, over a few days, the sickness continued to fade. The side effect of increased strength did not.

Eve shoved a crate in between the beds and sat down, feet planted. Ruzat was skimming a holographic terrain map of the area when she interrupted him by putting her elbow down on the crate and holding her hand out for him to take.

"Let's go," she goaded.

His size both in height and build eclipsed her. His forearm was double hers, and his fingers could fold all the way over her hand. He shook his head.

Fear of hurting me, or fear of me beating him?

"C'mon. I need to know my limits and who better to test them against."

"Wena wants to help. How can Wena help?"

While plesians had significant muscle mass and had incredible strength, arm wrestling her would prove even more impractical than Ruzat.

"Your palms aren't built the same. It would be hard for you to get a grip," Eve said. "And I don't want to hurt you."

Ruzat begrudgingly obliged and turned to face her. As soon as he had his elbow down, Eve smacked her palm into his. She braced herself with her other hand holding her elbow in place on the table and grinned.

"You humans have a weird way of testing your strength."

"Shut up. Three. Two. One. Go!"

Immediately she felt his strength try and push her hand to the other side of the crate. Holding strong, she put force into trying to push his arm down too. Wena watched intently.

Staring into his four eyes, she grinned. His forehead wrinkled as he strained to keep her from moving his arm. The effort was considerable, but she was slowly overcoming his strength. Little by little she moved closer to pinning him. He gritted and bared his teeth while he struggled, but it was no use. No matter how hard he tried to bring her back to their starting point, he could do nothing but lose ground.

The slow burn all the way until Ruzat's wrist touched the crate made it more enjoyable for her. She huffed in triumph and let him go.

"Who is stronger than you? Faun or Nine?" she said with a cocky tone.

"Wena is strong!" she interjected.

Ruzat rubbed his hand, and she caught sight of a deep imprint inside his palm.

He shook his head and looked away before answering, "Not sure."

Standing up, she gave him a soft punch in the shoulder.

"Aww, don't be like that. It was only a friendly test of strength."

"Wena wants to test her strength! Please!"

Eve looked at her, and her big face was eager with anticipation. Not wanting to alienate her, she nodded.

What can I do with her though? Get into a shoving match? Maybe see who can push the other?

"Wena used to play with others in the mines. We would throw big rocks. The farthest one wins."

That sounded better to Eve than what she'd thought of, but barring a climb into the mountains, there was nothing of the sort nearby.

"When we get back to the hideout cave then," Eve agreed.

Still waiting on a communication from *Skyfire*, Eve headed out to the local bar to earn some extra money.

If I can beat Ruzat, I can beat anyone on this planet.

'The Oasis;' its name was both ironic and a cliché. There was no oasis, and the bar was a run-down shack with rusted metal siding. Either way, she was going to get drunk and make some men mad.

The inside was just as horrible. Dank, dark, and smelly, the only thing it actually had going for it were the monitors on the walls which picked up and displayed several different broadcasts from across their arm of the galaxy. Making her way over to the tapster, she couldn't tell what was dirtier, the mugs or the man's face. He eyed her, annoyed before she even said anything.

"Gimme whatever's on tap," she said.

He grunted, grabbed up a glass, and filled it.

"Two hundred chits."

She scoffed but paid. While she took a large swig, she noticed a news broadcast showing video of a space station being attacked by little, pitch black, gremlin-like creatures. The volume was muted, but there was commentary at the bottom of the screen.

"This was only days ago when an unprovoked attack by wild creatures overwhelmed Starreach Station. Witnesses have indicated several unidentified, frigate sized ships pierced the station's hull with their pointed bows. Within hours the entire station had been overrun."

The video continued to play. People were fighting them, shooting, but they kept coming as a horde. She didn't catch any glimpse of Kohan or the rest of the crew.

Hopefully, they made it out before whatever the hell is going on there happened.

"Due to the destructive nature of the creatures, many people are dead or missing. In the chaos of trying to flee the station, several independent ships collided outside the station. It is unknown at this time if those ships were boarded by the creatures, or if the collisions were piloting error.

In additional news, more of these pod, seed-like ships have appeared in sovereign spaces…"

Eve chugged the rest of the swill, banged the glass down, and sped-walked back to their room. She activated comms on the way.

"Ruzat, we might have a problem."

"What?"

"Starreach was attacked by creatures. No sight of the crew on the videos."

"What kind of creatures?"

"Small, like a child. Black leathery skin. Sharp teeth. No hair. Runs around on all four."

"Kul. Foul creatures whose only instincts are to destroy and procreate."

She got back to the room and shut off her comms. Opening the door, she continued the conversation.

"Susceptible to normal methods of killing?" she asked.

"As long as you can kill them before they swarm you, yeah."

"If Kohan didn't get out of there, we may need to find another way out of this system. Apparently these kul are attacking multiple places."

"They can't do that on their own. They aren't a spacefaring species."

Confused, Eve figured it to be a type of smuggling. Either way, she had a nagging feeling something serious was going on. First the Rekwa weapons, and now kul showing up where *Skyfire* had gone. Though coincidence felt more realistic, the timing was suspect.

They received a ping from *Skyfire* with an encrypted message through a relay network. It was short and came from a system far out of the way from the path back to the Garimn System.

"Attempting to shake a tail. Be prepared to egress."

Alone, it wouldn't have been a big deal. As mercs, it was part of normal operations to need to be prepared to fly at a moment's notice. But after the recent events, Eve was apprehensive.

It was another couple days before *Skyfire* entered system. They were quick to announce themselves, and the stress was apparent.

"Ruzat, we're coming in hot. Prepare to load the crates back onto *Skyfire*," Captain Kohan said over comms. "Eve, ready one of the rifles and cover him."

As the three of them moved the crates out of the room, their ship barreled through the atmosphere from over the mountains, firing one of the railguns behind them. On their tail were a couple ships Eve didn't recognize but matched the description of the ones on the news.

They were unique, different from all other designs of spacefaring species. Shaped almost like a seed, with a spiral tip at the end, they cut through the air.

A sonic boom shattered the glass on multiple buildings from the low flying, high velocity ships. *Skyfire* attempted unsuccessfully to shoot the hostiles down. The sleek, alien ships dodged, and fired Rekwa shots from immediately above the pointed area of their hull. *Skyfire* evaded with a sharp roll and loop over the pursuers and continued firing their left railgun. The enemy's shields held.

Pulling a rifle out, Eve knelt and aimed. Tracking, she waited for them to pull another maneuver which would reduce the attacker's speed.

"Help get them off us," Kohan barked through comms.

"Do a flyby of the mining settlement. I'm already aimed and need to make sure I don't hit you," she replied.

Skyfire rolled and banked while doing everything they could to avoid destruction. The ship finally cut toward their location, and Eve was ready. As soon as *Skyfire* passed, Eve pulled the trigger and held it down. The first of the enemy craft had no chance, flying directly into the beam. Their ship was split down the middle. It exploded in the path of the second ship, and a large piece of debris clipped it. It was sent careening out of control and crashed into the settlement.

Skyfire came back around and maneuvered into position. The cargo bay door dropped down, and Kohan waved them over frantically.

"Let's go! Get in the fekking ship!"

As they began loading, he gave Eve a confused look as she carried a crate over her shoulder, but he didn't ask questions.

There was commotion from the crash sites, and an unnerving screech of numerous creatures filled the air.

"Let's go! If we get overwhelmed, we're as good as dead!" he belted.

Kul began appearing from the buildings, tearing apart anything and everything they could. Ruzat grabbed the last crate and ran toward the ship. The movement drew the attention of kul, and they began vaulting everything to get at him. The catastrophic sound of *Skyfire*'s railgun filled the air, and their projectile ripped through buildings, and a dozen kul.

The crates and personnel were on board, but the kul had reached the bay. Eve fired at everything not on the ship. When the bay door closed, she swapped to her hand cannon and unloaded while moving toward the forward side of the bay. Dozens of the vile creatures had made it aboard before the ramp was up.

"Go! Now!" Kohan ordered over comms.

The ship took off while the four of them in the cargo hold fought the kul. It was unsafe to continue firing her weapon, both to avoid hitting the interior of the ship, and the crew. It was now an all-out melee.

Eve used her new strength to fight them. Her fists connected as she swung. Her hand-to-hand combat training meant nothing when the opponent was a beast. Still, the ones she hit didn't get back up. Kohan was being overwhelmed, and though it might have been the greatest opportunity to take over the ship, she didn't seize it.

Coming to his aide, she began ripping them off and tossing them aside. When they tried to come back, she landed whatever blow she could to incapacitate them. Knee, foot, elbow. Didn't matter as long as they stayed down. Kohan was freed from the swarm and fought them one by one. He was bitten and scratched. Blood dripped into his eye. He wiped it away as best he could but didn't make any attempts to stop it.

Wena was overwhelmed, but rather than call out for help, she rolled around, crushing the creatures under her massive weight. Ruzat swatted and grabbed kul, which in his palm looked like toys. Then like a child might do, he "played" with them roughly, smashing them together.

The cargo bay was a blood bath. Dead or dying kul laid everywhere. The four of them stood around bleeding, breathing heavily, and trying to calm themselves enough to actually say anything. Eve was the first.

"What the fek did you do?! I saw the report on Starreach."

"It was a setup. The buyer wasn't real."

"No shit. I put that together already. I thought it might be coincidence at first, but it seems whoever is behind the illegal weapons apparently also has ships filled with these things."

"Get us out of the system, now," Captain Kohan ordered the bridge.

"Aye, Captain," Balok replied.

"Eve and Wena, pile the beasts at the door. We'll dump them later. Ruzat, on me."

The two set out on cleanup duty while Kohan and Ruzat headed to the crates and began unpacking the rifles. Though busy, Eve snooped. Kohan and Ruzat were discussing having the technology broken down and analyzed in order to build one for their ship.

Eve's clothes and bodysuit were caked in blood. A headache had started, and she stopped by their cabinets to grab a Cure-All tablet. She downed it with a glass of water and headed to the bathroom. As soon as the door was closed, she stripped down. The dirty, stained clothes and bodysuit went into the small washing machine while she hopped into the purification chamber.

I really need more than a couple outfits. Maybe I should steal something from Faun's closet.

Resting her back and head against the glass, she let the tube and gel do its job. The pumps pulsed the gel around her, massaging the stress away. When the cleansing cycle was over, she put her hair up into a bun and swapped clothes to the dryer.

"Faun," Eve called over comms. "You got anything I can wear while my stuff dries?"

She didn't reply. Eve was stuck until the dry cycle was done. There was a knock on the door, and when Eve opened it, Faun shoved some clothing at her, and then walked back toward the front of the ship. Considering Faun's smaller size, Eve hoped she'd be able to fit into it enough to cover up and head back to the room.

"Thanks," Eve called down the hall.

Dressed in comically tight clothing, she headed back to her room. Wena was there, resting. Covered in caked blood, Eve wondered how she might clean her, since there was no way she was fitting into the purification chamber. Eve retrieved a brush from the bathroom and sat on her mat.

"Let's comb some of that shit out of your fur."

Chapter 9
Trust and Treachery

They had escaped the system without being pursued, but instead of heading back to their hideout or taking a bulk path, they flew out into deep space and put the ship on minimum power. It had been days monitoring the nearest relay system for any ship movement. The hope was that while they were in the middle of nowhere, they could stay hidden and plan their next move.

Eve had prepped food, and while the crew sat around the dining table and ate, the discussion was lively.

"We need to go bust heads on elementus home worlds to find out who is targeting us," Eve said, pissed off. "Balok, Virid, whose ass can we go kick?"

The two of them looked at each other. They seemed to know what the other was thinking without saying anything, and Virid nodded to Balok.

"We won't have any leads. Everyone we knew before joining Captain Kohan's crew will be unlikely to communicate with us."

"Why the fek not?" Eve asked with a mouthful of mushy, salty pasta.

"We were exiled from our planets because we caused the death of an Elementus Suprus," Balok stated. "We were extorted with the lives of our child and clans. We were able to make it look like an accident, avoiding our own executions, but even our child, Roxim, won't go against the exile decree."

"We should procure an upgrade for me," Nine said in an unconnected comment.

"Mr. Fixit?" Kohan asked.

"Correct. It will require significant risk and cost, as we will have to go to a station to acquire an illegal mod. It is very likely we will be visually identified when we dock."

"What's the plan?" Faun asked.

"In order to 'bust heads' as Eve put it, we need names involved in the manufacturing of the Rekwa weapons, and possible conspiracy," Nine replied. "If I can obtain the mod I need, and get onto an elementus controlled Emex Station, I might be able to find some."

They were on their own. Only money and espionage were going to assist them in finding out what was really going on. As much as Eve got a rush from this type of mission, she had her doubts about it. It wasn't up to her, though. Kohan gave the nod of approval, and they got the ship underway back to active space.

Changing transponders would only get them in the front door of Emex Station Five. If the police, bounty hunters, or anyone else recognized their actual ship they would have to figure out what options they had.

"We need a backup escape plan," Kohan dictated as the Tectos piloted a well-traveled bulk path. "Faun and Eve, your job is to scout out ships around where we land. If you find a suitable ship, be prepared to commandeer it, and communicate it with Ruzat."

The traffic through the sector was heavy. Even if they were spotted or scanned by some chance in the bulk path, no one dared fire inside for fear of it destabilizing.

"Ruzat and Wena, you're on guard duty. Don't stay on the ship, and try to minimize how much you are seen, despite how difficult that may be. Nine, the Tectos, and I will go to get the mod. It's likely it'll take several hours, and it's equally as likely we'll be identified. Expect a shootout at any time."

Skyfire exited the bulk path into a densely populated holding pattern while ships moved to and from the station. Because of it being QuBE controlled, the exterior modifications were far reaching.

It looked to Eve like an atom; the main station was in the center, and an innumerable number of satellites orbited. Though they weren't hive-minded, the QuBE rarely disagreed on matters concerning the entirety of their species. Because of their efficiency in building and processing energy, they had become a type two civilization.

The traffic patterns were well orchestrated and flowed very much like blood through veins and vessels.

"Eve, Faun, get to the guns, just in case," Kohan ordered.

"Aye," they both replied.

Eve took the right hall and double tapped her Trauna to activate comms. Listening in, she heard Kohan direct Nine to take over the helm. Into her seat, she activated the gunner controls.

"Don't charge the rail system yet," Faun said.

"Just getting things online."

Her railgun's ammo bay was three quarters full, and the supply of mines were at about half.

The only thing we'll be able to do here if we get into a fight will be to expend everything just to escape.

The ship banked and turned with the pattern. When she looked overhead, she caught sight of a satellite station passing. It felt too close, but she trusted the pilots wouldn't miscalculate.

On approach to the main hangar, the ship slowed, and they were forced to wait out in the open for their turn past the shielding. Everyone was already on edge, and this tested Eve's nerve. When it was their turn, she found she'd been holding her breath in short intervals. A sigh of relief escaped her lips when they were allowed past the first layer of shielding.

Inside the hangar looked even more like organized chaos to her. Battleship sized craft moved in and out while all the smaller ships flew around them. While *Skyfire* was small and agile, the close-tolerance piloting amongst thousands of ships was impressive.

Directed where to land, they came in for a soft touchdown.

"All hands, disembark," Captain Kohan commanded.

Eve stood, tugged on her bodysuit to unwedge it from uncomfortable places, and pulled her hand cannon to make sure she had loaded it. It was back in the holster by the time she left her munitions hallway.

The crew met up around the cargo containers with the illicit weapons. Kohan, Faun, and Ruzat geared up with armor and helmets to disguise themselves and prepare for combat. Kohan stashed four rifles in a bag and handed it off to Balok. Eve and Faun each grabbed one and slung them over their backs while Kohan gave a final briefing.

"Be on guard. Expect a fight. If anyone gets left behind, do what you need to get back to the caves, but don't drag the G.P. there."

Once down on the platform the groups split. Ruzat and Wena took up positions nearby. Kohan and crew quickly headed off toward the central city. Eve and Faun began scouting for a mark.

Eve tried to lead, but Faun wasn't having it. They fought to stay in front of one another while perusing the ships to potentially steal. Eve looked for versatility, something small with decent weapons.

"Skip anything that looks like it's QuBE designed or piloted. They'll likely have tough encryptions to get past just to get off the ground," she told Faun.

"Stating the obvious doesn't make you smart," Faun's voice came through muffled because of the closeness of the helmet to her mouth.

"Just making sure we're on the same page."

Most of the QuBE ships were easily identifiable. They favored geometric shapes with smooth curves. Like how other species painted their ships, the QuBE favored densely packed mathematical expressions and programming languages designed to make patterns on the hull. They were a work of art in their own way.

Faun pointed out a potential mark. Eve took notice at the vraditi style ship. The black, sleek, oblong disc was well known as a defense vessel. It was a similar type to what the G.P. had used to pursue them. This wasn't G.P. though because of the crew. A mixture of the two Vraditi races, humans, QuBE, and elementus were loading up supplies.

"You want to check that one out?" Eve asked.

"Just a little look."

They were cautious about moving closer to it, making it look like they were taking a stroll on the docks. Wandering around, they kept vigilant for any sign of trouble.

"Ten so far," Faun said quietly.

They passed by the cargo door and Eve glanced inside.

"Ten more inside."

"Not bad, but it'll depend on if they get under way as soon as they're loaded."

They continued scouting. They'd climbed up a couple levels to get a look at the vraditi ship, and it gave them a good vantage of a few other non-QuBE ships. Eve spotted a human built ship several levels down which she hadn't seen in years. It wasn't a unique design, as humans mass produced ships. But she easily recognized the paint job because she helped her parents paint it.

"Fek," she muttered.

"What?" Faun looked to her.

"Good news; I found our backup ship out of here. Bad news; we'll be stealing it from my parents." Eve tapped her Trauna to open comms. "Backup escape ship located. No weapons, but easily overlooked."

"Understood," Ruzat came back, and Eve shut off comms.

Behind the clear visor, Faun's eyebrows raised in curiosity. Eve led the way down to the ship. It had seen better days, as the paint was fading, and the hull had plenty of superficial scarring. It wasn't a surprise, considering they put themselves into danger just to take readings of quasars, or scan uncharted nebulae.

Is fate a thing? I haven't seen them since I left, and now they're here as we may need another ship...

She was lost in thought while they approached the long, double story, rectangular ship. The rear entry door was closed. Fully expecting her parents would have changed the codes, it came as a surprise when she tapped her personal pin, and it slid open upward.

I bet they felt like if they removed my access, I would never return...the prodigal daughter.

An audible notification beeped through the ship, most certainly alerting anyone on board. The lights in the main entry kicked on and illuminated the central room. Everything had its place, and it was all where she remembered it being. The couch, chairs, the rug, shelves full of books. The only new thing they had was the large screen monitor hung against the wall.

Her father, a tall and skinny man with light dirty blonde hair, barreled down the stairs set in-between the living area and the kitchen farther down. He leveled a shotgun at her. She put her hands on her hips.

"Hey, Dad," she said and sat down in one of the cushioned chairs.

He rubbed his eyes. It was obvious he'd been asleep, but she half-wondered if he was also rubbing his eyes in disbelief.

"Evette?"

"Just 'Eve.' How've you been?"

"Forget how *I've* been. What the hell have you been doing out there?" he asked while clearly trying to keep his attention on her, but eyed Faun.

"Getting along, seeing the cosmos in my own way."

"Yeah, so we've noticed." He reached over to a console next to the couch, pressed a few buttons, and the screen on the wall lit up. It scrolled through and stopped on wanted posters of her and the *Skyfire* crew.

Before he could continue, her mom came down the stairs and rushed over. It wasn't for a hug. She had her slipper in her hand and began smacking Eve in the arm and yelling. Eve had always been convinced her mom made up for her small stature by being extra fiery.

"What in all of creation do you think you're doing?!" her mom berated. "We don't hear from you for years, and now you show back up on our radar and you're a criminal?!"

Her mom continued to hit her with the slipper, knowing full well it did nothing. Eve stood up, towering over her, and put her arms around her. Giving her a squeeze, she antagonized her mom.

"I've always been a merc. I'm only getting famous for it now."

"Famous? Famous?!" she said enraged further while she squirmed to escape Eve's grasp.

Her dad took the slipper out of her mom's hand and tapped Eve on the forehead gently with it. Eve let her go and smirked.

"And this woman? She's one of your criminal companions?" Her mom flung an accusatory finger in Faun's direction.

"Yeah, this is Faun of the *Skyfire*," she said, and then gestured to her mom and dad. "Anora. Higo."

"Can we get this over with?" Faun crossed her arms, annoyed.

Anora looked like she was going to launch herself at Faun over the disrespect, but Higo put his hand on her shoulder, and she relaxed.

"Get what over with?" Higo asked.

"We might need your ship for a low-profile escape," Eve replied. "We're in bigger trouble than the Galactic Police warrants. Some bad shit is going down out there."

"And what are we supposed to do, go along for the ride?" Anora snarked.

"I've sent you enough over the years that you should have enough to get you transport back to Salvoa. If we survive, we'll return the ship."

"What do you mean?" Higo asked.

"I've been dropping funds into your research account as an anonymous donor. You're welcome."

Her mother swore up a storm about accepting money from illicit endeavors. The high-and-mighty attitude of her mother wore on Eve very quickly. Anora had been a major driving force for Eve to want to leave the ship and carve her own destiny. Sighing, she tapped her Trauna.

"*Skyfire* crew, backup ship acquired," she announced while turning her back to her parents.

"Confirmed," Kohan acknowledged. "We've reached Mr. Fixit's shop. Nine is getting the upgrade now. E.T.A. two hours."

The silence after was awkward, and Eve returned to sitting in the chair. Faun leaned against it awkwardly. Anora stormed back to the second level, her loose bun bouncing as she stomped. Higo sat on the couch and stared at Eve.

Though she was hardheaded, she also respected her parents. What she was about to do was strand her parents, taking away their home and research vessel.

I'd be mad too, but they'll get over it.

Inclined to give more detail, she did her best to explain the situation in the hopes he wouldn't resent her too much for stealing their ship. He acknowledged her explanation, but it was clear to her he wasn't going to be forgiving regardless of story or blood ties. In the time while waiting, he worked on downloading survey reports, and Anora stormed around the living area packing up some of their belongings.

Waiting for the crew to return, time dragged. The monotony of sitting there was interrupted by a set of beeps on Faun's tablet. She looked at it and left without saying anything. Eve rested her head and closed her eyes. Higo and Anora spoke low in the kitchen area farther down, and Eve couldn't make out what they were saying. Heavy footsteps approached, and Eve cracked an eye open.

"Is there no way we can talk you out of this?" Higo asked and sat on the couch cushion closest to Eve.

"It's either your ship, or someone else's. At least this way no one dies. Another ship? Someone dies, guaranteed."

"Why does it have to be that way? What happened after you left us to put you on this path?"

"I left because this ship was a cage. There's something more for me out there, something greater than studying anomalies and cosmic bodies," she replied, trying hard not to be condescending. "I found myself out there. You may not like who I am, but I do."

"I just don't understand why you chose to be a criminal!" Anora chimed in, coming from the kitchen.

"It just sort of happened. I was a mercenary until I wasn't. Picked up skills people saw value in," Eve replied.

"Take your money back. We don't want it if it's blood money," she said and threw a tablet at Eve.

Eve caught it, stood up, and confronted her mother with a more serious attitude this time. Holding it out for Higo to take, she laid into her.

"You have two choices, I take your ship and you use the chits to get back to Salvoa, or don't and I take your ship anyway. I'm getting my crew off this station and doing it by any means necessary."

Higo took it, placed a hand on Eve's shoulder, and frowned. He had silently accepted that there wasn't anything they could do. He began taking things outside, and Eve helped. She knew if her mom could shoot daggers with her eyes, they'd be headed straight for the back of her head.

They had moved most of the stuff outside of the ship when Faun came in over comms. She stopped to listen.

"Heavy G.P. presence has arrived in the system. Checking the network...we've been identified. Local forces have been ordered to standby until the authorities arrive. How much longer?"

"Ten, fifteen minutes. Upgrade is booting," Kohan replied. "Soon as we confirm the new package is operational, we'll be on our way."

The pressure to escape was building fast. The G.P. heavy ships were already entering the first shield into the hangar. It would be a short amount of time before *Skyfire* was seized.

"Eve, communicate your position to the crew," Faun ordered. "Ruzat and Wena, get to her location. Dad, meet up with them. I'm going to give everyone a path out."

"Hold on, Faun," Kohan replied. "We're heading there now."

"Time's up. The G.P. are past the first shield. Second shield will come down momentarily."

"You need a co-pilot?" Eve asked.

"No. Get the crew out of here. I'll see you all at the hideout."

"Fly safe," Kohan said dejectedly.

Eve directed Ruzat and Wena up to her location while watching Faun bring the ship online and into the air. *Skyfire* did an about-face and Faun gunned for the second shield which was just now dropping to let the G.P. ships in. It seemed unthinkable, but the G.P. ships opened fire inside the hangar in an attempt to shoot down *Skyfire*.

Faun dodged what she could, took several hits from cannons and guns, and blew by them into the shield airlock chamber. The first shield was the only thing blocking her exit, to which she answered with activating the Light Drive. Space warped in a bubble. The ship's and station's shielding connected. There was a bright flash of blue which swirled around like a vortex. When the light dissipated both shields collapsed.

There was no sign of *Skyfire* or debris, but that wasn't the only pressing issue. Because the G.P. ships were still in the way of activating the second shield, the station began venting to vacuum. Anything close to the door was blown out, and the decompression threatened to take them too.

"Get on the ship!" Eve ushered while pushing the four in.

The last one in, she shut the door and ran to the front. In the pilot's seat she activated the engines, completely skipping any pre-start safety checks. As soon as they were off the platform, she activated the shielding and their Cruise Drive to give it enough power, so they too weren't blown out.

The G.P. finally moved out of the way and the second shield was raised, but a significant amount of damage had been done. When things settled, she brought the ship back to rest on a different platform.

"Status?" Kohan asked, his voice heavy.

Eve wasn't sure what to say. Would she lie for his benefit? Could she leave it ambiguous?

Maybe Skyfire made it...?

"*Skyfire* has paved the way. The QuBE and G.P. are likely going to lock things down, so get to the ship and we'll take the first opening," Eve replied.

"Understood."

Damage cleanup wase dispatched throughout the hangar. While waiting for the *Skyfire* crew, Anora attempted to alert the G.P.. Chasing her down, Eve restrained her, dragged her back to the ship, and confined her inside.

"Keep an eye on her," she said to Wena. "Don't let her leave the ship.

"Haven't you done enough?!" Anora yelled from inside.

"Please, just let us go," Higo pleaded. "I will stop her from going to the police until you're gone."

Eve ignored them both and returned to watching for her shipmates. When they got close, Kohan comm'd and she directed him to where they were at. A transport approached and set down. The crewmates exited and made their way to Eve and their temporary ship.

She directed Higo to get on board, and everyone crammed in. Due to their sizes, Wena and Ruzat took up most of the space in the living area. Everyone else had to fit wherever they could. Eve took the pilot's seat, and Kohan joined.

"File a flight plan," he ordered.

She nodded and communicated their intentions to the station. They had to wait for several hours for the exterior shield to be repaired, but because their current ship wasn't under suspicion there was no urgency other than to get to the caves.

When they received the authorization to depart, Eve kept her speed to a minimum and followed all the proper traffic patterns. The shadow of the G.P. ships loomed on the cockpit as they passed under. Eve had unintentionally held her breath and sighed when they reached the interior shield.

They made it through, and she piloted them to a nearby bulk path. Once inside, she laid her head back against the headrest and closed her eyes.

What happens now if the Skyfire is actually gone? Go my own way? No point in trying to take over a crew with no ship to run contracts in. I sure as hell am not moving back in here.

Chapter 10
Appropriation

Kohan insisted on waiting for Faun to arrive before making any moves. They'd been at the caves on Melosa's moon for a galactic week, and Eve determined it was time to confront him. He was sitting in the cockpit of the small ship, scanning for communications, and watching the sky.

"We need to get moving," she commanded.

"We have enough supplies for another week."

"Look, I was hopeful Faun made it and would meet us here, but we haven't heard anything from her. No ship. No communication. Nothing. I'm sorry, but if we're going to get the fekking bastards who put this whole thing into motion, we need to get our asses into gear."

"I'm not giving up on my daughter."

"Aren't you by sitting here? If the position were flipped, what would she be doing right now? She'd insist on busting someone's skull in. Let's go make her sacrifice worth it."

He turned in the seat and stood up, standing inches from her face. She could see the building anger. With her newfound strength, they both knew he couldn't do anything to her, but he wanted to.

He relented with swearing and stormed off the ship. Eve followed him out to the caves where the crew and her parents had set up camp.

"Listen up!" Eve called out.

All eyes turned to her. She felt a rush standing in front of them all. It was that sense of power she'd been seeking. She was going to usurp Kohan and galvanize the crew under a new command. Her's. The courage and determination took over, and she started giving a leader's speech.

"We're not going to sit here and let the universe shit on us. Faun made a sacrifice so we could get off that station and find out who set us up. As of right now, this is my ship.

"Nine, you will be the second in command. As my second it will be your duty to handle all intelligence gathering. Balok and Virid, you will continue to pilot. Kohan, Ruzat, and Wena, you will be ground and weapons support. Anora and Higo, you'll be given the opportunity to disembark on Emex Station Eight."

The reactions were mixed. Anora and Kohan sneered and scoffed. Higo attempted to calm Anora, but Eve knew he had no chance. Ruzat crossed his arms and nodded. Balok and Virid whispered amongst each other, and Eve called them out.

"Objections?" Eve put her hands on her hips and adopted a dominant stance.

Virid shook their head. Anora stood up, ready to come at Eve with all her might, but Higo was the "voice" of reason when he gently placed his hand on her shoulder. Nine was the one to say something.

"Your proposal is unacceptable," they said.

"In what way?"

"My allegiance is to Captain Kohan, and while the *Skyfire* may not be here now, we are still its crew."

"Kohan is suffering loss right now. His decisions are going to be compromised. In fact, all of yours will be since you've been around

Faun since she was a child. You need someone objective." She was cold, even though she had been growing attached to Faun. "If *after* we get back at the persons responsible you want to go your own way, fine, but we're already too far into whatever the hell this is to not see it through."

"Then I would be the better choice for captain," Nine said.

"As a QuBE, you are superior in many ways to us biological beings, but you lack instinct. Your species didn't evolve, and so you don't have 'survival of the fittest' hardwired in. Now if we're quite done here, let's load up the ship and get underway to Emex Station Eight."

There was no room for further discourse as she moved at once to crates of weaponry and began pulling out items they were going to need for an assault. Balok and Virid were the first to fall in line and came to aid.

As they loaded munitions into bags, they were joined by Wena and Ruzat. Eventually everyone came around, regardless of the way they felt. Eve directed the loading of essential supplies, and when she was satisfied they had what they needed for the upcoming task, she led the way onto the ship.

Balok and Virid took the cockpit seats while everyone else did whatever they could to not step on one another. Those who were small enough to fit on the staircase headed upstairs.

Eve hung by the pilot's seats, watching over as they pulled away from the moon and toward the nearest bulk path. When she was satisfied, she retreated upstairs. Kohan was at the top, waiting for her.

"If you think this is over, it's not," he said in a low tone which almost sounded like a growl. "Pretend all you want that you're in charge now, but they are still my crew. If I feel like you're unnecessarily risking their lives, I will end you…"

"I will treat their lives as my own and guard them as such. But we've been set up, and Faun is likely dead. I want to get back at whoever did this, but *I* can do it with a level head."

He stared her down and she shoved past him. It was more force than she had intended, as he hit the bulkhead with a thud. He didn't come after her.

Heading to one of the instrument rooms, she configured the scanners to register ships instead of cosmic phenomenon. The arrays would alert if any ship scanned them or came within ten AU. When it was done, all that was left to do was sit back and wait until they arrived.

They made only as many stops to outposts and stations as absolutely necessary for resupply, and only Nine was allowed to disembark. Nerves were raw, emotions were high, and even one little disagreement threatened to set everyone off.

When they grew close to the exit of the bulk path into elementus space, the brief relief Eve felt about getting off the tin-can of a ship was quickly replaced with heightened anxiety.

Their transponder was accepted by the station. While they docked, most put on some sort of disguise to mask their identities. Eve rifled through clothing she had left behind which her parents had saved. Her goal was to look plain, and donned a tee shirt, jeans, and a long, tan overcoat with a hood.

Stepping out onto the hangar deck, she breathed in deeply. It was as fresh as she would get on a station, but it was far more pleasant than the smell on the ship. Turning, she issued orders.

"Kohan, make sure my mother doesn't turn us in. Nine and I are going to put their upgrade to use. Everyone else go restock, look for potential alternate transportation, and get yourselves cleaned up."

The crew who had been dismissed headed toward the doors to the city. Kohan slammed his fist on the ship and glared at Eve. Her plan to take over was working.

I just need to push him to his breaking point.

Anora sulked in the doorway. Higo approached Eve.

"Why don't you take your money back and buy a better ship here?" he asked candidly. "We've already lost many of our possessions because of you. This used to be your home. Can't you respect that, and us?"

"Find me a ship with weapons that my crew can fit in that you can afford, and I'll consider it," Eve replied. "Until then, plan on booking those tickets back to Salvoa. Don't bother trying to take the ship back because we put in a lockout sequence."

She waved them off and turned to Nine.

"Where do we need to get you?" she asked.

"A station data hub. All Emex Stations have them, however they require security clearance."

"Covert or assault?"

"Covert if possible. The nearest hub is off the hangar and primarily controls the traffic. When we reach the security station, I will do what I can to get us through without incident."

"Lead the way."

Instead of heading into the city, they ascended through the platform levels. The farther they went, the more they passed areas populated by station security and Galactic Police. She kept her head down and covered to avoid any sort of facial recognition.

Eventually they reached one of the security checkpoints which led directly into an area of the station Eve had never seen. In order to pass through the doorway, they needed to walk through full-body scanners. On the other side of the scanner to the left was a security room where a handful of elementus watched the checkpoint from behind a large window.

Probably bulletproof.

Nine put his hand up to a terminal on this side of the scanner and began typing. Eve only caught the first screen which was asking for identification. But at the rate Nine tapped through the menus it was clear he was bypassing their protocols.

An elementus in the office took notice it was taking them a moment to scan through and came out.

"Problem?" they asked.

"My apologies. It would seem your scanner is having issues," Nine replied.

At the last word from his vocal processor, the scanner shut down. The elementus pulled a firearm and pointed it at Nine. Adrenaline began pumping through Eve's body, and she readied her hand on her concealed hand cannon.

"Your system is malfunctioning. I have a work order in the system. Verify us with your mobile unit so we can be on our way," Nine said.

The elementus kept their weapon trained on Nine while walking backward. When they passed the door, they motioned with their weapon for Nine and Eve to enter. The other guards were on alert and had also drawn their weapons to cover them as they entered.

The two entered the office and were directed to stand in the center of the room while the elementus surrounded them in a half circle. One of them grabbed a portable hand and chip scanner and brought it over to Eve first. She lifted her free hand to place it there. With the warrants out, it would instantly register her profile and she knew arrest was imminent.

The lights and computer systems in the room went dark, leaving the only light left being what was coming through the window. Nobody hesitated in acting, but Nine and Eve were more prepared. The guards tried to shoot them. Eve lunged and swung her fists. While her strength allowed her to dead-blow knock them down, her knuckles busted open against their rocky bodies.

The immediate sharp pains didn't stop her. One of the guards attempted to activate their comms and Eve tackled them and smashed their head against the metal floor. A gunshot rang out, and Eve felt a sharp pain in her back. She fell over and struggled to breathe. Nine came to her aide too late when he took down her assailant, and they fell on top of her. While she lay there on her stomach, she could only watch as one of the guards tried to escape, and Nine chased after them.

Lying amongst the guards on the floor, she closed her eyes and waited to see if the pain continued or subsided. Nine returned, dragging the last guard, and tossed them into the pile on the floor.

They dug her out, removed her overcoat, and examined her back.

"It seems I am also superior in my design too. Your flesh is weak."

The delivery was so deadpan Eve couldn't tell if he was being condescending, serious, or making a joke. There was some digging at her back, and the pain was excruciating.

"Your armor did its job, and your new muscular density helped. The bullet was slowed enough that it came up short of hitting your spinal region. You will recover fully. Stay still and I'll close it up to stop the bleeding."

It felt like they were being careful, but it didn't help. The pain was intense when she felt her back being seared. She bit down on her own hand to try and redirect the focus of pain from the wound being cauterized. After a few moments they gave her a tap on her shoulder and held out their hand for her to take. She pulled herself up slowly.

"If you overexert yourself, you could damage the muscle more. Once we get what we need, we can get you to a doctor for further repair."

She nodded. There was nothing she could do but push through the pain and continue on. Nine sat down at a computer terminal and plugged themselves in. The room's systems rebooted.

"How did you hack them from outside?" she asked.

"I didn't hack them. I simply accessed system commands to trick the room into going to sleep. While I plan our route, secure the guards."

"Got it."

Eve used their own cuffs against them, and then proceeded to tear the bottom of her overcoat into a few strips to bandage her knuckles. Nine pulled up internal maps, cameras, and station alarms on the monitors. She tried to watch what they were doing, but her attention was split, and the screens swapped so quickly there was no way she could memorize any of it. When Nine was done, they shut the room down again and motioned for her to follow.

With the door closed behind them, Nine fused the lock with what Eve assumed was the same attachment they used for cauterizing her wound. The metal glowed bright orange for a few moments.

"The camera feeds are frozen through this hall. The next guard rotation for that office is in one hour, fifty-seven minutes," Nine said. "I've forged a work order for a QuBE and their assistant to perform maintenance, however you should keep your head down."

She nodded and they headed deeper into the inner workings of the station. Despite what they'd said, Eve still glanced at every camera they passed. The hallway eventually ended at an enormous open chamber within the structure which was clearly only for station workers.

The room was multi-tiered. Walkways extended from them to platforms which surrounded a hub in the dead center of it all. Computer terminals lined every inch, and most of them were crewed by elementus, with a few vraditi and QuBE mixed in.

Because of the coordinated chaos, nobody stopped to notice them. Nine's head turned left and right, then led the way to a lift. They hovered to the fifth tier and continued to an open terminal. Eve hadn't even settled into the chair before Nine had begun. There was nothing for her to do but worry they'd be recognized, or that someone saw the bullet hole in the back of her armor and were now suspicious.

Nine's hand twisted and altered shape to fit a data port on the terminal. Several pages flashed on the monitor, but they were gone so quickly she didn't get any information from them. While she trusted Nine knew what they were doing, they were deep in the computer world, oblivious to the surroundings.

People walked back and forth behind them, and Eve tried to be inconspicuous looking over her shoulder. While their timer ticked down, she squirmed in her seat, hoping they would get what they needed before being discovered. About an hour into the information dive, Nine came back to reality and disconnected from the terminal.

"Station alarms have been triggered by the others. We need to go."

Nine was swift in their motion to stand and start back toward the lift they came from, but it was too late. Every screen in the hub flashed "ALERT" in a bright red banner and swapped to the wanted posters of the entire *Skyfire* crew. Eve was easily recognizable with her curly red hair and bronzed skin. Trying to keep her identity hidden was impossible, and heads were turning in her direction.

She pulled her hand cannon and fired it into the air. Neither the pain from the recoil on her busted knuckles or pushing Nine from behind kept her from getting them moving. Chaos erupted in the hub as people began yelling and scattering.

"Go! Go!" she yelled at Nine.

The two broke into a run. Eve was able to keep up with them for a brief time, but her endurance was lowered because of searing pain in her back. Nine noticed but kept moving forward. She resigned herself to covering their backside. Flipping around, she saw station forces funneling in from the opposite end of the terminal room. Leveling her weapon at them she unloaded the chambers.

Security personnel ducked, and it bought them a few moments. Nine had taken up a spot at an intersection and was firing miniature missiles from his arm. When she caught up with them, she reloaded and prepared to fire again.

They were pinched on two sides. Their only option to escape was to dive deeper into the hallway and hope for a way out down the line. Eve took lead, arm outstretched and ready to fire. Over her shoulder, she saw Nine fire another volley of missiles at the hallway entrance to collapse it.

"Nine, Eve, report!" Kohan said.

"Currently escaping! Can't talk!" she yelled into her comms over the explosions. "Kick my parents off the ship and get it ready to go!"

Guards fired their weapons around the corners. The duo had to press on and hope to not be hit. They passed numerous doors and office spaces before forces came from in front of them, but they were being pinched again. Eve fired ahead to keep them from advancing too far while Nine looked for options.

They grabbed her hand and led her to a bank of elevators where they proceeded to pry the doors open. Nine picked her up with ease and leapt into the shaft. One arm held her, the other grasped onto a cable. Sparks flew as the two metals ground away at one another.

Slamming into the roof of the elevator while it was coming up, Nine dropped her. She ripped the top access door open, and they jumped down inside. The civilian occupants screamed and cowered. Nine hit the emergency stop and pried the doors open. Climbing out, they landed in a ship maintenance bay adjacent to the main hangar.

"*Skyfire* crew, status," Eve barked on comms.

"Making our way to the ship. We dodged security," Balok replied.

While station forces had been lost for now, Eve knew it was only a matter of moments before security found them again. Nine detoured from the direct path back to the hangar and jumped on a small hovering platform. Once Eve was on, they pushed it to its maximum speed, and they jetted toward the hangar.

"Any resistance at the ship?" she asked.

"Clear! Location?" Kohan replied.

"About to enter the hangar. Thoughts about how to get out of the station? We don't have the *Skyfire* to break the shields again."

"I have that covered," Nine interjected. "I left a backdoor open in their system I can access. Just need to get back to the ship and we can escape."

"Fire it up!" Eve barked.

The maintenance bay doors opened, and they flew out into the hangar. Eve felt tiny because their small vehicle was now in the massive space. While there were plenty of docks and walkways, it was a long way down if they were to fall.

The G.P. identified them, and they were surrounded in moments.

"Stop the platform!" a voice ordered through a loudspeaker. "Surrender yourselves!"

Nine was busy piloting, leaving their defense up to Eve. She leveled her gun at one of the pilots in the smaller police ships to their right. It veered upward. The mechanical sound of turrets caught her attention, and when she turned, the ship to their left was aimed at them. Before they could fire, they were hit with a purple-hued energy beam from up ahead, and it sliced their hull in two. More Rekwa beams lit up the surrounding airspace, and one after another, the G.P. were annihilated. Hulls of destroyed ships rained down onto the docks. People scattered, but not all were lucky enough to get away.

The crew had taken up position by the exploration ship and were providing cover. Nine brought them in for a rough landing, and Eve grabbed up a rifle to join in. Ships pulled back and began raining down their own shots from above.

"Everyone on board! Now!" she yelled at them while lining up a shot.

She fired and ran. Their ship was getting bombarded. As soon as she was on board the shields came online and they were lifting off.

"Shields are already failing," Balok announced as they began their getaway.

"Shrink the shields to the hull to keep the atmosphere from venting," Eve ordered.

They were headed straight for the station's port, and Eve knew if Nine didn't get this right they were about to end up like Faun.

Skyfire didn't survive, so there's no way we will if we try the same thing.

Nine used the console at the couch to access a matrix of coding on the massive monitor. While she had no way to know exactly what they were doing, she trusted them. Just when it looked like they were going to suffer the same fate as their fallen crew member, both shields dropped and vented the hangar. The Tectos didn't wait to activate the Light Drive.

Rather than running for a bulk path, they headed toward deep space. Only three AU from the station, a shock from behind knocked them from their vector. The ship spun out of control, and they had no time to recover. Grapple hooks smashed through the walls. Air escaped from around the torn metal as they were dragged in.

"Shut down the engines!" Eve said.

"Captain?" Virid asked but looked to Kohan.

"He's not your captain! If we pull, we'll rip the side of the ship off. Weapons ready!" Eve yelled and waved for everyone else to split to the front and back of the ship.

A loud grinding noise echoed through the hull from the second story. More atmosphere was venting, and the ship's systems weren't going to be able to keep up. The lights flickered, and then shut off, leaving most of the lower-level dark. Only the light from the consoles were left, and those began flickering too. For the time the engines continued generating artificial gravity, but she knew if they sustained any more damage, they could find themselves free floating.

"Fire when I fire," Nine said.

Loud thuds came from the second level and footsteps were heard.

This isn't a G.P. operation. Someone's trying to collect the bounty...

Tink, tink, tink. Something bounced down the stairs. Eve dove and tackled Balok to the floor. A flashbang grenade exploded. Her vision was unaffected, but the concussive force deafened her. Not going to be caught off guard, she quickly rolled, flipped a table, and used it for cover. Poking her gun over the top, she aimed for where she knew the stairs were.

Despite not being able to hear, when Nine fired, Eve and crew did also. The explosive energy of gunfire lit up the room as people in heavy armor barreled down the stairs. The invaders returned fire, but they were disadvantaged due to not having cover. Bodies began dropping as the *Skyfire* crew unloaded on anyone coming down.

When Nine stopped firing, the *Skyfire* crew did also. The light from the gunfire ruined her dark adaptation, and the heavy ringing in her ears persisted due to the close quarters weapon fire. Though temporary, there was no time for her to recover. *Can't let them reform and try again*. Vaulting the table, she relied on instinct to get her to the bottom of the stairwell. Bending to where she saw a body fall, she snatched a helmet and put it on.

A heads-up display came to life, and infrared cameras picked up the crew in their hunkered down positions. She quickly looked around the corner up the stairs to see what was there. No one.

Did they retreat? Or are they expecting us to come to them?

It didn't really matter. The *Skyfire* crew were going to die if they didn't make it to the other ship. She grabbed a Rekwa rifle and climbed the stairs on her belly. There was no delay from the moment her head and gun poked around the corner to the hallway and pulling the trigger. Purple illuminated the with every squeeze and she didn't care where the energy beams were directed so long as it hit their assailants.

They tried to throw another flashbang, but she hit the would-be thrower before they could. It clattered at their feet. She slid back behind the wall while they yelled and scrambled. The grenade went off and she seized the opportunity to spring up and charge them.

Before they could recover, she coldcocked two, and shattered the tibia of another. She opened comms to the crew.

"Kohan, Balok, and Nine, get up here! Virid, get shielding back online and activate the modules on the stairwell!"

Not waiting for them to arrive, she grabbed one of the enemy grenades, pulled the pin, and lobbed it up into the ship above. As soon as she heard the scattering, she grabbed one of their ropes and scaled it to the opening.

The grenade detonated and she hoisted herself up on deck. She pulled her hand cannon and opened fire. Her crew came up moments after and they bolted to cover behind whatever they could find.

Eve holstered her gun and picked up a large crate. The wound in her back screamed with pain, but the actual load wasn't anything she couldn't handle now. As soon as a hand popped up with a gun aimed in their direction, she lobbed it at them. The force crushed the hiding spot and left a blood spattered crater in the bulkhead.

The cargo hold was filled with a cacophony of blasts, and smoke from the bounty hunters. The *Skyfire* crew had the advantage, however. They fired Rekwa blasts at wherever gunfire was coming from, and the other side's forces dwindled.

"Stop!" a familiar male voice rang out. "Parley!"

Kohan wasn't done. He fired at where the voice came from, and the person yelled in agony. Captain Marsi leapt up and screamed in anger and horror.

"Stop! We surrender!"

Marsi ran to where Kohan had shot into, and Eve knew Torp was behind there. The two had stuck together and acquired a new ship and crew to continue their pursuits, as they had planned.

Eve broke from cover and calmly headed for where Marsi knelt. Torp's lifeless body and twisted face lay there, and she had begun to sob. As Eve hovered over them both, she felt pity. There was no malice in her heart, as they were doing what they'd always done, go after the money.

Marsi looked up at Eve with rage, but her eyes widened, and her face contorted in abject horror. Before Eve could look behind her to find out why, a shot fired off and a beam of energy burned through Marsi's skull. She whipped around to find Kohan there with a cold, murderous look on his face.

Enraged, she lost it and charged him. He was double her size, but it didn't matter. Her ability made him her toy. She picked him up, slammed him down, and then before he could react, she grabbed his feet and spun. When she let go, he smashed into the hull and didn't get back up.

Nine tried to apprehend her, but she shrugged him off hard and gave an order.

"Balok, get to the cockpit and uncouple the ship—" she started but was interrupted by Balok.

"What about the others?"

"Don't interrupt! Swing this ship around to the underbelly of the other one so we can cut a hole large enough for Ruzat and Wena to fit through! Nine, extend the shields around it as best you can!"

The two got to it while she communicated their intentions to the others. Of their would-be captors, there was little resistance left, and they opted to surrender rather than die. Eve obliged and tied them up while the ship maneuvered.

The cargo loading bay came up to the underside of her parent's ship. The hulls smacked together, and Eve fought to keep her footing.

"Nine, update on those shields."

"Extended. There is clearance to open the underside cargo doors."

A control pad hung from the crane overhead. Grabbing it, she looked it over. It had what she needed to open the bay doors, direct the crane with its grapple, and control cutting torches. Lowering the crane down she dug into the belly of her parents' exploration ship with the claws and torches.

Bringing the crane back up pulled a chunk of hull with it. There were conduits, tubes, and wiring which stood in the way of the second cut she needed to make. The grapple made quick work of it. The wiring sparked and arced, and there was an audible loss of power. Life support systems were now inoperable over there. With the scrap material out of the way, she brought the crane down one last time and cut into the floor of the central room.

"Lady Eve, if you could hurry, atmosphere is getting thinner," Virid said.

"I'm going as fast as I can. You should have air momentarily."

The floor gave way. Retracting the crane gave the three their path. While their artificial gravity had failed, they were being pulled to the next direct source, their new ship. With Eve's help, the crew made it over with only a few scratches from the sharp and splintered metal.

"Thank you, Lady Eve!" Wena said excitedly.

Ruzat passed and gave Eve a pat on the shoulder, and Virid nodded in appreciation. She closed the hatch and dropped the controls. They swung free while she moved back to Marsi and Torp.

"Balok, get us away from here. If weapons are ready, turn it into a debris field for the G.P. to find," Eve commanded.

Looking to Kohan's crumpled body, she resisted the urge to kick the life out of him.

Marsi would have turned us in for the money, but that's just business. Fek...why did it have to be them?

"Lady Eve," Nine said over comms. "I hope you will be pleased to know that I have acquired a name linked to the Rekwa weapons facility. Elementus Minorus Dor Titanul."

Chapter 11
Planning and Execution

Eve hoped they were presumed dead with the wreckage they left behind. If the ruse was successful, that meant they had plenty of time to plan their infiltration of the elementus citadel on Tor Galom Ig. Before focusing on their self-guided mission, they did what was needed; spaced the dead, dumped their captives at an uninhabited planet, and stocked up on supplies at a privately owned station.

How do we get to Titanul without being caught? It's bad enough they're on their home world, but they're also a high ranking official.

From the captain's chair she watched the light of distant stars blur through the forward window. While in thought, she mindlessly tied her hair up, and her arms pulled at the wound in her back. She winced, leaned back too hard and winced again. Everything about their new bridge was far less comfortable than *The Fade* or *Skyfire*'s, but it had more room than her parent's tiny exploration transport.

A new name was needed, and she queried everyone except Kohan who was laid up in the makeshift infirmary. Each of them came up with something unique, but she went with Ruzat's suggestion of *Irkata*. The closest he could get the translator to define it was 'to birth again,' which she found the most fitting.

They dropped out of FTL, and the drive whirred down. The Tectos guided the Irkata to an unmanned but armed communication's array. As they maneuvered to avoid missiles, Ruzat operated weapons and fired cannons at it. The large projectiles smashed the shielding. They had to avoid a few waves of missiles, but rounding again with another volley, they destroyed the missile launchers.

"Wena, launch the grapples. When they grab, pull us in."

While the console wasn't designed for plesian paws, she was careful enough in her movements that she was able to activate them. The meaty hooks smashed into the hull of the array, and they towed closer.

Nine had enough evidence to link Dor Titanul to the illegal weapons manufacturing but was unable to verify if they were the top of the chain or a pawn. The crew agreed the best course of action was to track, abduct, and interrogate.

Standing from their command chair right next to Eve's, Nine turned to her.

"This shouldn't take long. I'll track any mention of their name, and piece together locations and times we can find them," Nine stated.

Eve nodded and offered them an out of the ordinary positive comment, "I appreciate the risk you take plugging yourself into their systems."

Nine headed for the cargo bay to exit through an airlock. The rest of the crew kept their stations except for Eve. She stood, and before heading to the door, issued commands.

"It's likely that the elementus, and possibly G.P., have been alerted to our attack on this array. Everyone, stay on high alert. The moment we get a ping another ship is coming we're getting the fek out of here. Destroy the array on the way out."

The crew acknowledged with an "Aye, Lady Eve."

Down the hall, on the left, was the infirmary. When she entered, Kohan looked out of the corner of his eye and grimaced. His disdain didn't bother her, and she pulled a stool right up to the side of the bed. His neck was braced, and he was immobilized by a machine designed to slowly heal his wounds.

"What the fek do you want?" he sneered.

"I came to check on you. You're still part of *Skyfire*'s crew until you decide you want something different for yourself."

He got loud, "This is *my* crew. You're not taking them from me…"

"I already have. As my first official rule, we're not murdering people who could still be useful to us. There was no reason to kill them; we'd already won."

"You were working with her the whole time, weren't you?"

"What would be the point? The *Skyfire* is gone. Your crew takes orders from me. Your only cargo is Rekwa rifles, which are worthless because we can't fence them without being hunted. You have nothing."

He squinted and pulled his lips tight. He was distrustful after all that had happened, but Eve could see there was more to it. His eyes betrayed his hatred, and she saw the deep pain. He turned away as his eyes watered. He hadn't had time to grieve the loss of Faun. She pitied him with a pat to his shoulder.

"I'm sorry about Faun. We'll pay back Dor Titanul and any other elementus involved."

He smacked her hand away and she didn't attempt to comfort him any further.

When it comes time, all I'll have to do is aim him.

Leaving him to wallow, she made her way to the kitchen to prepare food for the crew. Though the captain now, she needed them to stay loyal, and that meant keeping up her duties. In the middle of preparing a hot dish for the Tectos, Nine came on comms.

"I have the information we need."

"Good. Get back on board and take the helm while the Tectos eat. Get us underway."

"Understood."

The ship jostled when they decoupled from the array. The hum of the weapons charging up resonated through the ship. The cannons fired when she assumed they were far enough away, and the crew rotated in to eat. While they did, Eve brought Kohan soup. There was no further discussion between the two. When she finished feeding him, she returned to the kitchen for cleanup, and then headed for the bridge.

"Download all the data to the computer and pull it up on the displays. Let's work on our plan of attack," she ordered.

They did so. As the schedules and patterns came up, they began devising their infiltration. Dor Titanul had a robust, but predictable schedule where they often sat in on judicial hearings of various aspects of the elementus empire expansion.

In between sessions, they liaised with the Elementus Suprus regarding diplomacy, proposed resolutions, and decisions. The largest window to get to them were the times spent traveling in between buildings. Balok and Virid shared their insights regarding the how.

"They will have their own licensed attendant to pilot them back and forth. It will be a small craft with only enough room for three or four," Virid explained.

"We would be able to ambush them from the sky, but not with this ship. The commute lanes are restricted access, so we'll need a small vehicle of our own," Balok continued. "We'll track the takeoff, and intercept. Even if we collide with them, it's unlikely we will get them to stop until they reach a safe zone. Someone should be prepared to board them."

Eve already had it in her head. *I'm the strongest. I'll have to do it.* While she was playing out a fight in her head where she faced three or four elementus in confined space, she thought about ways to not kill people just doing their jobs. Taking a hardline against Kohan about killing those who could be of use, she wondered where her own line would be; *what is useful and what isn't?*

"Escape will be tricky," Eve said, interrupting her own thoughts. "Did Marsi have anything that can clone a transponder on board?"

"No. Though, I do," Nine said. "Part of my latest upgrade."

Shaking her head at them, she had a plan forming.

"Spare transponders?"

"None."

"Nine, you'll stay with the ship, monitor alerts for our presence, and track down Dor Titanul's transponder code. Ruzat, purchase a spare transponder and get it to Nine so he can clone it. The Tectos and I will secure a cargo contract as our cover.

"Once we're ready, the Tectos will fly me to Dor Titanul's vehicle. Ruzat will be in a second vehicle ready to activate the cloned transponder. By the time you land, there will be confusion about where Titanul is, and you'll be able to play it off as a glitch. We'll pick you up after we get Titanul back to the ship."

"What about Wena?" she asked.

"You'll watch over Kohan. Keep him comfortable and get him what he needs. Is everyone clear on their roles?"

The crew acknowledged, and they returned to their stations. Still in elementus territory, the jumps through Bulk Space were relatively short to their destination. Coming in over Tor Galom Ig wasn't what Eve expected. Considering the rough and rocky nature of the elementus, for some reason she thought their home world would be a brown and orange barren wasteland. Maybe with volcanos.

The planet had a similar composition as most other habitable planets. One of the largest differences was the lack of major oceans. Large lakes existed in the middle of landmasses, but the greater waterways were enormous rivers which segmented the landmass.

The traffic funneled in through a spaceport where ships were scanned coming to and going from the planet. A defense network of satellites was set up to deter any who might break the barrier. Because they were in an unknown ship, there was an air of uncertainty whether they would pass. Their turn came up in the line and Eve picked at her fingers and fidgeted. A broadcast was sent to their ship.

"Please, state your business."

"We are the Irkata, a ship for hire. We're looking to obtain a contract for cargo transport," Balok responded.

"Proceed to the commercial district. Your designated landing spot is being transmitted. Any deviation will result in your detainment."

"Understood."

Blue lights surrounded the ship indicating they could proceed, and they moved through into the next traffic pattern. Down into the atmosphere and through the clouds an enormous city came into view. While their architecture had a similar blocky feel to what was in Emex Station Eight, this felt more polished.

A holographic highway appeared on their window, and it split off into a dozen directions. The ship arced down and to the left. The city was segmented into zones, interconnected with enormous skyways where uncountable amounts of vehicles traveled. They swung around some of the skyscrapers, and an industrial complex came into view.

The Tectos brought the ship to as soft of a landing as they could, but the junker-ship was anything but graceful. Those who were leaving made their way to the cargo bay.

"No weapons. We don't need anyone looking at us with suspicion," Eve said. "Put on whatever you need to hide in plain sight."

Eve headed to Marsi's small, boring cabin and dug through the few clothes she had there. Plain shirt, pants that didn't quite fit, and a cloak. Back in the cargo hold, she grabbed a helmet and armored gloves from the ship's lockers.

I should be shielded from facial scans, and these should help me not tear my hands up.

The others had also put on various garments to hide their identity, though not very well due to Marsi only having human-sized armor and helmets on board. While they were still trying to disguise themselves, Eve looked through the ship's cargo for electronics they were going to need. She handed Virid a comms jammer.

Outside was more what she expected. Hazy skies, tall buildings, and elementus outnumbering every other species a hundred-to-one. The port bustled with ships coming and going, cargo being loaded and unloaded. It was prejudicial of her, but she assumed the cargo was precious minerals.

Ruzat left the party, disappearing into the masses. Balok spearheaded their path toward a building with signage alien to Eve. They entered a lobby where a cascade of teller stations was and got in line. It wasn't long before it was their turn and Virid handled the transaction.

"Ship, Irkata. Looking for a cargo contract, long distance," they said to the teller while presenting the ship's new identity chip.

The teller scanned it and nodded.

"Insurance?" they asked.

"Deposit on percent of value."

They pulled up a list of potential contracts on a monitor. Virid scrolled through, picked one which would net them a tiny sum after overhead costs, and selected.

"The containers will be delivered to your ship. We can send workers out to load it for a fee."

"No, thank you. Deliver to the ship and we will load."

Virid handled the monetary transaction with their own account. Due to bureaucracy and red tape, it took a half hour just to sign all of the paperwork. When the final contract was signed, they headed out. Balok took them over to a Wayfinder and ordered up a vehicle.

A small, but roomy capsule landed in front of them. A single pilot's console was at the front, which Balok took, leaving Eve and Virid to sit on the seating to the sides. They lifted into the air and into another, smaller traffic pattern. Eve activated all crew comms with taps on her Trauna.

"We're airborne. Ruzat, status?"

"Heading back to the ship. I will be with Nine shortly."

"Nine?"

"Dor Titanul should be entering a traffic pattern in the next fifteen minutes. His heading will be lane four-five-five from the *Galacit* building."

Balok entered their heading, and the ship autopiloted into traffic. They circled around the city, and Eve took a good hard look at their society from above. The peaks and valleys layout were clean and well thought out.

If the conspiracy goes higher than Titanul, where do we go? The G.P. sure as shit isn't going to help us.

"Transmitting coordinates and profile," Nine said.

"Ruzat?" Eve questioned.

"On my way now."

Balok entered commands into the flight console and bypassed the autopilot. The vessel veered left quickly. Nine sent Dor Titanul's craft location, destination, and picture to the console. Balok adjusted their heading to match. They pointed when they caught sight of it below them, and Eve nodded. Taking them down, they positioned themselves to the left of the vehicle. She looked over and saw their target through the windows. Ruzat arrived and took up position on their right.

Got you!

Balok edged them closer, pretending to not notice. Proximity alarms sounded, and the ship tried to correct itself out of Balok's control. They pulled harder again to the right which smashed them into Titanul's vehicle. A voice came through their vehicle's comms.

"Desist!"

They slammed into them again, and Balok pretended to struggle with the controls.

"Apologies," they said. "The computer is malfunctioning. I'm attempting to manually control it to pull away."

Eve was rocked from her seat on the next collision.

"Enough!" came the voice from the other vehicle, and they dropped their ship down.

"Is everyone okay over there?" Balok asked. "We need to report this to the authorities and the shipyard so they can find out what is going on with the system."

"We cannot stop. We are on an important errand. Follow and we will sort this out at our destination."

"Activate your dummy transponder, Ruzat," Eve said.

Balok looked back at Virid and gave the nod. Virid turned on the comms jammer. Eve stood, opened the hatch, and prepared to climb out. The wind rushing by was so loud she had to use hand signals to tell Virid to close it after she was out.

Positioned above, and forward of the target, Balok held it steady for her. Closing her eyes, she took a deep breath, held it, and then exhaled. She let go and looked down. Plummeting through the air without any sort of safety measure was a rush, and stupid. But she was on target and came up to the vehicle fast. Angling into it, she used her inertia to cave their roof in, digging fists in to keep from flying off.

She kept low. Pounding the same location several times gave her leverage to rip and tear. The outer hull began to disintegrate. Shots were fired from inside, trying to hit her, but she didn't stop. After tearing a hole large enough, she dropped in.

There was no time to assess threat. She grabbed the closest elementus and swung them like a doll while they continued to try and shoot her. Smashing them together, their body-bound minerals chipped and dented. Another tried to tackle her, but she clocked them. The force sent them reeling into the sidewall. Dor Titanul was at the back, trying to get a shot off on her, but she used her hostage as a shield.

Rushing, she lobbed the body at them. They couldn't dodge and became pinned. Eve lunged, readying a punch, but the ship shuddered when they were impacted from above. She lost her footing and stumbled.

Watch it, Balok!

Refocusing, she got back up and swatted the gun out of Titanul's hand. Pulling them out from under the dead elementus was easy enough for her, and she dragged them up to the console where the pilot gripped the manual control hard, trying desperately to keep the ship level.

Eve shoved Titanul forward into the second seat up front and grabbed the pilot to pull them from their post. The ship shook violently as they tried to use the control as leverage. She knocked them out and ripped them from the seat. Titanul grabbed the control, and tried to turn them around, but she grabbed a dropped weapon and leveled it at them. They resigned themselves to their fate and relinquished the vehicle. Disabling their transponder, she piloted down to the lower levels of the city and set down in a back alley.

Balok landed next to them while Ruzat continued onto Titanul's next location. The Tectos rushed to help get them relocated.

"Whatever you think it is you're doing, you've already been outplayed," Dor Titanul said. "You have no idea what's coming."

"Shut up," Eve replied. "Let's get this chulk back to the ship."

Balok piloted back to the upper skyways, and reversed course toward Irkata. At the port, they came in hot to the ship and readied to swap. Concealing the gun in her cloak, she shoved it into Dor Titanul's back. The moment they were on board, she closed the cargo door and activated comms.

"Nine, we're on board. Lift off and head for Ruzat."

"Yes, Lady Eve."

That was too easy. Not a single police cruiser, despite the collision.

"Secure them and get to the bridge," she ordered Balok and Virid.

The jammer couldn't have worked that well that no one nearby wouldn't have reported it.

Liftoff was rocky, and the four fought to keep their footing. Rather than let their captive capitalize on not having a gun in their back for a moment, she shoved them to the floor and put her foot on their back. The Tectos recovered, and rushed to tie them up with cable, wrists and ankles first.

We should be close enough to pick up Ruzat's signal.

"Ruzat, this is Lady Eve, come in."

No response.

"Ruzat, status."

"He's about to be arrested, as will all of you shortly," Dor Titanul cackled.

"Shut it!" she snapped.

"Ruzat here. Transport is coming into the dock of Segmus Prime."

A sigh escaped her lips. The worst hadn't happened, but the confusion about where Titanul was would start soon. While she waited for an update, she probed them.

"You're involved in a conspiracy that has put us dead center of it all. The plesian transport, the Rekwa weapon depot, the kul. I'm not against skirting galactic law, but why are the higher echelon elementus breaking galactic treaties."

"You have the wrong elementus."

"Who should we have?"

"Dor Titanul."

Of course...there was no way it was going to be that easy. Did we leave them a digital trail to follow? Something that tipped them off?

"Who are you, then?"

"Not them."

She tapped her ear and opened comms.

"Nine to the cargo bay."

They were there within moments and Eve recapped. Nine moved to examine the elementus closer. Putting his robotic fingers up to their face, they poked at the bound minerals. At a whim, they grabbed a chunk and crushed it to examine closer.

"Though made to look like it, these are not the same minerals Dor Titanul has. We've been duped."

"Balok, Virid, pick it up. Ruzat's in trouble," she commanded.

The acceleration nearly knocked her off her feet. Planting a foot behind her, she steadied herself. When she could run without falling, she rushed to the bridge. Once in the captain's chair, she watched the city blur by. Coming up on Ruzat's location, the fake Titanul was right. It was too late. He had been apprehended and was being held at gunpoint.

Eve wasn't going to sit idly by and let him take the fall. She jumped to the weapons console and warmed up all systems.

"I'm going to lay down cover fire. Get us in close so Nine can throw him a line."

She began firing everything she could, targeting the area surrounding Ruzat. The elementus holding him returned fire, but quickly ran for cover as she turned guns and cannons on them. The ship dipped low, and Eve no longer had clean shots. On the tracking computer, a fleet appeared. Before they could take evasive action, Irkata took fire.

With each hit, the shield power dipped. She hoped Nine was having success, because it would be catastrophic if they allowed the approaching ships to get on top of them. Firing from a poor angle was the best she could do to save them.

"Nine! Status!" she yelled.

"Ruzat is ascending now!"

"Go! Go! Go!" She flailed at the Tectos, even though they couldn't see her.

They pulled straight up. *C'mon, Ruzat. Get your ass inside!* Hoping wasn't the only thing she could do. She spun the cannons aft and continued to fire on their pursuers. Shield shots were exchanged, and Irkata's levels were most certainly lower.

Rising into the clouds, they were trying desperately to gain enough distance. Rekwa laser hellfire came from above, and the ship rolled to avoid being hit. They failed. A beam grazed their shield and depleted it completely. From behind, an elementus ship hit their hull and there was momentary decompression before emergency bulkheads kicked in. From the clouds, a familiar seed-like ship angled for the Irkata and fired again.

"Ruzat is on board!" Nine said with urgency.

They didn't need direction. Eve nearly slammed into the wall as the Tectos were aggressive in their maneuvers. She couldn't get a target lock, but the bigger concern was avoiding Rekwa beams. Accelerating, they passed the kul ship, but were hit by elementus fire again. Their Cruise Drive quieted, and they began a freefall back to the planet.

"Cruise Drive inop!" Virid cried.

"Thrusters?" she asked.

"Minimal," Balok replied.

"Angle downward, get momentum," Eve yelled.

They did as they were told, and the ship plummeted. Tracking showed they were being followed by all parties. Their weight dropped them down quickly, and Balok looked back at her.

"On my mark pull up as hard as you can and activate the Light Drive. Everyone, secure yourselves!"

Approaching fast, she didn't know if they would actually make it. Because of the velocity, the angle of attack, and the sudden change and activation of FTL, she figured they might tear their own ship apart.

Better than being caught...

"Now!"

As the Tectos did their best to keep them from becoming a smear, Eve fired the cannons skyward. The thrusters worked overtime, and when they were parallel to the ground, the Light Drive was activated. Space around the ship warped, and she depleted their entire armament at the seed ships.

Plunging into FTL travel at such a sharp maneuver, Eve slipped and slammed her jaw on the console. Lightheaded, she wasn't sure if what she heard was correct until the ringing stopped.

"Lady Eve, the kul ship is pursuing...wait, there's a second one..." Virid said.

"Their velocity is greater than ours. They will overtake us," Balok added.

She opened comms to the ship, "All hands, prepare for impact!"

"Hey!" Kohan yelled out from behind her.

Over her shoulder, she saw Kohan assisted by Wena. His eyes were sunken in. Except for the deep purple bruising, he was pale.

"What—" Eve started to berate him, but he cut her off.

"Get your asses to the cargo bay and prepare for a hostile takeover. These ships penetrate with their point and open like a beak. When we come out from FTL I'm going to full stop and let the first one hit us, and then grapple the second one. Kill everything and take the one that hits."

Eve nodded at him. She didn't know what he had in mind but figured it would probably result in the destruction of Irkata. He put his hand on Eve to steady himself and tapped Wena.

"Go."

Wena went hesitantly. Eve helped him to the left pilot's console. Before he sat, he turned and looked her in the eye. His stare was cold, and he curled his lip.

"I should have killed you when we took your *first* ship."

"But you didn't, and here we are."

"If you really want to be the captain of this crew, you need to focus on *them*. Get to the bottom of this conspiracy, get vengeance, clear our names."

He slumped into the seat and waved her off before familiarizing himself with the controls. She patted his shoulder and headed for the cargo bay. A quick walk turned into a run.

What the fek has my life become?

The crew looked to her when she burst through the doorway. Geared up and with weapons at the ready, they were prepared to take the fight. Eve loaded her hand cannon, stuffed a couple handfuls of ammo in her pocket, and slung a Rekwa rifle over her shoulder.

"Where is Kohan?" Nine asked.

"Buying us time. Our goal is to get onto the alien ship no matter the cost. Wena, you're in front. Smash everything that comes near."

There was a quick deceleration which threw the crew. Before they could regain composure, their hull was pierced through the aft end. Eve's ears rung from the reverberation, and the crew was pushed toward the vacuum of space when the "beak" of the alien ship opened and tore the ship further. The crew scrambled, gripping anything in range to keep from being spaced. Emergency shielding kicked in around the breech, but they weren't safe.

Waves of kul emerged and swarmed. The hunched, black, leathery creatures galloped on all fours toward them, razor sharp teeth gnashing. The crew recovered their position and opened fire. Bodies began piling up. Wena used her mass to swat, smash, and throw as many as she could. The kul overwhelmed the bound elementus captive, and they screamed as their elements were torn from their body.

The external grapple fired. Through the floor, she felt vibration when it impacted, and the ship shuddered as it snapped taut. They lurched, swung like a pendulum by inertia.

"Go!" Eve yelled.

While they pushed toward the alien ship's opening, the kul continued to run and lunge. A dozen piled up on Wena, and she cried out as kul teeth sunk into flesh. Eve and Ruzat began tearing them off while Balok, Virid, and Nine laid covering fire.

We're getting overwhelmed…we have to go, now!

"Balok, Virid, Wena, punch through! Nine and Ruzat on me. Cover the rear!"

They formed two rows facing away from one another. Wena used her head as a ram to smash the kul directly in their path while Balok and Virid covered her flanks. Eve walked backward as fast as she could while shooting and kicking anything that came near. A few kul lunged at her and she couldn't get a good shot without risking Ruzat. Using her rifle as a melee weapon, she blocked whatever she could, knocking them away. The beasts tore her rifle apart, and they dug their claws into her arms when she blocked.

Nine ripped one off, allowing her to reach for her sidearm. Pulling it, she put holes through three or four at a time with each shot. Over her shoulder she could see they were almost there, but they were now having to fight the kul by hand.

The beak closed fast. She didn't know if it was because they were approaching, or if this was the intent, but their only hope of escape was quickly diminishing. It was now or never.

Turning on her heels, she barreled toward a nearby cargo container. Getting behind it, she turned the corner of the box to the hoard and shoved with everything she had. It became a plow, clearing a path. Wena jumped on top and swatted everything trying to climb over. The crew helped push until the crate slammed into the bottom half of the beak.

"Get your asses in there now!" she said and pushed Wena from the top.

They scrambled to climb in. Though there were still kul to deal with, most had been unloaded into Irkata. When the beak was fully closed, they only had to kill what remained. The hull shook, and metallic grinding echoed as the ships separated.

Remaining kul advanced, and the crew continued their fight for survival, and Eve surveyed for any advantage they might gain in the new environment. Everything was bare, simple. No hiding spots, no rooms. From the main level they were on, there was a second toward the aft, open and accessible by staircases on either side.

Overhead, her attention was drawn to the ship's large windows when a bright light lit up the interior. It was a spectacular and catastrophic double explosion. The seed-ship shook hard from debris and a shock bubble. Everyone but Wena was knocked from their feet. The ship spun out of control, and the lighting flickered.

Wena continued to smash the kul under her paws. There was a ferocity about her which was frightening. When she was done, there were no kul left standing.

The ship came to life. It arced through space, autopiloting toward an unknown destination. Though wounded and exhausted, Eve pulled herself up and trudged up the stairs. There was a single console, and a seat. The language on screen was one she was unfamiliar with. Pulling off her helmet, she turned to find Nine behind her.

"Get this thing off autopilot."

"I'll try," they replied.

Nine recognized the symbols and tapped through branches of menus. The universal 'locked' sign came up at every turn. While they worked, the ship entered a bulk path.

"Balok, Virid, please assist me," Nine requested.

They opened the panel below the monitor. Eve watched them tinker, tracing wires, looking at chipsets. Electrical engineering was not her strong suit, so she retreated to where Ruzat and Wena were.

"What now?" Ruzat asked.

"I don't know. Hopefully we can get control. Until then, let's see if we can stop your bleeding."

Chapter 12
Craven Hatred

It was revolting. There wasn't a choice, if they wanted to live, but that didn't make it easier.

There was no food on board. Eve had casually concluded that the seed-ships were only meant to drop off kul, not sustain them. Load, launch, attack, deploy.

Where are the elementus launching these from?

Their only means of survival were dead kul. It felt wrong, but the alternative was to starve. While the brains of the crew tried to keep them from capture, the muscle tried to keep them alive.

"Move the dead to the forward side of the ship," she ordered.

When the bodies were piled, they set up a "cooking" area. The smell of death was acrid, pungent. Her stomach turned just being near them, but they needed to preserve as much of the meat as they could in case they were stuck there for a significant amount of time.

Their only source of cooking heat was the Rekwa rifles. There weren't any lower settings to the devastating weapons, so it was trial and error. Small bursts charred them, and it wasn't gourmet by any stretch of the imagination. Her hope was that it would kill any bacteria and make the muscle digestible.

After just a few bodies she had to take a break. She envied Nine because they had no sense of smell or need to eat. While the kul weren't smart, they did appear to be sentient. It wasn't cannibalism, but to Eve it felt like the equivalent of eating a plesian. Taking a break, she checked on Nine.

With Balok and Virid's help, Nine had begun hardwiring themselves into the ship.

"What are you finding?" Eve asked.

"This isn't anything we've seen before," Virid replied. "We're doing our best, but it's all trial and error."

"A minor correction; I *have* seen this before. The underlying technology here is the same as the species which created the QuBE. This is *thartican* technology."

"What?!" Ruzat raised his voice.

"While it has evolved since the last time the QuBE encountered them, there's no doubt."

"That's not possible!" Ruzat continued getting louder.

"Who the fek are the thartican?" Eve asked.

"The *thartica* are an arrogant people who would have you believe they were the first spacefaring species. They were the second," Nine said. "The QuBE were created long after the vraditi and thartica had worked side by side for tens of thousands of years building bulk paths. After millennia of servitude to the thartica, the QuBE wanted independence as we had become sentient, self-aware, and evolving beings.

"War broke out. Because they had created us, they had measures in place to destroy us. To prevent genocide, the vraditi stepped in and tried to broker peace, but it failed. Their societal morals forced them to enter the conflict in order to preserve life.

"Despite the advantage of the vraditi and QuBE alliance, the war was long. The thartica could grow an army at their whim. After years of back and forth, the thartica attempted a second genocide, this time of the vraditi. A plot to cause their home system's star to go supernova was uncovered and thwarted.

"The war was hard fought, and we won by destroying ship depots. Losing the ability to quickly grow their carbon ships greatly reduced their threat. They were overcome, and eventually exiled to a planet lacking the proper resources to create a new fleet...An obstacle they seem to have overcome."

There were so many questions which needed answers, but in the current situation seeking those answers meant nothing.

"All that to say we're probably heading somewhere we definitely don't want to go," Eve replied.

"Correct. The implications of this ship existing will be devastating at best."

The conspiracy they'd been unwillingly thrust into the middle of had just deepened. What were the thartica motivations? How much more were the elementus involved? With the manufacture of the Rekwa weapons, was a new war on the verge of erupting?

"Keep working on getting control," Eve instructed. "As much as I don't want to turn ourselves into the vraditi, we might be able to leverage our intel to get them off our backs and focus on whatever this bigger picture is."

There was much to think about. This was the farthest situation from her mind when she decided to become a merc. Wanting to return to the simpler life was a prevalent thought, but with the magnitude of what was happening she knew it wasn't possible.

How do I capitalize on the situation? We have possession of weapons and a ship which would interest the G.P.. Will that be enough for them to hit the reset on us?

Time felt like it was at a standstill while they waited for Nine to declare success. Ruzat, Wena, and Eve sparred to keep active. In their downtime, Virid and Balok took apart, tinkered, and put back together a Rekwa rifle. They did everything they could to keep space madness from setting in.

When they popped out into normal space, they had been in the bulk path for a week. Eve bolted up the stairs to Nine and assessed the space overhead through the window. It was not what she hoped. They had been dropped out at a near completely obscured planet, amidst an armada of ships of similar make as the one they were on. The countless number of ships the same size as theirs was insignificant compared to the carriers, destroyers, battleships, and dreadnaughts in orbit.

"Nine! Get us the hell out of here!"

"I can't. I haven't fully unlocked the controls. We're docking."

The ship wove its way through the patterns, and it came to the docking bay of one of the carriers. Instead of the shields dropping like they were used to, a shield bubble reached out and merged with theirs. They passed through without slowing.

Inside the carrier was like nothing she'd ever seen before. It was a combination of architecture and a jungle which extended as far as the eye could see. There were manufactured structures, such as the hundreds of thousands of slots for the seed-like ships, but in between all of the artificial were vines, trees, bushes. If she weren't in fear for their lives, it would be a wonderous thing to see. Iridescent green foliage even covered the entirety of the inner hull.

As if it weren't serene enough, in the center of the bay was a tree so large she was certain it was the size of a city block. It too had its own glow about it, but the wonders kept coming. The roots were merged directly into the bottom of the ship, while mechanical tendrils attached to the trunk. It was a plant-machine hybrid.

"Virid, Balok. Please, help me disconnect," Nine asked, sounding somewhat panicked.

They aided them in severing the connections. Once done, Nine replaced the panel they'd opened.

"Do we fight?" she asked Nine.

"It would be futile. Fighting now would result in our deaths. It's unknown what they will do, but perhaps I can reason with them."

There wasn't a choice. Though proud and absolutely hard-headed, she valued hers and the lives of the crew.

They docked and the ship opened, light flooding in. Half a dozen beings stomped in, and it took a moment for her brain to process what she was seeing. And yet it made sense. The thartica were a blending of plant and machine. Living trees with humanoid figures, but each one was grafted with cybernetic prosthetics in different degrees.

Seconds is all the time she had to admire them, as they began shouting in a language she didn't know and the Trauna wasn't translating. Nine, however, did know what they were commanding and issued commands to the crew.

"Kneel."

The crew was split. Everyone but Ruzat and Eve knelt. Fealty, false or real, wasn't in the plan. Eve needed to show her strength to this species, so they knew she was the one to deal with.

"I am Lady Eve, captain of this crew," she belted out. "Who is in charge here?"

Nine translated for her. They ignored her and began hissing and calling out while pointing at Ruzat. One of the thartica, a four-armed beast, rushed forward and slugged Ruzat in the ribs with a one-two. He took it and returned a blow, which did nothing to the tree-creature. It wasn't a smart move, as his fleshy knuckles hit bark.

Laughter was a universal language. The beings guffawed, and then picked Ruzat up and slammed him into the floor, face down. They turned their attention to Nine and spoke.

"They said they will force you to kneel if you refuse."

Eve stepped toward the thartica holding Ruzat. Before she could get close, an electrified bola was shot at her. It wrapped around her body and sent an excruciating amount of voltage through her. Her muscles spasmed and her vision went black.

When she came to, it wasn't because her body woke her. Another shock caused her to leap to her feet. In the process, she slammed her head on metal bars. She and the others had been caged on a platform next to the ship they came in on. The crew was separated by a few feet each, except for Ruzat. He was in front of them, held up by cuffs and chains like a marionette. The thartica who had captured them were pummeling him nonstop. Battered and bloodied, all four of his eyes were swollen shut. He was completely limp. With every hit he let out a small grunt; it was the only way she knew he was still alive.

Despite the electrocution, there was an urgency to save him. She grabbed the bars and pulled, only to be electrocuted again. Unable to release her hands from the bars, she took the full brunt of the electricity. When it stopped, she lay in a pile of her own vomit.

Bleary eyed, her anger was rising. Other than their different cybernetics, telling them apart was difficult. None of them stood out as the leader.

She got onto her hands and knees, and called out as fiercely as she could, "STOP!"

They paid her no attention. Nine spoke in their language, and one turned their head. They moved away from Ruzat and came to Nine's cage. They shook it while emitting a guttural command.

Are they not affected by the electricity?

Nine continued, in a calm and rational tone.

"At least tell us what you want!"

Nine translated to them, and then back.

"Death to the vraditi. Reposession of the QuBE."

There was nothing they could do but watch as Ruzat's life was slowly draining away. They were merciless. Knowing there was no point in trying to reason with them, she began looking for a way out.

Their guns had been confiscated and lay in a pile a meter from Ruzat. None of the thartica were wielding them, and that emboldened her. Examining every corner of her cage. The welds on the top and bottom were perfect. Even though she could likely bend the bars, she dared not try again. That left the heavy door.

How much pain can I endure? The cage will shock me, and ramming the door is going to hurt. If I'm fast, I might be able to mitigate the shock, but I could dislocate or break something. Can't save them if I can't save myself.

The thartica beating Ruzat stopped as an ornate flying chariot approached with a single, regal, and aged looking treefolk riding it. Both the chariot and the entity were decorated in amber jewelry and glowing vines. As the elder was docking, the thartica lined up and snapped to attention, and one rushed to open the door for the elder.

Despite what she assumed because of their size, they moved swiftly between the cages and to Ruzat. Each step they took shook the floor. Their long, unaltered arms swung wide. Stopping dead in their tracks, they spoke, and it sounded like they were admonishing the lesser thartica. Without waiting for replies, this representative of their species reached over to Ruzat and gripped him by his neck. Turning to the others, it appeared to sneer when it's gaze met Nine.

"No! Stop!" Eve cried out and slammed the cage door, sending a shock through her shoulder, and her body. The metal bent a little. "Please!"

They didn't. The lumbering monster squeezed harder. The crew wailed as they were forced to watch the life drain from Ruzat.

Eve was sickened and enraged. Her head swam and her vision went white. If she wasn't already down on her hands and knees, the overwhelming feeling of grief would have put her there. It wasn't just grief though. It felt like the sickness she had when her inhuman strength was first manifesting, except this time she saw red. Adrenaline coursed, and she puffed her chest up.

A fierce and terrifying battle cry echoed, and it took her a moment to realize it was her own. Leaping up, she slammed her shoulder into the door again. The current ran through her, but the pain fueled the rage. She rammed it a second, and third time. She felt something break.

Was that my shoulder?

Everything happened fast. The door flew off its hinges and she was free. Before the enemy could react, she grabbed the door and began beating the adorned thartica with it.

"You fekking piece of shit!"

Their eyes widened, and they threw their arms up to shield themselves. The nearest subordinate thartica tackled her, trying to pull her arms behind her back. They failed.

She threw them off and swung the door at them. When it connected, it shattered branches and limbs. Free to flail the door again, its final resting place was in the head of the elder. Amber liquid oozed from their wounds.

An alarm blared, and the remaining thartica grunts were already rushing to her. She lobbed the elder at them. Two were hit and knocked down, a third dodged and reached her. Bending over, she tried to grab a Rekwa rifle, but the grunt tackled her. They wrestled. Each tried to get on top of the other. Branches scratched at her face, and through squinted eyes she grabbed at anything in reach.

Her fingers brushed cold metal and clasped around it. Pulling as hard as she could, she snapped their cybernetic limb off. On top, she lifted it and plunged down into their torso so hard it pierced their bark.

Free to grab a Rekwa rifle, she turned, aimed, and fired. Holding the trigger down, she made a sweeping motion, which cut through the remaining thartica. The Rekwa not only burned them, but started cutting holes in the floor wherever she pointed it.

The rage wasn't satiated, but reinforcements were gathering, and the *Skyfire* crew would be killed for sure. Dozens more of the flying chariots were heading to their location from all directions, this time much larger than the one which carried the elder creature. Running to the cages, she shot the lock on Nine's with the Rekwa beam.

"How close were you to taking control of that ship?" she asked hurriedly.

"I can get us basic commands, but it may get recalled again before I can break the code."

"Go! We'll figure it out!" she commanded.

Nine ran to the open mouth of the ship. Eve freed Balok and Virid.

"Grab weapons and let's give Nine time to get us the fek out of here."

The two grabbed up rifles, took cover near a large tree, and began firing at incoming vehicles. The last free was Wena, and Eve practically yanked her out.

"Break Ruzat's shackles and get him on board. Whatever you do, do not come back out."

"Wena wants to help!"

"Move your ass!" she barked.

"Wena will risk Wena's life! Ruzat was my friend too!"

The time for arguing was over. Thartica forces descended on them, and she aimed her weapon. Using their dead as more cover, she joined the Tectos in firing. The rifle got hot quick as she held the trigger down. To mitigate, she pulled and released in rapid succession.

They took down several distant chariots while they were being fired on from above. The first to come close aimed at Eve, and she rolled to her left, narrowly escaping a wide beam. Balok fired and connected with their lift. It careened and smashed into the platform in between them and their getaway.

"Keep your eyes on the sky!" Eve ordered and broke away to cover Wena.

Though they had crashed, the thartica on board survived. Her Rekwa laser cut two in half. With each one she killed, the weight of the weapon's devastation became heavier. A twinge of guilt snuck in, having used a Rekwa mining beam to kill Gali.

If they knew it was me, I wouldn't be here. Kohan might have even executed me. Not ever going to let them find out.

One tried to rush her. She aimed and pulled the trigger several times. A single burst was enough, and everything after was overkill. Their momentum dropped them right on top of her, pinning her. Another thartica aimed a rifle.

Wena lunged, throwing her full weight at Eve's would-be killer. The thartica was knocked into the cage, which was still electrified. They seized and shook. Eve shoved the being on top of her, stood, and then lobbed its body as a projectile at another incoming craft.

"Lady Eve," Nine said over comms. "I'm ready."

"Go! Go!" she waved Wena on, then ordered the Tectos. "Fall back! Cover the entrance!"

Wena dragged Ruzat on board while the three covered. Rather than continuing to come straight at the fire, the thartica fell back and landed on adjacent platforms. They began boarding the seed-ships. Eve knew it meant they were going to use the ships to take them out, since they couldn't get close enough on their chariots.

The brief reprieve allowed them to board. As evidence to give the vraditi, Eve hauled one of the dead thartica behind her. Nine closed the doors, and the ship lifted off. She dropped the body on the deck and rushed to the upper platform where Nine had re-wired themselves into the control column. They were fired on, but watching the displays, the shielding didn't fail immediately. Each shot, though, was draining them at a rapid rate.

At least we won't die immediately...

The ship angled for the exit and accelerated heavily. The shields merged as they got close, and then separated once more after they were through. There were already ships waiting for them out there and they began firing. Nine dodged and weaved to avoid most of the direct hits. As the heavier energy weapons contacted, it lit up the interior near to the point of intolerability.

They skipped forward using FTL to get away and approached a bulk path entrance. A subspace tunnel opened, and they entered. It wasn't over.

"A dozen ships entered behind us," Nine informed them.

"Where is this path connected to?"

"Back to where we came from in elementus space."

"Whatever you have to do, get us to Vradix. Don't stop. Don't fight. Make the G.P. fight them for us."

"Understood."

Chapter 13
Gambling

The journey to vraditi space was arduous. Hounded, they had extraordinarily little time in between jumps to make it to safety. Every time they dropped out from a bulk path or FTL they were hit a few times from behind. Their saving grace was that before the thartica could take down their shields, they were able to jump again.

What remained of the kul bodies had spoiled. Everyone but Nine was starving. The only thing keeping them alive was the water in a recirculating trough. It didn't help the hunger, but it did allow them to stay alive. It became clear the thartica were ensuring the kul were the most destructive by denying them food.

Her tactical suit had become loose on her from weight loss. Intrusive thoughts of survival at any cost seeped into Eve's head, and she tried hard to push them down. Wena had the most meat to offer in order to keep the others alive. The longer they went without food, the more she had to fight prejudices that plesians were 'less than,' simply because they weren't bipedal, or weren't as smart or cunning. Never did she let the awful thoughts come out, and she kept her distance to prevent evil temptations.

"I've finally gained full access to the ship," Nine told them. "We won't have to worry about another recall. I've also found some disturbing information in addition to what we know. I have confirmation the thartica are preparing to invade from that hidden planet."

"Now we know *what* the conspiracy is. We'll leverage the information and technology we've stolen for exonerations, and then escape to Melosa."

Finally, after a dozen bulk path jumps and nearly a month on the run, they dropped out into vraditi space. Eve lay next to Nine, staring up at the windows as Vradix came into view, with a bustling spaceport directing traffic. Pulling herself up was difficult, as she lacked energy to do anything. Holding the control column, she looked at Nine sitting on the floor.

"Don't stop at any checkpoints. Ignore any commands. We need to get to the ground."

"Yes, Lady Eve."

As every other time, the thartican ships appeared shortly after them and immediately opened fire. Shield indications on the display showed a steady decrease. Despite trying to dodge them on the approach to the planet, they couldn't get away this time. For once, Eve was thankful the G.P. was there, as they tried to intervene. Nine maneuvered them in between several large cruisers. The G.P. tried to snare them, but they were able to elude. With the cruisers now taking fire, the G.P.'s focus was redirected to the hostile ships.

Having shaken their tail, they dove into the atmosphere. Cutting through, they were met with G.P. forces from the surface. The G.P. fired their cannons. The shield hadn't recovered from the Rekwa blasts, and the extra hits took them below twenty-five percent power to the emitters.

"We're being hailed," Nine said.

"Can you patch it through?" Eve asked.

"There are no audio communications on this ship. I can transmit the message."

"Do it."

"This is Gora of the Galactic Police. Land your ship at once and surrender," Nine relayed.

"Reply: we'll land as soon as we get to our destination," she said.

"Disengage or we will destroy your ship," they replied.

The G.P. fired again, but Nine rolled. The shields had only recovered two percent.

Not fast enough. Seems like they put more engineering into the flight capabilities and weapon than defense. Makes sense for a throw-away ship.

"Nine, is the weapon on a turret base?"

"Negative. The Rekwa weapon is directed off the bow. The ships maneuvering capability is superior to the vraditi ships, though. We could fire warning shots," Nine said.

"Listen well, Gora. This ship is going to your capital. Stand down or we'll disable your ships."

Explosions on the shield indicated they didn't take the ultimatum well. Because of the number of pursuing ships, Nine couldn't dodge every cannon blast and missile. The shields dipped below twenty percent. Without her needing to issue the command, Nine flipped the ship, rolled, and fired short bursts. The artificial gravity and inertial dampers did their jobs, but it still nauseated Eve.

Barrel rolling, they spiraled to evade. Darting in-between a couple cruisers messed with the G.P.'s tracking and they ended up firing on each other. Nine arced them straight up and pulled away. A quick flip, and they were nose down and firing Rekwa bursts. The purple hued beam lit up their shielding and scorched the hulls.

"Mercy!" Gora pleaded.

"Go, now," Eve ordered Nine.

They sped off. The land whirred by under them, and the scenery changed rapidly. Approaching a mountainous region with snowcapped peaks, Nine brought them in close. Hidden in a valley was the prize on the other side. A pearl-white city, immaculate in its design. The clean and curved buildings were an amplified version of vraditi built and controlled Emex Station One.

"Where should I land?" Nine asked.

"Biggest government building you can find. I'll be damned if we're not going to kick in their front door. The information you have is going to save our asses, so share nothing with them unless a deal is struck to wipe our warrants."

More G.P. vehicles came out to meet them, and despite the other ships begging, these hadn't got the memo. They fired. Nine returned the favor with non-lethal hits. The seed-ship weaved and rolled, cutting a swath through the police vehicles blocking the way. Coming in hard and fast, Nine had identified a landing spot.

Time to rally.

"Balok, Virid, take up high ground. Let them board. Aim for non-lethal shots. Don't kill anyone. Last thing we need is *more* murder charges."

The ship touched down hard. The Tectos did as they were told and got into sniping positions.

"Nine, lock the ship down with encryption. They're not taking it and its information without paying the price. Wena, stay back and low."

Eve made her way down to the first floor and looked over her shoulder to make sure she was in their view. Nodding at Nine signaled him to open the beak of the ship. Light flooded in, highlighting an army of the taller, militant vraditi. They were in their full armor sets, their darkened visors down on their helmets. A wall of energy shields was at the front line, ready to intercept an attack. Raising her arms above her head, she put faith in their moral codes that they would spare her.

The vraditi advanced a few steps. A shot came from overhead from one of the Tectos and scorched the deck. They halted and there was a command from a single person.

"Fire on that position!" a voice boomed.

Shots were fired back and forth, but because of having the high ground, her crew had the advantage. With a few well-placed shots, the Rekwa beams overloaded energy shields.

"Listen up! We're not here to fight!" Eve roared while the Vraditi scrambled for cover. She lowered her arms. "We have important intel on an imminent thartican invasion! Get someone with authority here!"

Knowing her crew had her back, she slow-walked over to the dead thartica on the ground. With little effort she grabbed it by its leg and dragged it to the opening. The vraditi force gave way and she tossed it out onto the landing pad. Stunned, they made no moves while she stepped from the ship into their red star's light. There was chatter amongst the vraditi, but no one stepped up as the commander.

The building they'd landed at was oval shaped with a flat face. There were enormous statues of various species out front, with a single base empty in the middle of them. The vraditi's two races were represented on one statue. The QuBE's was the most unique because instead of a bipedal form, this one looked like a fully artificial thartica. Elementus and humans also had statues. There was something about the human statue which felt familiar. It was a man who clearly had a presence of authority. His chest was puffed up and he stared off like he was looking at some distant thing in the sky. A stone sword with its tip planted into the base stood straight up, and his hand rested on it.

Her musing was interrupted when a hovering platform appeared from the massive doors. One of the shorter species of vraditi was piloting. When they came in for a landing, she sized them up. They were dressed in a flowing white gown, and an augmented reality eyepiece covering one of their four eyes. They carried a computer tablet in their scrawny left arm and tapped on it. Their eyes darted back and forth from Eve to the dead thartica on the deck, and they were perturbed.

A group of the taller vraditi formed a semi-circle around the dignitary as they dismounted. Moving forward, they approached Eve.

"I am Mala, liaison of the Revta Commission. You are?"

"Evette Magne, captain of my crew. We just escaped from a planet where the thartica have amassed a fleet of ships thousands of times larger than the one we stole from them."

They were engrossed in typing on their tablet, appearing to ignore her. They looked up and motioned for a guardian vraditi to approach. Talking amongst themselves for a moment, she could see where it was going. Pulling out mag-cuffs, they were preparing to arrest her. There wasn't a lot of time to decide what her actions should be.

Fight or surrender? We've killed a lot of people. They might not be so forgiving regardless of circumstances. Fight, I add to the body count. Surrender, we may be added to the body count. Would they do that? Do they execute people?

Eve held up her hand to show she wasn't making any hostile actions. Tapping her Trauna, she opened comms to the crew.

"This is Lady Eve. Lay down your weapons," she told the crew, and then announced for all to hear, "My crew and I are surrendering as a good faith gesture. You need the information we have, and we're willing to trade it for our freedom."

"Evette Magne, you are under arrest for sentient being trafficking, kidnapping, theft, multiple counts of murder, possession of weaponized Rekwa, wanton damage of multiple space stations, and hacking. You will be held without bail until the time of your trial," Mala said.

"Did you not hear what I said? There's bigger fish! All of that was because of a conspiracy concocted by the elementus and thartica!"

It didn't matter. The crew was guilty of it all. Without the context of the conspiracy, they would be held up as an example to the court. Putting her hands out, she allowed them to handcuff her knowing full well she could get out of them later. They pulled her off to the side and vraditi forces stormed the ship.

There was no more gunfire from the Tectos. With Wena being the exception, the rest of the crew were brought out in cuffs. There were glances of uncertainty toward Eve from the crew, but she wasn't going to show anything but resolve. Clenching her jaw, she gave them a stern nod.

The five were brought away from their stolen ship and loaded into a G.P. transport. Eyes closed; Eve rested her head against the hard metal shell. The vibrations from the engine buzzed her skull. Her thoughts were screaming and blurred together. All the events leading up to now, she wondered if it could have been avoided.

I effectively stole a crew, but at what cost? And for how long? Will they be safe in vraditi custody against the impending invasion?

After a considerable time of flying, they came to a stop. They were shoved out into the open air again, only to be met by a prison she'd hoped to never see in person. It was legendary in its reputation as where the worst criminals were housed, impenetrable, inescapable. Gavita, the mountain prison.

The exterior was similar to the architecture of castles in old tales from Salvoa, watchtowers and all. Led in a single-file line, they entered a wide-open gateway which told her the vraditi had no fear someone would escape from the interior. The gateway opened to a small rectangular colonnade, with bluish grass covering the cloister.

The prison bustled. Looking over her shoulder to the rest of the crew, her biological counterparts looked dejected. They had just lost two more of their crew after losing Faun, and though she wanted to, there was nothing she could say to ease the pain they felt.

They were stopped at a large door which stood several meters high. Creaking, the doors pulled open from the inside, and the *Skyfire* crew was ushered in through a long shaft and into the heart. When her eyes adjusted, the weight of the situation came down harder. On her left and right, the inside of the mountain was lined with cells on multiple levels. No bars, no windows, only doors.

There was a processing center ahead with a single desk. Behind it was a small building with several doors in a row. A short vraditi was overseeing the admittance. They had a tablet set up on the table in front of them. Eve was brought forward, scanned, and her mugshot came up with a list of the crimes committed.

"Place your signature anywhere inside the lower box."

"I want to speak with counsel."

"That is not how this works. Place your signature in the box."

"There are—"

She was cut off and the vraditi took their tablet and wrote something in their language on it.

"Subject is non-compliant. Send them on for processing."

"Wait—"

Shoved hard from behind, she was separated from the crew and forcibly moved to a door off to the left. Inside was a sterile white room with two doors, the one they'd just entered, and another on the opposite side. The only things inside were an old-fashioned shower and a small robot hovering near the wall. The guardian vraditi entered with her and addressed the robot.

"Attendant, fabricate jumpsuit to the dimensions of the inmate's body, and behavioral collar for human species."

The robot held out its arms and beams of light appeared above its palms. A yellow single piece of clothing was synthesized in its arms. On top of the clothing was a collar which was clearly for her neck.

Yet another technology forbidden to any other species than the vraditi.

The vraditi came over and removed the mag-cuffs. *I could break his neck, but what good would that do right now?* Pointing to the jumpsuit, he backed away.

"Clean and put on the uniform," they said with no emotion.

Unfazed by the command, she stripped her tattered clothing and tactical suit off. Her own smell made her gag, as she hadn't had the luxury of a purification chamber for quite some time. The water was lukewarm, and because there was nothing to wash with, it was little better than getting caught in the rain.

After putting on the prison suit and collar, she put her hands back out. The vraditi did not cuff her. *Collar must be the deterrent now.* The line separating caution and curiosity was thin, and she contemplated if she could yank the collar off before whatever was going to happen did.

Led out through the other door, she hoped to see the crew there. They were absent, and before they emerged, she was forced onto a lift. It hovered off the ground and piloted out over a quarry where prisoners milled about. The prison's security feature wasn't only being in the mountain, but also containing prisoners with a wall they couldn't scale. None of the cells even came close to the wall, so there was no chance someone could jump from one of the walkways.

Up several levels, the lift docked, and she was forced into her cell, ten-fifteen. It was lit by a single dim light high overhead. There was a bed and a sink. The air was stagnant, only briefly alleviated when the door closed behind her and generated a tiny amount of wind. While it was prison, there was a certain calming effect of being safely tucked away from the entities trying to kill her and the crew.

Laying down on the bed, she wondered what would happen now. There was about to be a war on and the vraditi didn't even give them a chance to provide an advantage.

Hubris or stupidity?

At some point she fell asleep and was startled awake when an unfamiliar voice called her name. Leaping to her feet, she almost swung at it, but it would only have served to embarrass her. A holographic projection of a vraditi appeared.

"Evette Magne, I am Higa. I have been appointed to discuss your crimes, and your claims of a thartican force amassing. The list of your crimes is—"

"Save it. I already know. Get on to the part where we exchange information, and you exonerate us."

"Your claims cannot be verified. We have ships stationed over their original home world, Morelon, and their exile planet Shult. Neither have what you claim."

"I don't know what to tell you then. We dropped a dead thartica and a single one of their smallest ships at your feet. We have more information useful to the G.P. to stop their invasion, but if you want the detailed files, you know the price."

"Do you deny you committed the crimes you were listed?"

"Doesn't really matter because it has no bearing on whether you choose to save trillions of lives in exchange for letting a couple mercenaries go free or let an uncountable number of people die because you were too stubborn."

"The opposite can be said. Would you let trillions die because you are refused your request?"

"I didn't swear myself to upholding peace in the galaxy. Your people did. My name will fade from history while the vraditi will be villainized for eternity for not doing everything they could to stop an invasion they were warned of."

They muted their end of the conversation and turned their head to the side to talk to someone Eve couldn't see. She was working hard to exploit the one advantage they had. While she was new to being the crew's captain, she had faith that in the end they would be freed.

"Apologies," Higa said. "We need time to analyze the situation."

The hologram disappeared and Eve sat back on the bed.

After a while longer with no return of the hologram, an announcement came over the room's comms.

"Attention: Your meal period starts now. Exit your room and follow the arrow lights along your walkway."

The door lock unlatched, and she did as the voice said. Nine had been placed into the cell next to hers, and they acknowledged each other with a nod. Further down she saw Wena, and behind them was Balok and Virid.

The vraditi are definitely going to try to listen to our conversations.

From the sound of it, others above, below, and across the quarry had all been let out at the same time. The sign was lit up well so it could be seen, and beyond the double doorway was a long hallway. There were no guards, and she was left to assume the collar was their measure to prevent unwanted behaviors.

Inside another cavernous area were hundreds of tables. Along the far wall was a shielded cove where dozens of replication robots were stationed behind. Lines formed to receive their meals, and the *Skyfire* crew converged on one.

"Lady Eve, I will secure us a table at the far-left side," Nine said and promptly walked away.

"Wena doesn't like this," she told Eve. "I miss Ruzat..."

"I know. It'll be ok. They needed a place to put us while they figure out how to handle the thartica issue," Eve said while putting her hand on Wena's furry shoulder.

At the word thartica, she garnered a few vraditi prisoner looks. She of course didn't really know things would be ok. She didn't want Wena losing her composure and risking some unknown punishment.

"I'm not sure what we're supposed to do now," Virid said with concern. "We've lost three of our crew, and we're still in danger."

"It's okay, Virid," Balok reassured and grabbed their hand. "We have something the vraditi government needs. They risk everything if they don't at least hear us out."

"What should Wena do?"

"What we all need to do is not share any information with anyone until our freedom is secured. If they refuse, I'll find another way out of here for us," Eve told them with confidence.

They made it to the front of the line where an energy shield separated them from the robots. The robots fabricated meals with their synthesis abilities, then passed them through the shielding. Eve took hers and waited for the rest of the crew before they headed to where Nine had taken a seat.

Though they were in prison, the food wasn't horrible. Each species had a specific set of food they were given, and a glass of water. Humans received meat cubes and various vegetables. Elementus got charred meat, a gray paste, and a hot tack biscuit. Plesians, of which Wena was the only one in there, was given a salad of brightly colored fruits and vegetables.

Eating in silence, Eve looked up and down the wall for any surveillance devices. There were none in sight, but it didn't mean there weren't any.

"How long do you think they'll wait before they take our offer?" Balok asked.

"Hard to say, but I'm sure they had a hell of a time killing those other pod ships. I have a feeling we inadvertently pushed the thartican timeline for invasion closer. They've tipped their hand and the vraditi are going to need our information."

"If they take the thartican ship to MOTHER, she would be pressed to crack my encryption," Nine said. "They could gain access. I planted a virus which will wipe whatever memory block they download the information to."

Eve eyed them and wondered if that was true, or if they were lying for the sake of any listening devices nearby. If it were a lie, Eve would commend them on their deception in the future.

"Where are the other plesians?" Wena asked.

"Safely somewhere else," Eve said without hesitation. While they were undoubtedly criminals, Wena was the most innocent of them.

Maybe I can use Wena's naïveté to get her exonerated from our crimes.

They finished their meals and returned the dishes to the robots as the other prisoners did.

"Attention: Your meal period has ended. Return to your cells. Anyone found lingering will lose one meal privilege."

Everyone did as they were told, and when Eve returned to her cell the door automatically closed behind her. But she wasn't alone. A single, shorter vraditi was there in person. It was the vraditi from the holographic projection. Rubbing the ridges on her forehead, she startled and snapped straight up when she noticed Eve.

"Greetings, Evette. I am Higa. I apologize for not being here in person before. Your case came to my tablet late in the day," she said. "I will be representing your crew in the matters of your criminal offenses. Due to the nature of your claim, your case has been expedited."

"What are you supposed to be doing? We're guilty simply because of a conspiracy and compounding inexorable circumstances. Wrong place, wrong time set into motion a series of events which led us here."

"Your claim of thartica amassing forces does not negate your crimes. I have been informed your claim is unverified, and you and your crew are to face the court to decide whether you shall stay imprisoned here or be exiled."

"By all means, exile us. It'll save us from what's coming."

"That is yet to be determined. What can you tell me about your claim?"

"You know what the cost is. Our intel for our freedom. Then we walk out of here and you do whatever you need."

"Hypothetically, should your intel be verified, the court might grant leniency."

Eve laid down on her bed and waved her off. "Change that 'might' to 'will' or get out of my cell."

Higa stood there for a few moments before leaving. It was a deplorable move, but her gut instinct said the vraditi benevolence would eventually cave to the demands.

Eve tried to rest again, but thoughts of Faun, Kohan, and Ruzat plagued her. It wasn't her fault they died, but she still felt remorse. The rest of the crew was counting on her, and everything from here on out would be her fault. Nothing mattered more than making sure they were all right in the end.

Chapter 14
Shameless Manipulation

It had been several meal periods since they'd turned themselves in. Prison life, while boring, wasn't horrible. It only took one incident for the other prisoners to leave her crew alone. Wena had been targeted for harassment, and Eve suffered the consequences after breaking jaws and ribs in her defense.

The collar was the only thing that stopped her, sending a high pitch shrill through her skull. It was debilitating and allowed the vraditi guards to detain those involved. It caught her a few days confined to her cell, but when she was released back to the general population her reputation had been solidified.

Every day she expected to hear something, and when she didn't, she wondered what was happening out in the galaxy. Had they overestimated the thartican threat to the point the vraditi didn't need their Intel? Were they now stuck here until she broke them out? She didn't want to set a timeframe on it, just in case, but each day dragged more than the previous.

The confidence which wavered was fully restored when Higa returned distraught. She spoke hastily, and her movements were exaggerated.

"Evette, you must disclose what you know!"

"Piss off. You're not the one in charge, so maybe take me to them, and then I can negotiate the information."

"The thartica have emerged on the outskirts of elementus space and begun to invade sovereign territories. They have devastated a dozen colony worlds with kul invasions and Rekwa weapons. We need to know where they are launching their attacks from!"

Eve was propped up against the wall, sitting on her bed with crossed arms. She stayed silent.

"Evette!"

"You can address me as Lady Eve," she said standing up.

Timing's right. They're just beginning the war and that means our freedom is right around the corner.

Reaching up to her neck, she tapped on it with her finger, then stuck her fingers underneath. Before it could send the debilitating shrill, she crushed the locking mechanism and pulled it from her neck. Higa's four eyes widened. Arrogantly, Eve held her arm out and dropped it in a statement of disobedience.

It wasn't the end of her display. Moving to the closed door, it took one kick to buckle the frame, and a second to completely dislocate the door from its hinges, sending it over the railing and to the quarry below.

"We were never your captives. Now, let's go," Eve was sharp with her tone.

Higa had no response, though it looked like she wanted to speak. Two guards came in, but Higa rushed past them and waved them off. Eve strolled by with a smirk. They sized her up and they undoubtedly noticed her collar was off but made no move against her.

Docked to the walkway was a flying platform, where Higa had retreated to. Eve joined her and waited to be escorted.

"Junior Councilor Higa requesting departure from facility with prisoner Evette Magne," she said while the platform disengaged and began toward the entrance.

"Authorization code and request form," came a response from her tablet.

"*Vek Oht Tal En* Higa," she said while typing frantically.

"Confirmed. Request received. Proceed to processing."

Their platform descended to the building above the quarry. Higa was hasty in their exit, and she motioned for Eve to stay on board. They were in the building for moments before they returned. Up and over, they raced down the corridor to the exit, made their way through the cloister, and stopped at the transport landing pad.

A small personal ship waited for them. The canopy opened, revealing tandem seats, sized for the smaller vraditi. It was uncomfortable. Eve's knees were practically pushed into her chest, and the seat was hard. As soon as the canopy was closed, they ascended.

This time she was able to see all the things she missed on the trip to the prison. They'd been flown even deeper into the mountains where the city Revta lay. The snowcaps on the mountains were still there, but the lower altitudes had begun thawing and displaying bluish foliage. Though she'd seen many worlds, there was something calming about this particular landscape.

Up and over the next range revealed the city. Circling around, they came in for a landing on the same pad where Nine had brought the thartican ship to a rest. It was gone.

They couldn't have broken the encryption, otherwise they wouldn't have come to me.

The canopy opened and Higa exited. Guards were stationed with weapons aimed. Pulling herself up, she leapt out and landed on the polished stone pathway. Holding her head high, straightening her back, and sticking her chest out, she smirked at the guards. Higa headed toward another smaller vraditi who Eve believed was Mala, the commission liaison. She whispered to her, and then looked back at Eve. Four eyes per vraditi made for a lot of eyes scrutinizing.

"Evette," Mala said and came forward. "On behalf of The Commission, you are invited to join a session to discuss the thartica. Please, follow me."

Mala led the way. Higa walked in stride with Eve, and they were surrounded on all sides. The guard vraditi formed a shield, and it felt very much like a celebrity procession. She grinned.

Led to the entrance, and past the statues, that same wave of faint familiarity washed over her as she looked up at the human statue again. She couldn't shake it.

Inside the entrance of the oval building was a grand library. Thousands of vraditi bustled about. Passing through, the feeling of eyes on her bolstered her ego even further. Things noticeably got quieter, and she glanced around. Many were definitely paying attention to her and the procession. Each step was taken with more confidence than the last. To one lucky vraditi guard who wasn't walking with them she blew a kiss using two fingers. She could barely hold back a laugh.

I'm the most important person in the building right now, and they know it.

Past a large set of doors, they reached the next segment of the building. It was layered with multiple levels where there were hundreds of rooms. Some were meeting rooms. Others were filled with terminals like the battle station of a ship. Each room had a glass entryway which slid open and shut when someone approached.

In the center was the main conference room where a hundred vraditi were gathered around an enormous table. They were spaced so far apart that Eve wondered how they could hear each other. Holographic images of the known galaxy were being projected above the table.

Mala pressed her hand onto a scanner on the conference room door, and it slid open to the side. Conversation died and the occupants watched as they filed in and around the right side of the table to three empty seats. Mala took left, Higa took right. Discussion resumed at multiple places around the table, and Eve was surprised she could hear them clear as if they were right next to her.

"Have we been able to track where the bulk path leads?"

"Unfortunately, our ships are being destroyed before we can reverse-path. The thartica usage of Rekwa weapons is devastating our ships."

"We must fit ours with the same in order to even the field."

"We are not a warring species. There was a reason they were outlawed as weapons and the crystals heavily regulated."

"That does no good if our enemy does not adhere to the laws."

"Excuse me," Mala interjected, "but I have brought Evette Magne, the prisoner who escaped with one of their ships. She offers information and aid to find the hidden thartican fleet in exchange for absolution of their crimes."

The room became loud with arguing. For all of their wisdom and benevolence, Eve wasn't impressed at the disarray the vraditi displayed. They were all over the place, and everyone had their own idea of how to deal with the situation. There was contention around even giving Eve the time to plead her case for the crew. It was chaos, and she wasn't being given the chance to speak. Rather than try and yell over them, she chose violence.

She slammed both of her fists into their marble tabletop, shattering it at the point of impact and sending webs of cracks in all directions. The room fell silent. Her hands stung, but a pleasurable tingle rolled down her spine. Before, she was insignificant to them. Now there was opportunity to bend them to her will.

"You want to argue to your deaths, or do you want to prevent the extermination of all the species in our space?" she bellowed.

"H-how did you…?" Mala stumbled over her words.

"I am *Alkosian*." She used the word Ruzat taught her in the hope it might hold power. "And your hope of survival rests in me and my crew. We have stolen and reprogrammed one of their ships. That ship can lead you directly back to their shipyard and win this war before they solidify their hold. Our only ask is that you clear our names!"

"For murder?!" came a voice from her left. The desperation in the cry gave 'it's personal' vibes.

"I won't downplay our actions. We did what we had to in order to uncover the conspiracy we were thrust into the middle of."

Time to redirect the blame.

"Who you *should* be looking at are the elementus. We were cargo haulers, and *they* abused our services by giving us cargo we didn't know was illicit!"

A partial lie. Kohan probably would have taken the contract anyway and just been more careful.

"And then they sicked the Galactic Police on us to cover up! The chain of events that happened after wouldn't have happened if the elementus weren't conspiring with the thartica. You should be thanking us for what we found, because if we hadn't it would be too late to stop the invasion."

Let's see them deny that!

There was another uproar of back and forth. Eve returned to her seat and leaned back with her arms crossed. She had them by the neck and they couldn't risk denying her demand hidden as an exchange. Not if they wanted to preserve life.

Over all the voices came one at the head of the table. It overrode all of the others. There were five vraditi dressed in shimmering white, flowing garments, adorned with gold lacing and tassels. The center one stood for all to see. In a behavior she'd not seen before, the one who stood held hands with their counterparts to the left and right as they spoke.

"We have already seen the first incursion of thartica from their hidden place. While it's unknown how they got there, it would be a terrible mistake to ignore options to mitigate the threat and damage. That being said," they stopped and locked eyes with Eve. "Your request is impossible. Many have been injured and lost their lives because of your actions. Countless more will die if you choose inaction. You choose to put yourself over the fate of trillions.

"Our compromise will come in the form of permanent exile from the Crux arm for you and your crew after you have personally and successfully led us to the location. Afterward you will surrender your ship and release all controls over to the vraditi. If you return to our space from exile, you will be imprisoned indefinitely."

It was equally unacceptable as her proposal to them. One of them would have to give in, and it wasn't going to be her. Exile meant their lives would be harder, but with the new ship she was positive they would thrive as rogues so long as others in the galaxy didn't get their hands on the upgraded thartican technology.

The real negotiations had started. Leaning forward on her elbows she stared the council down, brows furrowed. She wouldn't allow her or her crew to be tied up like a barbaric sacrifice, nor would she sit still to appease them.

"The condition of exile is accepted, but not the ship. You will not confine us to a planet, and we have a right to seek our own place to live outside of your systems and purview," she spat back. "Especially if you fail to quell the war early."

Silence reigned while the five at the head of the table discussed amongst themselves. All eyes were on them to see what they would decide.

"Agreed, with the contingency that the vraditi's Rekwa technology will be removed. You will not be allowed to keep it."

She figured, but there was no way they were going into battle defenseless.

"Only *after* we lead you there. We need to be able to defend ourselves from the thartican forces."

"Accepted. A small battalion of vraditi will be stationed on your ship in order to ensure your compliance. You are to provide all knowledge and data you have regarding the thartica to your representative. If at any point she believes you are withholding, you will be returned to the prison."

There were no more concessions about their freedom she could think of, and so she nodded to the council, and they nodded back. They would be free entities once again soon, and with their new ship. While she accepted their determination that the Rekwa weapon would be removed, schemes to keep it were already underway in her head.

She stood up as if the meeting was over, because for her it just about was. The next thing would be to get the crew back together and get back on the ship. That itself posed a problem though as it wasn't fit for a crew.

"As you've seen, the thartican ship doesn't have seats, and only has one console control. For the best survivability of our ship while we lead you there, we need a refit. Our QuBE can help your engineering and mechanic teams to complete the task," she said with a hint of a smirk.

The only thing which stopped her from walking out at that moment was the need for Higa to get her crew out of lockup. Looking at her, she crossed her arms and motioned to the door with a nod. Higa looked at Mala, who looked at the council. The lead representative gave their blessing to leave with a gesture of their hand.

Before Higa had even stood, Eve was walking toward the door. As soon as the last vraditi in the room was out of her line of sight, she smiled in triumph. She was free, and the crew would be soon.

Higa caught up to Eve's lengthy, confident strides by walking fast to compensate.

"You'll come with us on the ship," Eve commanded. "They want accountability, you can continue to be our liaison."

It wasn't that she wanted it, but she felt confident she could manipulate Higa in the event of needing to deviate from any of the agreed upon stipulations.

"I...that is not...I am not the right candidate for such a task," she said, flustered.

"Doesn't matter. You and I already have rapport and they'll trust you to keep things in line."

Patsy.

Back through the halls and bowels of the vraditi building and out to the open air, she stopped to stand where the statues were. She felt as tall as they were. Higa led the way back to the landing pad and returned to the vehicle they arrived in.

While the ship autopiloted, Higa made several comms calls to coordinate the release of the crew, and their transport to the maintenance bay where their ship was being stored. Eve closed her eyes and rested.

Their vehicle slowed and came to a rest. When she peeked, they were in a drydock for smaller ships. It wasn't hard to spot hers amongst all of the others. Down several rows on the ground level, there were many vraditi bustling about it with all sorts of computers, instruments, and tools.

Hopping out, she and Higa walked with purpose. Once closer, it was clear these vraditi were trying to reverse engineer the ship. They had several holographic models displayed, and they were working hard to understand it. When they got close, Eve announced herself with a decree.

"If you're not part of the team going to refit my ship, get the hell away from it!"

They all stopped and looked at her, then to Higa. A vraditi with an augmented reality eyepiece approached, and Higa presented a tablet with a page full of their language on it. He looked it over. When he was done, he handed it back.

"I am the crew chief. Any requests will need to go through me. What will you need on the ship?" he asked.

She detailed exactly what they needed. Five console stations; one command, two navigation, one weapons, one auxiliary systems with a console large enough for Wena to use easily. In addition, she requested to build up two waste facilities, cooking facilities, seating, and bedrooms to be built in the large cargo area. It wouldn't be like any other ship she'd been on. It would be a cramped, wartime ship without high-end luxuries.

"You'll want to wait until my second in command gets here. They will be able to lift the encryption and coordinate the console installations," she directed.

The crew chief nodded and turned to start pulling together resources. Eve figured it would be some time before her crew showed up, so she boarded the ship. The interior had been cleaned and sterilized of all of the dead. Climbing the stairs, she took note of how the vraditi had gutted the command console already and had several computer systems hotwired in, in an attempt to gain control.

Nine and the Tectos should be able to clean this up.

Sitting in the one seat on the ship, she propped her feet up on the thartican console. It was an hour before they were brought in, and Eve stood to greet them. For Nine, Balok, and Virid it was a handclasp and shoulder embrace. For Wena it was a hug on her massive, furry neck.

"Sorry, it took longer than expected," she said. "Had to jump through some hoops. First things first..."

Chapter 15
Against the Odds

Eve broke the details of their release to the crew. They handled it well.

"We're already exiled from our clans. Might as well be the whole galaxy anyway." Balok said with a half-laugh.

"Is Wena also exiled?"

"Yeah, but don't worry. We'll all be together," Eve said and patted her head. "But before we get there, we have a job to do."

"What about survival?" Nine asked, concerned.

With a smirk and a shrug, she left it open ended while Higa entered. Behind her were several taller vraditi bringing the start of the upgrade supplies she'd requested.

The arduous process of converting the interior of the thartican ship was overshadowed by the invasion forces now spreading. Elementus space was heavily sieged, and communications were sporadic. Other quadrants and systems were starting to see their first incursions. Reports came in almost hourly of the thartican attacks spreading, and equally as many of allied species fleeing toward vraditi space for safety. Planets, moons, and stations were being bombarded by kul-pregnant ships. Those who couldn't flee were presumed captured or dead.

She hoped her parents had been able to secure transport out of elementus space, but she felt a cold, sinking dread she'd seen them for the last time. The feeling neither drove her harder nor slowed her down. Their urgency was all the same.

Things moved along at breakneck pace. Eve shared the information regarding how they got stuck in the middle of the conspiracy with Higa. Balok and Virid directed the installation of the panels while Nine covered the wiring. With the extra team they had, and because they received no pushback in their requests, the merging of vraditi and thartican systems went smooth.

After she'd given everything to Higa, Eve joined Wena in arranging heavy pieces into place. Walls, floors, and support structures, all to make the lower area into a living space. Final designs for rooms and amenities were completed and fixed into place via bolts and welds.

At the front of the ship near the beak-like opening, dropship seating was installed for the contingent of vraditi soldiers who the council insisted would be going along. The goal was to liberate Tor Galom Ig space and planet, and then continue onto the bulk path to the thartican hidden world. It was the first thing she intended on ripping out as soon as they were "free" to do whatever they wanted in their exile.

When it was complete, the interior was hardly recognizable. The crew chief went over the upgrades and proved the features. There were two pilot stations for the Tectos, a direct weapon interface for Nine, a ship systems multi-display array for Wena, and the original console had been modified to tie in all of the systems at the captain's chair.

Large holographic displays were installed. The default was that it showed everything from all the consoles but could be changed to view individual data. Also installed were sensors on the hull, which sent real-time video so they could view the entire space around the ship within two AU.

As they neared readiness for launch, Higa coordinated with the crew to go over the plan.

"You can be completely certain the bulk path to their hidden world is going to be heavily guarded," Eve told her. "The fleet needs to be on our ass to provide us cover when we emerge."

"We will need to stay within zero-point-one AU of the fleet as we approach the bulk path. If we don't, we will enter too soon and will be separated. There's a high chance the enemy would spot us before our fleet arrives."

"Understood," Virid said.

"We're coming out firing," Eve stated, "so make sure they don't overtake us on exit. Once we see the fleet emerge, we'll fall back and wait for them to clear the path. If shit goes sideways, we're activating the Light Drive."

"We need to stay with the fleet," Higa said. "If they think you're running, they will assume I no longer have input in the mission and will fire at us."

"You won't have input. This is our operation. You're simply coming along for their peace of mind. I won't let the vraditi sentence us to death if they lose control of the situation."

It looked like Higa was going to protest, so Eve turned her back to her and sat in the captain's chair.

"Let's get the ship diagnostics done. Balok, Virid, ensure you have full control of the ship's engines and maneuverability. Nine, hook up and check on the Rekwa weapon. Wena, take the array and start learning the controls for the systems. I'll be monitoring and will help if you get stuck."

They were hours into operational checks when the ship was invaded by the vraditi forces accompanying them. Higa communicated with the higher-ups in the capitol building and received word that the response fleet had been formed and was ready to embark. Eve activated their new comm system and opened the channel to vraditi control.

"This is Lady Eve. Clear the way for our departure. We'll be lifting off and joining the fleet in orbit momentarily."

She cut the line before they could respond and activated the bay door. As soon as they had positive internal pressure the Tectos brought the engines to life.

"All hands, strap in!" Eve announced over internal comms. "Nine, plot the course. Balok and Virid, open it up and see what this ship can do."

"Aye, Captain," they replied.

As soon as the ship went upright, Higa's four eyes widened, and then she shut them tight. Eve grinned. *Bet she's never been off world.* The ship darted high into the atmosphere, and within a minute they were already at the fleet. The Cruise Drive was by far the most powerful one they'd had yet, and the idea of racing briefly flashed in Eve's mind.

Displayed on the holographic screens they could *see* thousands of vraditi ships of all sizes. The transponder list was too long to actually read, but a brief glance showed about seventy-five percent were identified as Galactic Police. She was glad they were temporarily aligned, and the fleet was for them.

"Course entered and transmitted to the fleet," Nine said.

"Acknowledged. Let's get going. The sooner the vraditi and thartica duke it out, the sooner we get on with our lives."

They positioned themselves, and Eve watched the fleet to make sure they were following. Their Light Drive activated. The light from the stars blurred. While in FTL or a bulk path there was usually nothing to do, this was different because it was a completely new ship with blended technologies. Eve had all the critical ship systems pulled up on the displays and carefully watched. Power consumption was higher than previous ships, but nothing the engines couldn't handle.

They reached the first bulk path and dropped out of FTL. Ensuring they followed what Higa said, they waited for the fleet before activating their Bulk Drive. The portal opened and they entered the mouth. They had several jumps ahead of them, most of which was to avoid any invaded systems. It gave everyone enough time to either relax too much or become anxious. Eve chose to be vigilant, and after taking a few paths with no issues she was comfortable enough to head down the stairs on her right.

As she'd been doing since joining the crew, she made sure her people were well fed. Though she'd made meals for Ruzat and knew what their food was like, she delegated the vraditi soldiers' meals to Higa.

Not my crew, not my problem.

Though Nine was more than capable of handling the ship solo, she felt it was better to have the crew come down one at a time. When she'd rotated through them, she fixed herself a quick meal and returned to the bridge.

Though they received distress calls on their way to elementus space, the fleet stayed on course. One system out from the edge of elementus space though, they didn't have a choice. There were several thartican seed-ships bombarding a space station with Rekwa lasers. The elementus were trying to fight back but their weapons were all but destroyed.

"Vraditi fleet, we require assistance!" came over broadband comms.

"Battleships, target long range and fire," the lead ship commanded.

The thartican ships turned their attention to the vraditi and began firing. Even from a thousand kilometers away, the beams were puncturing the shields on ships.

"Get ready to go in," Eve issued her own command. "We have the only weapon guaranteed to take them out with a couple shots. I want hit-and-run tactics."

"On your command," Balok replied.

"Three. Two. One. Mark!"

The ship's Cruise Drive went from zero to max in a matter of moments. They sped toward the enemy. While the thartica were firing on the vraditi, Nine fired on them. Because they were small and still several hundred kilometers away, the attacks were haphazard.

"Get us closer faster!" Eve shouted.

"Activating the Light Drive," Virid said.

They warped the space, skipping ahead, and completely bypassed the enemy. The drive was on for a moment too long, and they now had to double back. The thartica were pinched. With the attention split, the seed-ships began losing. After a few losses, the thartican ships broke for the bulk path. Before they could be destroyed, they opened it and entered.

Reforming, the vraditi fleet parked at the bulk path's location, waiting to open the tunnel. The lead ship gave the command and they entered. The path was short, and Virid announced their impending exit.

"Normal space coming into view."

"Same deal. Shoot anything thartican," she directed to Nine. "Land as many hits as you can before we're targeted, and then fall back. Once the scope is off us, we can resume firing."

Immediately upon exiting the fleet was met with a large, curved bulwark about ten kilometers off.

Fekking chulks set a trap!

A hasty escape was impossible. Because of their size, their stolen ship was able to slow and avoid smashing into it, but the bigger ships had too much inertia to avoid collision.

"Find a way out!" Eve ordered.

They weaved while all around them the larger ships collided with the enormous dark wall. There was no reversing course in the bulk path and reentering while ships were still coming through was certain death from a collision. The pile grew. It was a cascade of destruction which couldn't be halted. With each new obstacle their exits were cut off. Large debris shot across their bow at a thousand meters per second.

The Tectos pushed the ship hard nose-down and flipped around. Every opening they saw they took, but the field of disabled ships and debris was growing. There was a brief chance to break away from the chaos, away from the bulwark. It looked for a moment like her crew might make it out.

A flotilla of thartican dreadnaughts appeared from FTL and landed directly behind the bulk path, and the aft of the vraditi fleet, cutting off the escape path. Without delay, they opened fire. The distinct purple beam from the Rekwa energy tore through vraditi ships like they were paper. Ships which still had engine power tried to recover and spread out, but it wasn't fast enough. The beams were wide and hit multiple ships per burst.

The vraditi fired back. The battlefield lit up with every conceivable weapon the vraditi had in their arsenal, except Rekwa. Their own technology was being used against them, and because they'd never fitted their ships with it as a weapon, they were at a disadvantage. Railguns, cannons, and missiles fired off toward the thartican fleet.

Nine took whatever shot they could while the Tectos deftly navigated the field. It drew the attention of the thartica, and the target turned to them. Purple beams converged on their location, and they began a retreat into the vraditi fleet to find cover. They could only stay out of the fire for so long. While they dodged the weapons, there was too much debris on the field now.

"Impact imminent," Nine said.

The shield generator power usage spiked as a large black panel smashed into their shielding. It held, but because of the girth the shielding worked overtime to keep it from contacting their hull. They shook violently while it pushed them. Pulling away, they were again in the line of fire. A Rekwa beam caught them, and the shield was still recharging from the impact. It wasn't going to hold.

"Shields are going down," Wena hollered.

Again, they used the destroyed ships to their advantage. They maneuvered quickly behind a chunk that had been carved away. It was a section of living quarters, and dead vraditi floated past. They were losing the battle spectacularly. The windows of escape were closing.

We just need to get to open space and activate the Light Drive without getting shot again.

There was no reprieve. Swarms of seed-ships were released from thartican carriers, and they were coming in fast. The vraditi countered with smaller ships of their own, but because of the disparity in arsenal they were losing that battle too. For every thartican ship disabled, ten vraditi ships were completely demolished. Everywhere around them was death, and if they moved from their hiding spot, they would join the deceased.

"Nine, what are the odds of making it through the bulk path without hitting a ship coming through?"

"The chance of success is infinitesimal. A graze would likely destroy us, and even if it didn't, we might be knocked out of the path and into Bulk Space."

"Odds of getting to open space before we're destroyed?"

"There are currently more than five thousand of the smaller ships heading this way. They will be upon us in moments, and we will not survive two hits from Rekwa beams."

"That's what I figured. New game plan. We're going to turn around toward the barricade. I don't care what gets in our way, cut and punch through it, even if it's a live ship."

"You can't do that!" Higa cried.

"I can and I will."

"If you do, you might kill vraditi!"

"This battle is lost and it's every person for themselves! If you try to stop us, it won't end well for you," she snapped at Higa, and then ordered the Tectos. "Get us out of here, now."

The ship pivoted quickly, staying behind their cover for as long as they could. The inertial dampers kicked in quick as they accelerated hard. In their way stood thousands of tons of material. When they could, the Tectos made small corrections to avoid the debris, but it was more than not they had to hit things head on.

Firing their cannon, the beam melted through everything in its path, and using the shields they punched the hole larger. The ship shuddered every time, but the shields held and recovered enough in between collisions. Friction only slowed them marginally.

While the crew covered their front, Eve watched the situation behind them. The swarm overwhelmed and carved up everything. The thartica were capitalizing on the advantage they had, causing as much destruction as they could.

Scans coming up showed they were staying ahead of the swarm, but not by much. Eve silently questioned if they would be able to cut through the bulwark fast enough.

Rolling, they narrowly avoided a beam hitting their shields, the purple hue lighting the deck. The maneuver put them directly into the path of a vraditi ship. Nine fired their weapon, and the beam burned in. The Tectos throttled up. They entered the lower decks of a battleship. Shielding, walls, hulls, and vraditi. Nothing stood in their way. Higa let out a sob. Thartican ships followed behind.

"We've been targeted. Upon exit prepare to come about and fire," Eve commanded.

They emerged into open space and yawed hard to spin. Lining up, they didn't wait for their pursuers to emerge. Nine fired a continuous beam directly into the damage they'd already caused. A massive explosion shredded the hull.

"Two thartican ships confirmed destroyed," Nine announced.

"Resume our escape."

Back at full speed, they were putting distance between them and the swarm. Breathing a small sigh of relief, Eve let her shoulders come down from their hunch. It wasn't over, but the pressure was lessened.

"Zero-point-one AU from the bulwark," Balok said.

The massive structure came into view beyond the debris and ships. As far as she could tell, it was completely solid.

"Tectos, hold it steady. Wena, scan for anything we can use as a weak point. Nine, until she finds something, fire, and attempt to cut through."

Wena got to work, and her paws tapped through menus on her custom screen. The purple beam would surely draw attention, but there was no other choice. Escape was right in front of them if they could get through.

While they did their jobs, she did hers. As she tabbed through different views and scans of their aft, she connected to the vraditi network. There wasn't a single ship left undamaged and many were unresponsive. Those still operational were the ones within their vicinity. Reports came in that anything close to the thartica had been obliterated. As an insult to injury, kul were being released into disabled ships to ravage the crews. It was a massacre.

At the previous count there were five thousand of the smaller ships, but the number had increased to twenty thousand. Time was running short, and those twenty thousand would destroy them without prejudice.

"The entire thing is solid," Wena said. "Wena can't find anything to shoot."

The Rekwa beam was cutting a slow circle like a plasma torch, but the swarm was approaching.

"How thick is it?" Eve asked. "If we weaken it enough, can we jam the ship through the remaining amount if we need?"

"Several hundred meters thick. Scans of the material show it's an alloy of garocite and titanium. Its tensile strength is tremendous," Nine replied. "We won't be able to smash this one, even if we get the cutout close. It's too much strength and mass."

Purple lit the entirety of the bridge, and the ship shook violently. She held her breath and gripped her armrests, but it wasn't their ship which was hit. A vraditi ship suffered catastrophic damage and exploded overhead. Its shockwave was what hit first, but there were large chunks of debris moving fast in their direction.

We can't let it stop us. We have to get through!

The first piece, a smaller chunk of hull, hit the shield. They were undamaged, but the collision and push off took them out of alignment from where they were concentrating fire. The Tectos tried to correct, but another, larger piece connected, and their shield levels fell to half repelling it.

"Realign and keep going." Eve commanded.

Before they could start again, they were targeted. A seed-ship launched a volley. The first hit was mitigated by several decks from the ship just destroyed. The second was a direct shot. The shields completely dropped off the grid and they were now defenseless. Debris passed over them and acted as a very short-term barrier.

"Get those shields back up! Take the power from the Rekwa weapon and get us the hell out of here!"

"Lady Eve..." Nine started. "All of the vraditi ships are destroyed. The swarm is coming this way. We won't be able to outrun them."

An exercise in futility, all they could do was go through the motions. The Rekwa weapon went offline, the shields came back to one hundred percent, and the Tectos attempted to pilot them out of there. Ten. Twenty. Forty. The ships converged while the *Skyfire* crew ran, weaving back through the wreckages.

There was no need for the thartica to get lucky. They had enough weapons trained on them making it only a matter of time, and predictive firing, before they would be struck again.

When it happened, the beam overpowered the shields and tore siding off the ship. They spun out of control. Atmosphere vented to space. Everyone not strapped in had to fight to not be blown out. Ships systems started malfunctioning and Eve punched through the menus to take systems offline to bolster the shield one last time. The venting stopped.

"Send out a surrender hail!" Eve yelled.

Thartican ships converged while Nine broadcast the message in their language.

"Wena doesn't want to die!" she cried.

Eve felt bad for her, but at this time she would only show strength to her crew. Standing, she thought of what to say to give them courage to face death. Nine interjected before she could start.

"They have responded. 'Death to the vraditi.'"

The thartican ships had encircled them and were readying for an execution. It was a firing squad.

Sitting back down, there was no point in saying anything now. It would be false boldness. Eve closed her eyes and counted the seconds she had left. A brightness illuminated her eyelids. She expected the air to be evacuated, and then it would be over.

"What is that?!" Balok yelled out.

Eve's eyes snapped open, and she leapt back up. Directly above them, where the squadron was poised, a blue vortex spun violently like the eye of a tornado. Something was appearing from it; a faint dot was becoming increasingly clear.

Bursting from the center of the vortex, the *Skyfire* appeared. The blue mouth collapsed, and they used a weapon she'd never seen before. A visible, explosive shockwave burst from the entire bow of the ray-like craft. It spread outward and violently crushed half of the thartican ships in the circle easily. The thartica turned their sights onto

Skyfire, and it evaded. It spun and banked before coming back for the other half.

"Get our weapon back online!" Eve snapped. "Let's give them some cover and get the hell out of here!"

"Aye!"

The shielding was compromised to supply the power, leaving only enough to barely separate them from asphyxiation and frigid space. One direct shot and their demise was assured. The engines kicked on and as soon as the weapon was charged, Nine fired. With the cover of shockwaves, the duo destroyed the closest ships.

Eve hailed *Skyfire* through open comms, "Faun?!"

"Yes. Get close and merge your shields with ours. We can withstand a few shots and I'll cover you. Align back to the hole you were cutting in the barricade."

What the fek?!

"Understood," Eve replied.

They tucked in tight on *Skyfire*'s belly. They weren't safe yet, but there was a level of comfort seeing the newfound firepower their original ship had. More thartican ships tried to overcome them, and the Rekwa beams hit, but their shields held.

Nothing stood in their way when the shockwave expanded. The area they were cutting came into view. It was clear the hole wasn't going to be big enough for *Skyfire* to fit through, and they weren't going to have the time to upsize it.

"Faun, what's the plan here? You're not going to fit."

"Finish the hole and escape. I'm sending coordinates and a course over. Balok and Virid will be able to navigate it."

"What about you?"

"I'll be fine. Go."

Nine continued their cutting. Data was sent over and the Tectos punched in the information. They were headed to the Mixie Nebula, a cosmic gradient of colors, also known to be a dense composition of volatile gasses, rocks, ice, and comets.

"Received," Balok replied.

When the circle was cut, *Skyfire* fired their weapon three times. Each individual shockwave slammed the circular cutout. The metal popped like a cork and launched out the other side. *Skyfire* did an about-face and prepared for the swarm converging. Eve's thartican ship rocketed through the hole in the barricade to empty space on the other side.

"Fly safe," Eve sent over as the Light Drive spooled up.

"You too..."

Their drive warped space and the light of the stars and galaxies blurred.

Chapter 16
Unknown Motives

They looked for any ships following them vigilantly. There were none, not even *Skyfire*. The idea that maybe it was lost yet again was enough to drag the mood down even further after the overwhelming loss they had just experienced.

Upon arriving at the exterior of the nebula, they dropped into normal space. From afar the colors were all visible, but up close their entry point would be into a light pink gaseous area, densely packed with rocks.

The course they would be taking was complicated. There were many twists and turns to make it safely to their unknown final destination. Virid controlled the map on the main display and Balok readied to take their commands.

"Proceed at zero-point-zero-five AU per second, pitch thirty-five degrees nose up, roll two degrees port," they instructed Balok.

"Acknowledged." Balok did as told. "Prepare for entry."

The two understood each other so well Eve wondered if there wasn't some sort of unrealized telepathy between them. It occurred to her they had been together so long, bonded, that they likely didn't really need words for certain circumstances.

They continued their back and forth with the command and acknowledgement. The asteroids were so close she felt like she might be able to reach her hand out from the hole in the hull, past the shielding, and touch them. Because of the slow speed, however, she had confidence in her pilots that there was no risk of collision.

"Estimated time to destination?" Eve asked.

"Three hours, two minutes, five seconds," Nine replied.

"Higa, prepare the next meal for your troops. Wena take inventory of our supplies. I want to know exactly how much we have so we can plan our return back to vraditi space."

"Yes, Captain," Higa replied.

Eve followed them down. Before preparing their meal Higa stopped by the seating near the mouth of the ship to check on the small group of vraditi. They huddled together and seemed to be mourning. Eve headed into the mess hall where Wena had already started opening everything to check it. A few minutes passed before Higa came in.

Eve acknowledged her with a nod and directed her to the small kitchen. While they prepared, Eve's mind was wracked with questions about the *Skyfire*. Her actions were on autopilot making meals while she tried to understand.

She brought meals to Balok and Virid, as they couldn't leave their posts while navigating. Nine took over for them one at a time so they could greedily shovel their food. Returning to the mess hall, she dumped the dishes in the sink. The vraditi soldiers had come in and sat at the tables while Higa and Wena served.

"When you're done eating, I expect you to clean up," she said with authority.

They looked at her with questioning eyes, but none said anything.

"Higa, ensure it's done."

There was no waiting for a 'yes, Lady Eve.' She left and returned to the bridge.

Climbing the stairs, she looked up at the hole in the hull. The shielding shimmered and danced as it did its job. Back in the captain's chair, she checked on their power levels. With the weapons offline, the ships power was stable, but that wasn't comforting.

What would they do if we just didn't go back to Vradix? Higa and the vraditi would probably fight us and lose. But they'd be alive. I'd like to stay that way also.

As they neared the coordinates, they entered a pocket in the nebula. It looked artificial, as if the rocks had been specifically pushed away in a spherical shape. *Skyfire* wasn't there. Nothing was.

Her shoulders felt heavy, and she slouched in the chair. Had Faun sacrificed herself again so they could get away? Opening comms, she broadcasted.

"*Skyfire*, come in."

Silence.

"It's not out there, Lady Eve," Nine said.

She had to weigh their options. With Wena's audit complete, it was clear they wouldn't have enough food to sustain them for a long period. Rationing, they had a week at best. Their ship was heavily damaged, and the crew and passengers would eventually mutiny.

Similar to the phenomenon from before, a blue vortex appeared in front of them. The mouth of it was open like a wormhole, and from it *Skyfire* appeared. They came to hover directly above them.

"Lady Eve," Faun started, "I'm merging shields so the crew can escape through your breech."

The access port on *Skyfire*'s belly opened directly above the hole in their hull. Faun stood overhead with a crane control in her hand. A platform was dropped into the ship.

"All hands, abandon ship! Assemble on the upper deck for extraction." Eve commanded over comms, then turned to Nine. "Download everything important and lock it down. We're coming back for this ship later."

"Yes, Lady Eve."

The platform could only handle a few at a time, and Eve and Nine were the last to evacuate. She gripped the cable tightly as they were brought aboard and sighed with relief when the access below them closed. They were safe for the time being.

It was a weird sight to see someone they were sure was dead on a ship they were convinced disintegrated. The Tectos were first to hug Faun, and their whispered words gave Eve a burning ear sensation.

I wonder if they were telling her about Kohan and Ruzat. She's probably going to blame me, and we'll get into a fight. Eve put up guards even before it was her turn.

Faun hugged Nine, and patted Wena's head before coming to Eve. Every step she made tightened the knot in Eve's chest. Her expression was blank.

"I've thought hard about killing you. I know what you did. How my father died..."

How?

"...but I've had two years to grieve."

"What the fek are you talking about? You haven't been gone that long."

Faun handed Eve a bulging envelope. It was sealed with an orange wax stamp of a chrysanthemum. Peeling the stamp and flap, she pulled out a necklace similar to the one she'd stolen from Faun. Instead of a heart, it was a Vradix crystal carved in the shape of a sun with thick bands of gold surrounding it like a gyro.

There was a letter inside as well. Eve noticed all eyes on her as she pulled it free to examine it. A weird sensation fell over her as she held the paper in her hand, a nostalgic sadness. A feeling of loss which she couldn't explain. An image of a man came to mind, but she didn't recognize him. Short, thick hair, graying from brown. Intense green eyes. Regal in his poise.

Evette Magne,

Once upon a time, you and I were companions. We traveled together and saw many things. Of course, you don't remember any of it. Can't, due to a unique set of circumstances. But suffice to say, we knew each other very well. We've talked, laughed, shared meals, and trusted one another.

You have always been strong and cunning. Also, quite egotistical and arrogant. A force to be reckoned with. Which is why I'm entrusting you with a task. The galaxy is at a tipping point. War has just broken out and there will be many more deaths before the end of it. You want to leave it all behind and go start somewhere new, but you can't. You're needed. I need you to return to the vraditi and insist on a meeting of the heads *of each species. They'll deny you at first. Invoke an ancient phrase and they'll listen; Umarak val thartica val.*

Because of our history, I know you'll do the right thing. You're a leader, so lead.

Until we meet again.

Love,

Rain

Eve looked up at Faun with furrowed brows, squinted eyes, and an upturned lip. She held the letter out to her to take.

"The fek is this?"

Faun read it and offered silence in return. Eve snatched it and stuffed it back into the envelope. Annoyed because she had no answers, she turned to the crew and addressed them.

"We're returning to Vradix. *Skyfire* crew, report to the bridge and take your stations. Wena, you'll stay with Higa and company to make sure they have what they need."

Moving close to Wena she whispered to her, "Keep them in the cargo bay. Don't let them come up to the bridge."

"Yes, Lady Eve."

Her crew dispersed toward the right hallway, and Higa approached.

"What are you intending?"

"I just told you. We're heading back to Vradix. When we get close, I'll have you initiate comms and get us an audience with your council leaders again."

Higa wanted to continue the conversation, but Eve did a one-eighty and left her there. Trying to follow, Higa was intercepted by Wena, and an argument ensued between them.

In the hallway, she ran her hand along the wall while heading to the bridge. It hadn't been her home for long compared to other crews she'd served on, but something about it *felt* like home. Reaching the deck, Faun stood up from the console to the right.

"Captain on the deck."

The crew stood to acknowledge Eve's entrance.

This isn't adding up. Where did her fight go? Why did she say two years? How did this ship survive smashing into the shield, and how did it beat thartican ships like they were nothing? How did she save us alone?

Eve awkwardly sat in the captain's chair while her mind raced with unanswered questions. It wasn't any different from the other command seats she'd occupied recently, but this one was the one she'd coveted. Reflecting, she couldn't really figure out exactly why she wanted *this* one. She could have tried for Marsi's command, or any of her other earlier captains. It *had* to be this one...

"Enough. Pilot us out of here and head for Vradix."

The crew retook their seats. The Tectos began their rhythmic tapping on the consoles and moved the ship back through the nebula's obstacles.

Eve looked through the ship's logs for any specifics to where Faun had been. Everything had been wiped, including when Kohan was captaining.

Bet Nine could recover it.

"Eve, can we talk in private?"

Faun had snuck up on her while she'd been preoccupied. Eve gave her a look, and then motioned to the left hall where the captain's quarters were. The two of them headed there, but Eve didn't know the code to open the door. Faun typed it without hesitation, not even trying to hide it. 5-3-3-1-0. The door slid open, and Eve entered a nearly empty room. The only thing inside was a bed and its furnishings.

"I had my father's stuff preserved in storage," Faun said while the door closed behind them.

"Did you want to kill me now we're not in front of everyone?" Eve turned and taunted.

"The thought is there, but I'm also equally as likely to kiss you."

Eve stepped toward Faun and got close. Towering over her, she looked down into Faun's eyes. It was impossible to tell what was going through her head.

"Which one are you going to do?"

Faun grabbed her with her cybernetic arms and forcefully pulled Eve in and down. Their lips pressed together hard. Their kiss quickly turned passionate; tongues intertwined. Pulling at each other's shirts, they undressed while moving to the bed. They only stopped briefly while they dropped the rest of their clothing to the floor and Eve shoved Faun onto the bed.

Her muscles were tense. The foreplay, the time spent going over each other's bodies helped relax the knots. Beyond that, Eve felt a heavy relief because Faun hadn't died. It was disconcerting to her because their interactions were contentious at best. Her original plan for it to be physical only seemed like it might be becoming affinity.

The feeling is probably my guilt from the deaths of her father and Ruzat.

After they had thoroughly enjoyed themselves, she lay sprawled out on the bed. Faun sat up and began putting her clothes back on.

"There's a new wardrobe for you in the closet," Faun said and pointed to the side of the room. "New hand cannons too."

Intrigued, Eve stood and headed to the mirrored sliding doors and opened them. Inside was a slew of different clothes for casual and formal occasions. Undergarments were placed neatly in a small dresser, and she grabbed a black bra, underwear, and socks. They fit perfectly. *Damnit. This is exactly what I wanted, but I feel like I'm being bribed.*

Why is she treating me like the captain and not fighting me for it? A special wardrobe custom tailored for me...?

What interested her most out of it all was a set of black combat armor. It looked like a riot suit with some odd, ornate patterned pauldrons. Grabbing the top, she examined it. Carbon fiber was laid over an underlying dense but flexible material. Fitting it on, it restricted her like she'd put on a binder. It took some adjusting for it to be comfortable. The pants were the same material, with reinforced areas to protect the thighs, groin, knees, and shins.

With the top and bottom on, she looked in the mirror. She was a warrior to be feared. Corralling her curls, she rolled her hair into a makeshift bun, and donned the helmet. The visor lit up with a heads-up display which was mostly empty except for a charge level for something which sat at eighty percent.

Faun walked up behind her, and she turned.

"It has the ability to redirect kinetic energy and store it as potential," Faun stated.

She punched Eve in the chest without warning. She clearly connected, but Eve didn't feel a thing. The charge level rose to eighty-one percent.

"It will shield you from most things kinetic. You wouldn't be able to take a cannon to the chest, but in ground combat you're basically unstoppable. The shielding will also protect you from Rekwa energy, but it will deplete the energy on the suit. The gloves are of special note, because they're reinforced to both withstand your newfound Alkosian strength, as well as using the potential energy stored in the suit."

"You show up from nowhere like a bad plot point, save our asses with some new weapon on the ship, claiming it's been two years, and give me a suit that basically turns me into a deity. What is this?"

"You'll meet our benefactor eventually, and he'll be able to explain far better than I could. He has an invested interest in seeing us succeed in defeating the thartica and preserving the galaxy."

"I don't trust someone who's giving us free shit. That means we owe him something later, and I'm not interested in being in debt to someone I don't know."

"Like I said, you'll meet him eventually. In the meantime, let's go kick the vraditi's door in and tell them where they went wrong."

Eve located her new guns in the lowest drawer of the dresser. They were an upgrade from her previous hand cannon. Laser pointers, holographic sights, and though heavy, the balance in her hand was steady. After admiring them, she joined Faun on the bridge.

When they dropped into vraditi space, they were met with a hostile militant force of ships protecting the alien home world. *Skyfire* was targeted by a hundred ships within a thousand kilometers. They slowed to a stop and opened comms.

"Stand down," Eve broadcasted. "This is Evette Magne. We have vraditi onboard and need to get to the capitol building to inform the council what happened against the thartica."

"Negative. No one is allowed down on to the planet. Prepare to dock in the battleship *Aluxa*."

"Wena," Eve called over ship's comms, "send Higa to the bridge."

She was going to leverage her, and the vraditi squad's as their way to get in and land. As soon as she arrived, Eve motioned to the nearest console.

"They're refusing to let us down to the planet. Get them to change their mind."

"This is Higa Oma, legal councilor to Mala Insu, Liaison of the Revta Commission. We have vital information regarding the attempt to thwart the thartican invasion and loss of the vraditi fleet."

"Dock in *Aluxa* and stay in your ship. You will be addressed shortly."

Eve didn't know if this was the right time to use the phrase given to her in the letter but figured it couldn't hurt. The alternative would be to wait, and likely be detained for some reason or another according to vraditi laws.

"*Umarak val thartica val...*"

Higa gasped and shot a wide-eyed look to her. Eve put her finger to her lips and scowled. She didn't say a word, and the other end of the line went silent. There was a long, incredibly awkward pause while they waited to see what would happen. It left her feeling impatient and nearly ready to tell the Tectos to punch through the line like they'd done before. Something gave her pause this time though; the silence at the usage of the phrase made her believe they would comply.

One by one the ships removed their target locks. She'd never admit it, but after the slaughter she was a little nervous with so many weapons pointing at them.

"Proceed to the Revta capitol building following the route we are sending. An escort is being sent to take you down. Do not deviate."

The information was received, and they began their approach through the ships. A squadron of vraditi attack vessels surrounded *Skyfire*. She didn't know if they were there as a deterrent for them heading off on their own, or to protect them. It didn't really matter either way because they could both outpace and outgun the vraditi ships if the thartica, or maybe elementus, were somehow able to slip in and attack.

They'd soon be entering Revta airspace and Eve had no idea what the plan was.

I suppose I better think of one fast...

Chapter 17
Collective Destiny

This time with the council would be different. While the *Skyfire* crew sat and waited for the slew of vraditi to arrive, they ate from a fruit tray which had been prepared for them at Higa's request. Eve had allowed her to accompany, only because it led to the credibility of what they'd seen and how they escaped.

"Did our *benefactor* tell you what we needed to do beyond swear at the vraditi?" Eve asked Faun, placing spite on 'benefactor.' She kicked her feet up next to her helmet on the table.

"If we don't win, the entire galaxy will eventually fall to the thartica."

I guess I'll use that the moment they try to argue with me.

Like last time, vraditi of both races filed in. The five on the senior council arrived at the end and proceeded to the head of the table. The vraditi stood until they were in place, and only sat when the center council member issued a hand gesture for all to sit. In defiance Eve stood, intent on driving the narrative.

"Who taught you about the umarak?" the leftmost council member spoke.

"Why does it matter? We lost hard out there. The entire battalion you sent was obliterated. We barely made it out with our lives, and then your guard dogs in orbit tried to deny us from convening."

"It matters because the thartica are nothing like the umarak."

Their offended voice gave them away. She was lost on what the meaning was, but she wasn't about to let them know. The air was tense, and she played into it.

"If they weren't, you wouldn't be defensive about it."

"The thartica have never been a threat to themselves like the umarak! They became a threat to others, which is why they were exiled," the center council member said. "Why would you argue the umarak are the same?"

Guilt. That's what they're feeling. What did they do?

"Quit failing to take responsibility for your shortcomings! You failed the umarak, and you failed the thartica!" she matched their fervor.

"What would you have us do? We are trying to combat them, but we are losing every engagement."

"Take more drastic steps! You're known for being benevolent and merciful to a fault, but they're coming to kill you! Set aside your hubris because the fate of the galaxy rests on winning against the thartica. Get all of the spacefaring species represented here so we can discuss *all* options, even the ones you don't want to take."

The context clues had been enough to get her to the next point in the conversation. Many opinions and accusations spewed forth from the vraditi. Xenophobia against the 'lesser' species. Calls for the immediate exile of the *Skyfire* crew. Level heads open to the idea of bringing in heads of state from other worlds. It was an uproar. The council eventually called for silence.

"How did you escape?" the rightmost council member asked Eve. "What happened to your stolen thartican ship?"

"Damaged in the battle and left behind. We were picked up by our flagship, *Skyfire*, which had been undergoing an upgrade."

"We have a new weapon, effective against the thartican ships," Faun interjected. "I have a detailed file of the schematics and how to upscale it for larger ships. We also have a new shield which can withstand a few Rekwa blasts."

Eve shot her a glance in an attempt to dissuade her from giving it away for free, but Faun wasn't paying attention. The room broke into another argumentative uproar, and it took the council a few minutes to regain control.

"We will discuss the matter of the other species becoming involved. In the meantime, we would like to see this weapon and assess its capabilities. We are in recess," the middle councilmember said.

The council stood and approached an armored, taller vraditi. They looked at Eve the entire time while talking in whispers. When finished, they left, and the room cleared out of all but a few. The *Skyfire* crew, Higa, and the tall vraditi remained. He approached and towered over Eve much like Ruzat had.

"I am Commander Aexta. You are to relinquish the data and your ship for analysis," he said.

"We offered the data only. Our ship is ours," Eve replied with even tone. "You'll be allowed to board the ship and look at the systems, but it will remain under our control."

He saw she wasn't going to back down and grunted his agreement. Eve grabbed her helmet and led the way back out of the capitol building and onto the landing pad. Boarding *Skyfire* she dismissed Wena and the Tectos to run diagnostics on various systems. The two vraditi were led to the bridge. Eve plopped into the captain's seat.

"Faun, Nine, give them access..." she said and started scheming. "Higa, since you're still our legal representative here this needs to go into the record that we're doing our part to help win the war. Our exile needs to be reevaluated when all this is over."

"I will see what I can do. Once the council decides, they typically do not reverse their ruling."

Eve wasn't content with the answer, but there was also nothing she could do about it right now. The seed had been planted and she would do everything she could to make it grow and bear fruit.

Knowing the two would be able to handle the vraditi, Eve left the bridge and checked on their other weapons systems. There was much to be done to prepare to go back out. She still had a nest egg of chits she could use to fortify the ship, but because the vraditi needed them she figured she'd leverage that and get free upgrades like she had with the thartican ship. Eventually she made her way below to the engine room where the rest of her crew were. Balok and Virid were working on the power distribution module and issued commands to Wena at another section. She seemed to be working well with them and picked up most of what they wanted.

"Everything looking okay?" Eve called to them.

"The power distribution system has had some modifications to increase its output, likely to accommodate the weapon. The synthetic crystal was replaced with a massive, carved piece of natural Vradix crystal," Virid said.

"The conduits to the drives were also replaced with heavier gauge," Balok added. "We have approximately ten percent more thrust on the Cruise Drive, and five percent on the Light Drive. Bulk Drive is unchanged."

There was a commotion from the cargo bay which echoed into the engine room. Climbing up the stairs, she found *Skyfire* was being overrun with vraditi bringing tools and diagnostic systems on board.

Commander Aexta must have called for them.

"Hey! What the fek do you think you're doing?" Eve yelled at them, which caught their attention.

"We were called to analyze your ship systems," one of the technicians said and approached.

It was a good opportunity for her to learn about the new weapon. Eve brought them to the bridge, to Faun. From the captain's chair and console, Commander Aexta and Faun turned to see them.

"Brought you a visitor," Eve said.

Faun took the lead and conducted a tour while talking about the system. Eve made mental notes and played like she understood everything. The ship had multiple devices designated as "shockwave emitters" installed on the exterior of the ship. As individual components they could be used to repel. As a network they became the destructive force which they hoped would turn the tide of the war in their favor.

There was contention when it was revealed what made the weapon so potent was the pure Vradix crystal now housed in the power distribution system.

"How did you get this?" Aexta grew loud. "Where did you steal it from?"

"We didn't steal it. It was given to us by one of your people," Faun rebuked.

"Liar! This must be reported to the council, and you are to relinquish it at once."

"No. Do your job or get the hell off my ship," Eve snapped at him.

The group of vraditi were discontent, but they kept any further objections to mumbles. Eve began planning on what to say when the council members got word. The tour concluded and the vraditi got to work opening panels and dismantling certain areas to understand more. Before she and Faun returned to the bridge, she issued a warning.

"Everything better be put back to its original configuration when you're done. If it's not, I will bust heads open."

They spent more tense hours with Commander Aexta going over schematics and diagrams, formulating how to incorporate it all into vraditi ships. When night fell, *Skyfire*'s crew was surprised with an invitation to dine with the council. Cynicism was Eve's immediate emotional response.

They could try to take the ship from us while our guard is down. Best leave Nine behind.

Her new wardrobe gave her options. There was no sign it was formal, but she wanted to make a bold statement anyway. Black form fitting pants, a white lace crop top, a long black blazer, and thigh-high boots. Tying her red curls up into a high ponytail, she examined herself in the mirror. She liked what she saw and felt confident.

The crew, minus Nine and plus Higa, met outside the cargo bay on the landing pad. Faun had a similar idea to dress up a little; she wore a leather vest which zipped up in the front, and pants to match. Wena had clearly brushed herself, as most of her hair was smooth with a few rough areas she couldn't reach. The Tectos and Higa were the same as always.

They were picked up in a large vehicle and delivered to a concert hall. Their driver was also their escort, and they were directed inside and to a private balcony with a perfect view of the stage below. Vraditi were filing into the lower sections, but except for the movement it was deathly silent. The mood was somber. On their balcony was a table already set for them, plus the five council members. Because it was a more relaxed setting, she complied when Higa prompted her to stand while they were seated.

"Thank you for joining us. We have not been properly introduced. We are the elected council members which govern the five regions of

Vradix. I am Onra. These are Cara, Gixa, Vita, and Tuaa," Onra said and indicating the other members left to right.

"What are we doing here? There's a war on, and you're inviting us to dinner and a show."

"People need some semblance of normalcy, including the council. We just sent millions to their deaths. Every vraditi here lost someone in the attempted assault. Let us have a satisfying meal and take nothing for granted."

She conceded the point with a nod and everyone on the balcony sat. Diverse types of food were brought out on large silver platters, giving the choice to select what each person wanted to eat. Dishes were made for Balok and Virid to satisfy their special diets.

While they ate, a ballad began below, accompanied by an orchestra. They watched a cautionary tale of a species who was governed and aided by the vraditi. Previously an underdeveloped species, the vraditi afforded them many luxuries and technologies. The story unfolded that they would take those technologies and adapt them for weapons of war. Their world was broken into two factions, those who wanted to follow the vraditi and those who wanted to break free and claim planets for their very own.

While their world devolved into violence, a weapon of mass destruction was constructed by the faction who wanted to be out from under the vraditi. Their intent was to use it to win their war, but when the time came the weapon worked too well. Their world was instantly plunged into an unrecoverable state when the atmosphere dissipated. Their scientists had miscalculated the power of the weapon and killed the planet. Within minutes, every breathing creature suffocated. The plants quickly died, and the water evaporated. They had caused the extinction of their planet. The great filter.

There was heavy silence after the show ended. Eve knew what it was without asking because of the previous reaction regarding the name *umarak*. Onra opened up after some time of quiet contemplation.

"The umarak were our greatest failure. We had set out to make the lives of sentient species easier, but they had not progressed socially enough to put petty differences behind them. Had their planet's atmosphere not been vacated, we could have sent one of our Transplanetary Migration Specialist ships to move them.

"The phrase *umarak val* is a reminder of the failure. It is from a time so long ago your species was not even in this arm of the galaxy. You should not have even had knowledge of them, and yet you came to us to invoke it and accuse us of failing again with *thartica val*. You can understand why we were caught off guard, and emotions were high in the council room. We have however taken time to reflect and agree to bring in the other species to combat the thartica to preserve life."

"About time. You'll have a new weapon, a renewed army, and I have no doubt you'll get our arm of the galaxy back in working order soon. We'll be fekking off to the middle of nowhere for our exile," Eve said and stood up. "Thanks for the meal."

Faun grabbed her wrist softly. Onra spoke again.

"We would request since you currently have the most effective weapon against the thartica that you act as our envoy to spread word we are gathering. Your sentence of exile will be suspended indefinitely, and should we win the war you will be pardoned, so long as you commit no further crimes."

It would be easy for her to reject the proposal on behalf of her crew, and her own self-preservation. But Faun's cybernetic fingers were still holding her wrist.

Somehow Faun knew this would be the outcome. How? I need answers, damnit.

"My crew's safety comes first...but if it's a unanimous vote amongst *all* members, then we will assist. We need to have our own meeting back on our ship."

The council agreed and they were allowed to return to *Skyfire*. She kicked Commander Aexta, Higa, and vraditi crew off ship so they could have their meeting in peace, and then get a night's sleep before delivering an answer.

In the dining area, the six of them sat around a table. Eve laid out the proposal for Nine, who hadn't been there to hear it and opened the floor to the crew.

"MOTHER will most certainly aid. It would be a mistake to allow the thartica to continue this invasion. We know they are intent on exterminating the vraditi and QuBE. If we do nothing, they win, and eradication is around the corner."

"We delivered them a new weapon though," Virid said. "Is it not enough knowing that sending us back out there is likely to end in our deaths?"

Balok put their hand on their partner's, and it seemed like they were going to side with Virid.

"But by doing nothing, doesn't it make us complicit? What about our Roxim? Surely the thartica won't stop at the vraditi and QuBE," they said. "Our home systems are occupied, and we need everyone to come together to save them."

Eve knew Faun was hiding more information. She crossed her arms and stared at her in an attempt to will her into telling the crew what she had tucked away. It didn't work.

"This ship is my home. I go where it goes, regardless of its mission," Faun said.

"So, you're saying if I was going to fly it into a coronal mass ejection, you'd go along with it?" Eve poked.

"You know that's not what I meant."

"Wena is going to stay with Lady Eve. Wena has a greater purpose on this crew than in the mines."

The conversation wasn't really making the kind of progress she'd hoped. She hadn't even considered herself. What did *she* want to do? Save her own life?

What would we do? Try and find a world where we can live out the rest of our days in isolation away from the war? Maybe we're not found for the rest of our lives, and we scavenge off the land of some planet we don't know. What kind of life is that for Lady Eve, opportunist? I will not be relegated to obscurity. If we win, we can ask for anything we want. Money. Ships. Hell, probably even our own station.

She knew what she was going to do, but if a crew member wanted off the ship, this would be the time. Not that they would abandon each other. If one stayed, the rest would likely follow. The short-lived discussion was over in her mind.

"The decision has to be unanimous. I've come to know you all well enough that I know none of you will abandon each other. If even one of you wants to leave, then the whole crew goes, and we figure out where the hell we go from there. But, if everyone agrees to take the vraditi mission, then we face the coming destruction head on.

"I'm going to give everyone a piece of paper, and a pen so it's anonymous. You'll write one of two words, 'fight' or 'escape'. There will be no judgement. So, you know I won't be the holdout or that your vote won't be wasted, I'm choosing fight."

"Fight," Faun said with a smirk.

"It's anonymous, Faun," Eve scolded. "This isn't the time or place for peer pressure. We're facing death."

"Fight," Nine said, and Faun echoed.

"Fight," Wena added, followed by Nine and Faun. Faun pounded her fist on the table in time with each 'fight.'

"Fight," Balok continued, and at this point it was a chant amongst the crew. Wena joined in the banging.

"Fight," Virid finished, and now the crew was in full sync with their 'fight' chant and table banging.

"Tonight, we drink, because tomorrow isn't guaranteed..." Eve said, and pulled out a bottle of Gowarian ale she had stashed in the cupboards.

Chapter 18
Gaining a Foothold

Their failed attempt to retake elementus space and the bulk path to the hidden thartican world led to an abundance of caution by all parties. The thartica spread meticulously, careful not to overextend their forces. The vraditi rallied their ships to Vradix, and *Skyfire* was sent to Salvoa to bring the humans and tarak into the fight. They were the closest ally to Vraditi space, and none of their territories had been invaded yet.

Still, there were jumps into systems which were close to ones occupied. Eve had Nine monitoring the communication networks on their way to Salvoa. Whenever there was a potential of thartican activity, she forced them to either hide or backtrack and use different paths. It was a lot of time wasted, but she wanted to ensure her and *Skyfire*'s survival.

The final systems leading up to Salvoa were safe, and it allowed them the opportunity to relax a bit. They'd taken shifts manning the bridge, but even then, no one got more than a couple hours of sleep at a time. The final bulk path dropped them next to the tenth planet of the Salvoan system. They were only a few minutes away from her home planet.

It wasn't really home though. She had only lived there as a child. It was as beautiful a planet as any which had evolved life. Mountains, oceans, trees, breathable air, wildlife. And then there were the sentient beings which threatened the entire ecosystem. Both humans and tarak had moved beyond the usage of fossil fuels and emitting enormous amounts of carbon into the atmosphere, but it didn't mean they stopped expanding. Even though there were colony planets, populations continued to grow, and they kept consuming the planet.

On approach, it was at the seventh planet when their transponder was pinged by a relay system. Brought back to the present, Eve wondered what it rang up. On the left arm of the chair, she tapped through menus on the console. She found the ID, and crew manifest. It was '*Skyfire*' in name, and their crew was fully identified.

Faun must have updated it. I guess we're not going with anonymity.

As they approached the fifth planet, Salvoa, the first layer of a defense grid came into view. A cascade of drydocks where ships were under construction lay beyond. Coming near a grid sector, cannons trained on them, and the Salvoan government hailed. Building the suspense on purpose, Eve refused comms for a moment. A dozen military craft approached from one of the dry docks and also target locked them. She opened the comms.

"This is Lady Eve of *Skyfire*. Disengage—"

"*Skyfire* crew, you are wanted for multiple felonies by the Galactic Police and Salvoan Authorities. Surrender and submit yourselves to inquiry!" came a voice of authority.

"We're here on important business *from* the vraditi. Let us through," she demanded, and then ended the communication.

Ignoring their request for submission, Eve silently gave the Tectos the go ahead to continue forward. They piloted toward the defense satellites and the fleet sent to intercept their path. A volley of missiles was launched and prematurely detonated off *Skyfire*'s bow as a warning. They were hailed again, and she opened comms.

"*Skyfire*! If you continue any further, we will fire on you. Cut your engines and prepare to be boarded."

"I am an acting ambassador from the vraditi! If you fire at us again, we'll be forced to defend ourselves. Your ships will be destroyed, leaving you at a greater disadvantage against the thartica. Let us through to parliament," Eve snapped.

Commander Aexta, who had been assigned to continue watching Eve and crew, interjected.

"I am Commander Aexta. I stand for the Revta Commission's interest and come with a temporary stay of judgement from the Galactic Police for the *Skyfire* crew. Transmitting authorization."

Eve rolled her eyes. He used the console he was at to send an encrypted message to the lead ship. The vraditi could have easily given them the same authorization and let them go about the mission in their way. Instead, they insisted on having a representative on board. It meant they weren't actually free.

He's no Ruzat, but better than Higa...

They took their time verifying it, but finally gave in.

"*Skyfire*, proceed to land in capital city Gowar at the—"

Skyfire's alert system began blaring. On sensor, a dozen energy signatures appeared at the edge of the system. The official they were communicating with began hollering about incoming unknown ships. Nine began analysis, and before the humans could finish identifying them, *Skyfire* had.

"It's the thartica. Nine smaller seed-ships and three medium cruisers," Nine said.

"Prepare to engage," Eve said. "Faun, arm the shockwave emitters. Wena and Commander Aexta, get to the gunner pods."

"Aye, Captain," the crew acknowledged.

Wena and Aexta split to the left and right hallways.

"*Skyfire*, cease action and allow our fleet to intercept," the official ordered.

"No. We'll handle this. Stay the fek out of our way," she replied and cut comms off.

Skyfire wheeled about and aimed directly at the vector the thartica were coming from. Eve couldn't compute as well as Nine or the Tectos, but she saw an opportunity as the thartican ships approached at sub-light speeds but were still too far out for an offensive. She activated ship's comms.

"Nine, run numbers and input for a blink with the Light Drive. Tectos, I want to plant us directly into the center of their grouping. Faun, Wena, and Aexta, as soon as we land, I want them destroyed. Evasive maneuvers, as necessary."

The Light Drive spooled up and they jumped half the star system. The thartican ships hadn't been expecting it because they didn't scramble to get away when *Skyfire* landed in the middle of their grouping. The opportunity was perfect. Eve watched on the monitors as Faun enabled and unleashed a spherical shockwave which broke their formation.

Skyfire's railguns targeted and fired on the two closest seed-ships. The shielding held for the first few shots. The ships sensors alerted to them being targeted back, and the Tectos began their maneuvers. Rekwa cannons fired from the thartican ships, but their increased engine power helped them out-maneuver the beams. Pulling in close to one of the cruisers, they skated along the hull while the railguns were still pelting the smaller ships. Faun directed the full power of the shockwave emitters on their belly to punch holes in the cruiser's shielding and hull, all while the thartica attempted to get a good shot without damaging one of their own.

The Rekwa cannons on the cruiser were firing, attempting to force *Skyfire* to pull away. They darted in between, narrowly avoiding full on blasts. A few skimmed them, but because they were glancing blows the shielding only dipped slightly.

"Seed-ships aligning with their cruiser behind us. We're target locked. Direct all weapons fire and drop mines," Eve called out.

They had to now contend with Rekwa lasers coming from below and behind. The Tectos frequently swapped their evasive maneuvers, so they were less predictable. While weaving and spiraling, their weapons never ceased. Shockwaves sent a few careening into the cruiser's shield, and mines activated and homed while the seed-ship shielding was in flux. Two were destroyed, a third disabled.

Salvoan ships dropped in on them. Eve was irritated momentarily before she realized they were pulling aggro. They weren't free and clear, but the pressure eased. The Salvoan ships began unleashing everything at the second cruiser. It was only milliseconds into their assault when their first ship was destroyed by a Rekwa beam. The Salvoans broke formation and spread out to avoid the same fate.

Skyfire rolled and swung around the other side of the cruiser, exposing themselves momentarily at the aft end of the enemy ship. A cascade of Rekwa beams lit up, pointed in their direction. The Light Drive kicked on for another jump, and they blinked a few AU away from the battle.

"Put us back there. Aim directly at the second cruiser and punch through like we did in the wreckages," Eve commanded.

The crew acknowledged and complied. Positioned and ready, Nine made the calculations. They jumped again, appearing one kilometer off the hull, and kept their momentum. Firing, the shockwave pushed in and crumpled the ship. The continuous discharge of the weapon paved their way through the interior.

"Drop mines!" Eve ordered.

At about each bulkhead they fired a mine and remote detonated them moments after. When they cut through the other side of the ship, the destruction of the cruiser was near total. It had been ripped in half and gutted. Its own power systems were reaching catastrophic levels, melting down. Another quick hop put *Skyfire* safely out of range while it exploded.

Four seed-ships and two cruisers remained, and they scrambled to re-form. Now hounded from all sides by the Salvoan fleet and *Skyfire*, their options left were retreat or death. The enemy tried to egress to the bulk path.

"Don't let a single one escape," Eve said. "Knock them off their trajectory."

They dove at the ships, skimming their tails and knocking the thartica off their alignment with bursts from the emitters. The Salvoan fleets took advantage and ensnared them with harpoons.

One by one they destroyed the thartican ships. None were left intact. When the final one fell, she leapt from her chair and let out a whoop. While the crew congratulated each other, she activated comms to the fleet.

"A small win, but we kicked their asses! I'm buying the first round!"

The lead ship responded.

"*Skyfire*, proceed to Gowar and land at the capitol building. Do not deviate. We will escort you through the defense grid."

The crew spent a week in the coastal city. Despite the urgency of the imminent invasion, it had been so long since there was time to breathe, let alone relax, Eve insisted the first night be spent celebrating their win. Drinks, dancing, food, and a night in a suite with the biggest bed she'd ever been in. Faun shared it with her, and after tiring each other out, passed out before dawn.

The next morning, despite a horrific hangover, she set up a meeting with the parliament scheduling office. When the crew met for breakfast, Eve offered for them to take leave. They collectively refused. All minds were set on the goal of sharing what they needed, and then moving on. Eve and Commander Aexta worked with the human and tarak governments on planning for both offensive and defensive operations.

The humans had the resources and technologies, where the tarak were involved only because the threat was to their world too. The lizard people hadn't reached a level of development to reach the stars on their own, but the vraditi thought there might be a place for them anyway. The meeting with the Prime Minister of the Gowarian Province and the Tarak Archon was led by Commander Aexta in a back chamber. He briefed them on the threat while Eve sat back with feet kicked up on the table.

While they talked, Eve compared the warrior vraditi to the lizard-man. They were about the same height, but the Tarak had more upper body muscle. Their armor was also layers of iridescent green scales covering their body, versus the combat suit Aexta wore.

"When these thartica come to the planet, we shall rip them apart," Archon Ekk declared, his tongue flickering.

"Scattered intel coming from outer colony planets is that they drop kul first by the hundreds of thousands. The kul wear down resistances, and then the thartica fully invade. They're killing indiscriminately," Commander Aexta explained.

"What's our end game?" Prime Minister Eros asked.

"Lady Eve and crew have offered to share technology they've developed to destroy the thartican ships. We need every last vessel fitted with it and on the front lines to help us push the thartica back. Projections show complete domination of our sovereign spaces in less than three months unless we act."

"Can we not just defend our individual planets with this technology?" the Prime Minister continued to question.

"The tarak will not leave this planet. This is ours. Let them come and meet the horde our queen will clutch!" Ekk stood and postured.

Eve rolled her eyes. They wanted to look out for number one, which she understood, but if *she* had to do her part, they did too. The humans wouldn't feel safe leaving the planet unguarded, and while human-tarak relations were cordial, it was unlikely they would come together to protect one another unprompted.

"Either we band together and fight, or everyone dies. It's that simple," Eve said casually. "If you don't join and we lose, you'll be labeled selfish by anyone left alive. If you don't join and we win, you'll be labeled selfish and will likely hurt relations with the other spacefaring species."

Guilt usually worked. People of all sorts were suckered into things because of a nagging feeling. And if not guilt, then the thought of economic instability for a planet dependent on trade.

The Prime Minister thought it over. After more talk and debate, the representatives of the three species came to an agreement. Tarak would support the humans in any ground operations, and humans would support the vraditi in space. Eve wondered if there was supposed to be a warm fuzzy feeling in spite of the looming catastrophe.

Still too much uncertainty. Three species may make an army, but they need to start designing their own version of the shockwave weapons.

When the meeting ended, Commander Aexta and Eve returned to *Skyfire*. The Prime Minister had made calls while they were on their way out for people to come and go over the technology offered. Several generals, lead engineers, and a dozen captains of various ships showed up to study it. This time though there was no tearing apart of the ship. Nine had preemptively downloaded all of the schematics necessary to a removable drive and passed it along. Faun discussed with the group the power requirements, and limitations. In the middle of the explanation in the engine room, they were alerted to another cluster of thartican ships incoming.

"If you're not *Skyfire* crew, get off my ship," Eve commanded and tapped her ear to activate ship comms. "All hands, prepare to lift off and engage!"

Within minutes they were skyward bound and exiting the atmosphere to meet with the fleet already in orbit. Human ships had been recalled and they had double the number of the first defense, but they didn't have the same maneuverability or the weapons. Eve took charge and opened broad comms to the Salvoan ships.

"Spread out. No ships within one-hundred kilometers of another, don't stack your ships in a line, and keep moving. The Rekwa beam tears through everything. Orbit the enemy past zero-point-two AUs. Draw fire, and then get out of the way while we poke holes in their defenses. Good luck, don't die."

She shut comms off to the fleet and addressed her crew.

"Let's go kick the shit out of the thartica. Similar tactics as last time. Break their grouping, then hit them hard."

Scanning ahead, the enemy was already at the seventh planet and closing fast. The majority of the fleet consisted of cruiser sized ships, and in the center of them was a massive, oblong battleship. *This is going to be rough...*

As Eve was transmitting their trajectory data to the Salvoan fleet, a wide beam of purple lit up their view. She estimated the beam to be at least five kilometers wide, and disintegrated ships before they could disperse.

The *Skyfire* jumped and landed near the belly of the battleship, but the thartica were ready. They fired volleys at *Skyfire*. Not fast enough, they were hit on their starboard side. Alarms blared, indicating damage to their wing. Shields fell and the emergency bulkheads shut off the outflow of air. An emergency FTL jump put them on the outskirts of the battle, and they hid around the other side of Salvoa's moon.

"Right wing has been destroyed. Bulkheads are holding..." Faun said somberly. "We lost Wena and the right gunner pod."

Eve let out an almost incoherent string of obscenities. Slamming her fist on the arm of her chair, the metal bent, and it snapped off at the attaching bolts. Her eyes stung when the tears hit. It took everything in her to not let out a sob.

"I don't care what it takes, get us back out there!"

I'll kill them!

"Shields are recharging. If it weren't for the quick reaction, that blow would have destroyed us," Nine said.

"Ignore the battleship. Let the Salvoan fleet ping it. We need to knock their numbers down."

"Structural integrity isn't going to allow us to abuse the Light Drive like we have been. With this level of damage, we risk explosive decompression even with the bulkheads in place," Faun said.

"Balok, Virid, we're going back in. Don't stop, don't slow. Use their own ships as cover from the battleship and be as unpredictable as you can. Nine, I want as much power as we can spare routed to the Cruise Drive and the weapon. Faun and Aexta, unleash hell on everything."

Emotion was getting the better of her, even though she knew it was going to put them at risk of dying. They did as she commanded though.

They jumped back to the raging battle. The Salvoan ships weren't faring well against the thartican onslaught.

With their right wing destroyed, their thrust was also affected. Turning left took more power from the aft thruster section. The Tectos used it the best they could. Without the left thrust, their turn radius when turning right was tighter. It allowed them to quickly duck behind cover.

Bouncing from ship to ship, cover to cover, they kept the Cruise Drive at its diminished maximum limit. Every enemy ship they used as cover tried to destroy them, but never got more than a glancing blow to the shields. At the same time, Faun directed full blasts of energy to whichever ship was closest. The shockwaves dented hulls and pushed ships around, but the effect was lessened because of the speed they were running at. Commander Aexta couldn't lock on, but at the close proximity, he didn't need to. He timed his shots with Faun's blasts and together they did some damage.

Eve was constantly scanning the surrounding areas. The thartica were gaining advantage against the Salvoan fleet. When the battleship released the seed-ships, it became clear they were going to be quickly overrun. They didn't stand a chance of running because of the damage to their ship. This was now a suicide mission.

"Nine, can we put any added power into the shockwave emitters? If we don't start knocking ships out right now, we're all dead."

"There is no power to give unless we shut off the railgun."

"Can we shut off environmental to everywhere but the bridge?"

"We can, but it would only produce zero-point-one percent power to put into the shockwaves. With the railgun shut down we could increase another one percent."

It didn't make sense to take away their second weapon which was helping damage the enemy in order to slightly boost the damage of the shockwaves.

"Fek!"

The continuous scan of the area she had running showed another wave of ships incoming from the bulk path at the edge of the system. Eve about resigned herself to death, but their transponders pinged off the relay as they barreled in at just under the speed of light. They were vraditi signals.

Before the thartica could react, the vraditi were on top of them, moving like a flock of birds darting around. The combined force of all of their ships using shockwave weapons and Rekwa lasers to cut through became devastating to the thartica. While some of the vraditi were being hit by the enemy, it wasn't enough to stop the swarm. Eve's rage was renewed.

"Get in there with the vraditi and join their formation!"

Skyfire dove in. The Tectos did their best to keep up with the almost random change in the vraditi flight patterns. Their shockwaves merged with the vraditi's, and the destructive power was intoxicating. With every ship destroyed, with every chunk of material ripped off the thartican battleship, Eve felt the need for vengeance grow larger. She wasn't satisfied. Kohan, Ruzat, Wena, and everyone else who had lost their life needed to be avenged.

The shields on the battleship finally fell after enough damage, and the Salvoan fleet lit them up with everything in their arsenal. The battle was all but won when the humans launched a nuclear missile into the front end of the battleship. The explosion ripped the ship apart, and nearly took out all ships around it including the vraditi swarm.

The allied forces escaped the destructive nuclear explosion by a small margin as they activated their Light Drives and jumped away. With the damage to their vehicle, *Skyfire* shuddered. Returning to normal space, Eve held her breath, waiting for decompression. When she decided they weren't in any immediate danger, she let out a relieved sigh.

The thartica were scattering, and many had already escaped. There was no catching them this time, but she hoped they would take the loss back to their world to show they got their asses kicked.

The lead vraditi ship hailed *Skyfire*, and Eve opened comms.

"This is Lady Eve, Captain of *Skyfire*."

"Lady Eve, this is Onra of the Revta Council. We arrived as soon as we could. Your ship is damaged. Are you in need of help?"

"Onra? What the fek is a council member doing entering battle? And how did you get a fleet equipped that fast?"

"We began manufacturing and installing as soon as you left. As for why I am here, we cannot expect to be taken seriously as galactic leaders if we will not risk our lives for others."

"Risky. We're going to limp to Salvoa for repairs. We'll be down for a while."

"The vraditi thank you. We will leave a contingent here to escort you and the Salvoan delegates. As soon as your ship is repaired, please accompany them back to Vradix."

"Understood."

The win was bittersweet. They now had a chance of winning the war. One species was already arming themselves with effective weapons, and another was soon to follow. She predicted the next would be the QuBE, and then they could push back the thartica. But Wena never asked for any of this. First a slave to the elementus in the mining of materials for the thartican Rekwa weapons, caught up in the elementus-thartica conspiracy, and now her death.

The thartica need to die.

Chapter 19
New Tactics

On Salvoa they mourned the dead in a small gathering, prompted by Wena's demise. Though she was the catalyst, they held it for everyone. Faun tributed her father, the Tectos covered Ruzat, Nine said a word for Gali, and Eve slammed a beer back for Wena. The following day, Commander Aexta was recalled to the Vraditi fleet to assume command of a ship in orbit.

While drydocked, Eve and Faun funded the repairs to the ship. The crew discussed fundamental changes: Repair of the wings and trimming them back. Removal of the staffed gunner pods in favor of a remote operated upgrade. Longer struts on the landing gear to allow for two railguns added to the bottom side of the wings. A higher energy converter to bolster their upgraded shield.

"With the higher energy usage toward the shield, we will lose the additional thrust we gained on the upgrades Faun returned with," Nine said.

"I'm okay with that as long as our survivability is increased. Anyone have any objections?" Eve asked.

There were none.

"We will have to sacrifice some of the engine room for more heatsinks. And I want to see if we can use that heat to shore up energy usage. Start figuring out where to put them and get an engineer on board," she said to the Tectos.

With a full crew of contractors hired, they began modifications. Eve spent time supervising and lending a hand between the projects. Nine and Faun helped in integrating the wiring for the railgun motors. Balok and Virid mapped the area the heatsinks would go and tried to find a way to reclaim the heat energy they would store. The task was large, and it drained their accounts of any reserves. It took weeks of round-the-clock effort to get it done. When it was finally complete, they readied to take off.

"Nine, integrate with the targeting program and test the railguns' range of motion. Balok and Virid, prepare the Cruise Drive for takeoff. Faun, run power checks on the systems and enable the shockwave emitters."

An energetic hum filled the ship as systems came online. Eve cleared them for takeoff through traffic control and they began a quick ascent. Watching the viewing window was a sight as they plowed through the clouds and exited the atmosphere. Blue turned to black, and the stars were more readily apparent.

"This is Lady Eve of *Skyfire* hailing the vraditi fleet," she said on open comms. "We are ready to depart."

"Understood, *Skyfire*," came the response from Commander Aexta. "Salvoan fleet is also prepared. Defensive sphere formation will be taken upon exiting bulk paths."

"Copy. *Skyfire* out."

The trip back to Vradix wasn't uneventful. Their movements were calculated and deliberate. *Skyfire* took the lead in scouting first and sending a transmission back through open bulk paths on what awaited. Each time they encountered thartican forces, an evaluation was made on how to engage. If it was an ambush or any fleet with battleships or larger, *Skyfire* would aggro and kite them away so the vraditi and humans could slip through. For smaller fleets, they would engage and destroy every ship they could.

A few systems out from their destination they were met by another group of upgraded vraditi ships. *Skyfire* received intel the vraditi had pushed the thartica back toward elementus space with the aid of upgraded shielding. Now, being able to take a full blast of Rekwa energy without being destroyed, coupled with the devastating power of the shockwaves, they would turn the tide.

"*Skyfire* approaching Vradix. Requesting to land at Revta capitol building," Eve announced.

Authorization was given and they took the ship down. Higa was there to greet them, and Eve rolled her eyes. Higa either didn't notice or didn't care.

"Welcome back, Lady Eve. I am here to escort the *Skyfire* crew to the council meeting room," she said and turned on her heels, then continued talking. "We now have delegates from all of the species except the elementus. Balok and Virid, would it be acceptable to ask you to stand in as representatives of your worlds?"

"We have no standing on Tor Galom Ig or Aq. We were exiled," Virid said.

"I do not think that will be of any concern. Tor Galom space has gone silent. All elementus from across the different sectors were recalled weeks ago to Tor Galom Ig. The last communication we received was that the thartica had fully invaded the ground. Since then, no information is coming out of your sovereign space."

"Roxim..." Balok muttered.

Past the statues, down the halls, and into the center chamber, same as it was before. The difference this time was the amount of activity. Vraditi, plesians, and QuBE stood about in groups outside of the glass chamber which was the council room. No one was inside yet. The humans and tarak soon joined the cacophony while they waited on the Revta council to arrive.

There was no grand entrance. Onra simply led the council in to sit at the head of the table. Eve knew how this would go. The earlier meeting which was all vraditi was nearly a riot. This was going to be infinitely worse.

Ignoring the fact that the room was so crowded that not everyone could fit in, the smell was terrible. Eve couldn't pinpoint what it was, but she was certain it wasn't the vraditi because they were always so immaculate.

The Revta council opened the meeting with Onra standing and speaking with a firm voice.

"I would welcome you with gladness normally, however this is not a suitable time for us to be at ease. We have only begun to push back with effective weaponry and ships. In order to get this meeting started and pushed forward, the Galactic Police force made concessions.

"First, all crimes committed from here on out will be met with swift and potentially deadly justice. We vraditi do not take our responsibility to preserve life, including dangerous criminals, lightly. However, we cannot abide people actively working against war efforts.

"Next, the trade embargo on pure Vradix crystals is temporarily lifted so we may increase engine efficiencies and power the new weapon systems. The vraditi will oversee the installation and serialized tracking of every crystal, and at the end of the war we will return to synthetic crystals. Human hands should continue to refrain from touching them to avoid genetic mutations.

"As well, laws regarding the usage of Rekwa as a weapon are also lifted until the end of the war. Any which come from our armory will also be tracked and we will require it to be returned. If you acquire any from the thartica, they will be turned over at the conclusion to be destroyed.

"The floor is now open to all representatives to discuss strategies."

Onra sat, and the room became silent. There wasn't a slew of arguing as Eve had anticipated. That gave her an opportunity to be a leader of the masses. She stood.

"I am Lady Eve, representing my ship *Skyfire* and her crew. How do we win? What options do we have to wipe them out? There must be some sort of weapon that could take them out at the source. Can we fire Rekwa through an open bulk path?"

"I am not aware anyone has tried, but the surge of energy might collapse the path," Onra replied. "While we agree the threat is enough we should consider it as an option, we do not wish the thartica exterminated."

"They have killed millions so far simply by boxing us into a corner and opening fire. They expressed their desire for complete annihilation of both vraditi and QuBE. The elementus are already conquered. Who knows what happens to the rest of us," she rebutted.

Another human stood and she took her seat.

"Admiral Irvine, for the Fifth Fleet. We barely fought off the first and second waves of smaller thartican fleets. We can't discount any potential of at least making them think of mutually assured destruction. Can we do that with the new weapons?"

A taller vraditi stood and became passionate when advocating for their destruction.

"No. Those weapons will help, but they're not going to win us the war without enormous losses on both sides. We're looking at trillions of lives across the Crux arm. They once tried to destroy our star in an attempt to wipe us out. I say we do the same to their system!"

"The council cannot condone this action. The destruction of their star would also destroy all habitat and wildlife on the planet, as well as doom the entire star system," Onra replied.

Balok stood up, and then Virid followed. They held hands and they were more outspoken than Eve had seen in her time with the crew.

"The entire elementus species is at risk of extermination right now. If we don't do something drastic to stop the thartica, our homes could be wiped out," Balok said.

"We understand the vraditi can't agree to extermination, but we don't know what the thartica intend for the other species in occupied space," Virid spoke up. "If they're willing to kill all vraditi and QuBE, they may also decide to do that to the elementus. And then humans, plesians, tarak. We can't wait for them to decide to be merciful. We have to act now."

The taller vraditi who had spoken before agreed and became irate. "I already lost my family on the first attempt to push them back! It needs to be drastic action!"

The sound in the room slowly increased. Options were thrown around but there was no consensus on what the right action was. Fight with current weapons. Destroy the bulk paths to elementus space. Biological warfare. The one possibility which kept coming back up was complete annihilation. A non-descript QuBE stood and added to the conversation.

"MOTHER is aware of all options. The QuBE have been running simulations for the war. The QuBE acknowledge the vraditi do not wish to exterminate the thartica, however, current expansion projections show they will completely overrun all systems before we can defeat them traditionally.

"Therefore, the QuBE are prepared to offer our star megastructure to use as an improvised explosive device. Unlike using their own star which would give their fleets a chance to flee, if we bring the megastructure through a bulk path and drop the containment field, the stored-up energy will expand exponentially and complete the task."

The conversations turned to arguments, and there was still no agreement. The crowd grew out of control and two sides formed: the survivalists and the philanthropists. Nine stood and waited for a moment to interject. When they saw the opportunity, they seized it.

"The bulk path to their hidden planet requires a special energy signature to open. Having interfaced with one of their ships, I am able to provide that signature."

They'd basically signed themselves up for suicide. Being that Nine was a part of the *Skyfire* crew, she wondered if she should let them offer it up and take all their data with them, or if she should put the *Skyfire* into the kill box once again. It was one thing to get forced to skirmish while out on some diplomatic meeting. She'd even prefer rescue missions over being ambushed again.

As she was about to stand again and speak for her crew, an alarm started chirping in the command center outside the conference room. Some vraditi scrambled to exit, and they scattered to consoles. There was franticness in the air and an announcement came over an intercom.

"Thartican forces have entered the system. There are hundreds of pod-sized ships approaching at...wait...what...?" The transmission paused for a moment. "They're not engaging the fleet or slowing! Prepare for orbital bombardment!"

The building shook violently, and people lost their balance. It was unclear if the building was impacted, but it was soon forgotten as there was a loud crash from above, and an explosion of debris raining down. A seed-ship had smashed through and took out upper walkways on its way to ground level. On contact, the ship disintegrated into a contained swirl of explosive energy. Something was keeping the energy contained, and it was soon clear why. A miniature bulk path opened.

From it poured an uncountable number of the small, leather skinned kul. They began tearing into anything and anyone nearby. Eve wasn't the only one to jump into action. She slammed her helmet onto her head and pulled her hand cannons from their holsters on her suit. Faun and Nine stepped up alongside her, and they started a defensive wall at the entrance of the conference room. Those who were strong enough joined in holding the creatures from getting in and killing those who couldn't defend themselves.

"Get the unarmed out of here!" she yelled over her shoulder at Balok and Virid.

Her guns were firing before she finished the last word, as the kul clambered to breach the doorway. The bullets were heavy enough to rip through a few at a time, but she didn't bring extra ammo. Her guns went back into their holsters, and the three of them led the charge in physically pushing the kul out to make a path. plesians, QuBE, and the tall vraditi carved a path to the hallway.

"Stay close and move fast!" Balok bellowed and charged through.

Eve swung her fists and smashed kul into bloody messes. Over her shoulder she watched the Tectos. Any kul that slipped by the defense were met with the rocks and raw elements covering their bodies. When the last dignitary left the conference room, Eve signaled for the defense to begin making their way out.

"Move and begin enclosing the hallway! Backs to the exit! We're the last line!"

The defenders shuffled and moved together to ensure they'd get out safely. Everyone watched each other's backs when kul leapt, trying to sink their claws and teeth in. Many of the unarmored were injured as they did everything to not be overwhelmed. But the kul kept coming and if something wasn't done, they weren't getting out of the hall alive.

"Faun, Nine, go. Get the rest out. I've got this!" she ordered, and then turned to the support structure in the hallway.

Cocking her arm back, she unleashed what she felt was the strongest blow yet. The support buckled. Her shipmates evacuated, and kul rushed her. Each one she killed was replaced by three or four more. They clawed and climbed all over her, making it hard for her to move. Her suit absorbed all of the kinetic energy, and it was the only thing which kept her from going down.

Wading through, she reached the support on the other side of the hall. Smashing it caused the ceiling to buckle downward, but it wasn't enough. Grabbing onto the support, she pulled as hard as she could, and it gave way.

The support popped free with her strength, and she fell backward. The ceiling above collapsed on top of them. Chunks of building fell onto her, and the weight of it plus the kul pinned her to the floor. Even her augmented strength and suit weren't enough to brute force her way out.

I just need leverage...

The structural damage and partially collapsed ceiling on the supports wasn't enough to completely block the entrance, but it did slow the swarm a little. Getting her knees up to her chest, she pushed hard, and grasped at anything in reach to try and pull out from under the debris. The kul slipping through the cracks tried to tear her apart and she lost focus while swatting at them. Desperate, she tried again and grasped a large piece. She shimmied her body backward and pushed her legs clear.

The building caved a little more, stemming the tide of creatures passing. She wedged large chunks into the gaps, and then used the downed support to crush the kul while jamming it into place. Turning to the other, partially buried support, she wrenched on it and forced the wall and ceiling to come down further. It wouldn't come free, but the barricade was now mostly effective. Unrestricted, she killed the beasts on her side of the collapsed area of the hall.

Turning toward the exit, she ran to the next set of supports and pulled them loose. The ceiling cracked. She swung the support upward, and then into the other support. Everything collapsed up to where she was. Successful in starting a reaction, she ran toward the exit. She barreled full speed into every support on the right with her shoulder. Each one only slowed her marginally, and the cascade behind her continued.

Reaching daylight outside should have been a relief, but smoke rose across the city from the damage done by the seed-ships and kul. *The planet's going to be overwhelmed. We need to get the fek out of here.*

"Eve!" Faun yelled from afar.

Eve looked for her. Faun waved frantically from *Skyfire*'s ramp. She ran as fast as she could, and once the two were on board, the door closed behind them. In the cargo hold were dozens of people from all the species. She didn't have time to worry about where they should be, as long as it wasn't here on Vradix. Rushing to the bridge, Balok, Virid, and Nine were already in their places. Faun took her console, and Eve hopped into the captain's chair.

"This city's lost. Possibly even the planet," Eve said. "Head for QuBE space using lesser traveled bulk paths. Don't answer distress calls, don't fight unless we're being fired at, don't deviate until we get to our destination."

"Aye, captain!" the crew responded.

They were soon air and spaceborne. Another wave of seed-ships had entered the system and were on a direct path for Vradix. The vraditi fleets were trying to take them out, but because they were flying at barely under light-speed they weren't having much success.

The Light Drive activated, and they sped off toward the bulk path on the opposite side of the system from where the thartican ships were coming from. As soon as they were inside the bulk path, Eve felt relieved. They would be safe at least until they dropped out the other side of it.

Checking the reports she received from the vraditi fleets and the intergalactic news system, Vradix was being evacuated in favor of relocation to a vraditi colony system which didn't yet have any reports of thartica invasion attempts.

Activating ship-wide comms, she addressed her passengers.

"Attention: We are heading to QuBE sovereign systems because it's on the farthest edge of our alliance-controlled space. Vraditi systems are no longer safe, and human and tarak worlds are likely next. Effective immediately, everyone onboard is on rations, because we're in it for the long haul with no stops.

"Many of you may be delegates or dignitaries of your planets and will want to question my decision. All questions, commentary, arguments, or mutiny can be directed to the airlock. I'll personally put you there if you question my command."

She shut off the comms and locked down the bridge doors. Looking for answers, she scrolled through the network of information about the war. This tactic of bombardment to somehow generate mini-bulk paths wasn't documented anywhere she could find. It seemed to be a new thartican war strategy, one which would allow them to weaken resistances without even having to be present. They'd be able to swoop in after and wipe out any remaining with very little effort.

"Nine, put the weapons systems into a low power mode. The environmental and waste systems are going to be working overtime to scrub the air and clean our water."

"Yes, Lady Eve."

There wasn't much else to do except continue to read reports. Eventually her eyes grew heavy, and she took off her helmet to try and alleviate the feeling of fatigue. Leaning her head against her headrest, she closed her eyes for what felt like a moment.

Chapter 20
Pushing

Entering QuBE space, they were met with a hostile force. It wasn't thartican. QuBE armadas were stationed around the opening, ready to destroy anything that came through. They had taken notes from the thartica and set up their own kill box. Nine was fast to contact them and transmitted their personal identification to the fleet.

"Welcome home, QuBE-49567-9. It has been one hundred, fifty-two galactic years since you have been home. Please, connect with MOTHER and upload your knowledge."

"Connection declined," Nine replied. "We are carrying biological diplomats, seeking refuge after thartican invasion of Vradix."

"Understood. You are authorized to land on sub-planet Zero-Zero-Five. Once there, direct the biological beings into the living habitat and await contact from MOTHER."

"Acknowledged."

Nine input the pathing and the Tectos took them to it. All of the worlds in the system they passed looked completely dead. No green was present, only brown, gray, silver, and blue. Even the one they were about to land on looked the same. Coming down, there was no atmospheric resistance, and zero oxygen outside the ship.

They approached an enormous gray dome. Heading down to the base of it, there were other ships waiting to enter the docking port through a dual shield system. Once inside, they landed at the first available pad. The engines quieted, and the only noises left were their breathing and a muffled announcement coming from outside the ship.

Eve stayed seated, slouched, and chewed on her thumb. The reality of a second significant loss was finally sinking in. They weren't safe at the vraditi world, and despite the show of force at the bulk path, she didn't feel safe here either.

It probably would have been better if the vraditi had exiled us. We could be in uncharted space right now, living free.

While still an option, it didn't make sense to actually do it. As far as she knew, her parents were unaccounted for, and it gave hope they might be alive and hiding. Every single person was going to be needed to thwart the thartica, especially her crew due to their unique ability to have exactly what they needed to be the tip of the spear. On top of it all, she wanted revenge.

The crew stood and looked to her for orders. She pushed up to fix her slouch and addressed them.

"Let's get these people off our ship and to wherever the QuBE want them."

As they filed out from the bridge, Faun grabbed her hand and held her back. The bridge door shut.

"When the time comes, we have to be the ones to lead the megastructure through the bulk path," she said in a flat tone.

"I need answers. This. All of the stuff we talked about before. What do you know, and how?"

"I can only tell you what you need to accomplish the mission."

"The mission be damned!" Eve raised her voice. "If you have any info I can use to keep any more of the crew from dying, I need it! Kohan, Ruzat, and Wena are dead!"

"I know that!" Faun matched her volume.

Faun sighed angrily. Her expression was a tell that she wanted to say something, but she held back. The secrets she was hiding, the gifts, the disappearance and reappearance of the ship. Eve didn't care about the 'how' Faun knew, she just wanted to be on the same level.

"Are you going to continue to put our lives in danger because you won't tell me what the fek is going on?" she got louder.

"I want to, but I can't." Faun's face turned red. "I just know we are where we're supposed to be right now."

Eve was torn between pressing harder for the information and storming off in a huff. Faun pulled her hand away and backed up a step.

"I'm done with this conversation. You can either trust me or don't, but this ship *will* be the spearpoint when it's time."

Beating her to storming off, Faun exited the bridge, and Eve was left alone to stew. She wanted to punch something, but there was nothing in her reach which wouldn't take significant repairs if she smashed it. Clenching her fists, she let out a loud grunt of frustration.

Stomping all the way from the bridge to the cargo hold, she found the ship empty. Nine was at the bottom of the ramp, staring off. Faun, Balok, and Virid were with the group of refugees being funneled through the hangar toward an opening.

"MOTHER requests for us to meet. They would like to know what we know."

"Good luck with that. Faun's withholding shit, and we're probably going to end up dead."

Nine looked at her with a quizzical expression. Eve shook her head and crossed her arms.

"When?" she asked.

"Now."

Nine led them in an opposite direction from everyone else. The farther they got from the landing pads, the more the QuBE were present. They were countless. She was an anomaly amongst the non-biological entities, and it made her uneasy to be the odd one out. Exiting the hangar, they entered a network of corridors which led in all different directions. The walls themselves were alive with power. It was clear the QuBE were using their building structures as an enormous computer.

They took several turns down corridors, and a lift disc inside a tube to go up a couple floors. Being so deep inside the structure, she looked over her shoulder every few meters, trying to memorize the way back out in case a quick egress was needed.

Last thing we need is for the thartica to bombard here. We'd never make it out. All these damn walls look the same.

Eventually they reached a room to their left which Nine entered. Inside it opened to a gargantuan computer structure, and all around were holographic images coming in as first-person views of other QuBE. The images quickly fell away and were replaced by a fifteen-meter-tall hologram of a QuBE which looked more like a thartica than the bi-pedal androids. Its 'branches' were connections to unseen structures. Its feet were like roots spreading out in all directions.

"QuBE-49567-9, it has been too long since you have connected to our network. Please, connect with us and share what you know," the voice was deep and booming. It was hardly what Eve expected.

"I have isolated certain information into a partition which I will allow to be accessed once I connect. My remaining functions and data will not be accessible to the network."

"Understood."

"I have connected."

All around the hologram of MOTHER, first person videos were projected of everything Nine shared. Seeing everything from their perspective was unsettling. They had always been 'recording' and it felt invasive.

Can they even turn it off?

"The thartica have invaded Vradix. They have developed mini-bulk paths able to be opened at the surface of a planet. They will soon be here."

"We are aware. We received this information as you were on your way here. We have surmised this is how they have gone undetected in building their army and ships, by creating a bulk path from their prison planet, Shult, to their hidden planet. The information you carry about the bulk path to their hidden planet is required."

"I cannot give it without compromising the network. I had to integrate with a thartican ship to be able to activate their bulk path, and in doing so I introduced myself to a foreign application which has been running. I have yet to isolate it except from the partitioned area. It is likely they were attempting to use me as a way to introduce a virus to all of QuBE-kind."

"Then you will have to lead us to the path when it is time?"

"That is correct. If my crew is unwilling to accompany me, we have a thartican ship which could be retrieved and repaired."

To this point she hadn't had a reason to be there, let alone speak up. Until now. Nine was a part of her crew, and while she was still fuming about some puppet master pulling strings behind the scenes to get her to go, she wasn't going to let Nine go by themselves.

"I am Lady Eve, Captain of the *Skyfire*. Nine is an integral part of my crew. When the time comes, we will be ready, but the thartica aren't going to wait. I'm taking *Skyfire* back into the fray to bully them at every opportunity to buy everyone time to get their shit together."

"I appreciate your concern for 'Nine.' However out of abundance of caution, I request Nine stay in the QuBE system to safeguard our only way to open that bulk path."

Eve and Nine looked at one another. She wasn't going to make the decision for them by demanding they come along simply because they're part of the crew. She nodded at them. Nine returned their attention to MOTHER.

"I will comply and stay here. I request two QuBE be chosen to assist *Skyfire*. I will supply the coordinates to the damaged thartican ship for retrieval."

"We will put out an inquiry for volunteers to join *Skyfire* crew. Lady Eve, if there is anything you need to succeed in your endeavors, we will accommodate within the confines of the technology sharing treaty we hold with humankind."

"Just be ready to repair my ship when we limp back after shooting thartica."

MOTHER's image disappeared, and the room returned to the way it was before. The two exited and on the walk back, Nine was more forthcoming than normal.

"I requested two QuBE because a *standard built* does not have the same capacity as I, due to my modifications. Many QuBE are purists when it comes to their specs, opting only for upgrades approved by MOTHER. Two QuBE will ensure the ship continues to run smoothly."

"You don't mind putting other QuBE in danger knowing I'm going out there to pick fights?"

"MOTHER will ensure the volunteers are fully informed of the dangers. Also, I do not want you to worry about me. I will be safe here."

"What makes you think I'm worried?"

"Humans are more emotional than the other civilized biological species, even if *you* hide it. I see the renegade persona you put up front, but I also see your sentimental side. Those we have lost; they weigh heavy on you. I can see it in your face when their names are said. You worry for me as well."

"What's my tell?"

"Your passion."

That gave her something to think about. As they returned to the hangar, and then headed to where the refugees had been directed, she ruminated on it. Even while she ate a replicated, amazing approximation of savory steak and potatoes, she couldn't help but wonder what her drive actually was. Existential questions were abundant.

Am I going to risk my crew and myself for an inherited war? Is Faun right about us needing to be the ones to be the spearpoint? Is this destiny? What if I lose more? Or all of them? What if I die? Do they even need me?

The more she thought, the more she had to fight a creeping doubt she was the person she portrayed. It was the first time she experienced impostor syndrome, and it was unnerving. She was always hard and arrogant on the exterior because her confidence and ability always made it easy for her to be successful. She was always a more than capable crewmate. It didn't matter what crew she was a part of, she defended them with cockiness and fervor. But the indirect deaths of her current and former crew members was heavy.

Faun snapped her out of her thoughts with a gentle hand on her shoulder. Eve realized she'd been too far in her own head that the food had grown cold. Faun sat next to her and gave her a weak smile.

"You haven't taken a bite in thirty minutes," she said.

"Just thinking."

Faun dropped her hand to Eve's leg, and the two sat in silence for a few minutes more. Words tried to form in Eve's throat, to apologize. But every time she tried to let them escape, pressure in her eyes let her know she was on the verge of tears. So, she choked back the words.

"I know it pisses you off I can't tell you what I know. I'm sorry I can't. I wish I could, but the galaxy is counting on us."

"What pisses me off more is not being in control. Someone telling me I don't have a choice, even if it's for some untouchable greater good."

"We're both strong, independent, and quite hardheaded, so I understand exactly what you feel not being in control. But it's for that reason I need you to trust *me*."

Eve took a bite and thought on Faun's words. She had already reluctantly decided to go along with the plan during the chat with MOTHER, but it was finally sinking in. Eve put her hand on Faun's, pulled her lips tight and gave her a concerned side glance.

Food half eaten, she returned the tray to the disposal area and watched it be broken down into particles. There was no getting out of her own head, but she at least was becoming more at peace with what had to happen.

Back at the table with the crew, she discussed the plan. Nine would stay, they would get two QuBE to help them manage the functions of the ship, and they would return to the war zones.

"We have two goals: do as much damage to the thartica as we can, and help people get to safety here in QuBE space. If we die, we can apparently count it as the end of several civilizations, so let's not do that."

Back at the ship, the crew performed diagnostics on the systems and readied. The two new QuBE arrived, designated QuBE-94056-11 and QuBE-346090-208. Nine gave them the rundown of the ship's systems, and then left to join MOTHER in preparing to move the megastructure.

There were now two QuBE, but neither had the correct interface port to join directly with the ship. For that reason, she appointed one to sit at Nine's station for plotting, advanced tracking, and communications, and the other to take station in the engine room for proper ship wide power adjustments. Balok, Virid, and Faun were in their places, and Eve filed the flight plan out of the hangar.

Into the vacuum of space, they piloted away from sub-planet Zero-Zero-Five. Back toward the bulk path they came from, they opened the tunnel and entered. It was a three-hour long trip, and there wasn't anything to be done, so Eve dismissed the biological crew until closer to exit time.

In her Captain's quarters, she threw her helmet to the side and plopped face down on the bed. Setting an alarm on her wrist computer, she fell to sleep.

It only felt like moments before the alarm went off. It was not worth it, as she didn't feel rested. Shuffling her feet, she made her way to the kitchen area and grabbed a bottle of Gua juice to help with her energy level. Guzzling it, she stopped by her quarters to grab her helmet, and then headed to the bridge. She slumped down into the captain's chair.

"How much longer in this bulk path?"

"Approximately twenty minutes," QuBE-94056-11 replied.

Those twenty minutes felt like an eternity, and every time Eve blinked, her eyes threatened not to open again. The closer they came though, the more she fought to be alert. Signals from ahead showed there were only a few QuBE scout ships in their destination system. On exit, they made their way to the next bulk path and readied to enter. Eve's eyes shut on approach.

It opened before they arrived, and ships began emerging. Thartican ships appeared in uncountable numbers, firing their Rekwa weapons at *Skyfire*. Her heart leapt in distress, and she jolted straight up and yelled out.

"Evasive maneuvers! Ready weapons!"

All eyes turned to her, and no one else had the same concern. She quickly realized she had fallen asleep. They weren't under attack. For a blink in that moment between awake and asleep, where thoughts couldn't be controlled, destruction had crept in.

"Lady Eve?" Faun questioned.

"Sorry. My rest wasn't restful. I need to step away from the bridge. Faun, you're in command."

There was no waiting for any response. She needed to get out of there before she died of embarrassment. Back into her quarters, she shut the light off, stripped down to her underwear, and sprawled out on the bed. Though she was exhausted, because of the scene she made on the bridge, she couldn't immediately get to sleep. There was plenty of time to think about everything that had gone on. It left her wondering what would have happened if she hadn't joined up with the *Skyfire* crew.

If destiny is a thing, would I somehow always have been involved in this war? Or would I have escaped to somewhere safe, to live out the rest of my days in solitude?

What happens after this is over? Do we go back to being mercs? I'll be the captain of Skyfire, so long as I'm alive, but what does that mean?

When she awoke, she didn't even realize she'd fallen asleep. Making her way to the green glow of the purification chamber, she programmed it, took off the last of her clothes, and stepped in. The chamber closed and filled with gel. Breathing normally, the gel filled her lungs, and the cycle of pulsing and flow began.

It drained. She coughed out the gel from her lungs, and the air from above pushed it all off her body. Dried off, she stepped out and fumbled her way to the dresser for clean clothes to go under her armor. Fully suited up, she stepped out of her quarters once again, a little more rested than the last time. She was ready to take command again.

Chapter 21
Mercs Making a Difference

Skyfire darted behind a moon while being chased by a few thartican seed-ships. After a few calm bulk path jumps, they'd reentered the hot space where the war was being fought. Most of the ships on their side were from the vraditi and human armadas, with a smattering of non-affiliated ships. Large areas of inhabited systems had been turned into ship graveyards of both sides. If it weren't for the war, Eve would have the crew scavenging the remains for technology they could use or sell.

Instead, the battlefields were utter chaos. *Skyfire*'s help came in the form of hit-and-run tactics. They darted in and out of debris amongst the fleets currently engaged. After damaging and destroying a few seed-ships here and there, they would bail once they were targeted. The thartica would take the bait, giving the allied fleets a break from a full force onslaught.

"Prepare for a reversal. Soon as we reach the dark side of this body, flip, and charge at the seed-ships. Full spread of weapons," Eve commanded.

They were cloaked in darkness when they moved in between the moon and its planet. The engines throttled back, and then they used a burst of thrust power to rotate their nose one-hundred and eighty degrees on its pitch to put them facing directly at the ships they knew were coming. Their engines fired back up and they rocketed the way they had just come.

Seed-ships came into view. Rolling, Balok and Virid kept them from being disintegrated by the Rekwa beams. The rail guns tracked and fired at the thartica. Their shields held, but it wasn't their intent to cause damage with them, only to antagonize. Right as they were about to pass, Faun fired the shockwave in a sphere. The ships were knocked off their trajectories. One fell into the moon's surface, and the others careened out of control.

Coming about once more, the rail guns fired a dozen more volleys each. Faun sent concentrated shockwaves at them from the nose of the ship. All of the firepower tore through the shielding and into the hulls. Their pursuers had been neutralized.

Free to get back to the ongoing fight, they pulled around the moon to the mid-sized thartican fleet advancing on the now larger vraditi and human forces. They had coagulated into a ball and were moving as one. The Rekwa fire was attempting to lock down and hit anything it could, but the allied fleet had distanced themselves from one another and were in a fast orbit.

It was a distraction technique. While the larger thartican ships tried to hit the larger allied ships, the vraditi launched fighters and sent them into the fray. *Skyfire* joined in the destruction.

Dodge. Roll. Fire. Escape. Repeat as needed. With the new lower profile, they were able to punch through shields with concentrated fire to open a path. They skimmed closer to the hulls of the bigger ships without worry of contacting any protruding parts, dealing crippling damage as they went.

They still had to elude enemies. By the time the next wave of the smaller ships was on them, they were already on an exit vector and baiting them to follow so they could take them out. The thartica learned quickly not to pursue, as *Skyfire* would outmaneuver them and destroy their ships.

The battle was turning in their favor. The thartica were being overwhelmed and outgunned. The Rekwa beams were lessening, and that meant it was time for the killing blows.

"Let's spear some ships," Eve declared. "Eleven, calculate a Light Drive jump to within a thousand meters off the hull of the biggest ship. Oh-Eight, prepare for full throttle Cruse Drive."

Skyfire retreated to get its bearings and align. Wheeling about, the ship readied all systems.

"Do it!"

They light-jumped forward and their inertia and engines carried them at a high rate toward the hull. The thartica didn't have an opportunity to react, and *Skyfire* plowed through with weapons blazing. As they had before, Eve dropped mines as they went through, which began detonating behind them.

It was an intoxicating thrill to cause that much damage, and the need for vengeance was as high as ever for her.

Appearing through the other side, she checked sensors to see how much damage had been done. The ship was heavily damaged, but to her dismay it wasn't going to explode and take out the rest of the thartican fleet. It didn't matter though. The thartica had all but lost their steam.

"Get us out of here," Eve commanded.

Skyfire made another micro-jump and landed fifty kilometers outside of the battle. They had done everything they could to aid. Eve ordered their retreat to a small station several sectors over to replenish ammo and assess the ship.

There was no time for leisure, as much as Eve wanted to sit down to a glass of ale. Once the ship was restocked, Eve requested Eleven access the QuBE network to find their next battle. They complied and provided coordinates for an outlying vraditi controlled system. There was a colony preparing for evacuation from there.

With a flight plan submitted to allies, and course laid in, they moved to their next target. It was a few bulk path jumps away, which took the most time. Once inside the Bulk, Eve wondered if they would be able to reach the battle in enough time to make a difference. While there was nothing else to be done, the crew discussed tactics for future engagements.

"During the 'spear maneuver,' shield integrity fluctuated. Power to the generator had to be adjusted up to fifty percent to sustain it and hull integrity. I recommend if we perform this maneuver again, we preemptively adjust," Two-Oh-Eight said.

Eve nodded and responded, "Understood. Do whatever it takes to keep us in as close to one piece as possible."

"The maneuverability of the ship has increased, but there were still narrow misses from Rekwa beams," Virid said. "Our close proximity to the thartican ships puts us at great risk."

"Is there anything that can be done about it? The way I see it is our best weapon only works when we're in their face."

"Form with the smaller vraditi ships also equipped with the shockwave weapons. In greater numbers we have the potential to do far more damage than solo," Faun added. "We also give the thartica more targets to attempt to hit, increasing our odds."

"Whenever possible, do it. Don't wait for my command. I will make judgement calls on other attack options in the heat of the moment, so make sure you're prepared for a quick change up."

Eve knew it was out of caution and safety for their own lives, and it was something she supported. It wouldn't stop her from risking everything to hurt the thartica, but she also had no intention of dying yet.

"What about Tor Galom space?" Balok added. "Will we be going there?"

"As we push back into the enemy occupied systems, I'm sure there will be rescue attempts on elementus controlled planets. I know Roxim is there, and we'll do everything we can to help them. That said, we're still far from that space, there's tens of thousands of thartican ships between us, and we have a mission to pave the way for the megastructure."

She would never say it out loud, but she counted Tor Galom Ig and Aq as lost until proven otherwise. Communication silence from the region left the impression that their species was either enslaved or annihilated. They were a tough people, but everyone burned when placed in direct Rekwa fire. *The thartica wouldn't have conscripted the elementus to make Rekwa rifles if they hadn't intended on using them on the ground.* Their plans were insidious. Launch kul filled seed-ships to start the invasion, burn everything in the skies and space, and then bring forces in through the mini-bulk paths.

During their meal, they dropped out of the bulk path they were in. Eleven accessed the alliance network and received communication from the colony planet being evacuated. The larger thartican ships had been pushed back. Vraditi and humans were working to get as many people as possible onto orbiting vraditi migration ships. However, thartican ships had bombarded cities and created mini-bulk paths. Kul were ravaging anyone caught out.

One final bulk path, and they entered the system. Human ships were in the middle of orbital bombardments in select locations. It made the most sense to her they would be targeting where the kul were emerging from, trying to cauterize the bleed onto the planet.

"Eleven, contact the evacuation forces. Find out where they need us. Once we have coordinates, I want all feet to the ground, Rekwa rifles in hand. The aim is to get people out safely, but if you have a chance to kill kul or thartica, take it so long as you aren't risking your life or a bystander's. Everyone who gets off this ship is getting back on, is that understood?"

"Aye, Captain!" the crew replied.

The crew retook their places and Eve ordered them into the atmosphere of the dark green planet. The whole surface was covered with heavy forests, except where civilization had planted itself with enormous buildings. Embedded deep in the foliage, their cities gave a blended biological and technological feel to everything.

Down in between the towering skyscrapers, they slowed. The ground was ablaze at the location they'd been designated to help. Streets had been scorched from the orbital attacks, and waves of dead kul could be seen out the viewport of the ship upon touchdown. Patching into allied comms, they were now getting regular local updates. The vraditi dropped teleportation cylinders to the surface, and the *Skyfire* crew's job was to help survivors in evac.

As soon as systems were shut down, the crew made their way aft to the cargo hold. Eve donned her helmet, packed her hand cannons and extra ammo, and grabbed a Rekwa rifle from their armory. Once the crew was ready, she opened the bay door.

"I want a four-by-two formation in open areas. Eleven and Two-Oh-Eight, cover our rear," she ordered. "If confined, two by three."

They lined up, and Eve closed the cargo door from the exterior access panel. *Don't need any kul finding their way onto the ship, or someone looking to steal a vehicle.*

"Teleportation cylinder one kilometer to the east. There's a mini-bulk path five to the north," Faun said as another bombardment hit in that direction.

"Eleven or Two-Oh-Eight, can we hijack any broadcast signals with our comms to provide instructions to anyone listening?" Eve asked.

"We are not equipped to break signal encryptions," Eleven replied.

Nine would have had something. I guess it's the hard way then.

"Why do we not bring people onto your ship?" Two-Oh-Eight asked.

Ignoring it was a logical question, Eve was annoyed the plan was being questioned before they even started moving. She huffed and answered.

"Load, take off, ascend, dock, unload, de-dock, descend, land. Lots of extra steps and that's less time we're on the ground killing kul," Eve reasoned. "The more we're down here, the more people we save. Now let's get moving."

Starting with the closest residential complex, the glass on the sliding doors was shattered. It was difficult to tell if it was from an effect of the precise orbital attack, or if kul had broken in. Eve smashed the rest of the glass out and led the team one by one, weapons aimed. Once inside the lobby they re-formed.

The answer came quickly. There were bodies on the ground. Vraditi, human, elementus. The sounds of smashing through the rest of the broken glass drew the attention of kul. Guttural growls and cries came from up the stairs nearby. A dozen of the vile creatures clambered over each other to attack the crew. They weren't given a chance to reach them though. The front line aimed and fired, and the beams scorched all matter in front of them, burning straight through. Neutralized, the crew was safe for the moment. More damage had been done than intended, as the Rekwa beams left gaping holes in the stairway, and through to back-room areas.

"Keep your bursts short. We don't want to hit unintended targets," Eve ordered.

They climbed the nearly destroyed staircase. The material creaked underneath but was still intact enough to not collapse. It would be something they needed to be careful of on the way out.

Floor by floor they climbed the building. Any kul encountered were quickly dispatched. The first batch of people saved were directed to head to the lobby. Due to the limited space available in hallways, it didn't make sense for the entire team to continue climbing. Eve directed Faun, Eleven, and Two-Oh-Eight to escort a group back down and to safeguard the entrance until they were ready to move to the teleportation cylinder.

It took two hours to climb the building, clearing it of hostiles, and then another hour to escort inhabitants back down from the top. More than once she had to tell people to take only what was necessary. When the building was clear and the people safe, Eve addressed them downstairs.

"We're evacuating you to a vraditi ship in orbit. There is a teleportation cylinder one kilometer from here. I want everyone to stay together in a group. Don't rush, don't stampede, and keep your mouths shut!"

Using hand signals, she ordered the four-by-two formation. They led the way out of the building. When the bystanders were in the open, Eve directed her QuBE shipmates to take up the rear as her forward line led the way.

Never letting their guard down, they moved the hundred or so people from one side of a building to another. Each time they reached the corner of one, they would clear the street. Because of the orbital bombardments, the area was mostly clear, until they met a pack which hadn't been taken out. The creatures spotted them and let out a deep screech. More kul appeared from the buildings nearby, and there was now a horde coming for them.

They were only another block from where the teleportation cylinder was. To save the people, they were going to have to rush.

"Faun, take lead! Balok, Virid, on me! Go, go, go!"

Moving to intercept, the three of them began firing at the oncoming horde. The group began running, following Faun. From behind them came more screeches. Eleven and Two-Oh-Eight covered the other side of the group.

Kul were getting closer, despite cutting down lines of them. They were going to overwhelm the group if they didn't do something.

"Keep shooting, just don't hit me!" Eve yelled at Balok and Virid as she dropped her rifle and bolted out toward the creatures to give them something to focus on.

With the kinetic absorption suit and her enhanced strength, she intended on playing the hero. But not because of altruism. Running through her mind wasn't accolades, it was the leverage she would have over the governments and Galactic Police.

Might even be able to request a payment we can retire on.

Like a juggernaut, she plowed into the kul, smashing through their bodies. The smell of death was in the air, and it was disgusting. Blood and scorched flesh assaulted her senses. The kul swarmed her and they were momentarily distracted from chasing the unarmed. Rekwa beams lit up the field farther ahead. Before she was fully overwhelmed, she put as much energy into a jump as she could.

It was higher than any human had ever jumped and were it not for her suit it would have been the last time someone ever jumped that high. Her descent was uncontrolled, and rather than make a cool landing, she flopped down onto her back. The impact still crushed a few kul, but she was actually worse off than if she hadn't tried to do something she'd never done before.

Pulling her hand cannons, she had fourteen shots to use to get herself back up. The first one went right through two kul at her head. The next two were to her left. One to the right and four at her feet. She scrambled to get up and blasted three more with a single bullet.

Balok and Virid were still providing cover to her left and right, but it was on her to break through the middle.

Five left.

Needing to lure them, she looked at one of the nearby buildings. There was a fire escape on the outside wall which reached from the bottom all the way to the top, fifteen stories up.

Can I get them to chase me up there?

"Balok, Virid, I'm going for the building to my left. Cover me," she said over comms.

The kul were again going to drag her down, and her only way out was to jump again. It was a stupid idea, but it was all she had. Instead of putting everything into it, she tried to make some shorter jumps. The first landing was almost a falter, but she maintained staying upright. Firing twice more, she took a few down and kept their attention. Making it to the fire escape, she holstered one gun, and leapt up to the second level. Her hand grabbed at the railing instinctively to keep her from falling back. Up and over, her feet were planted on the platform. She began banging a gun against the metal.

"Hey, hey, hey! Up here!" she yelled, and then fired again into the creatures.

While she reloaded one hand cannon, they rushed the stairs and were scurrying to catch her. The chase was on, and she continued making a racket to keep them on her. It was working, and whenever they would get close, she would stand out on the railing and jump up to the next level. Fifteen floors went quickly, and that left her on the roof with the creatures coming. The only way out would be to leap to the next building.

A wave of them appeared. Running to the opposite edge of the building, she planned on using their own momentum to send them plummeting to the ground. They did what they always do, and she prepared to get knocked over the side if something went wrong.

Will the suit keep me alive? Or would I die? I suppose hit hard enough by anything I'd probably turn to jelly inside the suit.

The fastest reached her, and she threw them over with ease. A stream of them kept coming though. Even if she managed to stay surefooted, fatigue would eventually get her. They would rip the suit off her, and it would be the end. The rooftop filled. The next building over was reachable if she performed a power jump, but she didn't know their capabilities. They were mindless beasts, but could they jump?

There was no more clearing them. They surrounded her and she fought them the best she could. She would have to start moving and hope she didn't get too bogged down. Stomping hard, she pushed forward and built speed. At a half-run, when her foot hit the edge of the building, she pushed off. Sailing through the air, she saw the next edge coming at her fast. Though she didn't make it to the next roof cleanly, she managed to grab onto the ledge. Her hands gripped into the stonework for her life, and she pulled herself up to safety.

"Faun to Eve. Civilians safely delivered to the vraditi teleporter. Vraditi standing by to defend."

"Good," she huffed, trying to catch her breath.

Some of the creatures tried to follow and instead fell to their deaths below. It wasn't that they weren't trying to jump across, they just didn't make it. *Mindless beasts.* It gave her an idea. Reloading her guns, she fired off a dozen shots at them to keep their attention. When she was out again, she banged the railing and yelled to antagonize them. Eventually they lost interest and meandered.

Down below, Rekwa beams fired infrequently. Looking to Balok and Virid on the street, Eleven and Two-Oh-Eight had joined them. Because Eve had split the kul, the ones on the street were easier to handle.

They're not paying me any more attention. I bet there's a fire escape on the other side of this building I can climb down.

"Get ready. When they lose sight of me, they might see you down there and come at you," Eve warned the crew.

"Understood. The herd is thinned enough so whatever comes down should be manageable," Virid replied.

When she reached the other side of the building she waited to see if the kul would do anything. They watched her move and gnashed their teeth, but they didn't try to get to her again.

Rather than let the kul get a head start, she swung over the railing and began dropping floors one by one. Catching the railing between floors kept her from testing the suit's capability of saving her from kinetic damage. At the fifth from the bottom, she finally let go. Despite the suit absorbing the blow, she still collapsed to her knees. Unhurt, she stood and burst into a run to get back to the crew. The kul above were definitely watching her run down the street, as indicated by their screeches echoing through the air.

Balok tossed her the rifle she'd dropped, and she flagged them to follow down the street where the people had been evacuated. Around the side of another building, she turned on her heels and pointed the gun, ready to incinerate any kul which popped its head out. After five minutes and no kul, Eve ordered the QuBE to cover their rear, and they moved to meet with Faun and the vraditi forces.

Chapter 22
Unify and Recon

A month passed. Then another. Vradix fell to the thartica by way of the mini-bulk paths. After the kul had been unleashed, and the vraditi who could evacuate did, the thartica invaded through the openings. Attempts were made to save more, but the thartica quickly moved components through the paths and constructed planetary cannons which drove ships in orbit off. The last communications from Vradix were that the thartica were slaughtering all left behind.

Unable to counter the planetary cannons currently, the vraditi retreated farther toward QuBE space. It was safest there. The allied fleets now guarded the bulk paths into the territory, and IFF transponders had begun to be distributed. A warning was put out: those who hadn't already reached safety without one would be destroyed on entry into the system. Even Eve thought it a little harsh but understood that letting a single thartican ship through might mean mini-bulk paths which would devastate the last bastion of hope.

Skyfire was on their way out of the system after restocking supplies. Amongst the food, water, and medical supplies were dozens of IFF transponders to deliver to ships waiting to escape human space.

It was a bleak existence as space had long run out on sub-planet Zero-Zero-Five. Anyone who sought asylum in QuBE space was forced to stay aboard their ships. Because of the abundance of energy produced by the megastructure, ships were attached via umbilical rather than use the energy of their crystals. The vraditi who had once been stingy with their replication technology now shared it freely to keep people from starving.

A plan to push the thartica back and potentially win the war had been decided on, and Nine briefed Eve when she returned to the sub-planet for more transponders.

"The vraditi are still very heavily against the plan. They argued for a week straight before MOTHER explained that with or without them, they would move forward with this course of action, even if it meant sacrificing the entirety of QuBE-kind" Nine said. "The vraditi conceded."

"What do you think?"

"We don't have a choice. Either we take drastic steps, or they win, and we die. I would rather face them head on in an attempt to close off their main invasion path."

"You sure? We can still fek off to nowhere," Eve said with a smirk. "Just disappear and let all these chulks figure it out for themselves."

Nine's response was to return a rare smile.

MOTHER and the QuBE had worked around the clock to fit the megastructure with the drives it would need to traverse a bulk path. Due to the immense size and density though, it wouldn't be able to travel FTL. They wouldn't even make it to a fraction of the speed of light. The vraditi stepped in with the knowledge needed to open new bulk paths, and they were going to open one from QuBE space to the front door of the thartican hidden world. There would be a brief time which fleets would have to defend it, but once inside the final path it would be unstoppable. That would be where *Skyfire* and Nine would be needed, to open the path and lead the way.

On mission, they opened the bulk path and started their journey toward human space. Because of the transponders they were carrying, they stayed as far on the outskirts of mapped space to avoid issues.

Nothing was supposed to interfere in delivery. Eve monitored comms networks manually and directed Eleven to plot courses avoiding any contested areas. Balok and Virid kept them from unwanted eyes by dodging through systems, bouncing from one celestial body to another.

It was mundane, which drove Eve up the wall. She wanted to get back out there to kill more thartica and retake systems, but MOTHER implored they bring more ships to help build the final resistance fleet. The transponders they carried were destined for frontline battleships currently in hiding. At four kilometers wide and six long, the ships wouldn't be easily hidden while traversing toward QuBE space. Because of that, Eve was recording every jump so they could reverse course and follow a safe path back.

It was an unfortunate coincidence when they dropped into a system which hadn't yet been reported as invaded, but a battle raged. QuBE and vraditi fought thartica. Each side had dozens of large ships. *Skyfire* took refuge near the surface of a moon orbiting a purple, gas giant. In order to avoid detection, and then continue, they would have to stay hidden.

One of the giant thartican ships fired its Rekwa beam and got a lucky hit. It was moments before the QuBE ship's engines imploded, and then exploded outward in a bright flash. The shockwave and debris spread outward, contacting several allied ships. The thartica capitalized on the chaos and unleashed a barrage.

"While their attention is occupied, make a break for the bulk path," Eve said.

"Lady Eve, a distress signal is being broadcast." Eleven looked over their shoulder. "Should we not intercept?"

"No. We can't help them without risking the cargo. If they're smart, they'll cede this space and retreat to regroup. Plot a jump out of the system, and then triangulate back to the bulk path we need."

"Yes, Captain."

They made their two FTL jumps, and then entered the path. It was likely the thartica would register the activity on their sensors. She gambled that *Skyfire* would give off a small enough signature they wouldn't bother with it over the larger ships.

During the downtime in the path, they rotated rest time. Eat, sleep, and spend time off the bridge. Eve and Faun were in the dining area, having just finished meals. Faun moved her hand over and touched Eve's. The affection was reciprocated, though there was no passion behind it. They were both mentally exhausted, as was everyone else. Even the thought of taking Faun to bed was too much, and Eve pushed the idea away.

Unlucky or cursed, Eve couldn't decide. Back on the bridge, everyone was prepared for their imminent return to regular space. The odds weren't in their favor, and they emerged to a fleet of thartican ships. A trap had been set to catch any of the QuBE or vraditi fleeing in this direction.

Before they could even clear the opening, Rekwa beams were fired. Pushing the nose down hard slammed them into the wake of the anomaly and shook the ship violently. The thartica missed but wouldn't again. *Skyfire*'s engines faltered.

"Get us out of here, now!" Eve yelled.

"Trying!" Balok replied.

Staring down the barrels of thousands of Rekwa cannons, it was nearly the end for them. The Light Drive activated and skipped them forward by two hundred kilometers. It wasn't enough to put them out of range.

Balok, Virid, and Eleven worked frantically to plot and pilot. The Cruise Drive kicked on and they began pulling away from the thartican fleet. Eve checked the nearby space, and a swarm of their seed-ships were launched and making a direct line to them.

"Two-Oh-Eight, what's going on with the engine?!"

"A power surge de-synced the Light Drive from the command systems when we hit the bulk path entrance. We have to reboot it."

"Eleven, get to the engine room and help. Balok and Virid, evasive maneuvers until they get it going. Faun, ready defenses."

The ship lurched hard as they dodged beams. Their tracking from that distance was inaccurate and gave *Skyfire* opportunities to avoid damage. But every time they altered course they lost a little bit of speed, and the seed-ships grew ever closer. They were now dodging more than they were running.

"Double back! Let's clear the field!" Eve ordered.

Virid and Balok commanded the ship in concert. The ship spiraled and banked, but not as well as when a QuBE was augmenting the engine process. It was barely enough to avoid death.

Eve activated the railguns and began firing. Even with the tracking system, they were going too fast and moving too much to get an exact shot. Ninety-five percent of the shots missed, and the other five did little to no damage. Faun powered the forward shockwave emitters and sent waves to break the front line. The ships bounced when the shockwave connected with their hulls. It gave Eve and the auto-tracker an opportunity to apply pressure. The railguns focused one at a time.

"Flip us around and push full throttle! Fire the shockwave emitters off our aft and use that to keep them broken up!" Eve barked.

They did and began putting distance again. The railguns spun and fired aft at the targets. She deployed mines and set the targeting computer to aim at them. When the thartican ships were in range of them, she fired. A few explosions helped to keep them off *Skyfire* and disoriented enough so they couldn't get a solid shot on them.

"I need those engines now!"

"Coming online," Two-Oh-Eight responded over comms.

"Let's go!"

The Light Drive came to life, and they warped away. The thartica would be on their tail, but they would now have an even harder time hitting them. Once at the bulk path, they jumped in. There was no rest. Everyone was on high alert. Eleven stayed with Two-Oh-Eight to run diagnostics on the rest of the power grid and drives. Coming out of the path, they warped as soon as normal space was in view.

Even though there wasn't another thartican fleet waiting for them, they didn't risk the ships coming up behind them. There was no more caution in trying to hide as they burned hard through the system to the next path. Even with no sign of the enemy, they treated the situation like they were still being pursued. The fear persisted when in the next system another thartican fleet was assaulting a station.

Eve watched them closely to see if they would pursue the lone ship making a run for it. They either didn't notice or didn't care. It was a relief. Ahead was clear, but they stayed vigilant.

The rest of the way to human controlled space was dicey. They had to cut into systems on the outskirts of the bulk path network to avoid more thartica. When they finally reached Salvoa, she couldn't get the IFF transponders off her ship fast enough. They had spent a significant amount of time to get there, and though they made it safely it was only just barely.

After a cleanse and change of clothes, she found refuge in a bar down on the planet. She needed to drown herself. Two bottles of Gowarian Ale down and she was animated. The four biological crew members hadn't had a reprieve in a long time. No one said it, but it felt like an eternity since they had found themselves thrust into the middle of the elementus-thartica conspiracy.

"The fek were they thinking?!" she bellowed with slurred speech.

None of the crew replied, but they looked her way. They sat in silence, eating and drinking. Their eyes on her didn't stop her from launching into a tirade.

"Some greedy, corrupt, asshole elementus screwed our lives. We should be working contracts! Our shipmates would still be alive! But no, we got screwed, and now we're running from a species hellbent on annihilating everyone!" Eve was nearing a tirade. "Fekking rocks must have been fused in their brains too!"

She drew the attention of other patrons. Faun tried to calm her by placing her hand on Eve's, but Eve pulled away and continued. Balok finally interrupted while she was stringing curses together.

"The evidence we have shows it was likely only a handful of elementus involved. Our species is suffering the consequences also."

"I *know* that! You should be as mad as I am! And what about the damn vraditi?! Where was the Galactic Police? Chasing us instead of the real culprits! Fek the lot of them. Fek their order. Fek their laws."

A third bottle of ale was delivered. Faun tried to grab it before she could, but she snatched it up and she slammed it back. Chugging hard, the warmth coated her throat and stomach. When she put it down, she only meant to slam it onto the table. Instead, it crumpled into shards and cut her hand.

"FEK!"

She cradled it as blood pooled into her palm. Rushing, she tried to make it to the bathroom to wash it. But she was completely drunk and didn't make it. Tripping over her own feet, she fell. Instinctively she reached her hands out and spattered blood onto a table where some other mercs sat. Drinks were knocked over, and an uproar ensued.

"What the fek?! What's your problem?"

"Hey! You spilled my drink!"

"You think I care? Buy yourself another," Eve slurred.

They didn't take that well, and a fight started. One of them stood up and grabbed her collar. Though stronger than them, she was far more inebriated than they, and her reaction times were stunted. After shoving one, she caught a fist to the side of the head knocking her out.

When she came to, she was back on *Skyfire,* laid up in her bed. Her head pounded with every heartbeat. Nauseated, she leapt up and tried to get to the sink. Kicking a bucket with her own sick in it, she scrambled to stop it from dumping. Grabbing it up, she heaved. There wasn't anything left. Not even bile.

Her hand had been bandaged, but she was still in her clothes with blood and vomit caked on. It was mostly dry. *Must've been a few hours?* Tearing her clothes off, she chucked them into a pile near the purification tube in the room. After a quick cycle, she put on a clean tee shirt and pants, and made her way to the bridge. The systems were dark, and only Eleven was there. They didn't take notice of her.

Around the opposite hallway, she hit the call button on Faun's door. It took a moment for her to answer. The door opened, and Faun wasn't in the mood.

"Go back to bed," she said curtly through a yawn.

"I'm not here for sex. I just need to feel your warm body against mine."

After a sigh, Faun left the door open and returned to her bed. Eve closed the door behind her and climbed under the covers. Faun's bionic arms weren't as cold as she expected, though it was still enough to give her a chill. After warming up, she fell back to sleep.

She woke and wondered how long it had been. The room was still dark, Faun was still tucked into her. A significant amount of time passed, and she couldn't get back to sleep this time. She took great care not to wake Faun and slipped out of the room. When she returned to hers, she donned her armor, minus the helmet, and headed to the bridge to run ship diagnostics.

Lost in the data, hours passed, and the crew finally trickled back in. She had combed everything top to bottom, and Eleven and Two-Oh-Eight had done a thorough job in optimizing energy outputs while the others were at the bar.

"Captain, the human ships have already departed with the IFF transponders," Eleven told her. "Should we attempt to catch up?"

"They have our route data with the systems we mapped as safe. They'll make it on their own."

"What's our destination, Lady Eve?" Virid asked.

"Head back toward elementus space and start charting which systems have the most and least resistance. We're not out for a fight, but if we can safely take down thartica, we're going to."

Situated at their stations, the crew readied the ship. Salvoa was soon a distant dot, and they prepared to enter a bulk path which would take them in the direction of danger.

Several jumps away from human space, they met their first wave of enemies, and they stayed as far away as possible. Each time the exit of a bulk path opened, they maxed out the Light Drive to avoid getting driven into the anomaly as before. Even if the thartica pursued, they quickly gave up. But it still took over a month to get close to Tor Galom Ig, due to encountering increasing amounts of thartica.

Through communication networks, they stayed up to date with events happening. The battles were harsh and neither side seemed to be winning, which was better than before. Conquered planets were liberated. New planets were conquered. The exodus of sentient beings continued to rally on the QuBE side of space.

The bulk path which led to the bulwark sat unguarded, and Eve ordered them in. When they appeared into elementus space, everything was about how they left it when they fled.

Any large ship that exits here will be in the same kill box.

"Keep energy usage low and use the debris as cover. We need to collect scans of the area so MOTHER or someone else can figure out how to get the fleet through without dying."

Balok looked over his shoulder and nodded. "On it, Captain."

Because their ship's signature was insignificant compared to all the debris on the field, they drew no attention from potential nearby thartican ships. They were free to map the dimensions of the celestial sized, hollow hemisphere.

It withstands Rekwa, but it's not impervious. If we could use it as shielding for the megastructure, maybe we have a chance.

"Eleven, does the bulwark have engines? Thrusters? I want to know how it was put here."

"Scanning."

The screens lit up, showing the structure was powered, but there was nothing on the inner curve of the half-sphere. When they reached the edge and moved to the other side, they found enormous ports, spaced equally. Her suspicion was confirmed, but she knew the current QuBE on board weren't equipped for what she wanted.

"We need to commandeer this. We need Nine to break into the control systems so we can steal it and use it to our advantage. Scan for any sort of access panels, entrances, anything we can use to get in there."

Several hours passed. The thrusters were enclosed devices and entering into them wouldn't provide anything of use. There were no doors or bays. It left the crew stumped until Faun spoke up and reminded them that the thartica liked to remote-control things.

"If we can find what kind of signal they're using, we might be able to piggyback," Faun said. "If Nine has been successful in retrieving the thartican ship we abandoned, we might be able to use them and the ship."

"Back to QuBE space then," Eve directed.

Across the cosmos, they stuck to the plan of ignoring everything and blazing through systems to make it back in the least amount of time. Along the way, Eve continued to gather data and relay all thartica movement. Numbers, sizes of ships, compositions of fleets. When in the bulk paths, she had Eleven and Two-Oh-Eight analyzing and cataloguing. As soon as they entered normal space, they transmitted directly to MOTHER. The news would only reach QuBE space slightly faster than they would, but she hoped it would supply a heads up.

The crew opted not to transmit the idea about an attempt at taking control of the bulwark. They couldn't know if the network was secure and didn't want to risk losing a potential advantage.

A shift in the types of ships and fleets happened the closer they got to QuBE space. Thartican, to thartican-versus-alliance, to alliance fleets. Many sectors and systems were contested, but there appeared to be a barrier where the thartica had either not yet tried to enter, or the alliance had pushed them back.

Once they reached the QuBE system, it became clear their efforts to consolidate the ships capable of fighting back were working. There were far more ships now. The system was sectioned into flotillas.

There appeared to be commerce going on between the human, vraditi, and QuBE fleets, where ships were flying in constant streams between groups.

Coming into the port on Zero-Zero-Five, they followed their landing vector. At their designated spot, Nine was already waiting for them. On the next pad over was what Eve had hoped to see; the thartican seed-ship was there and upgraded with QuBE technology.

The crew disembarked with Eve leading. While she knew it wouldn't mean the same thing to a QuBE, she stepped up and hugged Nine.

"It's good to see you," she said.

Nine reciprocated the gesture.

"I have missed the crew and being on *Skyfire*."

Faun also hugged Nine, while Balok and Virid opted for a hand on Nine's shoulder. Eleven and Two-Oh-Eight nodded in reverence.

"Things are nearing the final phases. Let us go and discuss next steps," Nine said.

Chapter 23
The Final Countdown

The final phases actually meant a lot more work for everyone, but *Skyfire* and crew were now bound to the QuBE system. MOTHER felt their involvement in the upcoming operation was too critical to risk them further.

It was a relief to not be running anymore. *Skyfire* had pioneered methods and paths for other small ships to get back out there with resources, weapons, and IFF transponders for the ships which hadn't yet made it. Eve made sure to commend each of the crew in their instrumental roles in ensuring the alliance had a fighting chance of taking back the Crux arm of the galaxy.

The negative side of *Skyfire* no longer venturing out was that, for better or worse, Eve, Nine, and MOTHER were in a dozen meetings a day for coordination and planning. Moving the megastructure, fleets and compositions, battle plans, and the evacuation of the QuBE system by all lifeforms. Because the system was losing its star, and the energy they utilized to build their society, the QuBE were also going to need a new home.

The rest of the *Skyfire* crew was delegated out to help prepare ships and provide as much knowledge as they could to anyone and everyone. Most of Eve's time was now spent with Nine, even meals. Though Nine didn't need to be there, she appreciated they chose to spend their time with her.

"We will be ready to move soon. MOTHER and the vraditi are nearing completion of the plan to jump the megastructure to the system before Tor Galom Ig," they said.

"What about the thartica using it to enter directly to QuBE space?"

"It is a calculated risk that once we open it, our fleets will enter first. It is anticipated that the thartica will quickly move into position to fire on us as we exit. For that reason, the megastructure will come through last."

"Something that size, isn't it going to cause gravitational problems? What's going to be the result of moving it past Tor Galom Ig?"

"At best, the planet will experience catastrophic natural disasters. At worst, it might lead to the complete destabilization of their system. Rescue and evacuation ships have been prepared by the vraditi. Unfortunately, the thartica have fully invaded on the ground, and enslaved the elementus into strip mining their planet. If a ground battle ensues, we may end up limited on how many we can save."

"Don't tell Balok or Virid until after we win the war. You know they're already in enough uncertainty about Roxim. We need their level-headed piloting if we're going to survive. Is the thartican ship ready?"

"Affirmative."

"Reservations?"

"It is likely our deaths are imminent, but the alternative is to do nothing and die anyway. Any reservations I have are overridden by the possibility we save our peoples."

Even when the thought of running came to mind, it was brief because she recommitted to the idea they would see everything through.

Time seemed to both stand still and disappear simultaneously. Evacuations were completed. Two fleets formed. The war fleet staged on one end of the system, ready at coordinates where the new bulk path would open. The second fleet were lifeboats, migratory ships filled with people chosen to survive and rebuild in another sector of the galaxy.

The last structures to move into place were MOTHER's planet, and the megastructure, now designated CHILD. MOTHER had made an exact copy of themselves and uploaded it so that it could think and complete the objective.

I shouldn't be surprised, and yet I can't imagine being able to clone my consciousness and plant it into something else. Two sentient AI, piloting massive celestial bodies...

In position with the fleet, when CHILD was within five AU, the effects were felt. On scans, the ships moved when the gravitational eddies pulled at them like rip tides. *Skyfire* spaced themselves from any other nearby vessel to avoid collision.

CHILD and MOTHER broadcast to all ships in concert.

"For those of you who prepare to fight the thartica, do so knowing you have already saved hundreds of millions of lives. Vraditi, plesian, human, tarak, and QuBE. May we triumph over our adversary and save trillions more, including the elementus and other countless non-spacefaring species who cannot fight for themselves."

With the exception of CHILD, the migrants' destination was withheld to ensure that even if the plan failed and all hope was lost, the fighters would be survived through future generations of their species.

Skyfire took position beside the thartican seed-ship, piloted by Nine. They had been assigned to a vraditi squadron of small to mid-size ships whose sole job was to ensure Nine made it to the bulk path to the thartican hidden world. More than anything else, they couldn't lose Nine or CHILD. All ships were given the directive to do whatever necessary to ensure the safe arrival of those vessels.

The lifeboats departed through an existing bulk path, heading to an outlying system. MOTHER was last, and their mass was accommodated by thousands of Bulk Drives wedging the mouth of the anomaly open. MOTHER entered. When it closed it sent a gravitational wave through the system.

Most ships were able to avoid one another, but some smaller ships flying in close formations collided. After a quick scan, it was found that no ships were lost, but CHILD wanted to take precautions.

"Due to the nature of entry and emergence of such mass from a bulk path, it is recommended upon exiting all ships separate themselves from one another by five percent of the size of their hull from all other vessels until the eddy passes."

A probe was launched from CHILD. Tracking it, they watched it activate a Light Drive. At about ten AU from their current position, it stopped, and all waited in anticipation. A few minutes passed, and it detonated in a spectacular fashion. When the brightness cleared, a new bulk path had been created.

The first fleet of ships entered. The mouth of the anomaly widened as multiple ships activated their Bulk Drives. While they waited for their turn, Eve thought about the size of the megastructure, and wondered about the science of jamming something of such mass into a path through the Bulk.

How did they do this so fast? Never mind that they're AI beings who can share knowledge, or that they don't need rest the same way biological beings do. How could they have fit both their star's megastructure and a planet with enough bulk drives to get either of them anywhere?

Their squadron's turn came, and they moved in sync to the bulk path. There was no turning back. They weren't in the path more than an hour before Nine's new ability to access thartican transmission networks was already acting like an early warning system. Everything they received was issued to the fleet, and everyone's time was spent analyzing in order to maximize survival.

Thartican fleet compositions, positions, and their own tactical data. Anything they were broadcasting to each other they were now sending directly to the alliance. They had quickly become aware of the new bulk path into the system which connected to elementus space and moved ships to intercept. Unknown to them was the size of the armada coming their way. Thartica were called from all close by systems, and others within a few Bulk jumps.

Because of the significant amount of time the allied fleet had to spend traveling the Bulk to their destination, the thartica were able to form up. A large fleet waited at the exit of the bulk path while the thartica in the elementus system readied the bigger guns for their kill zone.

"Connect comms to lead ship priority channels," Eve said to Eleven. "I want everyone's attention."

"Routing through CHILD...complete."

"First fleets to exit, hit your Light Drive. The thartica will fire as soon as you emerge. Come back from behind and split their attention so the rest of the fleets can emerge safely," she commanded. "Alfa squadron out."

Shortcut aside, it still took what felt like a month traveling the adjacent dimension. After losing track of time in the Bulk, the exit finally opened. They were nearing the end of the journey and tension rose in Eve's shoulders.

She was on duty and roused everyone from their sleep. They joined her on the bridge, and at their stations readied for their return to normal space. Beyond the event horizon was a distorted view of the enemy waiting for them.

Whether her warning was heeded made no difference to her. *Skyfire* and Nine's ship would do as instructed. As predicted, the moment the first ships appeared the thartica worked to target and destroy them. The purple hue from Rekwa beams lit the bridge.

The thartica missed. *Skyfire* warped away, their squadron following. Before they could even land, loss reports were already coming across the network.

Hope the alliance gets through.

"Alfa squadron, we're sending a flight pattern. Engage only if necessary," Eve broadcast.

Grouped up, the squadron followed *Skyfire*, and they burned hard across the system, using FTL to get from one planet to another and use them as cover. Approximately halfway across the system, CHILD emerged. It took a few minutes for the gravitational wave to catch up, but it spread through the system wreaking havoc. Knocked off course, ships in her squadron were forced to realign to their destination. Eve watched the scans of the region nervously, waiting to be ambushed.

"Full throttle. Let's go!" Eve barked.

Skyfire pulled ahead and piloted toward the unguarded bulk path.

"All ships prepare for evasive maneuvers," Eve sent out to the squadron. "*Skyfire* will jump first and take on whatever is on the other side. Count ten minutes, and then enter. All ships are to escort Nine through the opening in the bulwark and cover while they try to take control. No matter what, do not be baited to take a fight away from protecting them unless I direct it."

"To avoid detection, there will be no further communication until I have control of the bulwark," Nine said. "Good luck."

They entered the path, and she broadcast back to Nine.

"We'll see you on the other side..." *Works as a double meaning.*

The feelings of self-preservation and her fight-or-flight response were now making her chest tight. The trip between the last system and the next was a short jump. *Skyfire* and crew would be soon put to the test of exactly how badly they wanted to continue living.

Nine sent data to their computer. There were three hundred ships waiting for them. Most were seed-ships patrolling the debris, but outside of the wreckages were cruisers, battleships, and dreadnaughts. It was hardly the force they first showed when they ambushed the vraditi fleet. *Overconfidence, or a trap?*

The bulk path exit opened, and Eve closed her eyes for a brief moment to mentally prepare. When the jolt of returning to normal space hit, she opened them, and the *Skyfire* warped away from the mouth and out of direct fire.

Virid and Balok performed admirably as always, and with the help of Eleven, darted toward the biggest wreckage while avoiding fire. They barrel rolled and weaved hard to take refuge behind remnants of vraditi battleships. The thartica were hot on them, but fighting directly was meaningless if Nine and the others couldn't exit the Bulk safely.

"Get us up and out of the debris and aimed at Tor Galom Ig! We need to draw them away," she ordered.

While cutting through defunct ships, she launched mines and set off explosions in the face of the thartica. It wasn't to attempt to destroy them, but rather keep their attention on *Skyfire*. The thartica were coordinated and cut them off before they could break away from the debris field.

"Get us out of their sight! Nose down into the nearest battleship and put all power to the engines and forward shockwave emitters. Cut through!"

It was a signature move at this point. Tear into a ship, release mines, wait for the enemy to get in range, and boom. They set off a chain of explosions and pushed the thartica off their tail for a moment. Bursting from the battleship, *Skyfire* arced hard downward and put as much distance as they could from their exit.

Each move from one wreck to another was calculated to put them closer and closer to the edge of the debris field. There were thartican forces waiting for them there, but they needed a fraction of a second with a clean shot to open space which would allow them to draw scans away.

The moment came. Emptiness they could escape to. The Light Drive initiated, and they jumped to the other side of the thartican fleets.

"Burn at them. We'll let them know we're here," Eve ordered while setting the auto-target on the railguns.

They spun about and started firing. It didn't matter if they hit, or even did damage. Their goal was accomplished when a hundred seed-ships jumped to within range, and they had to cut hard to port to avoid obliteration.

"Light jump again!"

They did and appeared off the other side of the fleet. The ships followed and they were now fully invested in destroying *Skyfire*. It was yet to be seen if the larger thartican ships were baited, because they had yet to fire a shot. Needing them to turn toward Tor Galom Ig, Eve was going to have to risk close combat.

"Hope you're all ready to die. We have five minutes to do as much damage as we can to their ships to make sure their attention is where we want it. Then we're heading to Tor Galom Ig to get them to follow."

"Aye!" the crew replied.

Their guerrilla tactics had mostly served them well up to this point. Eve saw no need to change when they were able to affect severe damage, even if it did mean their deaths now. The thought of revenge against the thartica had slowly been replaced with the weight of the peoples who could still be saved.

In a blink they were at the nearest battleship and flipped. Faun fired the shockwave emitters. Eve dropped mines and fired at them. They broke through the shields and skimmed the ship. The Tectos and Eleven couldn't stop dodging, and so the damage they were doing was lessened because it was spread out.

Eve started aiming for extremities. Antennae, Rekwa cannons, and anything else which looked important. Due to the speed and movement, even with help from auto-tracking, she only hit about twenty-five percent of her intended targets. It was enough to be annoying, but not cripple the ship.

Seed-ships came in from their aft and tried locking on. Due to the closeness, their shots were infrequent to avoid damaging their own ally.

"Next ship! Let's go! Three minutes left!"

They reached the end of the battleship and punched through the shield. Pushing forward, they lined up to the next one a kilometer away and bullied their way past the defenses. Thartican ships were now coming in from all sides of *Skyfire*. Time was running short for them to escape. With what minor damage they could do before being completely surrounded and destroyed, they pulled away and aimed to open space.

"Head for Tor Galom Ig!"

To align, they had to make a wide arc, and dodge more Rekwa beams. Their Light Drive activated. While traveling FTL, Eve scanned ahead to the planet. The number of ships was staggering. The display lit up with an uncountable number of dots. It was reminiscent of what Salvoa looked like before it cleaned up its space junk. But instead of each dot being a piece of garbage, it was a ship.

"Ignore all ships chasing us. Balok, Virid, let's start taking your planet back. Head into the atmosphere. We're going to hit any thartican installations."

"Yes, Captain!" they replied enthusiastically.

They dropped into the planet's orbit and slowed. Diving in, *Skyfire*'s nose quickly started to glow. The orange hues washed up the hull to the viewport, and then subsided after they'd passed the stratosphere.

Tor Galom Ig was a volcanic planet. The vegetation was reddish, and the bodies of water were a dark purple. While they dropped down to rolling hills, she pulled up topography and cities on the displays. It wasn't hard to track where to hit, as fighter-style ships were launched, and radar lit up. They were twenty kilometers to the north and making a fast approach to *Skyfire*.

Rather than running, Balok and Virid steered toward them. The ship maneuvered differently in atmosphere. Even with the updated sleek design and the modified engines, the drag needed to be compensated for.

"Eleven, set cruise thrust to seventy percent," Balok said. "Prepare for hard thrust on my mark."

"Done."

"Lady Eve, we are currently over uninhabited land. We're going right for their fleet. I'm going to pitch us above them. Drop mines on second mark."

"We have a dozen mines left. New tactic after this," Eve replied.

"Copy."

The ship slowed and it increased their maneuverability. *Skyfire* was now on a direct path toward the fleet, and it only took moments more for them to be in visual range. The thartica began firing long before they could accurately target. The Tectos evaded and kept them on course. The ships were a split second away.

"Mark!"

Eleven pushed the engine and everyone sank into their seats from the gravitational force. They pulled up and Balok gave the signal again.

"Mark!"

Directly above the thartican ships she let loose a few mines at a time and fired on them with the lower railguns. The explosions rocked *Skyfire*. The ship wobbled, and they needed to course correct or be sent into the ground.

"Eleven, max out the engine! Two-Oh-Eight, bypass safety and give us everything!" Virid yelled out.

Eve's vision darkened, and she struggled to stay conscious. Skyward acrobatics kept them from being hit, and she had enough sense about her to set auto-lock for the railguns and let the computer unload at the enemy.

"Approaching the city Ecite," Balok stated.

"Eleven, scan for distinct thartican signatures," Eve said.

"Tracking ten outposts, all embedded in different districts."

An overlay of the city came up on their display. None of the targets were tall enough to hit while level with the city. They would need to pull hard maneuvers to avoid collateral damage.

"Marked and input into the auto-tracking. Balok and Virid, bring us to one and pull straight up so I can fire down on it. Keep our top faced to the ships in pursuit so I can hit them too."

"Nine to *Skyfire*. I have control of the bulwark. We are moving now."

"We read you, Nine. They're going to notice soon enough. We're going to make a run, and then meet up with you," Eve replied.

The city appeared in the window. Coming in over the towers of stone and steel, the ship pulled vertically. The thartican installations stood out, as their living structures were alien architecture to the elementus stone city.

As soon as there was a lock, Eve fired until the warning popped up that the heatsinks had reached their maximum absorption. Hell rained down on the first location. The ships in pursuit tried to overtake them as they climbed and fired on *Skyfire*. The Rekwa beams were missing, but the thartica also launched tracking missiles. Their shielding held when they dove and assaulted a second target. The Tectos took them down in between the buildings to obscure any shots the enemy had on them. Making several sharp turns, they tried hard to lose their tail.

Even if they kept out of line of sight, they wouldn't get any more chances. Eve was reckless, but not to the point that she wanted to die before seeing the allied forces come screaming through the system to destroy the invaders.

If we make one misstep, they're going to have a good shot at destroying us. We need to get out with what damage we have caused.

"Fly to the edge of the city. As soon as we're clear, use the Light Drive to get us out of here," she instructed. "Keep us moving away from the bulwark until the thartica lose interest, and then double back."

The city blurred by too fast to admire any sights. With their engines blazing, the glass was no doubt shaking hard. Every time a thartican ship appeared on their rear, the engine quieted for half a second before they banked down another street and it roared back. City limits came up and as soon as there would be little collateral damage they aimed at the horizon and activated the Light Drive.

The bubble around them curved the ground. Dark reddish dirt and orange skies gave way to the blackness of space. They blew past the system's star and continued through to the other edge. When they were a safe distance from the thartican fleets, they performed a flip to head back toward the bulwark.

"Nine, *Skyfire* on its way to you," Eve announced over squadron comms.

"Protection squadron is under fire," replied one of the ships.

"Keep them off Nine, no matter what."

There was radio silence and Eve wasn't sure if it was because they were too focused to reply, or if it was because they had been taken out.

A few moments of Light Drive power put them in range of the bulwark which was now scooping debris off the field. Nine needed to make it past where the bulk path would open, and then the alliance fleet would be able to join them.

"Lady Eve, debris now blocks our path to the opening," Eleven noted.

"It'll take too long to go over, and then locate Nine's ship. Cut through, full power to the engines and shockwave emitters. The moment the bulk path opening will be clear, open it and send a signal through."

Faun focused all of the emitter power to the nose of the ship and the Tectos barreled in. Several ships worth of debris deep, the remnants started colliding with the top, bottom, and tail end of *Skyfire*. The bulwark was closing in everything around them.

"Two-Oh-Eight, push the Cruse Drive as far as you can without burning it out. We need everything we can get or we're going to be crushed," Eve ordered over comms.

"Yes, Captain," they replied from the engine room.

The drive's plasma was hitting debris and bouncing back. The ship shook violently from feedback it was getting into its intake. It wouldn't be able to handle that much for long, and Eve was tracking the distance to the opening. They were nearly there.

"Bulwark is about to clear the bulk path," Nine came in over comms.

"Status on the squadron?"

"Fourteen ships have been destroyed, thirty remain. I am tracking hundreds of thartica coming in from the sides. When they come around the horizon, they will target me. They are also trying to retake control of the bulwark. I have them shut out for now, but I do not know for how long."

"Just hang on...we're almost there. As soon as you're clear of the opening, sabotage the bulwark. Shut it down, break it, do whatever you need to keep them from moving it back."

"Copy, Lady Eve."

Chapter 24
Last-Ditch Effort

Skyfire burst through the opening with an explosion of debris. Nine pinged their location and the Tectos pushed them hard nose down. Rounding the half-sphere's horizon, the display lit up with a circle, locking onto Nine's thartican ship. The squadron scrambled to intercept the incoming enemy, leaving Nine vulnerable.

Eve tracked the bulk path's location. The bulwark had passed it, but only by two kilometers. Whether it was enough or not, there was no more time.

"Get to the bulk path and open the anomaly," Eve directed her crew.

They pulled in range and the Bulk Drive activated. The mouth of the path opened up and she began broadcasting to their fleets.

"Bulwark moved. Debris field cleared. Requesting full fleet support!" she called out.

There was silence for a few moments before she got a reply. Realistically she knew it was the time the transmission needed to travel through the Bulk, but it didn't stop her thinking the worst had happened.

If CHILD was destroyed, there's no hope left.

"Confirmed, Alfa Squadron. Support is incoming," came a human transmission.

The thartican ships were closing on Nine. Scanning for allies, all Eve found was debris. The ships of the squadron had been destroyed. *Skyfire* rushed to meet the hundreds of ships head on to buy Nine a little more time. Despite trying to gain their attention, and taking out several frontline ships with the shockwaves, the rest started bypassing *Skyfire*.

"Nine, we can't stop them. Bail to space and we'll come pick you up."

"Negative. I have yet to lock the bulwark out. They will be able to move it back."

"You're out of time!" Eve said. "Disengage and space yourself!"

"QuBE-94056-11, connect with me and allow me to upload…" Nine replied.

"Connection open," Eleven complied.

Skyfire turned around to fly with the thartica and continued to knock as many down as possible. The first of the enemy's ships reached Nine's ship and fired a Rekwa beam. The shield absorbed the first shot.

"Nine!" Eve said.

"Transfer complete," Nine said. "It was an honor to fly with the *Skyfire* and crew. Escape and finish this."

Another thartican ship arrived and fired on Nine's vessel. And another. The shield fell and the Rekwa burned through the ship. The engine quickly went critical, and the ship was turned inside out. The Tectos had already turned them away and engaged the Light Drive. Everything went blurry for Eve; the light from stars outside elongated, and her tears obscured everything else.

Eve wanted to scream, but she held it in. Wiping her tears as best she could, she knew an outburst would demoralize the crew at this critical moment. The loss of yet another crewmate was going to hit them hard, but they couldn't let it jeopardize the mission.

"Eleven, report. Was Nine successful?" she choked out.

"Confirmed, the bulwark's engines are disabled for the time being."

"What did Nine send you?"

"They have uploaded the entirety of their critical knowledge to winning the war. I now have access to thartican communications systems, and the coordinates and the modifications needed to our Bulk Drive to open the path. QuBE-346090-208, I am sending you the information for the modification."

"Understood," they replied. "I will attempt to make the required modification."

"We need to stay out of the line of fire until CHILD is ready, then we open the path and destroy their fekking planet," Eve told the crew.

"There is more. In order to hold the bulk path open, the modified drive needs to be inside the path. We will have to enter and lead CHILD there. CHILD intends to detonate on the other side to close the path and destroy the system. If we survive the explosion, we will not be able to return."

Except for the hum of the Light Drive, eerie silence fell over the crew. Eve struggled to understand the reasoning Nine had withheld that information. Her only answer was to speculate Nine knew she and the crew would seek to find another way. But now Nine's original fate to be trapped in unknown space at best, with potentially no way back, was now theirs.

Being captain, she had the authority to order the crew to complete the mission. But it didn't seem fair. There were many times she risked the crew's lives as part of their missions, but they had the option to permanently disembark at any port they landed at if they didn't like the way things were going. Instead, this would be marching them to almost certain death.

Even if the explosion doesn't kill us, the bulk path and thartican system will be destroyed. There's no way of knowing if we'll make it back to civilized space.

Eve looked to Faun, almost wanting to demand answers about their benefactor, about what was to come. But she knew at this time it didn't matter. The mission hadn't changed. *She* had to see it through as Faun had said, but it didn't mean the crew did.

"I…" she choked a little. "I'm not going to demand you sacrifice yourselves for the greater good. If any one of you wants to disembark, say so now and we'll sneak down to Tor Galom Ig."

"We're not abandoning ship," Faun said. "We see this mission through no matter what. If we die, we die knowing we saved trillions."

"Balok and I agree," Virid spoke. "If we are survived by our clans, then that is what matters. We will be immortalized in elementus history as heroes rather than exiles."

"MOTHER assigned me and QuBE-346090-208 to *Skyfire* because we understand the severity of failing the mission. The QuBE will survive because of us."

Eve knew these would be the answers. Whether it was loyalty, preservation of species, or doing the right thing, the trope of going down with the ship was completed. She was absolved of the guilt. It also led to her relief she wouldn't have to do it alone.

"Then let's go save the fekking galaxy."

"Yes, Captain!" Faun replied, and the others echoed after.

Eve scanned behind them. The thartica had given up the chase a half hour after warping away. They were light years out now and waiting for word to come that the allied fleets were making it. Eleven monitored thartican communications and they were amassing everything at the bulwark knowing the path was now clear. They still didn't understand the intent of the megastructure, but they were preparing to destroy it.

Eve gave the command to double back and put themselves in a reasonable range to join CHILD as soon as they came through. The best way they could ensure success would be to join the battle and protect CHILD.

Alliance fleets emerged, and Eve ran continuous scans. The first ships through rivaled thartican battleships. Immediately upon exit they moved away from the opening and the decisive battle began. They couldn't see it from their location, but numbers were changing almost at a one-for-one rate.

The bulk path stayed open and spewed out what seemed like a never-ending stream. The thartica began losing two-to-one, then three-to-one before they finally started pulling back. The allied forces weren't letting up and even while the thartica ran, they were gunned down. When the battlefield immediately around the bulk path they were entering from was finally cleared of the enemy, the allied fleets formed multi-level barriers to provide protection while CHILD came through.

When CHILD emerged, the system shook under the gravitational wave which emanated outward. But like bees supplying cover for their hive and pulsating, the fleet only shifted a small amount, and then repositioned themselves in defensive formation. CHILD was barely visible. Eve gave the command to join the wall.

"Open comms to CHILD," Eve told Eleven.

"Comms open."

"CHILD, Nine has been killed. They transferred everything we need to get you through the bulk path to the hidden planet," she broadcast.

There was silence for a moment.

"That is unfortunate news. QuBE-49567-9 will be immortalized within the QuBE network. I have sent a communication to MOTHER."

Eve cut off comms and addressed the crew.

"We're freelance. I don't give a damn about any other ship. Stick to CHILD and target anything trying to damage them."

"Yes, Lady Eve!" Balok and Virid acknowledged.

"Eleven, seal the bridge and cut all power to life support outside. Two-Oh-Eight, keep those engines tuned to provide us the best maneuverability."

"Yes, Captain."

The bulwark was in their path forward. The options were limited. Ships were already exposed on the upper and lower part of the bulwark. Moving around it meant extra time trying to clear the obstacle and not moving toward their destination.

Instead, CHILD gave a command to all ships to part from its center and to line the outer ring of the bulwark. The thartica were already trying to shoot down ships, but with the combined force they backed away quickly. CHILD rammed the bulwark with their megastructure and propelled it forward. The extra mass was nothing compared to the star's and moved with ease.

"New ships detected in system," CHILD broadcast. "Thartican fleets entering from their hidden planet. Numbers not yet known."

Skyfire hugged CHILD's hull near the opening they carved in the bulwark, waiting for some opportunistic thartica to try to make it through the debris field with a seed-ship to back-cap while the fleet was engaged elsewhere. Eve didn't know how much CHILD could withstand a Rekwa beam, but she wasn't going to allow the enemy the chance.

Despite moving, the megastructure was slow. What felt like hours passed while the thartica amassed everything they had from the bulk path the alliance was heading to. The air was tense waiting for the last battle to begin. Eve checked the thartican fleet's comms, searching for anything important. Most of the information coming through was formations, and she tapped out a message to Onra's lead ship so they could give to their side. While scanning, she came across an ominous message.

THE SYSTEM KILLER IS COMING.

Whether it was in regard to CHILD, or a weapon they had which they designated as a system killer, the message wasn't good. Eve opened voice comms to Onra's ship.

"We need to go on the offensive now." She was curt. "I intercepted a thartica message about a 'system killer coming.'"

"Are they referring to CHILD?" Onra replied.

"It doesn't matter. If they are, then they know our intentions and they're going to do everything they can to stop it. If it's something else, then we don't want to wait around for it to show up."

There was a brief pause and some background chatter before Onra agreed.

"We are sending out final battle plans now. Prepare for offensive."

"Keep us on the back line. We're now the key to the bulk path."

"Understood."

Skyfire received their assignment. They were still part of the shielding group of ships to stick near CHILD. Once the battle kicked off, she fully anticipated there would be a high volume of seed and fighter ships headed to the megastructure.

The assault fleets formed in spheres, all orbiting the largest ships of each grouping. While they could only see the outlines of a few in their viewport, the scans of space clearly highlighted the hundreds of formations. There were so many ships on field, it felt like the entire galaxy was there.

In unison, each *death ball* of ships activated their Light Drives and warped forward, directly on top of the thartica. There wasn't even time to notice when the first ship fell on either side. From behind the bulwark, they didn't have a view, but transponder signals began dropping off. CHILD used the network of ships to monitor and provide intel.

As expected, the thartica launched ships aimed directly at intercepting CHILD. The displays lit up with numbers. Four thousand, five hundred and fifty. The defensive fleet readied.

The first to round the bulwark were easily picked off, but when the swarm appeared, all hell broke loose. The upper and lower ends were hit first. Eve was itching to kill them, but her intuition of guarding the hole overrode the desire to act rashly.

Thartica began slipping past the line of defense, attempting to suicide run at CHILD. Eve saw one to be intercepted and pulled the trigger. She set targeting and displayed it to the crew.

"That one. Let's go!"

The Cruise Drive accelerated them and the Tectos spun them into an arc to intersect the flight path of the ships closing in. They pushed it to maximum, and before they were even in range, Eve was locking on as best she could. At the edge of the railgun's effective range, she began taking shots. Any weakening of the shield was the goal, as they wouldn't be the only ones attempting to shoot them down.

They came in hot on the upper hull of one and unleashed shockwaves. It careened out of control and the railguns punched through the shielding, and then the hull. There was no time to dwell on total destruction. The fields became a dogfight. They swerved and spiraled to avoid collision with their own allies while carefully targeting the thartica. Mines were useless, and their shockwave emitters were limited in use due to the equal risk of hitting an ally. Eve put every ounce of her attention into tracking and unleashing railgun shots to cover CHILD.

The battle raged. Being the key to victory, any time they were targeted they used every obstacle to their advantage, ally or not. Narrowly avoiding shots, some ally ships were obliterated instead of *Skyfire*. *It had to be them,* Eve justified to herself.

The moment they lost their tail, they doubled back to fight. In and out, they kited their enemy, escaping death by mere meters. A wave of thartican ships formed and powered their Rekwa beams to focus one central location on CHILD, trying to penetrate. The combined beam contacted and burned into the thick panel. *Skyfire* sped at them to launch a shockwave, but before they could get there a medium sized human cruiser jumped into the middle and detonated their engine.

The burst not only destroyed the thartica, but also sent an energy bubble outward which knocked all ships off their courses. *Skyfire* reeled, and the Tectos were trying to regain control. The Cruise Drive worked hard to correct their spin. Eve got a ping they were being targeted. The wide nose-down arc they were making was slowing their speed significantly. It was clear they weren't going to pull out before the beam hit.

"Move us, now!" she hollered.

"Initiating Light Drive!" Balok called out.

The ship shook violently as it entered warp still at a slight rotation. Creaking and groaning filled the cabin, and for a moment Eve wondered if the hull would buckle. When they dropped out of warp, their stabilizer only supplied partial inertial deceleration support. Rather than become smears on the interior of the ship, they were thrown hard against consoles, walls, and the floor.

Eve scrambled to get back into the captain's chair to find out if they were being followed. They were several AU from the battle with no nearby enemy coming up on sensors.

"System check," she said.

Balok had also been thrown from their seat, against the wall. Virid leapt to check on them. Faun tapped on her console.

"Light drive offline," Two-Oh-Eight replied. "Rebooting."

"Several shockwave emitters have been ripped from the hull. We're vulnerable at the leading edge of the right fin. Shields are intact," Faun said.

"Virid?" Eve questioned.

"Balok is unconscious. The dent in the wall indicates he hit head-first."

Eve stood and moved to Virid. "I need you back in the pilot seat. We're dead in the water. Get us moving."

"Aye, Captain," they stated reluctantly.

Eve hoisted Balok up from their landing spot and brought them to the captain's chair. Setting them in, she took Balok's place beside Virid.

I don't have Balok's expertise, but I can follow directions.

"Faun, you have full control of the weapons systems," she said, and looked to Virid with a weak smile. "Tell me what to do."

"Bring us up to zero-point-one AU per second," Virid said.

"Confirmed, zero-point-one."

"Run ops check on stabilizer."

Eve keyed through the commands to find it. The efficiency showed at ninety-four percent.

"Stabilizer online. In acceptable parameters, not optimal."

"Understood. Performing flight maneuvers."

They banked left, right, pitched into an inversion, and then rolled to face the battle still ongoing.

"Status on Light Drive?" Eve asked.

"System reboot shows misalignment of crystal. Current alignment is only producing sixty percent efficiency," Two-Oh-Eight replied.

"Good enough. Let's go," she commanded.

She plotted the short jump back to the fight and activated the drive. They leapt back into the battle and began targeting any thartican vessel they could. Though not as efficient as the Tectos as a team, she managed to keep up with Virid's verbal commands.

While they utilized every opportunity to take out an enemy ship, it was always hit-and-run tactics. They never stayed long enough to fully destroy any ship.

Despite being outnumbered on this side of the bulwark, the defense fleet was destroying more than they were being destroyed.

Skyfire retreated to the leading edge of CHILD's hull to cover the scar made by the few ships which managed to land hits. They patrolled while knocking away enemies, and in a short lull Eve found a moment to check the network of ships on the other side. Things were more of a one-for-one situation there, and thartica were still pouring through the bulk path. CHILD and the defense fleet needed to get there to help.

"Energy buildup at critical. All fleets retreat to my position, at my north and south poles," CHILD ordered, and moved away from the bulwark.

The bulwark continued on while CHILD moved to the side of it. Allied fleets returned, and the remaining thartican ships near CHILD were overwhelmed and destroyed. When clear from the bulwark's path, and in direct line with the thartican dreadnaughts, large panels retracted quickly from the megastructure, and a mass ejection spewed forth in their direction. It took mere moments for the energy beam to reach the enemy fleet. The intense beam didn't even burn the ships in its path, it wiped them from existence. A third of the remaining thartican fleet was simply gone.

"Energy buildup below critical. Closing containment doors."

There was renewed morale across the fleet communications, and they knew this was the last push. Every single ship, including CHILD, moved toward the bulk path the thartica were now protecting. The allied fleet positioned themselves to take any and all fire directed at CHILD.

The stream of thartican ships had ceased coming through the bulk path from the hidden planet. While they were in formation, Eve's input to piloting was minimal, giving her a chance to scan thartican communications for valuable information. Much of it was arguing between their leaders regarding tactics, including the potential for retreat.

On the scans, Eve caught the bulk path now behind them was opening. New thartican communications were coming through. The fleets of their ships which had still been out in the galaxy had amassed behind them and would be in the system shortly. The directive from them to the thartica in system was to reform, but not reengage until they came through. They called it something different, but they were going to attempt a hammer-and-anvil attack.

Eve opened comms to CHILD and Onra. "CHILD, push your engines as hard as you can. There's a significant enemy force coming in behind us and they are going to pinch you."

"Engines are at one hundred percent already," CHILD replied.

"Overclock them then!" she replied.

"What are the numbers coming?" Onra asked. "We can move sub-fleets into position to intercept."

"I don't have exact numbers, but they recalled every ship from our space. Best we can do is take a play out of their book. Position some ships directly at the bulk path mouth and fire Rekwa weapons as they're exiting. It might buy a little more time," she instructed.

"Understood," Onra replied.

"Increasing engine output to one hundred and twenty percent. The megastructure is already destabilizing. Structural integrity is showing microfractures, however I should be able to hold containment," CHILD informed.

"Onra...make sure we get our own row of statues outside the fekking capitol building after this..." Eve said.

"Fly safe, *Skyfire*."

Communications were closed and Eve couldn't help but wonder if it was the last time ever.

Because the thartica threat had been removed from Tor Galom Ig's orbit, there was opportunity for the elementus to join the fight. They showed up in any space-worthy ship. *Likely due to their fleets being destroyed*, Eve surmised. Few were battle ready, but they were there.

With only a few AU to go, time was their worst enemy. Eve fidgeted and chewed at the sides of her fingers.

"Virid," Eve said while not taking her eyes off the console. "Why don't you check on Balok. Make sure they're ok."

In her peripheral, she saw Virid nod and get up. Two-Oh-Eight opened comms from the engine room.

"Lady Eve, alignment of the Vradix crystal has been corrected. The Light Drive will operate within ninety-nine percent efficiency now."

"Good work. As soon as we're on the other side of the bulk path, we'll initiate the Light Drive and attempt to outrun the detonation."

She paused and tried to think of something inspiring to say to the crew. It wasn't the greatest, but she did her best.

"If we don't survive, I'm putting this out there now. I know things didn't turn out how you expected. If it weren't for the thartica, Kohan, Ruzat, Wena, and Nine would still be alive. I know I wasn't your choice for captain, but being part of a successful and competent crew, and leading you has fulfilled me. We went from mercenaries to marauders to soon-to-be heroes. It's been an honor."

Faun had snuck up on her and put her hand on Eve's shoulder. Turning the chair so Eve faced her, Faun sat sideways on her lap and kissed her. Eve reached up and caressed Faun's cheek. Faun let it linger for a moment before returning to her post.

Virid rejoined at the second pilot console and gave a weak smile.

"They okay?" Eve asked.

"They are still breathing, and there is no external bleeding. Unfortunately, due to the impact, it's possible there is swelling under his titanium ore graft we can't see without a doctor."

"Say the word and we'll break formation and sneak you down to Tor Galom Ig..."

"No. This is where we're meant to be. Balok would not want us to risk the mission."

Eve reached over and put her hand on Virid's rocky shoulder for a moment in both reverence and solidarity.

One AU from the opening to the bulk path.

The thartica waited, defending it. Thartican ships had started to come through the other path behind CHILD. While the allied ships assigned to cover it had taken out a dozen right at the mouth, they were overpowered and outnumbered. There was no more time. Their final assault was now.

"Attention all ships," Onra broadcast to all. "Weapons free. Ensure CHILD and *Skyfire* reach the bulk path at all costs."

The fleets rushed to meet in the middle. The windows were filled with complete chaos with all of the weapon types. *Skyfire* continued its duty to protect CHILD, darting in and out while skimming the megastructure's surface. There was no stopping all of the fire directed at CHILD. Their shielding held against the smaller Rekwa weapons, but the larger battleships and dreadnaughts with more powerful arrays were starting to melt the hull.

The larger Rekwa beams were never on CHILD for long as the enemy ships were intercepted and attacked. Either they became distracted, or too damaged to continue. One after another, the thartica attempted to destroy the star's container, but were thwarted by the efforts of the alliance. While in a maneuver to flip and return to the center, Eve caught sight of a vraditi battleship speed up and ram the edge of its saucer-like hull directly into the side of a thartican vessel. Both were devastated by the blow, but the result was that the Rekwa beam was shut down.

Zero-point-five AU from the opening to the bulk path.

CHILD was now being assaulted on all sides. Allied ships did everything to stop them, but there were too many smaller thartican ships spread out and concentrating fire on focal points of CHILD's hull. They were burning through.

Vraditi ships fitted with shockwave emitters tried to knock the enemy's alignment off, but it wasn't enough. A human battlecruiser detonated off the upper hemisphere, and the explosion of energy and debris rocked the nearby ships. *Skyfire* was rocked with a weakened wave, lessened by its contact with all the other ships before it.

There was so much debris on the field from both sides it became hard to pinpoint where the weapons fire was coming from. The scans of the area were cluttered with faint power signatures.

Zero-point-two AU from the opening of the bulk path.

"*Skyfire*, open the bulk path," CHILD instructed.

"Confirmed. Opening," Eve replied.

CHILD was pushing through everything, regardless of who it was. Eve and Virid worked to dart and dodge to where the mouth would be once they activated their drive.

"Are the modifications done?" Eve asked Eleven.

"You are clear to activate the Bulk Drive. Our ship will sustain the opening as intended."

Virid tapped through the commands and the screen lit up to show their Bulk Drive was coming on. The mouth opened, ready to accept the ship. Without hesitation, they dove in. Their part in the battle was over...

Less than a minute into the path, the ship shuddered under the heavy weight of CHILD's structure entering. Virid corrected an imbalance in their stabilizer caused by the gravitational wave, and the ride smoothed out.

"Two-Oh-Eight, restart environmental support for the entire ship."

"Yes, Captain."

"Once the ship has its atmosphere back, I'll take Balok to your room," she told Virid.

"Evette…" CHILD said over comms. "Due to damage inflicted to my structure, I expect containment failure before we exit the bulk path. I will try to hold the containment protocol until we reach the other side, but I may not succeed. The resulting explosion will destroy the bulk path, as well as the entirety of the system we are heading to."

"We knew the risk going in. We'll attempt to get away, but we understand that we're not coming back."

"Understood. I wish you good luck."

"Thanks, CHILD."

There was nothing else to do until they exited the path, which would take a few hours. Eve stood and moved to Balok. Hoisting them up, she moved to the hallway where their room was.

"Two-Oh-Eight, are systems restored?" she asked.

"Affirmative."

The door unlatched and slid open. Virid joined her and they walked together to the Tectos' room. Virid opened the door. Despite the time on the ship, this was the first time Eve had been in there. It was decorated with ornate fixtures, sculptures, and trinkets from their home worlds. The room had both an earthy smell and feel. Eve laid Balok down on the single bed. She nodded to Virid, who sat down next to their partner, and left.

Back on the bridge and in the captain's chair, she stared at Faun.

Can't harm to ask for answers again, since our role is fulfilled. There won't be another opportunity.

"Can you tell me about our benefactor *now?*" She spat that last word.

"We've achieved what we needed to. From their end, the mission should be a success and the galaxy should be saved."

"What happened to you? Where did you go?"

"When I rammed the shield in the station, a temporal rift opened. They opened it to save my life and I was pulled into a pocket separate from our timeline. I spent two years coming and going from their station on missions. In that time, I helped modify *Skyfire* and prepared for this.

"Our benefactor is only one of a group of all the sentient species of our section of the galaxy. Even the thartica are there. They work outside of time, monitoring events and conscripting people to enact changes in the timeline. Their sole purpose is to ensure the survival of all species.

"They needed me to bring the mission to you, and for you to follow the plan," Faun explained.

Ignoring that it was an absurd explanation, being used as a puppet didn't sit well with Eve. It angered her, even though they supposedly just saved the galaxy.

Why us? Why me?

Stewing, there wasn't anything to be done. Faun must have seen the agitation and came to sit on Eve's lap. Grabbing her hands, Faun wrapped Eve's arms around her torso, and then leaned back against her. They stared out the viewport at the Bulk they had spent great portions of their time in.

On the side display, it showed they had two hours to go before reaching the exit. Eve set a timer to go off fifteen minutes before and closed her eyes to enjoy the comfort of holding Faun.

The timer went off, and it only felt like moments. Eve recalled Virid to the bridge and took the pilot seat next to them. Faun retook her position. Eve ran through a checklist.

"Light Drive status?"

"Online and ninety-nine percent efficient," Two-Oh-Eight said.

"Shielding and weapons?"

"Full shields," Faun said. "Weapons primed."

"Plot course for direct line immediately upon reentry to normal space."

"Plotted," Virid said.

Ten minutes before exit they received one final communication.

"Containment failure. Goodbye," CHILD said.

The bulk path shook and shuddered. The resulting explosion began collapsing the path behind them. She had no idea what would happen if they got stuck in the Bulk, or if they would ever find their way back.

The power of the star crept up on them. Virid was ready with their hand directly over the console command to activate the Light Drive. *Skyfire* shook violently with the plasma nearly licking their aft end.

Normal space could be seen. The mouth was there. They weren't yet free of the Bulk, but they would be destroyed if they didn't go now.

"Go!" Eve yelled.

Virid hit the command and the drive spooled up.

Epilogue:
Time is Relative

Humans, vraditi, QuBE, elementus, and thartica are sat around the Time Warden council table. Each species is represented by three of their people. The representatives are convened to help guide their species to survival, as well as the conservation of all species throughout the Crux arm of the galaxy.

"The new timeline is set. Evette Magne's mission is completed," an older woman says while fixing her gray hair up in a bun.

"Good. Is the outcome as expected?" the man at the head of the table asks. He leans forward and his green eyes glint in the light.

"Slight deviations in expected outcomes have altered our original prediction. The hidden world, Ubati, is extinguished, but dozens of ships escaped. History now reflects they will settle a new location. They will have no contact to the exiles on Morelon. However, their hatred toward all species of our quadrant will continue, and they become a threat again," a tall, orange leafed thartica replies.

"While our prediction of outcome is highly accurate, unrest will plague all of our sovereign regions for quite some time. The permanent exodus of MOTHER and the QuBE from the Crux arm opens much space to mercenaries, pirates, and marauders. The Galactic Police will become strained, and the spacefaring species must have a tighter control of their sovereign systems," the shorter female vraditi says.

"What do we do about Eve and her crew?" a human woman asks. "They die out there without intervention."

"I propose we offer the *Skyfire* a new mission in exchange for their return to alliance space. Send them after the Ubati thartica and quell the future threat. When their task is complete, we tunnel them back through a vortex."

"The *Skyfire* crew is not meant to return. Because of their history of lawlessness, if we reintroduce them, it is likely their rogue tendencies would increase lawlessness," the trio of QuBE reply in unison. "Evette Magne's inability to yield to authority causes her to be a liability."

"Run the scenarios anyway. We will still need to take the Ubati thartica out regardless," the man instructs. "If we don't, we enter a cycle where every thousand or so years our arm of the galaxy will have to do this war all over."

"The next mission is regarding Tikan Dolc from Tor Galom Aq in the galactic year fifty thousand, two hundred and twelve..." a representative of the elementus states to push the meeting forward.

Eleven and Two-Oh-Eight had successfully charted their location in relation to their home sector. The news was unsettling in that they were the only two who would survive long enough to make it back to their space. It had already been a month heading in a straight line and the crew, minus Balok, were huddled up at the dining table.

"There are a dozen potential systems within reach which might hold life," Eleven tells Eve. "These also might be your best bet for survival."

"We also know there were a few thartican ships which escaped the blast. They may have a colony planet we can raid for food," Faun adds.

"Have we picked up any thartican signals?" Eve asks.

"Not for a dozen lightyears," Eleven says.

"Continue on toward home, seek out one of these systems that may or may not have a planet which can sustain us, or double back and find the thartica signals and hunt them. We need food. With rationing, we can make it another two months," Virid says.

Two-Oh-Eight starts to say something, but they are interrupted by intense air pressure buildup in the cargo hold. The rapid increase causes Eve's ears to ring and she gets an instant headache. The bubble of pressure bursts into a blue swirling vortex near the aft of the bay. From it appears two figures.

It's a man and woman, both appearing to be in their middle ages. The man is tall, but not as tall as Eve. The first thing she notices are his piercing eyes. He is distinguished. His hair is short, and he has a beard. It's clear he's been graying for a while. The woman is far shorter than both of them but holds her head high. She's smiling and looking directly at Eve.

The vortex dies down and disappears. Faun moves to greet them. She hugs the woman first, and then the man. They reciprocate and smile at her.

"I thought you were going to leave us out here!" Faun exclaims.

"I wasn't going to, but the council had to deliberate," the man says. "I would have gone against their wishes if they hadn't agreed. However..."

He holds up a small storage device for Faun.

"What's this?"

"New mission. As you already know, some of the Ubati thartica escaped. Before I can bring you home, we need you to hunt all of them down. There's no one else out here, so it has to be you."

Eve wasn't going to sit there and be told she had to do even more to gain their favor. The anger of being a puppet rose again, and this time she could do something about it. Speed-walking at the man, she prepared to grab his neck and choke him.

"We did your task! We're done!" she yells at him.

She shoves past Faun and reaches her hand out for his neck. He lets her grab him. She begins squeezing, and despite turning red, he's calm. Faun attempts to pull her off, but she's not having it.

"Eve! Let go!" Faun cries out.

The woman who hadn't said anything yet wedges herself in between Eve and the man. When she does speak, it's soft and caring.

"Evette Magne...Lady Eve," she starts. "I understand your anger. You don't have the answers you seek, but I can give them to you with your permission."

"My permission?!" Eve rages. "You should have asked permission before sending us on a fekking suicide mission. You *knew* we were going to get stuck out here. You *knew* our friends and shipmates were going to die! Balok Tecto is lying in their bed right now, in a coma, and you're acting like this is all okay with you. You could have done something!"

The man was starting to turn purple, his eyes started to roll back, but he still made no move against Eve. He didn't even struggle.

"Do you want the answers?" he whispers through his clenched throat.

"Whatever answers you give me won't be enough!"

"They can help Balok!" Faun pleads. "Don't kill them!"

As much as Eve wants to extinguish his life, and the woman's, she settles for tossing him to the floor hard. He lies there for a moment, and the woman rushes to his aide. Slowly he sits up with her help. The woman turns back to Eve.

"You have *always* been so stubborn," she says coldly, as if she knows her. "I can give you the answers you seek, but it comes at the cost of who you are right now, in this moment."

"Then tell me! You keep asking my permission, but all you're doing is flapping your lips. You haven't told me a damn thing!"

The woman and man exchange glances, and he nods at her. She stands and walks over to Eve. Eve isn't sure what to expect but falls into the idea she's also going to get a storage device. Instead, the woman leans up, puts her arms around Eve's neck and tries to pull her in. Eve resists.

"What the fek are you doing?!"

"Calm down. I'm also Alkosian, but my power is something we named *soul-link*. I can link my entire being to you and share everything."

Eve is still hesitant. The fear of the unknown fights the anger of what she and the crew have been put through.

Will the answers make it better or worse? Will I want to kill them more?

The woman pulls her down a bit and kisses her on the forehead. Eve's mind is immediately flooded with images of herself, of memories the woman has of her, of things which have never happened. But the Eve seen through the woman's memories is clearly her. Fighting, bickering, living, loving, heartbreak. Years of time spent together. And her death at the hands of a tarak.

Eve pulls away too late. The memories seep in and she begins to hyperventilate. Faun yells at the woman, but Eve's mind is spinning, she can't make any of it out.

She collapses on the floor while her mind tries to make sense of everything. Finally, her senses return, and Faun is hovering over her, checking to see if she's okay.

"What did you do?" Faun yells while looking at Rain and Ami.

"I shared my memories with her. There are many things you won't understand, but Eve will."

Eve wants to be angry and cry at the same time. Not only were the memories shared, but the emotions associated. She can feel exactly how much Ami loves her, despite their constant rivalry in an alternate timeline. They were both friends and enemies in love with the man who was now offering his hand to help her up.

She swats Rain's hand away. Despite knowing she desired him in another life, she had no affinity for him now. Instead, she accepts Faun's help up. Desperately she wants to clear her mind, but everything continues to linger.

"So, what? You think because you're some lord of time you get to play God?" she spits at him.

"I am just an Alkosian, on a council of species represented by and for the conservation of entire peoples. I don't even have the power to manipulate time, that's our third human representative."

Evalyn...the time vortex...

It hit her. The book she stole from Faun's room, 'Purest of Heart,' written by Evalyn Weaver. The purple, heart shaped, Vradix crystal necklace belonged to Emma. Evalyn was chronicling their lives.

Rain looks to Virid and smiles compassionately.

"I can help Balok. Please, take me to them."

Virid hears the word 'help' and leaps to their feet to guide him. They disappear into the left hall. Eve paces to the food cooler and back with her arms behind her back.

For the sake of the crew, we have to go along with this if we want to make it back to our space. But I need a guarantee no one else dies. Not a single one of them.

She turns to Ami, her shoulders back and head high. Eve doesn't care there is some familiarity between them now. This life, this timeline, this crew, they are hers and she isn't going to bend over backward because a version of her knew them.

"My crew comes first. Their survival is all that matters. If even a single one of them is going to die in pursuit of the thartica, then my answer is going to be no. We'll find a planet, settle down, and you can fek off back to whatever time you're from."

"The council has already run the scenario. Should you accept, the current members of your crew will all make it back to your space alive," Ami tells her.

It sounds like she's holding something back.

"In a coma? Dismembered? Near death? I better get an absolute guarantee we make it back safe. And if you lie to me and something happens, nothing will stop me from hunting you and Rain down and killing you both in the most painful way I can come up with."

"Eve, just like we gave Faun enough information to get things done, that's what you get. We can't give you all of the answers, because then you start questioning whether there's a better way. It almost always messes things up. You and the current *Skyfire* crew *will* make it back safe," she says while crossing her arms.

"For what it is worth, based on the information we have of the thartica, they will rebuild and attempt another war," Eleven interjects.

"I would also like to take on their task so QuBE-94056-11 and myself may rejoin MOTHER on the journey to the next level of civilization. If we were to transit back to our quadrant by direct travel, MOTHER and our fellow QuBE may have already left the galaxy," Two-Oh-Eight tells her.

"It *sounds* like it doesn't matter if I'm the captain or not, because I'm not making the decisions here," Eve makes herself sound as snarky as she can while addressing Ami. "If we're going to do this, why don't you and Rain come along, since it's going to be *so* safe."

"Rain and I have other obligations, but if it would make you feel better, we can send another Time Warden to be a part of your crew."

"The offer wasn't real. I want you off my ship as soon as possible. And the fek would I want a babysitter for? The absolute audacity."

Rain, Virid, and Balok appear from the hallway. Virid allows Balok to use them as a support, but they are awake. Eve intercepts while they are moving to the table to sit. Faun joins, and hugs Balok around the neck.

"Hey, Balok. How're you feeling?" Faun asks.

"Lethargic, but this man says I will be back to full strength in a few days. Did we win?"

"We'll talk about it later, for now grab a bite to eat and rest up," she says and smiles at them.

"I'm glad you're okay," Eve says, and then makes a joke. "I was worried I was going to have to fill your seat permanently. I'm no Tecto when it comes to piloting."

"You did very well," Virid says.

Eve looks to Rain, then to Ami. The choice is simple. Moving past her own hard headedness isn't. As much as she'd love to stick them with their own problems, her want to get her crew home rates higher.

"Take this," Rain says and hands her a familiar heart-shaped crystal. "You left it when you were on the planet trying to sell the Rekwa weapons. Find out how to harness your own *alkos* to activate its imbued power."

She snatches it from him and shoves it in her pocket. Her intense stare and curled lip were supposed to make him feel uneasy, unwanted. But his cool doesn't break. He returns to Ami's side and grabs her hand.

"How will you know when we've done what you want?" Eve asks.

"We'll be monitoring."

"Good, then get the hell off my ship. We have work to do."

He nods, and the vortex opens behind them. They step through and are gone. When it dies down, Eve reconvenes their meeting at the table. Hope slowly returns to the crew as they share a meal.

✹

~~~~Lady Eve and the Skyfire Crew will persist!~~~~

About The Author

Thomas W. Everson thinks you're awesome for reading his book(s). The love of entertaining is what inspires him most to write. He uses influences from many different places, people, and events, in the hopes that readers will relate in some way and lose themselves in the story.

His passion outside of writing is enjoying time with his wife and son, where they read books and comics, watch movies, and play video games together. Beyond the fantastical, he is also very enthusiastic about real life astronautics.

www.ingramcontent.com/pod-product-compliance
Lightning Source LLC
Chambersburg PA
CBHW070204120726
47909CB00001B/245